# THE PL
# HUBERT HENRY DAVIES

VOLUME TWO

HUBERT HENRY DAVIES.
*at the age of four and a half*

# THE PLAYS OF
# HUBERT HENRY DAVIES

WITH AN INTRODUCTION BY

## HUGH WALPOLE

VOLUME TWO

LONDON
CHATTO & WINDUS
1921

**NOTE**

All rights reserved. The Amateur Fee for each and every representation of any one of these plays is five guineas, payable in advance to the Author's sole agents, Messrs. Samuel French, Limited, 26 Southampton Street, Strand, London, W.C.

# CONTENTS

| | PAGE |
|---|---|
| THE MOLLUSC | 1 |
| A SINGLE MAN | 65 |
| DOORMATS | 143 |
| OUTCAST | 207 |

# THE MOLLUSC

A COMEDY IN THREE ACTS

COPY OF THE "FIRST NIGHT" PROGRAMME

AT THE

CRITERION THEATRE, LONDON

ON OCTOBER 15, 1907

## THE MOLLUSC

A NEW COMEDY IN THREE ACTS

BY

HUBERT HENRY DAVIES

| | |
|---|---|
| *Tom Kemp* . . . . . | CHARLES WYNDHAM |
| *Mr. Baxter* . . . . . | MR. SAM SOTHERN |
| *Mrs. Baxter* . . . . | MISS MARY MOORE |
| *Miss Roberts* . . . | MISS ELAINE INNESCOURT |

*The scene of the Play is laid in Mrs. Baxter's Sitting-room at a house some twenty or thirty miles from London.*

# THE MOLLUSC

## THE FIRST ACT

SCENE.—MRS BAXTER'S *sitting-room. A pleasant, well-furnished room. French windows open to the garden, showing flower-beds in full bloom, it being summer time. As the audience looks at the stage there is a door on the left-hand side at the back, and from the door a few stairs lead down to the room. Nearer and also on this side is a fireplace. Against this same wall is a flower-pot on a table containing a plant in bloom. There is plenty of comfortable furniture about the room.*

*It is evening after dinner. Lamps are lighted and the windows closed.* MR. BAXTER, *a man about forty, is seated near a lamp reading "Scribner's Magazine." The door opens and* MISS ROBERTS *comes in. She is a pretty, honest-looking English girl about twenty-four. She comes towards* MR. BAXTER.

MISS ROBERTS. Mr. Baxter—are you very busy?
MR. BAXTER. No, Miss Roberts.
MISS ROBERTS. I want to speak to you.
MR. BAXTER. Yes. Won't you sit down?
MISS ROBERTS. Thank you. (*She does so.*) We shall soon be beginning the summer holidays, and I think after this term you had better have another governess for the girls.
MR. BAXTER. You want to leave us?
MISS ROBERTS. I don't *want* to. I shall be very sorry indeed to go. You and Mrs. Baxter have always been so kind to me. You never treated me like a governess.

MR. BAXTER. You have been with us so long. We have come to look on you as one of the family.

MISS ROBERTS. I can't tell you how often I have felt grateful. I don't want to leave you at all, and it will almost break my heart to say good-bye to the children, but I *must* go.

MR. BAXTER (*anxiously*). You are not going to be married?

MISS ROBERTS (*smiling*). Oh, no—nothing so interesting—I'm sorry to say.

MR. BAXTER. Have you told my wife you think of leaving?

MISS ROBERTS (*slightly troubled*). I began to tell Mrs. Baxter several times; at the beginning of the term and three or four times since—but she was always too busy or too tired to attend to me; each time she asked me to tell her some other time—until I don't quite know what to do. That's why I've come to *you*.

MR. BAXTER (*slightly disconcerted*). But it's not *my* place to accept your notice.

MISS ROBERTS. I know—but if I might explain to *you*——

MR. BAXTER. Certainly.

MISS ROBERTS. It's this. I can't teach the girls anything more. Gladys is nearly twelve, and Margery, though she is only nine, is very bright; she often asks me the most puzzling questions—and the truth is—I have not had a good enough education myself to take them any further.

MR. BAXTER. Aren't they rather young to go to school?

MISS ROBERTS. I think you need a governess with a college education, or, at any rate, some one who doesn't get all at sea in algebra and Latin.

MR. BAXTER. I should have thought you might read and study.

MISS ROBERTS. I used to think so—but I find I haven't the time.

MR. BAXTER (*thoughtfully*). Too much is expected of you besides your duties as the children's governess. I've noticed that—but I don't quite see how I can interfere.

MISS ROBERTS. Please don't trouble, and don't think

I'm complaining. I am always glad to be of use to Mrs. Baxter. It's not for my own sake I want a change ; it's for the girls'. This is their most receptive age. What they are taught, and *how* they are taught *now*, will mean so much to them later on. I can't bear to think they may suffer all their lives through *my* ignorance.

MR. BAXTER (*politely*). Oh—I'm sure——

MISS ROBERTS. It's very kind of you to say so—but I know what it is. I have suffered myself for want of a thorough education. Of course I had the ordinary kind, but I was never brought up to know or do anything special. I found myself at a great disadvantage when I had to turn to, and earn my own living.

MR. BAXTER. Gladys and Margery won't have to earn their own livings.

MISS ROBERTS. No one used to think that I should have to earn mine—till one day—I found myself alone and poor—after the shipwreck—when my father and mother—and my sister——

(*She turns her head away to hide her emotion from* MR. BAXTER.)

MR. BAXTER (*kindly*). We shall all miss you very much when you go. (*Leaning towards her.*) I shall miss you very much. (*She nods.*) We've had such good walks and talks and games of chess.

MISS ROBERTS (*brightly*). Yes ! I've enjoyed them all.

MR. BAXTER. I hope you have a nice place to go to.

MISS ROBERTS (*simply*). I haven't any place to go to. I hoped Mrs. Baxter would help me find a new situation. I can't get one very well without her help, as this is the only place where I have ever been a governess, and after being here four years (*smiles*) I must ask Mrs. Baxter to give me a good character.

MR. BAXTER (*meditatively*). Four years—it doesn't seem like four years. I don't know, though—in some ways it seems as if you had always been here. (*Looking at* MISS ROBERTS.) It is very honest of you to give up a good situation for a conscientious reason like this.

MISS ROBERTS. I don't know.

MR. BAXTER (*as an afterthought*). I suppose it really is your reason for leaving ?

MISS ROBERTS (*laughing*). It's not very nice of you to

compliment me on my honesty one minute and doubt it the next.

MR. BAXTER (*seriously*). No, Miss Roberts, no. I don't doubt it. I was only wondering. I thought perhaps there might be some other reason why you find it difficult to live here—why you think it would be wiser not to stay——

MISS ROBERTS (*innocently*). No——

MR. BAXTER. I see. Well—as I leave everything to do with the girls' education to Mrs. Baxter—perhaps you will tell *her*. Tell her what you have told *me*.

MISS ROBERTS. And—will you sit in the room?

MR. BAXTER. Why? What is going to be the difficulty.

MISS ROBERTS (*embarrassed*). I can't explain very well to you—but if you wouldn't mind sitting in the room. (*She rises.*) I think I hear Mrs. Baxter coming.

(MRS. BAXTER *enters. She is a pretty woman about thirty-five, vague in her movements and manner of speaking. She comes down the room as she speaks.*)

MRS. BAXTER. I've been wondering where *Scribner's Magazine* is.

MR. BAXTER. I have it. Have you been looking for it?

MRS. BAXTER. No—not looking—only wondering.

MR. BAXTER. Do you want it?

MRS. BAXTER (*pleasantly*). Not if you are reading it—though I was just half-way through a story.

MR. BAXTER. Do take it.

MRS. BAXTER (*taking magazine*). Don't you really want it?

(*She looks about, selecting the most comfortable chair.*)

MR. BAXTER. It doesn't matter.

MRS. BAXTER (*smiling*). Thank you. (*She sits.*) Oh, Miss Roberts, I wonder if you could get me the cushion out of that chair?

(*Pointing to a chair near a window.*)

MISS ROBERTS. Certainly.

(*She brings the cushion to* MRS. BAXTER *and places it behind her back.*)

MRS. BAXTER (*settling herself*). Thank you. Now I'm quite comfortable—unless I had a footstool.

MISS ROBERTS. A footstool?
*(She gets a footstool, brings it to* MRS. BAXTER *and places it under her feet.)*

MRS. BAXTER (*without an attempt to move while* MISS ROBERTS *is doing this*). Don't trouble, Miss Roberts. I didn't mean *you* to do that. *I* could have done it. (*When* MISS ROBERTS *has placed the footstool.*) Oh, how kind of you, but you ought not to wait on me like this. (*Smiles sweetly.*) The paper-knife, please. Who knows where it is? (MISS ROBERTS *takes the paper-knife from* MR. BAXTER *and gives it to* MRS. BAXTER. *To* MR. BAXTER.) I didn't see you were using it, dear, or I wouldn't have asked for it. (*To* MISS ROBERTS.) As you're doing nothing, would you mind cutting some of these pages? I find there are still a few uncut. (*She gives the magazine and paper-knife to* MISS ROBERTS, *then says, smiling sweetly.*) Your fingers are so much cleverer than mine. (MISS ROBERTS *begins cutting the magazine.* MRS. BAXTER *leans back comfortably in her chair and says to* MR. BAXTER.) Why don't you get something to do?

MR. BAXTER (*rising*). I'm going to my room to have a smoke.

*(*MISS ROBERTS *puts the magazine on the table and goes to* MR. BAXTER *with the paper-knife in her hand.)*

MISS ROBERTS. No, Mr. Baxter, please, I want you to help me out. I want you to stay while I tell Mrs. Baxter.

MRS. BAXTER. What's all this mystery? (*Seriously.*) Take care you don't snap that paper-knife in two, Miss Roberts.

(MR. BAXTER *sits down again.*)

MISS ROBERTS (*to* MRS. BAXTER). I was telling Mr. Baxter before you came into the room——

MRS. BAXTER (*holding out her hand*). Give me the paper-knife.

(MISS ROBERTS *gives her the paper-knife, which she examines carefully.*)

MISS ROBERTS. I told you at the beginning of the term, and several times since——

MRS. BAXTER. It would have been a pity if that paper-knife had been snapped in two. (*She looks up pleasantly at* MISS ROBERTS.) Yes, Miss Roberts?

MISS ROBERTS. I was saying that I thought——
   (MRS. BAXTER *drops the paper-knife accidentally on the floor.*)
MRS. BAXTER. Oh, don't trouble to pick it up. (MISS ROBERTS *picks up the paper-knife and holds it in her hand.*) Oh, thank you, I didn't mean you to do that.
MISS ROBERTS. I was saying——
MRS. BAXTER. It isn't chipped, is it?
MISS ROBERTS (*nearly losing her temper*). No.
   (*She marches to the table and lays the paper-knife down.*)
MRS. BAXTER. It would have been a pity if that paper-knife had been chipped.
MISS ROBERTS (*facing* MRS. BAXTER *with determination, and speaking fast and loud*). I said I must leave at the end of the term.
MRS. BAXTER (*blandly*). Aren't you happy with us, Miss Roberts?
MISS ROBERTS. Oh, yes, thank you. Very.
MRS. BAXTER. Really happy, I mean.
MR. BAXTER. Miss Roberts feels that Gladys and Margery are getting too old for her to teach.
MISS ROBERTS (*glancing her gratitude to* MR. BAXTER *for helping her*). Yes. (*To* MRS. BAXTER.) I've taught them all I know; they need some one cleverer; there ought to be a change.
MRS. BAXTER. I think you do very nicely.
MISS ROBERTS. *You* don't know how ignorant I am.
MRS. BAXTER (*sweetly*). You do yourself an injustice, dear Miss Roberts.
   (MISS ROBERTS *turns appealingly to* MR. BAXTER.)
MR. BAXTER. It was the algebra, I think you said, Miss Roberts, that you found so especially difficult?
MISS ROBERTS. Yes. I've no head for algebra.
MRS. BAXTER (*cheerfully*). Neither have I, but I don't consider myself a less useful woman for that.
MISS ROBERTS. You're not a governess.
MRS. BAXTER. Who said I was? Don't let us wander from the point, Miss Roberts.
   (MISS ROBERTS *looks appealingly at* MR. BAXTER *again.*)
MR. BAXTER. The Latin——
MISS ROBERTS. Yes, I give myself a lesson at night to

pass on to them in the morning—that's no way to do, just keeping a length ahead.

MRS. BAXTER. Perhaps Mr. Baxter will help you with the Latin. Ask him.

MISS ROBERTS. I'm afraid even that——

MRS. BAXTER. Mr. Baxter's a very good Latin scholar. (*Smiling at* MR. BAXTER.) Aren't you, dear?

MR. BAXTER (*reluctantly*). I read Virgil at school. I haven't looked at him since. After a time one's Latin gets rusty.

MRS. BAXTER (*cheerfully*). Rub it up. We might begin now, while you're doing nothing. Ask Miss Roberts to bring you the books.

MR. BAXTER. Oh, no, dear.

MRS. BAXTER. Why shouldn't we improve our minds? (*She leans her head back on the cushions.*)

MR. BAXTER. Not after dinner. (*To* MISS ROBERTS.) I don't see why you want to teach the girls Latin.

MISS ROBERTS. Mrs. Baxter said she wished them to have a smattering of the dead languages.

MRS. BAXTER (*complacently*). I learnt Latin. I remember so well standing up in class and reciting " Hic —haec—hoc "—accusative " hinc—honc—huc."

MR. BAXTER (*correcting her*). Hoc.

MRS. BAXTER. Huc, dear, in *my* book. And the ablative was hibus.

MR. BAXTER. Hibus!

(MR. BAXTER *and* MISS ROBERTS *both laugh.*)

MRS. BAXTER (*making wild serious guesses*). Hobibus —no, wait a minute—that's wrong—don't tell me. (*She closes her eyes and murmurs.*) Ablative—ho—hi—hu— no; it's gone. (*She opens her eyes and says cheerfully.*) Never mind. (*To* MISS ROBERTS.) What were we talking about?

MISS ROBERTS. *My ignorance* of Latin.

MRS. BAXTER. I can't say that *my knowledge* of it has ever been of much service to me. I think Mr. Baxter is quite right. Why teach the girls Latin? Suppose we drop it from the curriculum and take up something else on Latin mornings——

MISS ROBERTS (*earnestly to* MRS. BAXTER). I wonder if you realise how much all this means to the girls? Their future is *so* mportant.

MRS. BAXTER (*with the idea of putting* MISS ROBERTS *in her place*). Of course it is important, Miss Roberts. It is not necessary to tell a mother how important her girls' future is—but I don't suppose we need settle it this evening. (*Wishing to put an end to the discussion, she rises, walks towards the table on which stands the flower-pot and says amiably.*) How pretty these flowers look growing in this pot.

MISS ROBERTS. Would you rather we discussed it to-morrow, Mrs. Baxter?

MRS. BAXTER. To-morrow will be my brother's first day here, and he will have so much to tell me after his long absence. I don't think to-morrow would be a good day.

MISS ROBERTS. The day after?

MRS. BAXTER. Oh, really, Miss Roberts, I can't be pinned down like that. (*She moves towards* MR. BAXTER.) Aren't you and Miss Roberts going to play chess?

MR. BAXTER (*rising*). Miss Roberts seems so anxious to have this thing decided. I told her that anything to do with the girls' education was left to *you*.

MRS. BAXTER. Need it be settled this minute?

MISS ROBERTS (*going towards* MRS. BAXTER). I've tried so often to speak to you about it and something must be done.

MRS. BAXTER (*resigning herself*). Of course—if you insist upon it—I'll do it now. I'll do anything any of you wish. (*She sits down.*) I've had a slight headache all day—it's rather worse since dinner; I really ought to be in bed, but I wanted to be up when Tom comes. If I begin to discuss this now I shall be in no state to receive him—but, of course—if you insist——

MISS ROBERTS. I don't want to tire you.

MRS. BAXTER. It *would* tire me very much.

MISS ROBERTS. Then I suppose we must put it off again.

MRS. BAXTER (*smiling*). I think that would be best. We must thrash it out properly—some day.

(*She leans back in her chair.*)

MR. BAXTER (*to* MISS ROBERTS, *sighing*). I suppose we may as well play chess?

MISS ROBERTS (*with resignation*). I suppose so.

(MR. BAXTER *and* MISS ROBERTS *sit at a table and arrange the chess men.*)

MRS. BAXTER (*finding her place in her magazine, begins to read. After a slight pause, she says*). What an abominable light! I can't possibly see to read. I suppose, Miss Roberts, you couldn't possibly carry that lamp over to this table, could you? (MISS ROBERTS *makes a slight movement as though she would fetch the lamp.*) It's too heavy, isn't it?

MR. BAXTER. Much too heavy!

MRS. BAXTER. I thought so. I'm afraid I must strain my eyes. I can't bear to sit idle.

MR. BAXTER (*rising*). I'll carry the lamp over.

MRS. BAXTER (*quickly*). No, no! You'd spill it. Call one of the servants; wouldn't that be the simplest plan?

MR. BAXTER. The simplest plan would be for you to walk over to the lamp.

MRS. BAXTER. Certainly, dear, if it's too much trouble to call one of the servants. (*She rises and carries her magazine to a chair by the lamp.*) I wouldn't have said anything about the lamp if I'd thought it was going to be such a business to move it. (*She sits and turns over a page or two while* MR. BAXTER, *who has returned to his seat, and* MISS ROBERTS *continue arranging the chess-board.* MRS. BAXTER *calls gaily over her shoulder.*) Have you checkmated Mr. Baxter yet, Miss Roberts?

MISS ROBERTS. I haven't finished setting the board.

MRS. BAXTER. How slow you are. (*She turns a page or two idly, then says seriously to* MR. BAXTER.) Dear, you'll be interested to know that I don't think the housemaid opposite is engaged to young Locker. I believe it's the cook.

MR. BAXTER. Very interesting, dear. (*To* MISS ROBERTS.) It's you to play.

(*After three moves of chess,* MRS. BAXTER *says.*)

MRS. BAXTER. Oh, here's such a clever article on wasps. It seems that wasps—I'll read you what it says. (*She clears her throat.*) Wasps——

MR. BAXTER (*plaintively*). Dulcie, dear, it's impossible for us to give our minds to the game if you read aloud.

MRS. BAXTER (*amiably*). I'm so sorry, dear. I didn't mean to disturb you. I think you'd have found the article instructive. If you want to read it afterwards, it's page 32, if you can remember that. " Wasps and all about them." I'll dog-ear the page. Oh, I never looked out Tom's train. Miss Roberts, you'll find the time-table on the hall table. (MISS ROBERTS *rises and* MRS. BAXTER *goes on*.) Or if it isn't there, it may be——

MISS ROBERTS (*quickly*). I know where it is. (*She goes out.*)

MRS. BAXTER. What has Miss Roberts been saying to you about leaving?

MR. BAXTER. Only what she said to you.

MRS. BAXTER. I hope she won't leave me before I get suited. I shall never find any one else to suit me. I don't know what I should do without Miss Roberts.

(MISS ROBERTS *re-enters with small time-table.*)

MISS ROBERTS. Here it is!

MRS. BAXTER (*cheerfully*). Thank you, Miss Roberts, but I've just remembered he isn't coming by train at all; he's coming in a motor car.

MR. BAXTER. All the way from London?

MRS. BAXTER. Yes, at least I think so. It's all in his letter—who knows what I did with Tom's letter?

MISS ROBERTS (*making a slight movement as if to go*). Shall I go and look?

MRS. BAXTER. Hush. I'm trying to think where I put it. (*Staring in front of her.*) I had it in my hand before tea. I remember dropping it—I had it again after tea; I remember thinking it was another letter, but it wasn't. That's how I know. (*Then to the others.*) I'm surprised neither of you remembers where I put it.

MISS ROBERTS. I'd better go and look.

(*She moves to go.*)

MR. BAXTER. I think I hear a motor coming.

(*He goes and looks through the window.*)

MRS. BAXTER (*in an injured tone*). It's too late now, Miss Roberts. Mr. Baxter thinks he hears a motor coming.

MR. BAXTER. Yes, it is a car; I see the lamps. It must be Tom.

MRS. BAXTER (*smiling affectionately*). Dear Tom, how nice it will be to see him again. (*To* MR. BAXTER.) Aren't you going to the hall to meet Tom?

MR. BAXTER. Yes, of course.

(*He goes out.*)

MRS. BAXTER. You've never seen my brother Tom.

MISS ROBERTS. No, I don't think he's been home since I came to you.

MRS. BAXTER. No, I was trying to count up this afternoon how many years it would be since Tom was home. I've forgotten again now, but I know I did it; you'd have been surprised.

TOM (*outside*). Where is she?

(*Confused greetings between* TOM *and* MR. BAXTER *are heard.* MRS. BAXTER *rises smiling, and goes towards the stairs.*)

MRS. BAXTER. That's Tom's voice.

(TOM KEMP *enters followed by* MR. BAXTER. TOM *is a cheerful, genial, high-spirited man about forty-five; he comes down-stairs, where* MRS. BAXTER *meets him. He takes her in both arms and kisses her on each cheek.*)

TOM. Well, child, how are you—bless you.

MRS. BAXTER. Oh, Tom, it *is* nice to see you again.

TOM (*holding her off and looking at her*). You look just the same.

MRS. BAXTER. So do you, Tom. I'm so glad you haven't grown fat.

TOM (*laughing*). No chance to grow fat out there. Life is too strenuous. (*He turns to* MR. BAXTER *and gives him a slap on the back.*) Well, Dick, you old duffer.

MRS. BAXTER. Tom.

TOM (*turning to her*). Yes?

MRS. BAXTER. I want to introduce you to Miss Roberts.

(TOM *gives* MISS ROBERTS *a friendly hand-shake.*)

TOM. How d'you do, Miss Roberts?

MRS. BAXTER. Are you very tired, Tom?

TOM. Tired—no—never tired. (*Smiling at* MRS. BAXTER.) You look splendid.

(*He holds her by her shoulders.*)

MRS. BAXTER (*languidly*). I'm pretty well.

TOM (*spinning* MRS. BAXTER *round*). Never better.

MRS. BAXTER (*disliking such treatment*). I'm pretty well.

(*She wriggles her shoulders and edges away.*)

MR. BAXTER (*to* TOM). Have you dined?

TOM. Magnificently. Soup—fish—chops—roast beef

—— (*To* MISS ROBERTS.) You must live in Colorado, Miss Roberts, if you want to relish roast beef.

MR. BAXTER. But you've driven from London since dinner. (*To* MRS. BAXTER.) I suppose we can raise him a supper?

MRS. BAXTER. If the things aren't all put away.

TOM (*turning from* MISS ROBERTS). No—see here—hold on—I dined at the Inn.

MRS. BAXTER (*smiling graciously*). Oh, I was just going to offer to go into the kitchen and cook you something myself.

(*She sits.*)

TOM. I was late getting in and I wasn't sure what time you dined. (*To* MR. BAXTER.) Now, Dick, tell me the family history.

MR. BAXTER (*scratching his head, says slowly*). The family history?

MRS. BAXTER (*calling out suddenly*). His! Ablative—his.

TOM. Eh?

MRS. BAXTER (*gravely to* TOM). Hic—haec—hoc. His —his—his.

TOM (*looking blankly at* MISS ROBERTS *and* MR. BAXTER). *What's* the matter?

MRS. BAXTER (*smiling as she explains*). I was giving them a Latin lesson before you came.

TOM (*amused*). You?

MRS. BAXTER (*conceitedly*). I never think we were meant to spend all our time in frivolous conversation.

TOM (*amused, turning to* MR. BAXTER). Dulcie, giving you a Latin lesson?

MR. BAXTER (*sadly*). I suppose she really thinks she was by now.

TOM (*walking about*). It's bully to be home again. I felt like a kid coming here—slipping along in the dark—with English trees and English hedges and English farms flitting by. No one awake but a few English cows, standing in the fields—up to their knees in mist. It looked like dreams—like that dream I sometimes have out there in Colorado. I dream I've just arrived in England—with no baggage and nothing on but my pyjamas.

MRS. BAXTER. What *is* he talking about?

MISS ROBERTS. I know what you mean!

## THE MOLLUSC

TOM. I guess you've had that dream yourself. No, I mean you know how I must have felt.

MISS ROBERTS. Like a ghost revisiting its old haunts.

TOM (*sitting near* MISS ROBERTS). Like the ghost of the boy I used to be. I thought you'd understand. You look as if you would.

MRS. BAXTER. I'm so glad you haven't married some nasty common person in America.

TOM (*chaffingly to her*). I thought you would be. That's why I didn't do it.

(*He talks to* MISS ROBERTS.)

MRS. BAXTER (*laughing as she turns to say to* MR. BAXTER). He's always so full of fun.

MISS ROBERTS. *I* once dreamed I was in Colorado—but it was only from one of those picture post-cards you sent. I have never travelled.

TOM. And how did Colorado look in your dreams?

MISS ROBERTS (*recalling her vision of Colorado*). Forests——

TOM. That's right. Pine forests stretching away, away—down below there in the valley—a sea of tree-tops waving—waving—waving for miles.

MISS ROBERTS. And mountains.

TOM. Chains of mountains—great blue mountains streaked with snow — range beyond range. Oh! it's grand! it's grand!

MISS ROBERTS. I should love to see it.

MRS. BAXTER. I think you are much better off where you are, Miss Roberts.

TOM. It's great, but it's not gentle like this. It doesn't make you want to cry. It only makes you want to say your prayers.

MRS. BAXTER (*laughing as she turns to* MR. BAXTER). Isn't he droll?

MISS ROBERTS. I know what you mean.

TOM. *You* know. I thought *you'd* know. Here it comes so close to you; it's so cosy and personal. They've nothing like our orchards and lawns out there. (*Rising suddenly.*) I want to smell the garden.

(*He goes to the window.*)

MR. BAXTER. No! Tom, Tom!

MRS. BAXTER. Don't open the window; we shall all catch cold.

TOM (*laughing, as he comes towards* MRS. BAXTER).
Dear old Dulcie, same as ever.
MRS. BAXTER (*smiling*). All of us are not accustomed to living in tents and huts and such places.
TOM. What are you going to do with me in the morning?
MRS. BAXTER. We might all take a little walk, if it's a nice day.
TOM. A little walk!
MRS. BAXTER. If we're not too tired after the excitement of your arrival.
TOM. What time's breakfast?
MR. BAXTER. Quarter to nine.
MRS. BAXTER. We drift down about half-past.
TOM. What! You've got an English garden, and it's summer time and you aren't all running about outside at six o'clock in the morning?
MISS ROBERTS. I am.
TOM. *You* are? Yes, I thought *you* would be. You and I must have a walk before breakfast to-morrow morning.
MISS ROBERTS (*smiling*). Very well.
MRS. BAXTER. Don't overdo yourself, Miss Roberts, before you begin the duties of the day. (*To* TOM.) Miss Roberts is the children's governess.
TOM. Oh? (*To* MISS ROBERTS.) Do you rap them over the knuckles? And stick them in the corner?
MISS ROBERTS (*answering him in the same spirit of raillery*). Oh, yes—pinch them and slap them and box their ears.
MRS. BAXTER (*leaning forward in her chair, thinking this may be true*). I hope you don't do anything of the sort, Miss Roberts.
MISS ROBERTS. Oh, no! not really, Mrs. Baxter. (*She rises.*) I think I'll say good-night.
TOM. Don't go to bed yet, Miss Roberts.
MRS. BAXTER (*yawning*). It's about time we all went.
TOM (*to* MRS. BAXTER). You, too?
MRS. BAXTER. What time is it?
TOM (*looking at his watch*). Twenty minutes past ten.
MRS. BAXTER. How late.
TOM. Call that late?
MRS. BAXTER. Ten is our bed-time. (*She rises.*)

Come along, Miss Roberts; we shan't be fit for anything in the morning if we don't bustle off to bed.
(*She suppresses a yawn.*)
MISS ROBERTS. Good-night, Mr. Baxter.
(*She shakes hands with him.*)
MR. BAXTER. Good-night.
MISS ROBERTS (*shaking hands with* TOM). Good-night.
TOM. Good-night, Miss Roberts; sleep well.
MISS ROBERTS. I always do.
MRS. BAXTER. Will you give me the magazine off the table, Miss Roberts, to take upstairs? (TOM *goes to the table and hands the magazine to* MISS ROBERTS, *who brings it to* MRS. BAXTER. *To* MISS ROBERTS.) You and I needn't say good-night. We shall meet on the landing.
(*Turns over the pages of the magazine.*)
MISS ROBERTS. Good-night, everybody.
TOM (*following* MISS ROBERTS *to the foot of the stairs*). Good-night, Miss Roberts. (MISS ROBERTS *goes out.*) Nice girl, Miss Roberts.
MRS. BAXTER. She suits me very well.
MR. BAXTER. She says she is going to leave.
TOM. Leave—Miss Roberts mustn't leave!
MRS. BAXTER. I don't think she meant it. Don't sit up too late, Tom, and don't hurry down in the morning. Would you like your breakfast in bed?
TOM (*laughing*). In bed?
MRS. BAXTER. I thought you'd be so worn out after your journey.
TOM. Heavens, no, that's nothing. Good-night, little sister.
(*He kisses her.*)
MRS. BAXTER. Good-night, Tom. It's so nice to see you again. (*Then to* MR. BAXTER.) Try not to disturb me when you come upstairs. (*Speaking through a yawn as she goes towards the door.*) Oh, dear, I'm so sleepy.
(*She goes out.*)
MR. BAXTER (*smiling at* TOM). Well, Tom!
TOM (*smiling at* MR. BAXTER). Well, Dick, how's everything? Business pretty good?
MR. BAXTER. So so.
TOM. That's nice.

MR. BAXTER. I don't go into the city every day now, two or three times a week. I leave my partners to attend to things the rest of the time—they seem to get on just as well without me.

TOM. I daresay they would. (*Taking out his cigarette case.*) I suppose I may smoke?

MR. BAXTER (*doubtfully*). Here?

TOM. Well, don't you smoke here?

MR. BAXTER. You may. She won't smell it in the morning. (TOM *laughs and takes out a cigarette.*) Tom, if ever you get married don't give in to your wife's weaknesses in the first few days of the honeymoon—you'll want to then, but don't. It becomes a habit. What's the use of saying that to you? I suppose you'll never marry now.

(*He sits down.*)

TOM (*quite annoyed*). Why not? Why shouldn't I marry? I don't see why you think I shan't marry. How long has she been here?

(*He lights a cigarette.*)

MR. BAXTER. Who?

TOM. Miss Roberts.

MR. BAXTER. Oh!

TOM. Weren't we talking of Miss Roberts?

MR. BAXTER. No.

TOM. Oh, well, we are now.

MR. BAXTER. She's been here about four years. I'm so sorry she wants to leave. I don't want her to go at all.

TOM. Nor do I. Rather nice for you, Dick. A pretty wife and a pretty governess.

(*He nudges him.*)

MR. BAXTER. Tom, don't do that.

(*He defends himself by putting up his hands.*)

TOM. Very well, I won't.

MR. BAXTER (*embarrassed and slightly annoyed*). Why do you say that?

TOM. Only chaffing. (*He sees the chess-board.*) Who's been playing chess?

MR. BAXTER. Miss Roberts and I.

TOM. Does Miss Roberts play chess? I must get her to teach me—let me see if I can remember any of the moves. (*He sits by the table and moves the chess men about idly as he talks.*) She is far too good to be your governess.

MR. BAXTER (*enthusing*). You've noticed what an unusual woman she is?

TOM. Charming!

MR. BAXTER. Isn't she?

TOM. And so pretty!

MR. BAXTER. Very pretty.

TOM. She'll make a good wife for some man.

MR. BAXTER (*reluctantly*). I suppose so—some time.

TOM. I should make love to her if I lived in the same house.

MR. BAXTER. But if you were married?

TOM. I'm not!

MR. BAXTER (*slowly and thoughtfully*). No.

(*There is a moment's pause.*)

TOM. Let's change the subject, and talk about Miss Roberts. Tell me things about her.

MR. BAXTER. She's an orphan.

TOM. Poor girl.

MR. BAXTER. She's no near relations.

TOM. Lucky fellow.

MR. BAXTER. She's wonderful with the children.

TOM. Make a good mother.

MR. BAXTER. And so nice, so interesting, so good, such a companion. I can't find a single fault in her. She's a woman in a thousand, in a million.

TOM. I say, you'd better not let Dulcie hear you talk like that.

MR. BAXTER (*seriously*). I don't. (TOM *laughs.*) I was only saying that to show you how well she suits us.

TOM. Of course.

MR. BAXTER. How well she suits Dulcie.

TOM. Oh, Dulcie, of course.

MR. BAXTER. I can't think what Dulcie will do without her; she's got so used to her. Miss Roberts waits on Dulcie hand and foot.

TOM (*indignantly*). What a shame!

MR. BAXTER. Isn't it?

TOM. Why should Dulcie be waited on hand and foot?

MR. BAXTER. I don't know. She's so—well, not exactly ill.

TOM. Ill ? She's as strong as a horse, always was.

MR. BAXTER. Yes, I can't remember when she had anything really the matter with her, but she always seems so tired—keeps wanting to lie down—she's not an invalid, she's a——

TOM. She's a mollusc.

MR. BAXTER. What's that ?

TOM. Mollusca, subdivision of the animal kingdom.

MR. BAXTER. I know that.

TOM. I don't know if the Germans have remarked that many mammalia display characteristics commonly assigned to mollusca. I suppose the scientific explanation is that a mollusc once married a mammal and their descendants are the human mollusc.

MR. BAXTER (*much puzzled*). What *are* you talking about ?

TOM. People who are like a mollusc of the sea, which clings to a rock and lets the tide flow over its head. People who spend all their energy and ingenuity in sticking instead of moving, in whom the instinct for what I call molluscry is as dominating as an inborn vice. And it is so catching. Why, one mollusc will infect a whole household. We all had it at home. Mother was quite a famous mollusc in her time. She was bedridden for fifteen years, and then, don't you remember, got up to Dulcie's wedding, to the amazement of everybody, and tripped down the aisle as lively as a kitten, and then went to bed again till she heard of something else she wanted to go to—a garden party or something. Father, he was a mollusc, too ; he called it being a conservative ; he might just as well have stayed in bed, too. Ada, Charlie, Emmeline, all of them were more or less mollusky but Dulcibella was the queen. You won't often see such a fine healthy specimen of a mollusc as Dulcie. I'm a born mollusc !

MR. BAXTER (*surprised*). You ?

TOM. Yes, I'm energetic now, but only artificially energetic. I have to be on to myself all the time ; make myself do things. That's why I chose the vigorous West, and wander from camp to camp. I made a pile in Leadville. I gambled it all away. I made another in Cripple Creek. I gave it away to the poor. If I made another, I should chuck it away. Don't you see

# THE MOLLUSC

why? Give me a competence, nothing to work for, nothing to worry about from day to day—why I should become as famous a mollusc as dear old mother was.

MR. BAXTER. Is molluscry the same as laziness?

TOM. No, not altogether. The lazy flow with the tide. The mollusc uses forces to resist pressure. It's amazing the amount of force a mollusc will use, to do nothing, when it would be so much easier to do something. It's no fool, you know, it's often the most artful creature, it wriggles and squirms, and even fights from the instinct not to advance. There are wonderful things about molluscry, things to make you shout with laughter, but it's sad enough, too—it can ruin a life so, not only the life of the mollusc, but all the lives in the house where it dwells.

MR. BAXTER. Is there no cure for molluscry?

TOM. Well, I should say once a mollusc always a mollusc. But it's like drink, or any other vice. If grappled with it can be kept under. If left to itself, it becomes incurable.

MR. BAXTER. Is Dulcie a very advanced case?

TOM. Oh, very! ! !

MR. BAXTER. Oh!

TOM. But let us hope not incurable. You know better than I how far she has gone. Tell me.

MR. BAXTER (*seriously*). She's certainly getting worse. For instance, I can remember the time when she would go to church twice a Sunday, walk there and back; now she drives once, and she keeps an extra cushion in the pew, sits down for the hymns and makes the girls find her places.

TOM. Do you ever tell her not to mollusc so much?

MR. BAXTER. I used to, but I've given up now.

TOM. Oh, you must never give up.

MR. BAXTER. The trouble is she thinks she's so very active.

TOM. Molluscs always think that.

MR. BAXTER. Dulcie thinks of something to be done and tells me to do it, and then, by some mental process, which I don't pretend to grasp, she thinks she's done it herself. D'you think she does that to humbug me?

TOM. I believe there's no dividing line between the

conscious and subconscious thoughts of molluscs. She probably humbugs herself just as much as she humbugs you.

MR. BAXTER. Oh!

TOM. You must be firm with her. The next time she tells you to do a thing tell her to do it herself.

MR. BAXTER. I tried that. The other day, for instance, she wanted me to set a mouse-trap in her dressing-room; well, I was very busy at the time, and I knew there were no mice there, so I refused. It meant getting the cheese and everything.

TOM (*trying not to appear amused*). Of course. And what did she say when you refused to set the mouse-trap?

MR. BAXTER. She began to make me sorry for her; she has no end of ways of making me sorry for her, and I've a very tender heart; but that day I just didn't care. I had the devil in me, so I said—set it yourself.

TOM. Bravo.

MR. BAXTER. We got quite unpleasant over it.

TOM. And which of you set the mouse-trap in the end?

MR. BAXTER. Miss Roberts. (TOM *rises and moves away to hide his amusement from* MR. BAXTER.) It's always like that. She makes Miss Roberts do everything. For instance, Dulcie used to play chess with me of an evening, now she tells Miss Roberts to. She used to go walks with me, now she sends Miss Roberts. Dulcie was never energetic, but we used to have some good times together; now I can't get her to go anywhere or do anything.

TOM. Not very amusing for *you*.

MR. BAXTER. It does rather take the fun out of everything.

TOM. How did you come to let her get so bad?

MR. BAXTER (*simply*). I fell in love with her. That put me at her mercy.

(*There is a moment's silence, then* TOM *says with decision.*)

TOM. *I* must take her in hand.

MR. BAXTER. I wish you would.

TOM. I'll make her dance.

MR. BAXTER. Don't be hard on her.

TOM. No, but firm. I'll show her what firmness is. A brother is the best person in the world to undertake the education of a mollusc. His firmness will be tempered with affection, and his affection won't be undermined with sentimentality. I shall start in on Dulcie the first thing to-morrow morning.

MR. BAXTER. And now what do you say to getting our candles?

TOM (*following* MR. BAXTER *towards the stairs*). Come along. I'm ready—must have a good night's rest if I'm to tackle Dulcie in the morning. I don't anticipate any trouble. A woman isn't difficult to deal with if you take her the right way. Leave her to me, old man. You just leave her to me!

(*They go up the stairs.*)

CURTAIN.

# THE SECOND ACT

SCENE.—*The same scene on the following morning. The French windows are wide open, displaying a view of the garden bathed in sunshine.*
MRS. BAXTER *is lounging in an armchair reading a novel.*
TOM *enters with an enormous bunch of wild flowers, foxgloves, meadowsweet, etc.*

TOM. Look!
MRS. BAXTER. Oh, how pretty! We must put them in water. Where's Miss Roberts?
TOM. In the schoolroom. They are at their lessons.
MRS. BAXTER. Then we must wait. What a pity. I hope they won't die.
TOM. Is Miss Roberts the only person in this house who can put these flowers in water?
MRS. BAXTER. The servants are always busy in the morning.
TOM. Why can't *you* do it?
MRS. BAXTER. *I* have other things to do.
TOM. What?
MRS. BAXTER. Numerous things. Do you think a woman never has anything to do?
TOM (*coming to her and tapping her on the shoulder*). Get up and do them yourself.
MRS. BAXTER (*amiably*). While you sit still in this chair. All very fine!
TOM. I'll help you.
MRS. BAXTER (*rising lazily*). Very well. Bring me the vases and some water. (*She smells the flowers.*)
TOM (*pointing to two vases on the mantelpiece*). Will these do?
MRS. BAXTER. Yes. Get those.
TOM (*pointing to another vase on the table*). And *that*.

*You* must get that one. We will divide the labour. (*He gets the two vases.* MRS. BAXTER *has not stirred.*) Where's yours?

MRS. BAXTER (*smiling pleasantly*). I thought *you* were going to get the vases.

TOM. We were going to do this work between us. Get your vase.

MRS. BAXTER (*laughing*). Oh, Tom—what a boy you are still.

TOM. Why should I get all the vases? (*talking seriously to her*). You know, Dulcie, you'd feel better if you ran about a little more.

MRS. BAXTER (*pleasantly*). You'd save time, dear, if you'd run and get that vase yourself instead of standing there telling *me* to.

(TOM *puts the vases on the table. Then he goes and takes up the other vase.*)

TOM. Oh, very well. It's not worth quarrelling about.

MRS. BAXTER. No, don't let us quarrel the first morning you are home.

TOM (*bringing the vase and putting it before her*). There!

MRS. BAXTER. Thank you, Tom. You'll find a tap in the wall outside the window and a little watering-can beside it.

TOM. *I* got the vases.

MRS. BAXTER. *Please* bring me the water, Tom. These poppies are beginning to droop already.

TOM. I *won't* get the water. You must get it yourself.

MRS. BAXTER (*smiling*). Very well. Wait till I go upstairs and put on my hat.

TOM. To go just outside the window?

MRS. BAXTER. I can't go into the hot sun without a hat.

TOM. Rats!

MRS. BAXTER (*seriously*). It's *not* rats. Dr. Ross said I must *never* go out in the sun without a hat.

TOM. That much won't hurt you.

MRS. BAXTER. *I* don't mind, of course. But *you* must take the consequences if I have a sunstroke. Dick will be furious when he hears I've been out in the sun without a hat. You wouldn't like me to make Dick furious, would you, Tom ? (TOM *touches her and points to the window, then folds his arms. There is a slight pause while she waits for* TOM *to offer to go.*) If you think it's too much trouble to step outside the window I'll go all the way upstairs for my hat. I suppose all these pretty flowers will be quite dead by the time I come back.

TOM (*exasperated*). Oh, very well, I'll get the water.
(*He goes out into the garden.*)

MRS. BAXTER (*calling*). Try not to scratch the can, and be sure you don't leave the tap to dribble.

TOM (*outside*). Oh, the tap's all right.
(*She occupies herself by smelling the flowers.* TOM *re-enters almost immediately with a little watering-can.*)

TOM. Here's the water.

MRS. BAXTER. Thank you, Tom. Work seems like play when we do it between us. Fill the vases.

TOM. I won't.
(*He puts the can on the table.*)

MRS. BAXTER. Well, wait while I go and get an apron.

TOM. You don't want an apron for that.

MRS. BAXTER. I'm not going to risk spilling the water all down this dress ; I only put it on so as to look nice for you. I won't be a minute.

TOM. Stay where you are. (*Muttering to himself as he fills the vases.*) An apron to fill three vases. You might as well put on your boots, or get an umbrella or a waterproof.
(*He is about to set the can on the floor.*)

MRS. BAXTER (*quickly*). Don't put it on the carpet. Put it on the gravel outside.

TOM. Put it on the gravel yourself.
(TOM *holds the can for her to take. She elaborately begins to wind a handkerchief round her right hand.*)

MRS. BAXTER. It's no use both of us wetting our hands.
(TOM *grumbling goes to the window and pitches the can outside.*)

TOM. Now I hope I've scratched the can, and I'm sorry I didn't leave the tap to dribble.

MRS. BAXTER. Naughty, naughty. Do you remember

Tom, when we were all at home together, you always did the flowers?

TOM. I'm not going to do them now.

MRS. BAXTER. You did them so tastefully. No one could do flowers like you. I remember Aunt Lizzie calling one day and saying if we hired a florist to arrange our flowers we couldn't have got prettier effects than you got.

TOM. Get on with those flowers.

MRS. BAXTER. When I did the flowers, Mamma used to say the drawing-room used to look like a rubbish heap.

TOM (*loudly*). Get on with those flowers.

MRS. BAXTER. I should so like Miss Roberts to see the way you can arrange flowers.

TOM. Get on——

MRS. BAXTER (*wheedling him*). Do arrange one vase—only one, just to show Miss Roberts.

TOM (*weakening*). Well, only one. You must do the other two.

(*He begins to put the flowers in water.* MRS. BAXTER *watches him a moment, then she sinks into the handiest armchair.*)

MRS. BAXTER (*after a slight pause*). How well you do it.

TOM (*suddenly realising the situation*). No, no, I won't. (*He flings the flowers on the table.*) Oh, you are artful. You've done nothing; I've done everything; I got the flowers, the vases, the water—everything, and now not another stalk will I touch. I don't care if they die; their blood will be on your head, not mine.

(*He sits down and folds his arms. A pause.*)

MRS. BAXTER (*serenely*). If you won't talk, I may as well go on reading my novel. It's on the table beside you. Would you mind passing it?

TOM. Yes, I would.

MRS. BAXTER. Throw it.

TOM. I shan't.

MRS. BAXTER. I thought you'd cheer us up when you came home, but you just sit in my chair doing nothing.

TOM (*turning on her and saying gravely*). Dulcie, it grieves me very much to see you such a mollusc.

MRS. BAXTER. What's a mollusc?

TOM. You are.

MRS. BAXTER (*puzzled*). A mollusc? (*Gaily.*) Oh, I know, one of those pretty little creatures that live in the sea—or am I thinking of a sea anemone?

TOM. It's dreadful to see a strong healthy woman so idle.

MRS. BAXTER (*genuinely amazed*). I idle? Oh, you're joking.

TOM. What are you doing but idling now? (*Approaching her and saying roughly.*) Get up, and do those flowers. Get out of that chair this minute.

MRS. BAXTER (*rising and smiling*). I was only waiting for *you*. I thought we were going to do the flowers together.

TOM. No, we won't do them together; if we do them together I shall be doing them by myself before I know where I am.

(*He sits again.*)

MRS. BAXTER. I don't call that fair, to promise to help me with the flowers, and then just to sit and watch. I don't think Colorado is improving you. You've become so lazy and underhand.

TOM (*indignantly*). What do you mean?

MRS. BAXTER. What I mean to say is, you undertook to help me with the flowers, and now you try to back out of it. Perhaps you call that sharp in America, but in England we should call it unsportsmanlike.

TOM (*picking up the flowers and throwing them down disgustedly*). Oh, why did I ever go and gather all this rubbish?

(MR. BAXTER *enters and comes down the stairs.*)

MR. BAXTER. Half-past eleven, dear.

MRS. BAXTER. Thank you, dear.

TOM. Half-past eleven, dear—thank you, dear—what does that mean?

MR. BAXTER. Lunch.

TOM. Already?

MR. BAXTER. Not real lunch.

MRS. BAXTER. We always have cake and milk in the dining-room at half-past eleven. We think it breaks up the morning more. Aren't you coming?

TOM. Cake and milk at half-past eleven; what an idea! No, thank you.

MRS. BAXTER. I shall be glad of the chance to sit down. I've had a most exhausting morning.
(*She goes out.*)

MR. BAXTER. Have you been taking her in hand?

TOM (*pretending not to comprehend*). I beg your pardon?

MR. BAXTER. You said you were going to take her in hand, first thing this morning.

TOM. Oh, yes, so I did. So I have done—in a way—not seriously, of course—not the first morning.

MR. BAXTER. You said you were going to show her what firmness was.

TOM. Well, so I did, but never having had any firmness from you, she doesn't know it when she sees it. (MR. BAXTER *is about to put some of the flowers in a vase.*) What are you doing?

MR. BAXTER. They're dying for want of water.

TOM. But I said she must put them in water herself.

MR. BAXTER. Oh, I see, discipline.

TOM. Exactly.

MR. BAXTER. What happened?

TOM (*pointing to the flowers*). Can't you see what's happened? There they are still. (*Angrily.*) We've spent hours wrangling over those damned flowers. It may seem paltry to make such a fuss over anything so trivial, but it's the principle of the thing; if I give in at the start, I shall have to give in to the finish.

MR. BAXTER. Like me.

TOM. Yes, like you. When she comes back from the dining-room, I'll make her do those flowers herself if I have to stand over her all the morning.

MR. BAXTER (*looking at* TOM *with admiration*). That's the spirit. If only I had begun like that the very first morning of our honeymoon.

TOM (*with great determination*). I'll stand no nonsense. She *shall* do the flowers herself.

(MISS ROBERTS *enters.*)

MISS ROBERTS. Mrs. Baxter sent me to do the flowers.
(*She comes immediately to the table and begins putting the flowers in water.* TOM *and* MR. BAXTER *look at each other.*)

TOM (*to him*). Shall I tell her not to?

MR. BAXTER. Then Dulcie will tell her she is to.

TOM. Then we shall have to humiliate Dulcie before Miss Roberts.

MR. BAXTER. Yes.

TOM. I don't want to do that.

MR. BAXTER. No.

TOM. I'm not giving in.

MR. BAXTER. No.

TOM. Don't gloat.

MR. BAXTER. I'm not gloating.

TOM. You are. You're gloating because I've had to give in the way *you* always do.

MISS ROBERTS (*to* MR. BAXTER). The girls have been asking if I thought they could have a half-holiday in honour of their uncle's arrival.

MR. BAXTER. I don't see why not.

MISS ROBERTS. If you think they'd be in the way, I might take them off to the woods for the day.

MR. BAXTER. Yes.

MISS ROBERTS. I thought as it's so fine we might take our lunch with us, and have a picnic.

TOM. Why don't we all go a picnic?

MR. BAXTER. All who?

TOM. You and I and the girls and Miss Roberts and Dulcie.

MR. BAXTER. You'll never get Dulcie on a picnic, will he, Miss Roberts?

TOM. Why not?

MR. BAXTER. Too much exertion.

MISS ROBERTS (*still busy filling the vases*). I think Mrs. Baxter would go if Mr. Kemp asked her.

(TOM *looks at* MR. BAXTER *as soon as* MISS ROBERTS *has spoken and* MR. BAXTER *looks dubious.*)

TOM (*in a lower voice, to* MR. BAXTER). I don't want Miss Roberts to think that I can't master Dulcie; besides, a picnic, the very thing to make her run about, but we must approach her tactfully and keep our tempers. I lost mine over the flowers, otherwise I've not the least doubt I could have made her do them; we must humour Dulcie and cajole her. Whisk her off to the woods in a whirl of gaiety; you go dancing into the dining-room like this. (*Assuming great jollity.*) We're all going off on a picnic.

MR. BAXTER. Oh, no.

## THE MOLLUSC

TOM. Why not?

MR. BAXTER. It wouldn't be me.

TOM. Well, er—(*glancing at* MISS ROBERTS) go and—er—— (*Glancing again at* MISS ROBERTS.) Oh, go and say whatever you like. But be jolly about it; full of the devil.

(*He takes* MR. BAXTER *by the arm and pushes him towards the stairs.*)

MR. BAXTER (*imitating* TOM *as he goes*). We're all going off on a picnic. (*He stops at the top of the stairs and says seriously.*) It wouldn't be me.

(*He exits.*)

TOM. So you're not one of the cake and milk brigade?

MISS ROBERTS. No.

TOM. I thought you wouldn't be.

MISS ROBERTS. Aren't you going to join them?

TOM. No, I don't want to eat cake in the middle of the morning. I'm like you. We seem to have a lot of habits in common.

MISS ROBERTS. Do you think so?

TOM. Don't you?

MISS ROBERTS. I haven't thought.

(*She takes a vase to the mantelpiece.* TOM *watches her and follows with the other vase.* MISS ROBERTS *takes the vase from* TOM *and puts it on the mantelpiece.*)

TOM. Didn't we have a nice walk together?

MISS ROBERTS. Yes; don't you love being out in the early morning?

TOM. I'm up with the sun at home out West. I live out-of-doors out there.

MISS ROBERTS. How splendid!

TOM. You're the kind of girl for Colorado.

MISS ROBERTS (*pleased*). Am I?

TOM. Can you ride?

MISS ROBERTS. Yes, but I don't get any opportunities now.

TOM. Got a good nerve?

MISS ROBERTS. I broke a colt once; he'd thrown three men, but he never threw me!

TOM (*smiling at her*). Well done!

MISS ROBERTS. I didn't mean to boast, but I'd love to do it again.

TOM. I should love to see you mounted on a mustang, flying through our country.

MISS ROBERTS. With the tree tops waving down in the valley, and the great blue mountains you told us about, stretching away—away——

TOM (*watching her with admiration*). You certainly ought to come to Colorado.

MISS ROBERTS. Nothing so thrilling could happen to me.

(*She returns to the table and picks up the remaining flowers.*)

TOM (*following her*). Why? You've nothing to do but get on the boat and take the train from New York, and I'd meet you in Denver.

MISS ROBERTS (*laughing*). It's so nice to have some one here to make us laugh.

TOM (*a little hurt*). Oh, I was being serious.

MISS ROBERTS (*seriously*). Do you really think Colorado would be a good place for a girl like me to go to? A governess!

TOM. Yes, yes, a girl who has to earn her own living has a better time of it out there than here, more independence, more chance, more life.

MISS ROBERTS (*thoughtfully*). I do know an English lady in Colorado Springs, at least a great friend of mine does, and I'm sure I could get a letter to her.

TOM (*cheerfully*). You don't want any letters of introduction; you've got me.

MISS ROBERTS (*smiling*). Yes, but that is not quite the same thing.

TOM. No, I suppose not; no, I see: well, can't you write to your friend and tell her to send that letter on at once?

MISS ROBERTS (*amused*). You talk as if it were all settled.

TOM. I wish it were.

MISS ROBERTS (*not noticing that he is flirting with her, she says thoughtfully*). I wish I knew what to do about leaving here.

TOM. You told me you had already given my sister notice.

MISS ROBERTS. She won't take it.

TOM. She can't make you stay if you want to go.

MISS ROBERTS (*smiling, but serious*). It's not as simple as that. After Mrs. Baxter has treated me so well, I should be making a poor return if I left her before she found some one to take my place. On the other hand, my duty to the children is to leave them.

TOM. A real old-fashioned conscience.

MISS ROBERTS. One must think of the others.

TOM. It seems to me you're always doing that.

MISS ROBERTS. If you knew how I sometimes long to be free to do whatever I like just for one day. When I see other girls—girls who don't work for a living—enjoying themselves—it comes over me so dreadfully what I am missing. From the schoolroom window I can see the tennis club, and while I am giving Gladys and Margery their geography lesson, I hear them calling " Play ! Fifteen love ! " and see the ball flying, and the girls in their white dresses, talking to such nice-looking young men.

TOM. Um, yes. Don't *you* ever talk to any of those nice-looking young men.

MISS ROBERTS. Of course not.

TOM. How's that ?

MISS ROBERTS. Governesses never do. We only pass them by as we walk out with the children, or see the backs of their heads in church. Or if we are introduced, as I was to one at the Rectory one day—the occasion is so unusual we feel quite strained and nervous—and can't appear at our best. So that they don't want to pursue the acquaintance even if they could.

TOM. You don't seem strained and nervous as you talk to me.

MISS ROBERTS (*innocently*). You don't seem like the others. (*She meets his eyes—smiles at him and says.*) I must go back to the schoolroom.

(*She rises.*)

TOM (*rising and coming to* MISS ROBERTS). Not yet. Don't go yet. I want you to stay here—talking to me. You are sure to hear my little nieces shrieking about in the garden when they have done their cake.

(MRS. BAXTER *enters, followed by* MR. BAXTER.)

MRS. BAXTER. Oh, I hurried back to finish the flowers, but I see you have done them. Thank you.

MISS ROBERTS. You asked me to do them, Mrs. Baxter.

MRS. BAXTER (*smiling*). Oh, no, Miss Roberts—I think you are mistaken. I only said they were there waiting to be done.

(*She sits in an armchair and begins to read a novel.*)

TOM (*in an undertone to* MR. BAXTER). Have you told her about the picnic?

MR. BAXTER. There was no suitable opportunity—so——

TOM. You're a coward! (*He pushes past him.* TOM *then motions to* MR. BAXTER *to speak to* MRS. BAXTER. *He refuses.* TOM, *assuming great cheerfulness, addresses* MRS. BAXTER.) We are all going off on a picnic.

MRS. BAXTER (*pleasantly*). Oh.

TOM. Yes. We four and the girls. (*Whispering to* MR. BAXTER.) Back me up.

MR. BAXTER (*rubbing his hands together, and trying to assume jollity*). Won't that be fun?

MRS. BAXTER (*brightly*). I think it would be great fun——

TOM. Ah!

MRS. BAXTER. Some day.

TOM. Why not to-day?

MRS. BAXTER. Why to-day?

TOM (*at a loss for an answer, appeals to* MR. BAXTER *and* MISS ROBERTS). Why to-day?

MISS ROBERTS. In honour of Mr. Kemp's arrival, and it's such a fine day—and——

MRS. BAXTER. You will find the girls in the school-room—dear.

TOM (*very jolly*). Shall she go and get them ready?

MRS BAXTER (*innocently*). What for?

TOM. The picnic.

MRS. BAXTER. I thought it had been decided not to go to-day.

MR. BAXTER (*losing his temper*). Oh, Dulcie—you know quite well——

TOM (*signing to* MR. BAXTER *to keep quiet*). Sh! (*Turning to* MRS. BAXTER *and pretending to make a meek, heartfelt appeal.*) Please let us go to-day. It's in honour of my arrival. I shall be *so* hurt if I don't have a picnic in honour of my arrival.

MRS. BAXTER. Suppose it rains.

TOM (*at a loss for an answer, appealing to the others*). Suppose it rains?

MISS ROBERTS (*at the window*). I can't see a single cloud.

MR. BAXTER. The glass has gone up.

TOM. It won't rain if we take plenty of umbrellas and mackintoshes and our goloshes.

MRS. BAXTER. I think we are all too tired.

TOM (*scouting the idea*). Too tired!

(MR. BAXTER *and* TOM *get together.*)

MRS. BAXTER. I suppose it is the excitement of Tom's arrival which is making us feel so next-dayish.

TOM. Next-dayish!

MRS. BAXTER. *You* especially. You were very irritable over the flowers. You ought to go and lie down.

(*She takes up her novel and opens it as if she considered the argument over.* MISS ROBERTS *watches them anxiously.* MR. BAXTER *makes an emphatic gesture, expressing his strong feelings on the subject.*)

TOM (*clutching his arm*). We *must* keep our tempers. We *must* keep our tempers.

MR. BAXTER. Shall we poke fun at her?

TOM. No, no, we'll try a little coaxing first. (*He takes a chair, places it close beside* MRS. BAXTER *and sits. Smiling affectionately at* MRS. BAXTER.) Dear Dulcie.

MRS. BAXTER (*smiling affectionately at* TOM *and patting his knees*). Dear Tom.

TOM. We shall have such a merry picnic.

MRS. BAXTER. It *would* have been nice, wouldn't it?

TOM. Under a canopy of green boughs with the sunbeams dropping patterns on the carpet of moss at our feet.

MRS. BAXTER. Spiders dropping on our hats.

TOM. Dear, interesting little creatures, and so industrious.

MRS. BAXTER. Ants up our arms.

TOM (*laughing*). Lizards up our legs. Frogs in our food. Oh, we shall get back to Nature. (TOM *and* MRS. BAXTER *both laugh heartily, both in the greatest good-humour.* MR. BAXTER *and* MISS ROBERTS *also laugh.*) Then it's settled.

MRS. BAXTER. Yes, dear—it's settled.

TOM (*thinking he has won*). Ah!

MRS. BAXTER. We'll all stay quietly at home.
   (*She resumes the reading of her book.* TOM *is in dismay.*)

MR. BAXTER. The girls will be greatly disappointed.

TOM (*with emotion*). Poor girls! A day in the woods. (*With mock pathos.*) Think what that means to those poor girls.

MRS. BAXTER (*rising and saying seriously to* MISS ROBERTS). Miss Roberts, you might go to the schoolroom and tell Gladys and Margery that Mamma says they may have a half-holiday and go for a picnic in the woods.
   (TOM *winks at* MR. BAXTER. *The three look at each other agreeably surprised.*)

MISS ROBERTS (*moving towards the stairs*). Thank you. Thank you very much, Mrs. Baxter. I'll go and get them ready at once.
   (*She goes out.*)

TOM. I knew we only had to appeal to her heart.

MR. BAXTER. We shall want twelve hard-boiled eggs.

TOM. And some ginger-beer.

MR. BAXTER. A ham.

TOM. A few prawns.

MRS. BAXTER (*looking out of the window, to which she has strolled*). I am glad Miss Roberts and the girls have got such a fine day for their picnic.
   (TOM *and* MR. BAXTER *look at each other in dismay.*)

MR. BAXTER (*after a pause*). After leading us on to believe——

TOM (*in great good-humour*). Can't you see she's teasing us? (*Going to* MRS. BAXTER, *he playfully pinches her ear.*) Mischievous little puss!

MRS. BAXTER (*gravely to* MR. BAXTER). Dear, I should like to speak to you.

MR. BAXTER. Shall we go to my room?

MRS. BAXTER. I don't see why we need trouble to walk across the hall. (*Glances at* TOM.) We may get this room to ourselves by and by.
   (*She sits down.*)

TOM (*cheerfully taking the hint*). All right—all right. I'll go and make preparations for the picnic. Don't keep us waiting, Dulcie. Prawns — hams — gingerbeer——

(*He runs off.*)

MR. BAXTER (*slightly peevish*). I wish you would enter more into the spirit of the picnic. It would do you good to go to a picnic.

MRS. BAXTER. I don't like the way Tom is carrying on with Miss Roberts. Last evening they monopolised the conversation. This morning—a walk before breakfast. Just now—as soon as my back is turned—at it again. I don't like it—and it wouldn't do me any good at all to go to a picnic.

MR. BAXTER. Tom seems so set on our going.

MRS. BAXTER. Tom is set on making *me* go. Tom has taken upon himself to reform my character. He thinks I need stirring up.

MR. BAXTER (*embarrassed*). What put such an idea as that into your head ?

MRS. BAXTER (*looking him straight in the eye*). The clumsy way you both go about it. (MR. BAXTER *looks exceedingly uncomfortable.*) . . . It wouldn't deceive any woman. It wouldn't suit me at all if Tom became interested in Miss Roberts. I could never find another Miss Roberts. She understands my ways so well, I couldn't possibly do without her ; not that I'm thinking of myself ; I'm thinking only of her good. It's not right for Tom to come here turning her head, and I don't suppose the climate of Colorado would suit her.

MR. BAXTER. I don't think we need worry yet. They only met yesterday.

MRS. BAXTER. That is so like you, dear—to sit still and let everything slip past you like the—what was that funny animal Tom mentioned ?—the mollusc. I prefer to take action. We must speak to Tom.

MR. BAXTER. You'll only offend him if you say anything to him.

MRS. BAXTER. I've no intention of saying anything. I think it would come much better from you.

MR. BAXTER (*with determination*). *I* shan't interfere.

MRS. BAXTER (*trying to work on his feelings*). It's not often I ask you to do anything for me, and I'm not strong.

MR. BAXTER (*feeling uncomfortable*). I shouldn't know what to say to Tom, or how to say it.

MRS. BAXTER (*approaching* MR. BAXTER). You know the way men talk to each other. Go up to him and say, " I say, old fellow, that little governess of ours. Hands off, damn it all." (MRS. BAXTER *nudges* MR. BAXTER *in a masculine way.* MR. BAXTER *laughs and retreats a little.* MRS. BAXTER *is mightily offended.*) I don't consider that trifling with a young girl's affections is food for laughter.

MR. BAXTER (*trying to conceal his amusement*). I think I'll go and join Tom.

MRS. BAXTER. Will you tell him we wish him to pay less (MISS ROBERTS *enters*) attention to——

(*She sees* MISS ROBERTS.)

MR. BAXTER. We'll see.

(*He goes out.*)

MRS. BAXTER. I know what *that* means.

MISS ROBERTS (*coming to* MRS. BAXTER). If you please, Mrs. Baxter, I'm having such trouble with Gladys and Margery. They want to go to the picnic in their Sunday hats, and I say they must go in their everyday ones.

MRS. BAXTER. If there's going to be any trouble about the matter, let them have their own way.

MISS ROBERTS. Thank you.

(*She is going out.*)

MRS. BAXTER. Oh, Miss Roberts. (MISS ROBERTS *stops.*) I want a word with you before you start off on your picnic. Sit down, dear. (MISS ROBERTS *sits down.*) You know how devoted I am to my brother Tom.

MISS ROBERTS (*with smiling enthusiasm*). I don't wonder. He's delightful. So amusing, so easy to get on with.

MRS. BAXTER. Yes, but of course we all have our faults, and a man who gets on easily with one will get on easily with another. Always mistrust people who are easy to get on with.

MISS ROBERTS (*solemnly*). Oh—do you mean he isn't *quite* honest ?

MRS. BAXTER (*indignantly*). Nothing of the sort. You mustn't twist my meanings in that manner. You might get me into great trouble.

MISS ROBERTS. I'm so sorry, but I thought you were warning me against him.

MRS. BAXTER (*confused*). Yes—no—yes—and no. (*Re-*

*covering herself.*) I am sure you will take what I'm going to say as I mean it, because (*smiles at her*) I am so fond of you. Ever since you came to us I have wished to make you one of the family. When I say one of the family, I mean in the sense of taking your meals with us. Mr. Baxter and the girls and I are so much attached to you. We should like to keep you with us always.

MISS ROBERTS. I *must* leave at the end of the term.

MRS. BAXTER. We won't go into all that now.

MISS ROBERTS. But——

MRS. BAXTER (*smiling and raising her hand in protestation, says politely*). Try not to interrupt. (*Seriously.*) I should say that a man of Tom's age who has never married would be a confirmed bachelor. He might amuse himself here and there with a pretty girl, but he would never think of any woman seriously.

MISS ROBERTS (*embarrassed*). I can't think why you are saying this to me.

MRS. BAXTER (*plunging at last into her subject*). To speak quite frankly—as a sister—I find your attitude towards my brother Tom a trifle too encouraging. Last evening, for instance, you monopolised a good deal of the conversation—and this morning you took a walk with him before breakfast—and altogether (*very sweetly*) it looks just a little bit as if you were trying to flirt—doesn't it?

MISS ROBERTS (*with suppressed rage*). I'm not a flirt!

MRS. BAXTER. I didn't say you were—I said——

MISS ROBERTS. I'm *not* a flirt—I'm *not*.

MRS. BAXTER. We'll say no more about it. It was very hard for me to have to speak to you. You have no idea how difficult I found it.

MISS ROBERTS. Mrs. Baxter, you have often been very kind to me, and I don't want to forget it—but I'd rather not be treated as one of the family any more. I want my meals in the schoolroom, and I mustn't be expected to sit in the drawing-room.

MRS. BAXTER. Upsetting the whole machinery of the house.

MISS ROBERTS. I can't go on meeting him at table and everywhere.

MRS. BAXTER. I don't see why not.

MISS ROBERTS. I shouldn't know where to look or what to say.

MRS. BAXTER. Look out of the window and converse on inanimate objects.

MISS ROBERTS (*mumbles angrily*). I will not look out of the window and converse on inanimate objects.

MRS. BAXTER (*putting up a warning hand*). Hush, hush, hush!

MISS ROBERTS. Please understand I won't be one of the family, and I won't go to the picnic.

(*She goes hurriedly into the garden.*)

MRS. BAXTER. Oh, oh, naughty girl!

(TOM *and* MR. BAXTER *enter.*)

TOM. Cook thinks the large basket and the small hamper will suffice. She *said* suffice.

MRS. BAXTER. I'm very sorry, Tom, but it is out of the question for us to go to a picnic to-day.

MR. BAXTER. Oh, Dulcie.

TOM. Too late to back out.

MRS. BAXTER. *I* haven't backed out. It's Miss Roberts.

TOM. We can't have a picnic without Miss Roberts.

MR. BAXTER. What's the matter with her?

MRS. BAXTER (*solemnly*). Miss Roberts and I have had *words*.

(TOM *whistles quietly.*)

MR. BAXTER. What about?

MRS. BAXTER. Never you mind.

TOM. Oh, it can't be such a very dreadful quarrel between two such nice sensible women. I guess you were both in the right. (*To* MR. BAXTER.) I guess they were both in the wrong. (*Taking* MRS. BAXTER *by the arm and cajoling her.*) Come along. Tell us all about it.

MRS. BAXTER (*withdrawing her arm*). No, Tom, I can't.

TOM. Then suppose I go to Miss Roberts and get her version.

MRS. BAXTER (*in dismay*). Oh, no, that wouldn't do at all.

TOM. I only want to make peace. (*To* MR. BAXTER.) Wouldn't it be better if they told me and let me make it up for them?

MR. BAXTER. Why you?

TOM. A disinterested person.

MRS. BAXTER. But you are not.
                                      (*Putting her hand over her mouth.*)

TOM (*turns quickly to* MRS. BAXTER). What?

MRS. BAXTER. I'm not going to say any more.
                                      (*She sits down.*)

TOM (*seriously*). You *must*. If your quarrel concerns *me*, I have a right to know all about it.

MR. BAXTER (*motioning to* MRS. BAXTER). You are only putting ideas into their heads.

TOM (*turning sharply on* MR. BAXTER). Putting what ideas into their heads? (*It dawns upon him what the subject of the quarrel has been.*) Oh! (*To* MRS. BAXTER.) You don't mean to say you spoke to her about—— (*He stops embarrassed.*) What have you said to her?

MRS. BAXTER. I decline to tell you.

TOM. Then I shall ask *her*.                (*Going.*)

MRS. BAXTER (*quickly*). No, no, Tom. I—prefer to tell you myself. I spoke very nicely to her. I forget how the conversation arose, but I think I did say something to the effect that young girls ought to be careful not to have their heads turned by men years older than themselves. (*She looks significantly at* TOM, *who turns away angrily.*) Instead of thanking me, she stamped and stormed and was very rude to me—very rude. I simply said (*in a very gentle tone*), "Oh, Miss Roberts!" (*Rousing herself as she describes* MISS ROBERTS' *share in the scene.*) But she went on shouting, "I won't go a picnic, I won't go a picnic!" and bounced out of the room. It just shows you how you can be deceived in people, and I have been so good to that girl.

TOM (*coming towards* MRS. BAXTER). I'm very angry—with you—very angry.

MRS. BAXTER. I simply gave her a word of counsel which she chose to take in the wrong spirit.

TOM. You interfered. You meddled. It's too bad of you, Dulcie. It's unbearable.

MR. BAXTER (*watching* TOM). The way you take it any one would think you had fallen in love with our Miss Roberts since yesterday.

MRS. BAXTER. Yes—wouldn't any one?

TOM (*addressing them both*). Would there be anything

so strange in that ? Perhaps I have; I don't know—perhaps, as you imply, I'm old enough to know better. I don't know. All I know is, I think her the most charming girl I ever met. I've not had time to realise what this is; one must wait and see—give the seed a chance to produce a flower—not stamp on it. (*To* MRS. BAXTER.) You might have left things alone when all was going so pleasantly. I was just beginning to think —beginning to feel—wondering if perhaps—later on—— Now you've spoilt everything.

MRS. BAXTER (*tearful and angry*). I won't stay here to be abused. (*Going to the window.*) You've done nothing else all the morning. I'm tired of being taken in hand and improved. No one likes to be improved.

(MRS. BAXTER *goes out through the window.*)

TOM. I don't want to be unkind to her—but you know how a man feels. He doesn't like any one meddling when he's just beginning to——

MR. BAXTER (*showing embarrassment all through the early part of this scene*). I agree with Dulcie. It would not be suitable for you to marry Miss Roberts.

TOM. She's as good as any of us.

MR. BAXTER (*hesitatingly*). It's not that. Miss Roberts, from her position here—alone in the world but for us—and having lived here so long—is—in a sense— under my protection.

TOM. I don't see that, but go on.

MR. BAXTER. I feel—in a certain degree—responsible for her. I think it is my duty—and Dulcie's duty—to try and stop her making what we both feel would be an unsuitable marriage.

TOM. It's a little early to speak of our marriage, but why should it be unsuitable ?

MR. BAXTER. We don't wish her to marry you.

TOM. Why ? Give me a reason.

MR. BAXTER. Why do you press me for a reason ?

TOM. Because this is very important to me. You have constituted yourself her guardian. I have no objection to *that*, but I want to get at your objection to me as a husband to her. I'm in a position to marry. I'd treat her well if she'd have me. We'd be as happy as the day is long in our little home in the mountains——

MR. BAXTER (*unable to restrain himself*). You married to her ? Oh, no—oh, no, I couldn't bear that.
(*He sinks into a chair and leans his head on his hands.*)

TOM (*completely taken aback*). Dick, think what you're saying.

MR. BAXTER. I couldn't help it. You made me say it—talking of taking her away—right away where I shall never see her again. I couldn't stand my life here without her.

TOM. Dick, Dick!

MR. BAXTER. She knows nothing of how I feel; it's only this moment I realised myself what she is to me.

TOM. Then from this moment you ought never to see her again.

MR. BAXTER. That's impossible!

TOM. Think of Dulcie, and the girl herself; she can't live in the house with you both now.

MR. BAXTER. She's lived with us for four years, and no one has ever seen any harm in it; nothing is changed.

TOM. From the moment you realised what she is to you, everything is changed.

MR. BAXTER. There has never been anything to criticise in my conduct to Miss Roberts, and there won't be anything.

TOM. She is the object of an affection which you, as a married man, have no right to feel for her. I don't blame you entirely. I blame Dulcie, for throwing you so much together. I remember all you said last evening. Dulcie used to play chess with you, now she tells Miss Roberts to; Dulcie used to go for long walks with you, now she sends Miss Roberts. Out of your forced companionship has sprung this, which she ought to have foreseen.

MR. BAXTER. Nothing is confessed or understood; I don't see that Miss Roberts is in any danger.

TOM. She is alone. She has no confidant, no friend, no outlet for the natural desires of youth, for love, for some one to love. She finds you sympathetic—you know the rest.

MR. BAXTER. It is jealousy that is at the bottom of your morality.

TOM. It won't do, Dick. It's a most awful state of things.

MR. BAXTER. If you think that, I wonder you stay here.

TOM. Very well, if you mean I ought to clear out.

(*He goes towards the door.*)

MR. BAXTER (*following after* TOM). No, Tom. Look here, I didn't mean that ; but you see, you and I can't discuss this without losing our tempers, so if your visit to us is to continue mutually pleasant, as I hope it will, we'd better avoid the topic in future.

TOM. Then you mean to keep Miss Roberts here indefinitely,—compromised ?

MR. BAXTER. It's no use going over the ground ; we don't see things from the same point of view, so don't let us go on discussing. (*He goes up the stairs and then turns to* TOM.) Tom, you might trust me.

(MR. BAXTER *goes out.*)
(TOM *remains in deep thought, then suddenly makes a determined movement, then stops and sighs.*
MISS ROBERTS *enters from the garden. She hesitates timidly when she sees him.*)

MISS ROBERTS. Mrs. Baxter sent me to get her magazine

TOM. Where is my sister ?

MISS ROBERTS. Sitting in the garden.

(*She takes up the magazine and is going out again.*)

TOM. I—— (MISS ROBERTS *stops.*) I—want to tell you something.

MISS ROBERTS. I can't stay.

TOM. I ask you as a great favour to me to hear me.

MISS ROBERTS. I ought not to stay.

TOM. I didn't think you'd refuse me when I asked you like that.

MISS ROBERTS (*hesitating*). I can't stay long.

TOM. Won't you sit down while I tell you ? (*He indicates a chair.* MISS ROBERTS *comes to the chair and sits.*) I want to tell you about myself, and my life in Colorado.

MISS ROBERTS (*nervously*). I don't think I can stay if it's just to talk and hear stories of Colorado.

TOM (*smiling*). Did you have enough of my stories this morning ?

MISS ROBERTS. Oh, no, I was quite interested in what you said, but I——

TOM. You *were* interested. I knew it by your eyes. Why, you even thought you'd like to go there yourself some time.

MISS ROBERTS. I've changed my mind. I've quite given up that idea now.

TOM. You'd like it out there. I'm sure you would; it's a friendly country; no one cares who you are, but only what you are, so you soon make friends. That's right. That gives every one a chance, and it's good in this way, it makes a man depend on himself, it teaches him to think clearly and decide quickly; in fact he has to keep wide awake if he wants to succeed. That's the kind of training I've had. I've been from mining camp to mining camp—I've tried my luck in half the camps in California and Colorado. Sometimes it was good, sometimes bad, but take it altogether, I've done well. (*Making the next point clearly and delicately.*) I've got something saved up, and I can always make good money, anywhere west of Chicago. (*Laughing.*) Now I'm talking like a true American; they always begin by telling you how much they've got. You'll forgive me, won't you? It's force of habit. Now what was I saying? (*Seriously.*) We learn to decide quickly in everything; you find me somewhat abrupt; it's only that. I make up my mind all at once, and once it's made up, that's finished—I don't change. (*Hesitating slightly.*) The first time I saw you I made up my mind—I said that's the girl for me, that's the girl I want for my wife. (*Leans towards her.*) Will you be my wife?

MISS ROBERTS (*rising and very much moved and distressed*). Oh, no, I can't. I didn't know that was coming, or I wouldn't have listened, I wouldn't indeed.

TOM (*following her*). I've been too abrupt. I warned you I was like that: I make up my mind I want something, and the next thing is, I go straight away and ask for it. That's too quick for you. You want time to think—well, take time to think it over. (MISS ROBERTS *turns to him quickly.*) Don't tell me yet; there's no hurry. I'm not going back for a month or two.

MISS ROBERTS. I'm very much obliged to you for asking me to marry you, but I can't.

TOM. Never ?
MISS ROBERTS. No, never ! I don't think so.
TOM. Eh ? That sounds like hope.
MISS ROBERTS (*quickly*). I didn't mean it to sound like hope.
TOM. It didn't seem that way last evening when we were talking about the forests and the mountains, and I was telling you how it felt to be back—or this morning when we were getting flowers, or afterwards when we sat here, while they were eating their cake and milk ; it seemed to me we were getting on famously.
MISS ROBERTS (*appealingly*). Oh, please don't go on. I can't bear it. You only distress me. (*She sobs.*)
TOM. Oh ! (*Pausing and looking at her, he sees that she means it and is really distressed.*) I'm sorry.
> (*He goes out abruptly.* MISS ROBERTS *is weeping bitterly.* MR. BAXTER *enters. He comes downstairs towards her and looks down at her with affectionate concern.* MISS ROBERTS *does not notice his presence till he speaks.*)

MR. BAXTER. What is it ?
MISS ROBERTS (*trying to control her sobs*). Nothing.
MR. BAXTER. You are in trouble. You are in great trouble—can't you tell me ?—can't I do anything ?
MISS ROBERTS. No.
MR. BAXTER. Wouldn't it do you good to tell somebody ? Don't you want some one to tell it all to ?
MISS ROBERTS. I want—— (*She falters.*)
MR. BAXTER. What is it you want ?
MISS ROBERTS. I think I want a mother.
> (*The effort of saying this brings on her tears afresh; she stands weeping bitterly.* MR. BAXTER *puts his arm about her and draws her gently to him. She yields herself naturally and sobs on his shoulder.* MR. BAXTER *murmurs and soothes her.*)

MR. BAXTER. Poor child ! Poor child ! (*While they are in this sentimental position* TOM *and* MRS. BAXTER *appear at the window. They see* MR. BAXTER *and* MISS ROBERTS, *but are unseen by them.* MISS ROBERTS *disengages herself from* MR. BAXTER *and goes out sobbing without perceiving* TOM *and* MRS. BAXTER. MR. BAXTER *watches* MISS ROBERTS *off, then turns and sees* MRS.

BAXTER *for the first time; he becomes very embarrassed under her steady disapproving eyes. To* MRS. BAXTER.) Do you want me to explain?

MRS. BAXTER (*coldly*). Not at present, thank you, Richard.

MR. BAXTER. I was only——

MRS. BAXTER. Not now. I prefer to consider my position carefully before expressing my astonishment and indignation.

MR. BAXTER. Well, if you won't let me explain——

(*He turns to the window and sees* TOM. *He looks appealingly at him.* TOM *ignores him and walks past him.* MR. BAXTER *shrugs his shoulders and goes out through the window.*)

MRS. BAXTER. I don't know which of them I feel angriest with.

TOM. Dick, of course.

MRS. BAXTER (*tearfully*). For thirteen years no man has ever kissed me,—except you,—and Dick,—and Uncle Joe,—and Dick's brothers,—and old Mr. Redmayne, —and the Dean when he came back from the Holy Land. (*Working herself into a rage.*) I'll never speak to Dick again. I'll bundle Miss Roberts out of the house at once.

TOM. Do it discreetly. Send her away certainly, but don't do anything hastily.

MRS. BAXTER. I'm not the woman to put up with that sort of thing.

TOM (*persuasively*). Don't be hard on her; don't be turning her into the street; make it look as if she were going on a holiday. Pack her off somewhere with the children for a change of air, this afternoon.

MRS. BAXTER. It's most inconvenient; everything will be upside down. (*Calming herself, she sits in an armchair.*) You're right. I mustn't be too hasty; better wait a few days, till the end of the term, or even till we come home from the seaside, then pack her off. (*Pause.*) Unless it blows over.

TOM (*astonished and going to her quickly*). Blows over! It won't blow over while *she's* in the house. (*Very seriously.*) You're up against a serious crisis. Take warning from what you saw and save your home from ruin. (MRS. BAXTER, *awed and impressed by this, listens attentively.*) You've grown so dependent on Miss

Roberts, you've almost let her slip into your place; if you want to keep Dick, you must begin an altogether different life, not to-morrow—— (MRS BAXTER *shakes her head.*) Not next week—— (MRS. BAXTER *shakes her head again.*) Now! (MRS. BAXTER'S *face betrays her discontent at the unattractive prospect he offers her.*) *You* be his companion, *you* play chess with him, *you* go walks with him, sit up with him in the evenings, get up early in the morning. Be gay and cheerful at the breakfast table. When he goes away, see him off; when he comes home, run to meet him. Learn to do without Miss Roberts, and make him forget her.

MRS. BAXTER. Very well. (*Rising.*) She shall leave this house directly,—directly I recover.

TOM. Recover from what?

MRS. BAXTER. From the shock. Think of the shock I've had; there's sure to be a reaction. I shouldn't wonder if I had a complete collapse. It's beginning already. (*She totters and goes towards staircase.*) Oh, dear, I feel so ill. Please call Miss Roberts.

TOM. You were going to learn to do without Miss Roberts.

MRS. BAXTER. That was before I was ill. I can't be ill without Miss Roberts.

(*Puts her hand to her side, turns up her eyes and groans as she totters out.*)

TOM. Oh! Oh! You Mollusc!

CURTAIN.

# THE THIRD ACT

SCENE.—*The same scene one week later. The only difference to the appearance of the room is that there is the addition of an invalid couch with a little table beside it.*
TOM *is in an armchair reading a newspaper.* MISS ROBERTS *comes in carrying two pillows, a scent-bottle, and two fans. The pillows she lays on the couch.*

MISS ROBERTS. She is coming down to-day.
TOM (*betraying no interest at all*). Oh!
MISS ROBERTS. Aren't you pleased?
TOM. I think it's about time.
MISS ROBERTS. How unsympathetic you are—when she has been so ill. For a whole week she has never left her room.
TOM. And refuses to see a doctor.
MISS ROBERTS. She says she doesn't think a doctor could do anything for her.
TOM. Except make her get up. Oh, no! I forgot —it's their business to keep people in bed.
MISS ROBERTS. You wouldn't talk like that if you'd seen her as I have, lying there day after day, so weak she can only read the lightest literature and eat the most delicate food.
TOM. She won't let me in her room.
MISS ROBERTS. She won't have any one but Mr. Baxter and me.
TOM. It's too monstrous. What actually happened that day?
MISS ROBERTS. Which day?
TOM. The day you turned me down. (MISS ROBERTS

*looks at him, troubled. He looks away sadly.*) What happened after that?

MISS ROBERTS. I was still upset when Mr. Baxter came in and tried to comfort me.

TOM (*grimly*). I remember.

MISS ROBERTS. You know he's a kind, fatherly, little man.

TOM. Oh—fatherly!

MISS ROBERTS. Yes, I wept on his shoulder just as if he'd been an old woman.

TOM. Ah! An old woman! I don't mind that.

MISS ROBERTS. Then I went to the schoolroom. Presently in walked Mrs. Baxter. She seemed upset too, for all of a sudden she flopped right over in the rocking-chair.

TOM. The only comfortable chair in that room.

MISS ROBERTS. Oh, don't say that. Then I called Mr. Baxter; when he came, she gripped his hand and besought him never to leave her. I was going to leave them alone together, when she gripped my hand and besought me never to leave her either.

TOM. Did you promise?

MISS ROBERTS. Of course. I thought she was dying.

TOM (*scouting the idea*). Dying? What made you think she was dying?

MISS ROBERTS. She said she was dying.

TOM. Well, what happened after she gripped you both in her death struggles?

MISS ROBERTS. We got her to bed, where she has remained ever since.

TOM. And here we are a week later, all four of us just where we were, only worse. What's to be done?

MISS ROBERTS. We must go on as we are for the present.

TOM. Impossible!

MISS ROBERTS. Till you go. Then Mr. Baxter and I——

TOM. More impossible!

MISS ROBERTS (*innocently*). Poor Mr. Baxter; he will miss you when you go; I shall do my best to comfort him.

TOM. That's most impossible.

MISS ROBERTS. He must have some one to take care of him while his wife is ill.

TOM. You don't really think she has anything the matter with her?

MISS ROBERTS. I can't imagine any one who is not ill stopping in bed a week; it must be so boring.

TOM. To a mollusc there is no pleasure like lying in bed feeling strong enough to get up.

MISS ROBERTS. But it paralyses everything so. Mr. Baxter can't go to business; I never have an hour to give the girls; they're running wild and forgetting the little I ever taught them. I can't believe she would cause so much trouble deliberately.

TOM. Not deliberately, no. It suited Dulcie to be ill, so she kept on telling herself that she was ill till she thought she was, and if we don't look out, she will be. It's all your fault.

MISS ROBERTS. Oh—how?

TOM. You make her so comfortable, she'll never recover till you leave her.

MISS ROBERTS. I've promised never to leave her till she recovers.

TOM. A death-bed promise isn't binding if the corpse doesn't die.

MISS ROBERTS. I don't think you quite understand how strongly I feel my obligation to Mrs. Baxter. Four years ago I had almost nothing, and no home; she gave me a home; I can't desert her while she is helpless and tells me twenty times a day how much she needs me.

TOM. She takes advantage of your old-fashioned conscience.

MISS ROBERTS. I wish she would have a doctor.

TOM (*with determination*). She shall have me.

MISS ROBERTS. But suppose you treat her for molluscry, and you find out she has a real illness—think how dreadful you would feel.

TOM. That's what I've been thinking. That's why I've been sitting still doing nothing for a week. I do believe I'm turning into a mollusc again. It's in the air. The house is permeated with molluscular microbes. I'll find out what is the matter with Dulcie to-day; if it's molluscry I'll treat her for it myself, and if she's ill she shall go to a hospital.

MISS ROBERTS (*going to the bottom of the stairs*). I think I hear her coming downstairs. Yes, here she is. Don't be unkind to her.

TOM. How is one to treat such a woman? I've tried kindness—I've tried roughness—I've tried keeping my temper—I've tried losing it—I've tried the serious tack—and the frivolous tack—there isn't anything else. (*As* MR. *and* MRS. BAXTER *appear.*) Oh! for heaven's sake look at this!

(*He takes his paper and sits down, ignoring them both.* MR. BAXTER *is carrying* MRS. BAXTER *in his arms.* MRS. BAXTER *is charmingly dressed as an invalid, in a peignoir and cap with a bow. She appears to be in the best of health, but behaves languidly.*)

MRS. BAXTER (*as* MR. BAXTER *carries her down the stairs*). Take care of the stairs, Dick. Thank you, darling! How kind you are to me. (*Nods and smiles to* MISS ROBERTS.) Dear Miss Roberts! (*To* MR. BAXTER.) I think you'd better put me down, dear—I feel you're giving way. (*He lays her on the sofa.* MISS ROBERTS *arranges the cushions behind her head.*) Thank you—just a little higher with the pillows; and mind you tuck up my toes. (MISS ROBERTS *puts some wraps over her—she nods and smiles at* TOM.) And what have you been doing all this week, Tom?

TOM (*gruffly, without looking up*). Mollusking.

MRS. BAXTER (*laughs and shakes her hand playfully at* TOM). How amusing Tom is. I don't understand half his jokes. (*She sinks back on her cushions with a little gasp.*) Oh, dear, how it tires me to come down stairs. I wonder if I ought to have made the effort.

(TOM *laughs harshly.*)

MR. BAXTER (*reprovingly*). Tom!

(MISS ROBERTS *also looks reprovingly at* TOM.)

MRS. BAXTER. Have you no reverence for the sick?

TOM. You make me sick.

MRS. BAXTER. Miss Roberts, will you give me my salts, please?

MISS ROBERTS. They're on the table beside you, Mrs. Baxter.

MRS. BAXTER. Hand them to me, please. (MISS ROBERTS *picks up the salts where they stand within easy reach of* MRS. BAXTER *if she would only stretch out her hand.* MR. BAXTER *makes an attempt to get the salts.*) Not you, Dick; you stay this side, and hold them to my nose. The bottle is so heavy. (MISS ROBERTS *gives the salts to* MRS. BAXTER, *who gives them to* MR. BAXTER, *who holds them to* MRS. BAXTER'S *nose.*) Delicious!

TOM (*rising quickly and going towards* MRS. BAXTER). Let me hold it to your nose. I'll make it delicious.

MRS. BAXTER (*briskly*). No, thank you; take it away, Miss Roberts. I've had all I want.

(*She gives the bottle to* MISS ROBERTS.)

TOM. I thought as much.

MRS. BAXTER (*feebly*). My fan.

MR. BAXTER (*anxiously*). A fan, Miss Roberts—a fan!

(MISS ROBERTS *takes a fan and gives it to* MR. BAXTER.)

MRS. BAXTER. Is there another fan?

MR. BAXTER (*anxiously*). Another fan, Miss Roberts—another fan!

(MISS ROBERTS *gets another fan.*)

MRS. BAXTER. If you could make the slightest little ruffle of wind on my right temple.

(MISS ROBERTS *stands gently fanning* MRS. BAXTER'S *right temple.* MR. BAXTER *also fans her.* TOM *twists his newspapers into a fan.*)

TOM. Would you like a ruffle of wind on your left temple?

MRS. BAXTER (*briskly*). No, no—no more fans—take them all away—I'm catching cold. (MISS ROBERTS *takes the fan from* MR. BAXTER *and lays both fans on the table.* MRS. BAXTER *smiles feebly at* MR. BAXTER *and* MISS ROBERTS. TOM *goes back to his chair and sits.*) My dear kind nurses!

MISS ROBERTS. Is there anything else I can do for you?

MRS. BAXTER. No, thank you. (*They turn away.*) Yes, hold my hand. (MISS ROBERTS *holds her hand. Then to* MR. BAXTER.) And you hold this one.

(MR. BAXTER *holds* MRS. BAXTER'S *other hand. She closes her eyes.*)

TOM. Would you like your feet held?

MR. BAXTER (*holding up his hands to silence* TOM). Hush, she's trying to sleep.

TOM (*going to her, says in a hoarse whisper*). Shall I sing you to sleep ?

(MR. BAXTER *pushes* TOM *away.* TOM *resists.*)

MR. BAXTER. Come away—she'll be better soon. (*They leave her.*) Oh, Tom, if you knew how I blame myself for this ; it's all through me she's been brought so low,—ever since the day she caught me comforting Miss Roberts. How she must have suffered, and she's been so sweet about it.

MRS. BAXTER (*opens her eyes*). I don't feel any better since I came downstairs.

(MISS ROBERTS *comes back to the sofa.*)

MR. BAXTER. I wish you'd see a doctor.

MRS. BAXTER. As if a country doctor could diagnose me.

TOM. Have a baronet from London.

MRS. BAXTER. Later on, perhaps, unless I get well without.

TOM. Then you do intend to recover ?

MRS. BAXTER. We hope, with care, that I may be able to get up and go about as usual in a few weeks' time.

TOM. When I've gone back to Colorado ? (*He pushes* MR. BAXTER *out of the way and approaches* MRS. BAXTER.) I guess you'd be very much obliged to me if I cured you.

MRS. BAXTER (*speaking rapidly and with surprising energy*). Yes, Tom, of course I should. But I've no confidence in you, and Dr. Ross once said a doctor could do nothing for a patient who had no confidence in him. (*Smiling at* TOM.) I'm so sorry, Tom ; I wish I had confidence in you.

TOM. I have confidence in myself enough for two.

MRS. BAXTER. Dr. Ross said that wasn't at all the same thing. I wish you'd stand farther off ; you make it so airless when you come so close.

(*She waves him off with her hand.*)

TOM. I'm not going to touch you.

MRS. BAXTER (*relieved*). Oh, well, that's another matter. I thought you were going to force me up. Try to, rather. Do what you like, as long as you don't touch me or make me drink anything I don't like,—I mean that I ought not to have.

MR. BAXTER. I wish we could think of some way to make our darling better.

TOM. I've heard of people who couldn't get up having their beds set on fire.

(*He picks up a box of matches and goes towards* MRS. BAXTER. MR. BAXTER *runs excitedly towards her to shield her.*)

MR. BAXTER. No, Tom—Miss Roberts!

(MISS ROBERTS *also attempts to shield* MRS. BAXTER.)

MRS. BAXTER (*taking a hand of* MR. BAXTER *and a hand of* MISS ROBERTS—*serenely*). My dear ones, he doesn't understand—he wouldn't really do it.

TOM. Wouldn't he?

(*He puts the matches back.*)

MRS. BAXTER. To show him I'm not afraid, leave me alone with him.

TOM. Going to try and get round me, too? That's no good.

MRS. BAXTER (*affectionately to* MR. BAXTER *and* MISS ROBERTS). You need a rest, I'm sure—both of you. Miss Roberts, will you go to the library for me and change my book?

MISS ROBERTS. With pleasure.

MRS. BAXTER. Bring me something that won't tax my brain.

MISS ROBERTS (*soothingly*). Yes, yes, something trashy —very well.

(*She goes out.*)

MR. BAXTER (*impulsively*). I need a walk too. I'll go with Miss Roberts.

(*About to follow her.*)

MRS. BAXTER (*quickly pulling him back*). No, you won't, Dick. I want you to go upstairs and move my furniture. The wash-stand gets all the sun, so I want the bed where the wash-stand is, and the wash-stand where the bed is. I wouldn't trouble you, dear, but I don't like to ask the servants to push such heavy weights.

MR. BAXTER. I'll do anything, dear, to make you more comfortable.

MRS. BAXTER. Do it quietly, so that I shan't be disturbed by the noise as I lie here.

(*Closes her eyes.*)

MR. BAXTER. Darling.

(*He kisses her tenderly on the brow, then tiptoes to the stairs, motioning* TOM *to keep quiet.* TOM *stamps heavily on the ground with both feet.* MR. BAXTER, *startled, signs to* TOM *to keep quiet; then goes out.*)

MRS. BAXTER (*smiling and murmuring*). Dear Dick!

TOM. Poor Dick!

MRS. BAXTER (*plaintively*). Poor Dulcie!

TOM. Look here, Dulciebella, it's no use trying to get round me. I know you. I've seen you grow up. Why, even in your cradle you'd lie by the hour, gaping at the flies, as if the world contained nothing more important. I used to tickle you, to try and give you a new interest in life, but you never disturbed yourself till bottle time. And afterwards; don't I know every ruse by which you'd make other people run about, when you thought you were playing tennis, standing on the front line, tipping at any ball that came near enough for you to spoil (*he thumps the cushions*) and then taking all the credit if your partner won the set. (*Again he thumps the cushions. Each time* MRS. BAXTER *looks startled and attempts to draw them from him.*) And if a ball was lost, would you help to look for it? (TOM *gesticulates—*MRS. BAXTER *watches him in alarm.*) Not you. You'd pretend you didn't see where it went. Those were the germs of molluscry in infancy; and this is the logical conclusion—you lying there with a bow in your cap (*he flicks her cap with his hand*) having your hands held.

MRS. BAXTER (*in an injured tone*). You have no natural affection.

TOM. I've a solid, healthy, brotherly affection for you, without a spark of romance.

MRS. BAXTER. Other people are much kinder to me than you are.

TOM. Other people only notice that you look pretty and interesting lying there—they wouldn't feel so sorry for you if you were ugly. (MRS. BAXTER *smiles.*) You know that; that's why you stuck that bow in your bonnet. (*He flicks her cap again.*) You can't fool me.

(*Moves away.*)

MRS. BAXTER (*sweetly, yet maliciously*). No dear, I saw that the morning you made me do the flowers.

TOM (*exasperated at the remembrance of his failure*). Get up !

(*Thumps the table.*)

MRS. BAXTER. I can't get up.

TOM. Lots of people think every morning that they can't get up, but they do.

MRS. BAXTER. Lots of people do lots of things I don't.

TOM. How you can go on like this after what you saw—Dick and Miss Roberts a week ago—after the warning I gave you then. I thought the fundamental instinct in any woman was self-preservation, and that she would make every effort to keep her husband by her. You don't seem to care—to indulge your molluscry you throw those two more and more together.

MRS. BAXTER. I don't see how you make that out.

TOM. There they are, both spending the whole of their time waiting on you.

MRS. BAXTER. In turns—never together—and I always have one or the other with me.

TOM (*taking it all in, he laughs and says with admiration and astonishment*). Oh ! Oh ! I see. Lie still, hold them both to you and hold them apart. That's clever.

MRS. BAXTER. *Your* way was to pack Miss Roberts off; the result would have been that Dick would be sorry for her and blame me. *My* way, Dick is sorry for me, and blames himself, as long as Miss Roberts is here to remind him.

TOM. You can't keep this game up for ever.

MRS. BAXTER (*complacently*). When I feel comfortable in my mind that the danger has quite blown over—— (*She suddenly remembers she is giving herself away too much.*) Oh, but, Tom, I hope you don't think I planned all this like a plot, and got ill on purpose ?

TOM. Who knows ? It may have been a plot, or suggestions may have arisen like bubbles in the subconscious caverns of your mollusc nature.

MRS. BAXTER (*offended*). It was bubbles.

TOM. You don't know which it was any more than anybody else. Think what this means for the others —there's your husband growing ill with anxiety, neglecting his business—your children running wild when they ought to be at school—Miss Roberts wasting her life in drudgery,—all of them sacrificed so that you may lie back and keep things as they are. But you can't keep things as they are; they'll get worse, unless you get on to yourself and buck up. It's that, or the break-up of your home. Now Miss Roberts' presence in the house has ceased to be a danger (MRS. BAXTER *smiles*) for the moment. But you wait! Wait till this invalid game is no longer a novelty, and Dick grows tired of being on his best behaviour—or wait till he finds himself in some trouble of his own, then see what happens. He won't turn to you, he'll spare you—he'll turn to his friend, his companion, the woman he has come to rely on—because you shirked your duties on to her, and pushed her into your place. And there you'll be left, lying, out of it, a cypher in your own home.

MRS. BAXTER (*pleasantly*). Do you know, Tom, I sometimes think you would have made a magnificent public speaker.
> (TOM *is angry. He conveys to the audience by his manner in the next part of the scene that he is trying a change of tactics. He sits.*)

TOM. I wonder where those two are now?

MRS. BAXTER. Miss Roberts has gone to the library, and Dick is upstairs moving my furniture.

TOM (*gazing up at the ceiling*). I haven't heard any noise of furniture being moved about.

MRS. BAXTER (*smiling*). I asked him to do it quietly.

TOM. Miss Roberts has had more than time to go to the library and back.

MRS. BAXTER (*growing uneasy and sitting up*). You don't think he's gone too?

TOM (*in an off-hand way*). That's what I should do. Pretend to you I was going upstairs to move furniture, and I should move out after her.

MRS. BAXTER. It's the first time I've let them out of my sight together since—— (*She sits bolt upright.*) Go and see if they're coming.
> (*She points to the window.*)

TOM. They'd be careful not to be seen from this window.

MRS. BAXTER (*excitedly*). They may be in the arbour.

TOM. It's a very good place.

MRS. BAXTER. Go and look.

TOM. I won't.

MRS. BAXTER. Then I will!

(*She springs off the couch and runs towards the window.*)

TOM. I thought I should make you get up.

MRS. BAXTER (*brought suddenly to realise what she has done*). Oh!

TOM. Now that you are up, better go and look in the arbour.

MRS. BAXTER. If I do catch them again, of course there will be only one thing for me to do.

TOM. What's that?

MRS. BAXTER. The girls and I must come out and rough it with you in Colorado.

(*She goes out through the window.*)

TOM (*protesting vehemently*). No, you don't! I won't have that! Not at any price. There's no room for you in Colorado. Oh, dear! What a dreadful thought! (MISS ROBERTS *comes in wearing her hat and carrying the library book in her hand.*) Thank goodness, they were not in the arbour.

MISS ROBERTS. What?

TOM. Oh, never mind, never mind.

MISS ROBERTS (*surprised at not seeing* MRS. BAXTER *on the couch*). Why, where is she?

TOM. Gone for a chase round the garden.

MISS ROBERTS. A chase?

TOM. A wild-goose chase. Leave her alone — she needs exercise. You see I was right; she was mollusking.

MISS ROBERTS. And she wasn't really ill?

TOM (*quickly*). Now seize this opportunity to give her notice. Have a plan. Know where you're going to or we shall have—" Dear Miss Roberts—stay with us till you find a place "—and the whole thing over again.

MISS ROBERTS (*taking off her hat, says thoughtfully*). I don't know where I can go at a moment's notice. I suppose you don't actually know of any one in Colorado who wants a governess?

TOM. No, I can't say I do.

MISS ROBERTS. Then I suppose it must be the Governesses' Home.

TOM (*kindly*). We shall hear from you from time to time, I hope?

MISS ROBERTS (*pleased*). Oh, yes, if you wish to.

TOM. You'll write sometimes (MISS ROBERTS *looks up hopefully. But when he says " to my sister," she is disappointed*) to my sister ?

MISS ROBERTS (*disappointed*). Oh, yes.

TOM. And in that way I shall hear of you.

MISS ROBERTS (*sadly*). If you remember to ask. But people so soon forget, don't they ?

TOM. I shan't forget. I don't want you to forget me.

MISS ROBERTS. It won't make much difference to you in Colorado whether you're remembered or forgotten by me.

TOM. I like to know there are people here and there in the world who care what happens to me.

MISS ROBERTS (*faltering*). That's something, isn't it ?

TOM. It's a real thing to a man who lives out of his own country ; we spend a lot of time just thinking of the folks at home.

MISS ROBERTS. Do you ?

TOM (*looks at her face*). How young you are—there isn't a line in your face. (*She smiles at him.*) You will let me hear how you get on ?

(*Moves away.*)

MISS ROBERTS (*disappointed*). If there's anything to tell. Some people have no history.

TOM. Yours hasn't begun yet—your life is all before you.

MISS ROBERTS. A governess's life isn't much.

TOM. You won't always be a governess. You'll marry a young man, I suppose. I hope he'll be worthy of you.

MISS ROBERTS (*wistfully*). Would he have to be young for that ?

TOM. It's natural ; I suppose it's right—anyway it can't be helped. A man doesn't realise that he's growing old with the rest of the world ; he notices that his friends are. He can't see himself—so he doesn't notice that he, too—he gets a shock now and then—but . . . well, then he gets busy about something else and forgets.

MISS ROBERTS. Forgets ?

TOM. Or tries to. I almost wish I'd never come to England. It was easier out there to get busy and forget.

MISS ROBERTS. You'll find that easy enough when you go back.

TOM (*shaking his head*). Too much has happened; more than I can forget. But I must buck up, because I have to be jolly as a duty to my neighbours, and then your letters—they'll cheer me. And when that inevitable letter arrives to tell me you've found happiness, I shall send you my kindest thoughts and best wishes, and try not to curse the young devil whoever he is. So you see we can always be friends, can't we?—in spite of the blunder I made a week ago. Don't quite forget me (*taking her hands and shaking them*) when he comes along.

(*He goes and sits on the couch disconsolately.*)

MISS ROBERTS. Shall I tell you something?

TOM. What?

MISS ROBERTS. Oh, no—I can't!

TOM. You must, now you've begun.

MISS ROBERTS. I daren't.

TOM. I want you to.

MISS ROBERTS. Well, don't look at me.

TOM. I'm ready.

(*He looks at her, and then turns his back to her.*)

MISS ROBERTS. Suppose there was a girl, quite young, and not bad-looking, and she knew that her chief value as a person was her looks and her youth, and a man—oh, I don't know how to say this——

TOM. I'm not looking.

MISS ROBERTS. He had great value as a person. He was kind and sensible, and brave, and he had done things. He wasn't young, but he couldn't have lived and still had a smooth face, so she liked him all the better for not having a smooth face—his face meant things to a girl; and if he wanted to give her so much—such great things—don't you think she'd be proud to give him her one little possession, her looks and her youth?

TOM. You don't mean us? (*He turns to her.*)

MISS ROBERTS (*overcome with confusion*). Don't look at me. I'm ashamed. (*Covers her face with her hands.* TOM *goes to her, gently draws her hands from her face and holds them both in his.*) I wouldn't have dared to tell you, only I couldn't let you go on thinking what you were thinking. When you asked me to marry you a week ago and I said " No "—it was only because I was so hurt—my pride was hurt, and I thought—oh, never mind now—I wanted to say " Yes " all the time.

TOM (*looking at her and saying to himself, as if he scarcely believed it*). I am really going to take her with me to Colorado.

(*Kisses her. After a slight pause,* MR. BAXTER *enters, limping painfully.*)

MR. BAXTER. I've sprained my ankle—moving that wash-stand.

TOM. Oh, my poor old chap—what can we do for you ?

MISS ROBERTS. You ought to have some lint and a bandage. (*To* TOM.) You'll find it in a cupboard in the spare room—your room.

TOM. All right—hold on while I go and get it.

(*He puts* MR. BAXTER'S *hand on the post of the stairs ; then he goes out.*)

MISS ROBERTS. Hold on to me, Mr. Baxter.

(*She supports him.* MRS. BAXTER *enters from the garden without seeing* MR. BAXTER *and* MISS ROBERTS.)

MRS. BAXTER. They're not in the arbour. (*Catching sight of them.*) What—again ?

MISS ROBERTS. He's sprained his ankle.

MRS. BAXTER (*rushing to him*). Sprained his ankle— oh, my poor Dick !

MR. BAXTER (*looking surprised at* MRS. BAXTER). What, you up—running about ?

MRS. BAXTER. I've taken a sudden turn for the better.

MR. BAXTER (*mournfully*). I wish you'd taken it a bit sooner ; making me move that damned old wash-stand. (*Then suddenly.*) Oh, my foot !

MRS. BAXTER. Let me help you to my couch.

(TOM *comes in with bandages.*)

MR. BAXTER. You wouldn't know how. (*Pushes her away.* MRS. BAXTER *gives an exclamation of horror. Turning to* MISS ROBERTS.) Miss Roberts !

MRS. BAXTER. Let me !

MR. BAXTER. No, no—not now. (*As* MISS ROBERTS *assists him to the sofa.*) You see, she's used to helping people and you're not.

(MISS ROBERTS *kneels and begins to untie his shoe-laces.*)

# THE MOLLUSC

MRS. BAXTER (*to* TOM). He refuses my help.

TOM. He turns to the woman he has come to rely on. Now is your chance. Seize it; you may never get another.

MR. BAXTER. I want a pillow for my foot.

MISS ROBERTS (*rising*). A pillow for your foot?

TOM (*to* MRS. BAXTER). Go on—go on—get it.

MRS. BAXTER (*running for the pillow*). A pillow for his foot. (*She anticipates* MISS ROBERTS, *snatches the pillow and brings it to* MR. BAXTER, *then looking indignantly at* MISS ROBERTS *she raises* MR. BAXTER'S *sprained foot with one hand as she places the pillow under it with the other.* MR. BAXTER *utters a yell of pain.*) Oh, my poor Dick, I'm so sorry. Did I hurt you?

MR. BAXTER (*looking at her in wonder*). Why, Dulcie, but it seems all wrong for me to be lying here, while you wait on me.

MRS. BAXTER. I want you to rely on me, dear, so that when you're in trouble you'll turn to me, What can I do for your poor foot? We must get some—some——

TOM. Bandages.

(*Throwing bandages to* MRS. BAXTER.)

MRS. BAXTER. Yes, and some—some arnica. Miss Roberts never thought of arnica.

MISS ROBERTS. I'll go and look for it.

(*She makes a slight movement.*)

MRS. BAXTER (*pleasantly*). Don't trouble, Miss Roberts, I will go myself directly. (*Then to* MR. BAXTER.) You know, dear, we must learn to do without Miss Roberts.

TOM. You'll have to. She's coming back to Colorado with me.

MRS. BAXTER (*going to* MISS ROBERTS). Tom, this is news. Dear Miss Roberts, I'm so glad.

MR. BAXTER (*holding out his hand to* TOM). So am I.

(TOM *shakes hands with* MR. BAXTER.)

MRS. BAXTER. But oh, how we shall miss you!

MISS ROBERTS. I hope I'm not being selfish.

MRS. BAXTER. Oh, no, no, dear. I'm glad you're going to make Tom happy. We shall do very well here; it's high time the children went to school; I've been thinking about it for a long time. (*She kneels by* MR. BAXTER.) And now that I'm so much better, I shall be able to do more for my husband, play chess with him—go walks with him—— Tom shall never have another chance to call me a mollusc.

TOM. Bravo! Bravo!

MR. BAXTER. Dulcie!

MRS. BAXTER. Dearest!

MISS ROBERTS (*to* TOM). You've worked a miracle!

TOM (*quietly to* MISS ROBERTS). Were those miracles permanent cures? (*Shakes his head.*) We're never told! We're never told!

CURTAIN.

# A SINGLE MAN

## A COMEDY IN FOUR ACTS

COPY OF THE "FIRST NIGHT" PROGRAMME
AT
THE PLAYHOUSE, LONDON
ON NOVEMBER 8, 1910

## A SINGLE MAN

A NEW COMEDY IN FOUR ACTS

BY

HUBERT HENRY DAVIES

| | |
|---|---|
| *Robin Worthington* | MR. CYRIL MAUDE |
| *Henry Worthington* | MR. ERNEST MAINWARING |
| *Dickie Cottrell* | MR. LYONEL WATTS |
| *Lady Cottrell* | MISS FLORENCE HAYDON |
| *Maggie Cottrell* | MISS DULCIE GREATWICH |
| *Miss Heseltine* | MISS HILDA TREVELYAN |
| *Isabella Worthington* | MISS MARY JERROLD |
| *Louise Parker* | MISS NANCY PRICE |
| *Bertha Sims* | MISS DOROTHY DAYNE |
| *The Housekeeper* | MISS EMMA CHAMBERS |
| *The Parlourmaid* | MISS VERA COBURN |
| *The Nurse* | MISS DIANA SELLICK |

*The action, which covers a period of three weeks, takes place in Robin Worthington's house near Farnham in Surrey.*

ACTS I., III., & IV.—The Study.

ACT II.—The Drawing-room.

# A SINGLE MAN

## THE FIRST ACT

SCENE.—ROBIN WORTHINGTON'S *study. A broad French window affords a view of a large, well-kept garden. It is towards the end of the month of May, so that the garden looks at its freshest and brightest with flowering trees in bloom. The room looks comfortable and much used, and is distinctly a man's room. There are bookshelves on either side of the window. Almost facing the audience is* ROBIN'S *writing-table; a good-sized table, with all the necessary things for writing, and littered with letters and pamphlets. By the writing-table there is a small typewriter's desk. It has drawers down one side and a typewriter's machine, with a cover on, upon it. Other furniture completes the scene. Near a settee in front of* ROBIN'S *writing-table there is a cradle on rockers containing a baby. Lying near the cradle on the floor, as if they had been flung there, are a Teddy-bear, a rag-doll, and a rattle. On the settee lies a small case of needles and cottons and a baby's bonnet with rosettes and ribbon strings in the process of making.*

ISABELLA WORTHINGTON, *a bright attractive young woman of almost thirty, is on her knees beside the cradle.*

ISABELLA (*to the baby*). Coochy, coochy, coochy! (*Putting her head close to the baby.*) Bo! (*She picks up the Teddy-bear and holds it up for the baby to look at as she makes a poor imitation of a dog barking fiercely.*) Wow, wow, wow! (*She throws the Teddy-bear on the floor and bends solicitously over the cradle.*) Did muzzer fichen baby? Muzzer didn't mean to fichen baby. (CAPTAIN HENRY WORTHINGTON *enters from the garden.* HENRY *is a cavalry officer, a good-looking, pleasant man of thirty-five with conventional mind and manners. He wears a tweed suit and is smoking a pipe. He strolls down to the cradle.*) Dada! Here's dada! Here's baby's dada. (*Looking up at* HENRY.) Look at her, Henry. Doesn't she look sweet?

HENRY (*smiling at the baby*). Hullo, babs. (*He pokes the baby.*) Tsch!

ISABELLA (*in an ecstasy*). Did you see her smile?

HENRY (*giving the baby a series of little pokes*). Tsch, tsch, tsch!

ISABELLA. Don't do it any more, dear. It might not agree with her.

(*Rocks the cradle gently.*)

HENRY. I say, Isabella.

ISABELLA (*brightly*). What is it, dearest?

HENRY. Do you think you ought to be in this room?

ISABELLA. Why not?

HENRY. Robin may not like to have his study turned into a nursery.

ISABELLA. I shouldn't think he'd mind when it's for baby.

HENRY. Look at the floor.

ISABELLA. Those are baby's playthings. She threw them all there herself. (*Gushingly to the baby.*) Clever little girlie!

HENRY. Robin will be coming in directly and want to begin his morning's work. I think we'd better clear out.

ISABELLA. Very well, dear—we will—(*as she sits on the settee*) by and by.

HENRY. It's ten o'clock.

ISABELLA. A literary man has no fixed hour for beginning work. He waits till the spirit moves him. It's not as if Robin had to turn out on parade, punctual to the minute, like you.

(*Takes up her needle and cotton from the seat beside her and begins to stitch the rosettes and strings on the bonnet.*)

HENRY. No—but still—we must take care not to be in his way. It's very kind of him to have us here. I

# A SINGLE MAN

don't want him to think we are making too free with his house.

ISABELLA. I think it is so sweet of you, Henry, the way you never forget that you are the *younger* brother.

HENRY (*smiling*). I learnt my place at school when Robin was Worthington Major and I was Worthington Minor.

ISABELLA (*sewing as she talks*). I should think our happy little family of three makes a very bright spot in his dull, grey bachelor life. The other day—which day would it be? How long have we been staying with Robin?

HENRY (*without looking up from a newspaper he has picked up*). Four days.

ISABELLA. Yes. Then it was the day before yesterday —I was sitting here with baby, and I could see Robin, sitting at his desk, watching us. He didn't say a word —but I knew so well what was passing in his mind. He was thinking it must be very nice to have a young wife sitting in his study while he works, and a little baby-waby —lovidovickins!

(*She finishes her speech with her head in the cradle.*)

HENRY (*turning his newspaper*). I should think Robin will always remain a bachelor.

ISABELLA. Don't you think a man is much happier for being married?

HENRY (*smiling at* ISABELLA). Yes—if he finds the right woman.

ISABELLA (*smiling at* HENRY). Of course.

HENRY. Perhaps Robin hasn't had my luck, or perhaps he has been too busy writing books to think about getting married.

ISABELLA (*dropping her sewing, and saying thoughtfully*). He needs the idea put into his head. It's what you and I ought to do while we are on this visit.

HENRY (*shaking his head*). I never believe in taking a hand in other people's love affairs.

ISABELLA. What do you think of Louise Parker?

HENRY (*having forgotten who she is, echoes*). Louise Parker!

ISABELLA. You remember *her*. She was at school with me and she was to have been one of our bridesmaids, only she had influenza.

HENRY. Oh, yes. I remember.

ISABELLA (*resuming her sewing*). Poor Louise! She must be nearly thirty and she's never been engaged. I shouldn't think she's ever even had a proposal. I'm sure she'd have told me if she had. I thought it would be so nice for her if Robin fell in love with her.

HENRY (*good-humouredly*). I don't see why my poor brother should take up with an *old* girl who can't get anybody else.

ISABELLA. Louise isn't *old*, dear; she's *my* age—and she's very handsome. You've seen that photograph I have of her, with her hair done out at the sides, clutching a piece of white tulle in front. She looks lovely—and she isn't *very* much flattered—not if she is as handsome as she used to be—though of course I've seen next to nothing of her since we've been spending our winters in Egypt.

HENRY. No—I suppose not.

ISABELLA. Then I thought—having a little money of her own would make it so much better.

HENRY. Robin is well enough off now not to think about that.

ISABELLA. It would make Louise more independent.

HENRY. You are only looking at it from *her* point of view.

ISABELLA (*her hand on his*). No, dear, I'm not—but you see—poor Louise is the only one of the old school set who hasn't been able to find a husband.

(HENRY *laughs, and gives* ISABELLA *a little caress*.)

HENRY. I don't see how you propose to bring them together. If I remember rightly—Louise lives at Leamington, while here we are at Farnham.

ISABELLA. Louise might come from Leamington to Farnham.

HENRY. True.

ISABELLA. I don't see why she shouldn't be asked on a little visit.

HENRY. Where?

ISABELLA. Here.

HENRY. To this house?

ISABELLA. Yes; I thought if Robin saw Louise in his own home it might help to put the idea into his head.

HENRY. But Louise can't come on a visit to Robin!

ISABELLA. Yes, she can—with *me* here—Robin's sister-in-law and Louise's oldest friend. It would be quite all right. I'm sure Louise wouldn't mind.

HENRY. Robin might.

ISABELLA. I thought I could say to Robin, that as you and I have no fixed home in England, perhaps he wouldn't mind if I invited my old friend, Louise Parker, to spend a few days with me here. I don't see how he could say No to that.

HENRY. You haven't asked him yet?

ISABELLA. No—but I've asked Louise.

HENRY. You haven't!

ISABELLA. Didn't I tell you? I wrote to her the day before yesterday. I told her to put off *everything*, and come on here *immediately*. I gave her the most glowing account of Robin. I should feel so happy if I were the means of bringing them together.

HENRY (*gravely*). I think you ought to have spoken to Robin before inviting her.

ISABELLA (*penitently*). Yes, dear, I see that now.

HENRY. He may not want her here.

ISABELLA (*seriously*). That's my difficulty. I don't know what I shall do if Robin says he won't have Louise here.

HENRY. Put her off.

ISABELLA. It's too late. She's in the train. She'll be here in three-quarters of an hour. Yes; I received an eight-page letter from her this morning. Of course when I told her to come immediately, I never expected she'd come at once. (HENRY *smiles in spite of himself.* ISABELLA, *seeing* HENRY *smile, cheers up.*) Dear Louise! She's so delighted with everything I told her about Robin. She seems to look upon herself as engaged to him already.

HENRY. You'd better say something to Robin without delay.

ISABELLA. Yes, I suppose we had.

> (*She kneels and rocks the cradle.* ROBIN WORTHINGTON *comes in from the garden. He is a pleasant, wise, reticent and sweet-tempered man of forty-three years old.*)

ROBIN. Hullo!

HENRY. Hullo, Robin!

## A SINGLE MAN

ROBIN. Don't disturb yourselves. I can't do anything until my secretary comes.
  (ROBIN *turns over some papers on his desk, smiling broadly to himself.* ISABELLA *looks at* HENRY, *who makes faces at her, and nods, meaning that she must tell* ROBIN *about* LOUISE.)
ISABELLA (*with an effort*). I have a great friend—Louise Parker her name is—— (*She stops short when she looks at* ROBIN *and sees him smiling broadly to himself.*) What are you smiling at?
ROBIN (*diffidently*). I came in here for the express purpose of asking you both something—and now I don't like to.
HENRY. Go on.
ROBIN. You won't laugh?
HENRY. No.
ISABELLA. Of course not.
ROBIN. Well, then—— (*Looking from one to the other.*) Do you think I'm too old to get married?
ISABELLA. No.
HENRY. No.
ROBIN. I want you to say what you really think.
HENRY. We *are* doing.
ISABELLA. You are not at all too old to marry.
ROBIN. I don't mean—I mean a girl.
HENRY. Of course.
ISABELLA. So do *we*.
ROBIN. I don't think I've any time to waste. I'm forty-three.
HENRY. I thought you were forty-four.
ROBIN (*quite annoyed*). No, I'm not. I'm only forty-three.
ISABELLA (*complacently*). Is it seeing *us* that has made you want so much to get married?
ROBIN. Partly—and partly it's the spring. How can I keep my mind off marriage when all the woods and fields are filled with family life? I get the same unsettled feeling regularly every year.
HENRY. *I* used to get it before I was married.
ROBIN. All the bachelors do in the pairing season. I've no doubt *my* case *is* a good deal aggravated this year with watching you two and the baby. Do you know, before you arrived—I rather expected your

domestic happiness might irritate me, but—(*he smiles at them both*) I find it extremely attractive. It makes me quite jealous.

ISABELLA (*beckoning* HENRY *to her she whispers to him while* ROBIN'S *back is turned*). He's absolutely ripe for Louise.

HENRY (*as* ROBIN *turns to them*). I've often wondered how it is you've escaped so long. You used to be constantly falling in love.

ROBIN. That was before I could afford to marry. I got over them all. One can't miss for long something one never had. Since the days that *you* remember I've been so busy getting on in the world, and so afraid that marriage would interfere with my work, that I haven't encouraged myself to think of it. But now that I *have* got on—I seem to have come to a kind of full stop. Nothing matters as much as it did; my friends don't; my career doesn't. A great many bachelors experience the same sort of feeling round about forty. It's not pleasant: it's alarming. I ought not to be losing my grip on life *yet*—but to retain it I need a new interest—an interest outside myself. I need—(*indicating* ISABELLA, *who is gently rocking the cradle*) that's what I need.

(*He goes up to the window, and out into the garden a few steps, standing with his back towards* HENRY *and* ISABELLA. HENRY *goes to* ISABELLA *and sits beside her.*)

HENRY. Hadn't you better tell him about Louise?

ISABELLA. If I tell him *now*—after what he's been saying—he'll think I've asked her here on purpose for him to fall in love with—and that makes a man so angry.

HENRY. Pretend you've asked her here because *I'm* so fond of her.

ISABELLA. No, Henry, I won't!

HENRY. You *must* tell him she's coming.

ISABELLA. I know I must.

HENRY. Shall *I* tell him?

ISABELLA. No, I'll tell him.

HENRY. Well, tell him.

ISABELLA. I'm going to.

(*Enter* GLADYS, *a young parlourmaid.*)

GLADYS (*addressing* ROBIN). Miss Cottrell has called, sir, and would like to see you.

ROBIN. Oh! Show her in here, please.

GLADYS. Yes, sir.

(*She goes out.*)

ISABELLA (*in a quick whisper to* HENRY). How annoying: just when I was going to tell him about Louise!

ROBIN (*addressing them both*). It's Lady Cottrell's little girl—Maggie. They are neighbours of mine.

(MAGGIE COTTRELL *enters.* MAGGIE *is a very pretty, healthy, smiling girl of seventeen, full of vitality. She carries a basket of grapes.*)

MAGGIE. Good-morning!

ROBIN (*meeting* MAGGIE *and shaking hands with her*). Good-morning, Maggie.

MAGGIE. Mother thought you might like these few grapes.

(*She offers the grapes to* ROBIN.)

ROBIN (*taking the basket*). That's very kind of you. (*Lays the basket on his writing-table.*) Please thank your mother very much. Let me introduce you to my sister-in-law, Mrs. Worthington.

ISABELLA (*shaking hands with* MAGGIE). How d'you do?

MAGGIE. Quite well, thank you.

ROBIN (*introducing* MAGGIE *to the cradle*). My niece—Miss Pamela Grace Mary Worthington—Miss Maggie Cottrell.

MAGGIE (*peering at the baby*). What a sweet little kiddie!

(*Rocks the cradle violently from side to side.*)

ISABELLA (*alarmed*). Stop, stop! Don't do that!

(*She snatches the baby out of the cradle.*)

MAGGIE. I thought they liked it.

ISABELLA (*trying to be pleasant about it*). You were doing it just a trifle—violently.

MAGGIE. I'm so sorry!

ISABELLA. It doesn't matter.

MAGGIE (*peering at the baby*). It *is* a little love.

ROBIN. When you've done adoring the baby, this is my brother—Captain Worthington.

(HENRY *and* MAGGIE *shake hands.*)

HENRY. How do you do?

MAGGIE. Quite well, thank you. (*To* ISABELLA.) May I look at its toes?

ISABELLA (*proudly exhibiting the baby's toes*). There!

MAGGIE. Aren't they ducks?

(*She touches them with her forefinger.*)

ROBIN (*to* HENRY, *smiling as he watches* ISABELLA *and* MAGGIE). Isn't she charming?

HENRY. Isabella?

ROBIN. Maggie.

(*He continues smiling benevolently at* MAGGIE *as he watches her.*)

MAGGIE (*to* ISABELLA). *May* I hold it?

ISABELLA. Certainly—if you'd like to. (*She gives the baby to* MAGGIE *to hold.*) You'll be very careful, won't you?

MAGGIE. Trust *me*. (MAGGIE *sits smiling at the baby.* ROBIN *sits watching* MAGGIE *and smiling all the time.* MAGGIE *to the baby.*) Puss, puss, puss!

ROBIN (*murmuring as he watches* MAGGIE). Charming!

MAGGIE (*looking at* ROBIN). What d'you say?

ROBIN (*slightly confused*). Nothing—I was only thinking—nothing. (*To* ISABELLA.) Wouldn't she make rather a good study for a Madonna?

ISABELLA. Not in a hat.

MAGGIE (*to make conversation, says to* ISABELLA). What do you feed it on?

(ROBIN *and* HENRY *glance at each other, embarrassed.*)

ISABELLA. Beef and potatoes.

(ROBIN *and* HENRY *again glance at each other, then look away, trying not to smile.*)

MAGGIE (*suddenly thrusting the baby from her*). Oh! It's going to have convulsions.

ISABELLA (*hurrying to* MAGGIE, *snatches the baby from her. She tries to be polite, but is visibly annoyed*). It's because you are not holding her properly. Give her to me, please—thank you. (*She carries the baby towards the window, jigging it.*) Did she say we were going to have convulsions? Tell the naughty lady it was because she didn't nurse us nicely.

(*A* NURSE *appears at the window and remains a few minutes in conversation with* ISABELLA. *She carries a shawl.* HENRY *joins them.*

*After a few moments the* NURSE *takes the baby from* ISABELLA *and disappears into the garden with it. While they are thus occupied,* MAGGIE *speaks to* ROBIN.)

MAGGIE. I'm not much of a hand with a baby. I think I'd better be getting home.

ROBIN. Don't go yet. What have you been doing lately?

MAGGIE. Playing tennis most of the time and larking about generally. We had great fun last evening—tobogganing down the stairs on tea-trays.

ROBIN. Who was with you?

MAGGIE. Dickie, and one or two other boys, and Flossie, and Bertha Sims. We call ourselves the gang. (*Holding out her hand.*) Good-bye.

ROBIN (*taking her hand and retaining it*). Good-bye, Maggie.

MAGGIE. Shall I take the basket back with me, or call again?

ROBIN. Call again—soon.

MAGGIE. I'll come back for it in about twenty minutes. (*She withdraws her hand and goes towards* ISABELLA.) Good-bye, Mrs. Worthington.

ISABELLA. Good-bye.

MAGGIE. Good-bye.

HENRY. Good-bye, Miss Cottrell.

ROBIN (*moving to open the door for her*). When you come back—don't ask for the basket—ask for *me*.

MAGGIE. Right!

(MAGGIE *goes out;* ROBIN *closes the door after her, then turns to* HENRY *and* ISABELLA.)

ROBIN. That's the girl I was telling you about.

ISABELLA (*puzzled*). What girl?

HENRY. I don't remember you telling us about any girl.

ROBIN. I was beginning to, when—in she came. Wasn't it a coincidence?

ISABELLA (*after a look at* HENRY). You are not telling us you intend to marry Miss Cottrell?

ROBIN (*shyly*). I thought of doing so. (ISABELLA *and* HENRY *look at each other in surprise.* ISABELLA's *surprise amounts to dismay.*) Don't you like her?

HENRY. She's charming.

ISABELLA. Very *pretty*—but isn't she rather too young for *you* ?

ROBIN. No ; I may be too old for her, but she's not at all too young for me. That's what I want—youth and sunshine. It would keep me young. (*Taking* HENRY *by the arm and pointing to the garden.*) Think of Maggie running about that garden, springing over the flower-beds in pursuit of butterflies. (*Dropping* HENRY'S *arm he says with enthusiasm.*) The very vision of it makes me feel almost a boy.

ISABELLA. If you really were a boy——

ROBIN (*interrupting her*). If I really were a boy, I should see nothing so wonderful in youth. One needs to have reached *my* age to realise its charm.

(ROBIN *sits at his table and begins fussing with papers.*)

HENRY (*impressed with* ROBIN'S *last remark, says to* ISABELLA). There's a world of truth in that, Isabella.

ISABELLA (*much more impressed by her own idea, says carelessly*). Oh, yes, there is. (*Going nearer to* ROBIN.) But though you look so boyish for your age——

ROBIN. A man is as old as he looks.

ISABELLA. Feels.

ROBIN. *You* don't know how old I feel.

ISABELLA. But Henry and I can't help being a little afraid—that if you married any one so young as Miss Cottrell—you might miss the companionship we hoped you would find—in marriage with some older and more intellectual woman.

ROBIN. I don't want a wife with ideas. She'd argue with me.

HENRY (*speaking across* ROBIN *to* ISABELLA). I have noticed, Isabella, that clever men often choose stupid wives.

ROBIN (*indignantly to* HENRY). She's *not* stupid.

ISABELLA (*bluntly*). She has no idea what to do with a baby.

ROBIN (*a little shocked and embarrassed*). My dear Isabella—how you do run on ! I don't think we ought to discuss this matter so prematurely. I have no reason to suppose that Maggie takes the slightest interest in me. (*He smiles as he continues.*) At least—I hadn't—till this morning.

HENRY. This morning?
ROBIN. Yes.
ISABELLA. Something she said?
ROBIN. No.
HENRY. What then?
ROBIN (*pointing to the basket of grapes*). Those grapes! What do I want with grapes? I'm not ill. It's merely an excuse of Maggie's to come and see me. I feel greatly encouraged.
> (*He becomes absorbed in the papers on his desk.*)

ISABELLA. Didn't you hear her say it was her mother who sent her with the grapes?
ROBIN. Maggie is quite sharp enough and quite independent enough to send the grapes by the gardener if she didn't want to bring them herself.
ISABELLA. That may be, but——
ROBIN. Suppose we drop Maggie and the grapes. I'm rather sorry I said anything about either of them. I don't think I ought to have done so. (*Beside* ISABELLA *and very pleasantly.*) You were beginning to tell me something about somebody when I first came in.
> (HENRY *stands watching them to see how* ISABELLA *gets on.*)

ISABELLA. About my old friend, Louise Parker.
ROBIN. Oh, yes.
ISABELLA. Such a nice girl.
ROBIN. Really!
ISABELLA. I'm sure you'd like her.
ROBIN. I'm sure I should.
ISABELLA. I thought perhaps you wouldn't mind if I invited her to come and see me here.
ROBIN. Of course, my dear Isabella—any friends of yours would be most welcome.
ISABELLA. Thank you. Should you object if Louise stayed a few days?
ROBIN (*delighted*). The very thing! It would be an excuse to invite Maggie.
ISABELLA. Oh!
> (*She looks at* HENRY *in dismay.* HENRY *laughs at* ISABELLA'S *face of dismay.*)

ROBIN (*goes on without heeding them and delighted with his own idea*). Why, yes—don't you see—if you have a girl friend staying in the house, Maggie might be running backwards and forwards all day long. She has nothing to do. When do you want Miss—Miss—your friend to come?

ISABELLA. She's coming this morning. I took the liberty of——

ROBIN (*interrupting her*). I'm so glad you did. Nothing could be more fortunate. I'll go and tell Mrs. Higson to get a room ready. (*He goes towards the door.*) Maggie might come to tea this afternoon.

(*He goes out.*)

ISABELLA (*as soon as the door is closed*). Oh, Henry, can't *you* do something?

HENRY. Why shouldn't he marry Maggie?

ISABELLA (*indignantly*). Henry!

HENRY. I've known several cases of men marrying girls half their age that turned out very well indeed.

ISABELLA. But what am I to say to Louise?

HENRY. Louise hasn't got an option on him.

ISABELLA. Don't make jokes about it, dear; she'll be here in less than half an hour.

HENRY. Louise must take her chance. I should think when we've been here a little longer we shall find that the neighbourhood bristles with women who want to marry Robin.

(*Re-enter* ROBIN.)

ROBIN. I'm sorry, but I shall have to ask you to leave me now. Miss Heseltine is coming.

ISABELLA (*suspiciously*). Who's Miss Heseltine?

ROBIN. My secretary.

(*He sits at the writing-table and gets a pen and paper.*)

ISABELLA. Do you have a woman secretary?

(*She glances at* HENRY.)

ROBIN. Yes. I've been taking more or less of a holiday since *you* came. That's how it is you haven't seen her.

ISABELLA (*after another significant glance at* HENRY). Is she pretty?

ROBIN. I really don't know. I think so. I see her so much I forget what she's like.

ISABELLA. That's absurd!

ROBIN. It's quite true. You see—I'm always working when she's here. It's like thinking aloud to talk

to Miss Heseltine. I feel just as comfortable with her in the room as if she wasn't there.
(*He begins to write.*)
HENRY. Come along, Isabella. He wants to get to work.
ISABELLA (*joining* HENRY). Very well. I shall have to go to the station directly to meet Louise.
(*They go out.* ROBIN *is absorbed in his writing, and does not look up as* MISS HESELTINE *enters.*)
(*Enter* MISS HESELTINE. *She is a sweet-faced woman of twenty-eight, with unobtrusive manners but plenty of character and determination. She is neatly and very plainly dressed, and carries a note-book in her hand. She moves about in a quick, business-like fashion.*)
MISS HESELTINE. Good-morning, Mr. Worthington.
ROBIN. Good-morning, Miss Heseltine.
(MISS HESELTINE *expresses disapproval as she sees the Teddy-bear, rag-doll, and rattle lying on the floor.*)
MISS HESELTINE. Tsch, tsch, tsch!
(*She gathers up the Teddy-bear, rag-doll, rattle, work-box, and the baby's bonnet; pitches them all into the cradle; drags it to the corner. She then seats herself at her desk, takes the cover off her typewriter, and gets two sheets of paper from the drawer of the desk.*)
ROBIN. Where did we leave off last time?
MISS HESELTINE. We were writing that article on fossils.
ROBIN. I don't feel at all like fossils to-day.
MISS HESELTINE (*putting the paper in the machine*). We don't need to send it in before Friday.
ROBIN. I have an idea for a poem.
MISS HESELTINE. Some more of those topical verses?
ROBIN. No—just an ordinary little poem about love.
MISS HESELTINE (*taking a swift surprised look at* ROBIN *before she speaks*). Quite a new departure.
ROBIN. Take this down.
(*He paces the room, thoughtfully, before speaking. He then begins to dictate, soulfully.*)

Come hither, my beloved,

(MISS HESELTINE *makes a short, sharp, business-like attack on the keys of her machine.* ROBIN *continues as before.*)

With shining, smiling eyes,

(MISS HESELTINE *repeats the attack.* ROBIN *continues as before.*)

And soft, sweet lips.

(*Again* MISS HESELTINE *types.* ROBIN *drops the far-away voice in which he has dictated the poem.*)
ROBIN. It's no good. I can't concentrate my mind. It's all in a turmoil. Tear it up, please, will you? (*He stands at the window, looking out into the garden with his back to her.* MISS HESELTINE *takes the sheet of paper out of the machine, moves her lips as she reads the poem over to herself with an affectionate smile.* ROBIN'S *attention is obviously attracted by something he sees in the garden. He speaks without turning round.*) How pretty!
MISS HESELTINE. Are you still dictating?
(*She hurriedly folds up the sheet of paper with the poem on it.*)
ROBIN. No. I was watching the housemaid flirting with the postman. There's nothing so charming to see as a pair of lovers. (MISS HESELTINE *smiles to herself as she tucks the poem into the bosom of her dress.* ROBIN *comes towards his desk, idly turning over a sheet or two of paper to cover the embarrassment he feels in saying the following*). It may surprise you—what I am going to ask you (MISS HESELTINE *is very attentive*), but—I want to get married. (MISS HESELTINE *is so surprised she drops her ruler on the floor with a clatter.* ROBIN *hurries to pick it up for her. She rises, picks it up, and sits again.*) The girl I want to marry is some one I've known very well for a long time. I've been in the habit of seeing her constantly, but hitherto—we have only been on friendly terms. (MISS HESELTINE *nods her head gravely.*) I'd like to get on to sentimental terms with her. (MISS HESELTINE *nods her head, smiling.*) It's always a little difficult to change a long-established friendly relationship into a sentimental one—not difficult exactly—but it needs careful handling. You see what I mean?
MISS HESELTINE (*dropping her eyes*). I think I do.

ROBIN. I'm afraid I may make the transition too abruptly—startle her—perhaps even frighten her away. So I want you to help me if you will.

MISS HESELTINE (*looking up at him*). How?

ROBIN. Before asking her the definite question I should so like to find out—if possible—whether *she* has anything more than a friendly feeling for *me*.

MISS HESELTINE. Have you no idea?

ROBIN. None—at least—very little.

MISS HESELTINE. Perhaps you have given her no direct sign of the change in your feelings towards *her*.

ROBIN. No; I haven't.

MISS HESELTINE. Then I don't see what *she* can do.

ROBIN. You think, then, that she may be in love with me without showing it?

MISS HESELTINE. I'm quite sure of that.

ROBIN. She may want to but be afraid to?

MISS HESELTINE. That's it.

ROBIN (*moving about restlessly*). A man can feel just as shy about breaking the ice as a girl. It would be dreadful to get a rebuff. She might laugh in my face. Girls have been known to be very unfeeling towards middle-aged suitors. They think it's funny to lead them on till they get a proposal and give a refusal—and then they go and tell their friends about it. (*He picks up a letter and folds it nervously.*) I don't want to risk anything of that sort—so I was wondering if you'd be so kind as to say something first.

MISS HESELTINE (*taken aback*). Me speak first? (*Turning away from him.*) Oh, no—I couldn't!

ROBIN (*coming and standing close to her shoulder*). I only mean—if you could help me to find out in some way—what kind of an answer I should be likely to get. (*He pauses.*) It's Maggie Cottrell. (MISS HESELTINE *must express, unseen by* ROBIN, *the grief and disappointment she feels in learning that it is* MAGGIE *he has meant and not herself.*) You know Maggie Cottrell? (MISS HESELTINE *bends her head.*) She's a friend of yours? (MISS HESELTINE *bends her head again.*) A great friend?

MISS HESELTINE. We are not in the same position, of course, but she has always been kind to me and taken notice of me.

ROBIN. Has she ever given you any confidences?

MISS HESELTINE. Yes.

ROBIN (*shyly*). Anything about me?

MISS HESELTINE. No.

ROBIN (*with a little note of disappointment*). Oh! (*Moving away as he says, thoughtfully.*) That might either mean that she takes no interest in me at all, or that it's too deep for words. (*To* MISS HESELTINE *again.*) Are you sure you wouldn't mind?

MISS HESELTINE. I should like to do whatever would please you, but—do you think I'm the best person for this?

ROBIN. You are the *only* person. I don't know any one else I could ask such a thing of. I never feel shy with *you*. I was telling my brother just now—it's like thinking aloud to talk to *you*.

MISS HESELTINE (*quietly*). I'm glad you feel *that*.

ROBIN (*not noticing* MISS HESELTINE, *he says, smiling, to himself*). Dear Maggie—so young and so pretty. (MISS HESELTINE *rises. He had almost forgotten her presence for a moment in thinking of* MAGGIE. *He turns to her, smiling apologetically.*) I beg your pardon.

MISS HESELTINE. Forgive me for what I am going to ask you. (*She goes to him and says, very gravely.*) You are quite, *quite* sure that this would be for your happiness and your good?

ROBIN. Yes, I'm *quite* sure. I've thought it all out. It's so dull here, and I'm becoming *such* an old fogey. If Maggie would have me she'd cheer me up as nobody else could. She'd be the remaking of me.

MISS HESELTINE (*quietly*). I'll do what you want me to do.

ROBIN. It's very kind of you, Miss Heseltine. You can approach the subject quite lightly, you know—almost chaffingly.

MISS HESELTINE. Oh, no, I couldn't do it that way. If I do it at all—I must do it seriously.

(*The front door bell rings.*)

ROBIN. Maggie come back for her basket. I'll slip out and leave her with *you*. (*He goes towards the window.*) If you want an excuse for me not being in my study (*seizing the basket of grapes*) I've gone into the pantry to put these grapes on a dish. That'll look very natural.

(*He goes out hurriedly. Re-enter* MAGGIE *by the door.*)

MAGGIE (*coming just inside the room*). Isn't Mr. Worthington here?

MISS HESELTINE. He's gone to get your basket.

MAGGIE. Oh!

MISS HESELTINE. Will you stay and talk to *me*?

MAGGIE. Yes—with pleasure.

(*She sits on the settee watching* MISS HESELTINE *and waiting for her to begin the conversation.* MISS HESELTINE *slowly approaches* MAGGIE *and then sits beside her.*)

MISS HESELTINE. Have you ever thought of marriage?

MAGGIE (*cheerfully*). Oh, yes—often and often.

MISS HESELTINE. Thought what it means—to leave your present life behind you and go and live his life with *him*? You'd have to love him very much to do that.

MAGGIE. I should say so.

MISS HESELTINE. Perhaps you've already asked yourself whether there's any one you'd be willing to give up everything for? (MAGGIE *smiles knowingly sideways at* MISS HESELTINE.) Do you sometimes ask yourself that question?

MAGGIE. Every time I meet a nice-looking man.

MISS HESELTINE. Then you've never thought of any man seriously?

MAGGIE. Are you alluding to Mr. Worthington?

MISS HESELTINE (*rather taken back and embarrassed*). Well, yes—I—did mean——

MAGGIE. Did *he* ask you to—to?

MISS HESELTINE. Yes—to——

MAGGIE. Sound me.

MISS HESELTINE. That's it.

MAGGIE (*pleased and surprised*). Well, I never!

MISS HESELTINE. You may think it's funny for *me* to sound you——

MAGGIE. I didn't think of that. What made him pitch on *you*?

MISS HESELTINE (*with a touch of pride*). I know him better than any one else does. I'm only his secretary, of course, but I've been working for him for five years now, and what with dictating to me, and talking about his work to me, and saying his thoughts aloud to me——

MAGGIE (*with no idea of giving offence*). He has come to look upon *you*, I suppose, as part of your machine.

## A SINGLE MAN

MISS HESELTINE (*meekly*). That's it.

MAGGIE (*impulsively seizing* MISS HESELTINE *by the arm*). Go on—tell me—what else did he say?

(*Wriggling towards her.*)

MISS HESELTINE. That's all. He just wanted me to find out if there was any hope for him.

MAGGIE (*whispering loudly in* MISS HESELTINE'S *ear*). Tell him " Yes."

MISS HESELTINE. Have you made up your mind already?

MAGGIE. Ages ago. Mother and I have frequently discussed the probabilities. (*Giggling.*) " Mrs. Worthington "—just think of it!

(*She laughs and kicks out her feet in front.*)

MISS HESELTINE (*looking at her gravely*). I shouldn't have thought it would make you laugh.

MAGGIE (*sweetly*). Why shouldn't I laugh if I'm happy?

MISS HESELTINE. I thought when you heard that a man like Mr. Worthington wanted to make you his dear wife—you'd feel more like going on your knees.

MAGGIE (*impressed*). Of course it has its serious side.

MISS HESELTINE. That's what I want you to see—if you don't think I'm taking a liberty in saying so. I'm older than *you*, and I've had a harder life than *you*. There were many things at my home to make me grow up sad and serious-minded : it's all been bright for *you*. *You've* had no occasion yet to take life seriously—but you will have when you marry. You'll find him difficult to understand at times—moody, and even a little irritable, like all very clever people are ; then you must be patient, and remember that your husband is a great man. Some days he'll take himself off to the clouds, and then, if you think of yourself more than him, you'll be saying, " I might as well not exist for all the notice he takes of me." Those are the hardest times—the times when he doesn't seem to notice your existence. But if you take a kind of pride in keeping quiet and not bothering him, and not letting other people bother him— it'll make it easier for you. It'll all be quite easy if you love him enough. That's what it needs—real love— deep love (*bending forward she takes her hands*), love that knows how to wait patiently. Look after him well—won't you? (*Her voice falters.*) Excuse me preaching you such a sermon. (*Re-enter* ROBIN, *with the empty basket.* MISS HESELTINE *goes towards him.*) I've done what you wanted me to (ROBIN *smiles*), and now, if you don't mind, I'll go home. I've got a headache.

(*Exit* MISS HESELTINE *quickly.*)

ROBIN (*looking after* MISS HESELTINE). I'm so sorry, Miss Heseltine, so very sorry! (*He turns to* MAGGIE, *who rose when he entered. They are both exceedingly embarrassed and stand smiling foolishly at each other. After a pause he says.*) Well—Maggie.

MAGGIE (*looking at the ground*). Well—Robin.

(ROBIN *looks at the basket in his hand, then looks about him for a place to deposit it, makes a few hesitating movements, and finally puts it on the writing-table and comes towards* MAGGIE.)

ROBIN (*very nicely and gently*). You are very sweet. (MAGGIE *puts up her face, expecting to be kissed; he kisses her.*) Dear Maggie, I am very much touched that you care for me. (MAGGIE, *smiling, sits on the settee. He sits, taking her hand and looking at it.*) What dear little hands! (*He puts his arm round her waist and kisses her again.*)

(*The door is suddenly thrown open. Enter* ISABELLA, *followed by* LOUISE PARKER. ISABELLA *comes marching gaily in, dressed in her outdoor clothes.* LOUISE *is tall, graceful, affected, beautifully dressed, and twenty-nine.*)

ISABELLA (*speaking as she enters*). Here's Louise! (*She stops petrified, as she sees* ROBIN *and* MAGGIE *sitting in a sentimental attitude on the settee.*) Oh!

(ROBIN *and* MAGGIE, *very much embarrassed, jump up as they enter.* LOUISE *comes towards* ROBIN, *who goes towards her, holding out his hand.*)

ROBIN. How d'you do, Miss—Miss——

LOUISE (*languidly giving him her hand*). Parker—Louise Parker.

ROBIN. I hope you've had a nice journey from—from——

LOUISE. Leamington.

(*There is a pause of embarrassment.* ROBIN *looks at* MAGGIE *and goes to her.*)

MAGGIE (*whispering to* ROBIN). Hadn't you better tell them we are engaged?

ROBIN. Yes. (*Turning to* ISABELLA *and* LOUISE, *who look towards him as he speaks.*) Miss Cottrell has just consented to become my wife.

(*He takes* MAGGIE'S *hand. Another long pause of embarrassment.* ISABELLA *and* LOUISE *look at each other in consternation.* ROBIN *looks at* MAGGIE.)

MAGGIE (*going to* ISABELLA). I know without you telling me that you congratulate me. Thank you very much! (*She shakes* ISABELLA *warmly by the hand.* ISABELLA *does not respond. She does nothing but submit to have her hand shaken.* MAGGIE *then turns to* LOUISE *and shakes her warmly by the hand.*) Thank you very much. (LOUISE *submits in the same manner as* ISABELLA. MAGGIE *turns to* ROBIN.) I'll be off home now to tell the family the joyful news.

(*She takes her basket from the table and goes to the window.*)

ROBIN. I'll come with you. (*To* ISABELLA *and* LOUISE.) You'll excuse me, I'm sure—under the circumstances. I shall be back to lunch. Come along, Maggie.

(ROBIN *and* MAGGIE *go off.* LOUISE *looks after them, then at* ISABELLA.)

ISABELLA (*in great distress*). My poor Louise—what *must* we do?

LOUISE. We must lay our heads together, dear, and see if we can't wean him away from her.

(*She unfastens her coat.*)

CURTAIN.

# THE SECOND ACT

SCENE.—ROBIN WORTHINGTON'S *drawing-room. A large French window stands wide open and all the windows afford a view of* ROBIN'S *garden; a different view from that seen from his study window. The fireplace is banked up with ferns and flowering plants. There are plenty of comfortable armchairs, a cushion seat and two settees. Against the wall a cabinet. Up by the window a good-sized oval table is laid with a white cloth and tea-things for eight people. Chairs around this table.*

*Three weeks have passed by since the first act. It is half-past four on an afternoon in June.*
HENRY *and* ISABELLA *and* LOUISE PARKER *are in the room.* HENRY *is looking off from the window.* ISABELLA *is seated on one sofa and* LOUISE *on the other.* HENRY *wears tennis flannels, and* ISABELLA *and* LOUISE *are charmingly dressed for a garden party.*

*Laughter and noise are heard off in the garden; the loud young voices of* MAGGIE *and* DICKIE COTTRELL *and* BERTHA SIMS. *The voice of* BERTHA *is then heard above the laughter.*

BERTHA (*in the garden*). Stop it, Dickie! Come on, Mag! Play!

(*The laughter and noise die away.*)
HENRY. Robin's engagement really *has* rejuvenated him. There he is, running about the tennis court like a boy of fourteen, picking up balls for Maggie in the most gallant way. (*To* ISABELLA.) There's no doubt about it—he's tremendously in love with her.

LOUISE (*languidly*). He has only been engaged to her for three weeks yet. (HENRY *looks at* LOUISE *with marked disapproval.* ISABELLA *merely looks resigned and bored.* LOUISE *goes towards the window, saying graciously to* ISABELLA *as she passes her.*) I'm going out to talk to Lady Cottrell.

(*She goes out.*)

HENRY (*indignantly*). However much longer does that woman intend to stay ?

ISABELLA (*resigned*). I wish I knew.

HENRY. It's monstrous ! Lingering on week after week, uninvited — making up to Robin in this extraordinary fashion.

ISABELLA. Louise has not improved since she left school.

HENRY. The way she manœuvres to get him alone, insists upon reading everything he writes, and is always trying to give the conversation an intellectual turn.

ISABELLA (*letting herself go in irritation against* LOUISE). Oh, yes—and the way she keeps coming downstairs in one elaborate gown after another, gliding about so gracefully—and he takes no notice of her.

HENRY. A good thing for *us* that he doesn't see what she's up to—since she's *our* friend.

ISABELLA (*meekly*). Mine, dear.

HENRY (*stamping about*). What is her object in it all ? Does she think she'll get Robin away from Maggie ?

ISABELLA. That was what she said she meant to do when she first came. But, as you know, dear, I soon let her see I couldn't countenance anything of that sort. It's one thing to try and make a match, but it's quite another thing to try and break off an engagement.

HENRY. Doesn't she see that ?

ISABELLA. When a woman doesn't wish to see a thing she has very little difficulty in persuading herself that it is not so. I can quite understand that it *was* very disappointing for Louise to come all the way from Leamington for nothing—but it wasn't *my* fault that Robin got engaged just before she arrived.

HENRY. He probably wouldn't have taken any notice of her anyway.

ISABELLA. That's what I told her to try and console her.

HENRY. What troubles me most is that it looks so bad for *you* for her to be staying here so long and behaving in this way. It looks as though you encouraged her.

ISABELLA. I know. It presents *me* as a most repulsive character. But what can I do? She simply won't go.

HENRY. You've given her some good strong hints, haven't you?

ISABELLA. Dozens!

HENRY. What does she say?

ISABELLA. She doesn't say anything. She just stays. It looks as if she meant to stay for ever.

HENRY. I'm afraid you'll have to be rude to her.

ISABELLA. I've been ruder to her already than I ever was to any one in my life.

HENRY. I don't see how any one else can say anything to her. *You* invited her.

ISABELLA (*troubled*). Don't reproach me, darling. You don't know how I regret writing that letter.

HENRY (*going towards her to comfort her*). I'm not reproaching you, dear.

ISABELLA. I can't help feeling you are displeased with me.

(*She begins to cry.*)

HENRY. No, dear.

ISABELLA. I'm afraid you are—but you know, Henry —(*she swallows her tears and looks up at* HENRY) I do love you and baby.

(*They embrace.*)
(*Enter* LOUISE *and* LADY COTTRELL. LADY COTTRELL *is a strong, alert, opinionative woman of fifty; her clothes are loose and comfortable without being eccentric.*)

LOUISE. Lady Cottrell and I have come in to see if tea is ready.

HENRY. I suppose we must wait for Robin.

LADY COTTRELL. Not at all. Ring the bell. (*She sits on the sofa.* ISABELLA *obediently rings the bell.*) He's forgotten all about *us*. He thinks only of Maggie. (*Addressing* ISABELLA.) Have you heard? We are going to have the wedding quite soon.

ISABELLA (*interested*). Oh—no—I hadn't heard.

HENRY. Nor had I. When is it to be?

LADY COTTRELL. In six weeks.

(LOUISE *places her hand to her heart.* LADY

COTTRELL *stares at her without betraying emotion of any kind.* HENRY *and* ISABELLA *exchange glances.* LOUISE *totters towards* ISABELLA.)

LOUISE (*to* ISABELLA). Have you got your vinaigrette about you ?

ISABELLA (*irritably detaching a vinaigrette from the long chain which she wears round her neck*). There !

LOUISE. Thank you, dear. (*She sniffs the vinaigrette as* ISABELLA *glances at her with the utmost disapproval.* LOUISE *smiles wanly at* LADY COTTRELL.) I felt a little faint.

LADY COTTRELL. Your dress is too tight. (HENRY *giggles.* LOUISE *glances haughtily at* LADY COTTRELL, *turns from her as if not deigning to reply, as she sniffs the vinaigrette, and sits down.* LADY COTTRELL *addresses* ISABELLA.) That's the cause of nearly all the fainting—tight-lacing. (*She pulls her dress away from her in front to show that she is not tightly laced.*) I don't faint ! It's the cause of a great deal of bad temper, too—not to mention biliousness—— Yes. In six weeks. August the tenth. Why should we wait ? Nothing to wait for except the clothes.

LOUISE. Do you think it's wise, dear Lady Cottrell, to let your girl be married so young ?

ISABELLA (*angrily under her breath*). Louise !

LADY COTTRELL. Wise ! Of course I think it's wise or I shouldn't let her do it.

LOUISE. It seems to me to be thrusting responsibilities upon her almost *too* early. (*With a rapid, affectedly impulsive movement, she darts to the cushion seat and drops gracefully upon it almost at* LADY COTTRELL'S *feet.*) *Do* let her remain a child a little longer.

(ISABELLA *looks at* HENRY, *who shrugs his shoulders.*)

LADY COTTRELL. *Every* girl ought to be married by the time she's twenty. *I* was—so were my two sisters ; so was my eldest daughter, and so shall Maggie be. Marriage comes natural to a girl at that age. She loves her husband and obeys him instead of sitting up and criticising him as they do if they haven't acquired the wifely habit in good time—the good old habit of subjection. It's all due to this present craze for late marriages that we have so many hysterical spinsters. *They* don't know what's the matter with them, but their

mothers do. Nothing infuriates me more than the way our modern young women spend the time when they ought to be having children, in thinking and reading and writing and talking about marriage ; deciding among themselves what *men* ought to be like. By the time they think they are ready to put on their orange blossoms, they've grown so exacting they can't settle down to one man. Maggie shall marry in good time. (*Enter* GLADYS *with the tea, and plate of hot buns, which she places on the oval table up stage.*) Tea ! (*cheerfully*) I feel about ready for it after that harangue.
    (*Goes up to inspect the tea-table.* GLADYS *goes out.*
     HENRY *joins* LADY COTTRELL *at the tea-table.*
     LOUISE *remains drooping upon the cushion seat*
     *the picture of despair.* ISABELLA *goes towards*
     *the window, passing between* LOUISE *and the sofa.*)
 ISABELLA (*as she passes* LOUISE). Get up !
 LOUISE (*slowly rising to her full height and saying tragically to herself*). August the tenth !
     (*She presses her hand to her temples.*)
 ISABELLA (*at the window*). They've finished their game.
 HENRY. Are they coming in ?
 ISABELLA. Yes. Racing to see who'll get here first. Bertha Sims is last.
 LADY COTTRELL. Who's first ?
 ISABELLA. Your son.
    (*Enter* DICKIE COTTRELL *carrying a racquet. He*
     *is a bright-faced, merry boy of eighteen. He*
     *wears tennis flannels. He enters running.*)
 DICKIE. Here we are ! (DICKIE *runs in, then turning to look at the others who are following.*) Come along, Mr. Worthington !
    (ROBIN *and* MAGGIE *enter, hand in hand, running.*
     ROBIN *is rather blown.*)
 MAGGIE. I'd have won if you hadn't held me back.
 ROBIN (*protesting*). I can run as fast as any of *you*.
 DICKIE. Are you out of breath, Mr. Worthington ?
 ROBIN (*who obviously is out of breath*). No, of course I'm not out of breath.
 MAGGIE. Shall we all sprint back to the tennis lawn and back again ?
 ROBIN (*very positively*). No ! Certainly not !

DICKIE (*dancing up stage and looking off in the direction they have come*). Here comes Bertha! Go it, Bertha! Run, Bertha!
(*He claps his hands.*)
MAGGIE (*clapping her hands and dancing about with* DICKIE, *screaming*). Bertha! Bertha! Bertha!
(*Enter* BERTHA SIMS. BERTHA *is a fat girl of sixteen. She is puffing and blowing as she runs in.*)
BERTHA. I didn't get a fair start.
ROBIN (*laughing*). Poor Bertha!
DICKIE. Good old Bertha!
(*He slaps* BERTHA *soundly on the back.*)
BERTHA. Don't!
LADY COTTRELL. Dickie! You mustn't do such things as that.
(DICKIE *is momentarily subdued.*)
MAGGIE (*dancing up to the tea-table*). Come on, come on, come on. Tea!
(*She seats herself at the tea-table.*)
ROBIN. Come on, Dickie. We'll have tea at the big table.
DICKIE (*making* ROBIN *pass in front of him*). You must sit beside your inamorata.
ROBIN (*going to the seat by* MAGGIE, *he says before he sits*). Come along, Bertha.
BERTHA. Where shall *I* sit?
ROBIN. Anywhere.
(ROBIN *and* MAGGIE *pour out the tea together.*)
DICKIE. Don't make a fuss, Bertha. It doesn't matter in the least where *you* sit.
(BERTHA *sits down.*)
LADY COTTRELL (*to* LOUISE). I think we may as well let the gentlemen wait upon us; don't you, Miss Parker?
LOUISE. August the tenth, did you say?
LADY COTTRELL. Yes; I suppose you'll have gone away by then?
LOUISE (*mysteriously*). I don't know.
(*There is some general chattering and laughter at the tea-table.*)
HENRY. May I give you some tea, Lady Cottrell?
LADY COTTRELL. Thank you.
(*She takes a cup of tea from* HENRY.)

HENRY (*giving another cup to* LOUISE). Tea ?
LOUISE. Thanks.
LADY COTTRELL (*calling out*). Dickie ! Bring Miss Parker and me some buns.
>  (*Shrieks of laughter come from the tea-table. They all look towards it.*)

ROBIN (*rising and scarcely able to speak for laughter*). Bertha—has just stuck her thumb in the strawberry jam.
>  (*He sits down, shaking with laughter. All the others laugh, too, except* LOUISE. BERTHA, *sucking her left thumb, laughs round at them all, delighted with herself.*)

LADY COTTRELL (*turning to* LOUISE, *says, laughing*). Bertha has just stuck her thumb in the strawberry jam.
>  (LOUISE *doesn't laugh.*)

DICKIE. Oh, Bertha, you are a disgusting girl !
MAGGIE. Sit down !
>  (*She throws a piece of food at* DICKIE. *They all laugh and chatter round the table.*)

LADY COTTRELL (*to* LOUISE). How delightful it is to see Mr. Worthington unbend with the young people ! No one would think, to look at him now, that he's a clever man.
>  (LADY COTTRELL *and* LOUISE *turn to look at* ROBIN, *who is whispering with* MAGGIE, *his face nearly under the brim of her hat.* LOUISE *rises hastily and goes up towards the window.*)

ISABELLA (*anxiously to* HENRY). What is Louise up to now ?
LOUISE (*calling*). Mr. Worthington. (ROBIN *is so engrossed in* MAGGIE *he doesn't hear* LOUISE. *She calls louder.*) Mr. Worthington !
ROBIN (*turning to* LOUISE). Yes ?
LOUISE. *Do* come here. I want to show you something.
ROBIN (*to* MAGGIE). Excuse me a minute.
>  (*He joins* LOUISE.)

LOUISE (*affectedly, indicating the view from the window*). Aren't the various lights and shadows in the garden lovely ?
ROBIN. Lovely !
>  (*He hurries back to his seat beside* MAGGIE.)

LOUISE (*gazing across the garden*). They remind me of Bruges.
(*She looks round and finds him gone, then she gets a book and sits down.*)
ISABELLA (*to* HENRY). Trying to make out she's so travelled.
BERTHA. I say, can any of you do this ?
(*She throws a lump of sugar in the air and tries to catch it in her mouth, but fails.*)
MAGGIE. Yes.
(*She throws a piece of food at* BERTHA.)
BERTHA. Pig !
(*She throws a piece of food back at* MAGGIE. MAGGIE *throws a bun at* BERTHA. LADY COTTRELL *laughs heartily.*)
ROBIN. Can you do this ?
(*Juggling with some lumps of sugar.*)
MAGGIE (*taking lumps of sugar from the sugar-basin*). Oh ! I must try that. One, two, three !
(*Juggling with them.*)
DICKIE (*also juggling with lumps of sugar*). One, two, three !—don't jog me.
BERTHA. Look !
(*She tries to balance her teaspoon on her nose.*)
(*Enter* MISS HESELTINE *with a type-written letter in her hand. She remains near the door, a little timid among all the noise and laughter which seems to greet her. They subside when she enters, and all look towards her.* ROBIN *comes down to* MISS HESELTINE.)
ROBIN. What is it, Miss Heseltine ?
MISS HESELTINE. You asked me to bring you this letter as soon as it was written.
ROBIN. Oh, yes. (*Taking the letter from* MISS HESELTINE *he reads it over to himself.*) That seems all right. (*He looks at* MISS HESELTINE *and says kindly.*) You look tired. You'd better leave off for to-day and go home.
MISS HESELTINE. I haven't finished typing the American article.
ROBIN. Won't it do to-morrow ?
MISS HESELTINE. You promised to send it off to-night.
ROBIN. But I don't want you to overwork yourself.

MISS HESELTINE. If I didn't overwork myself—*I might lose my head, too.*
> (*She takes the letter out of his hand and goes out quickly with it.* ROBIN *looks after her till she has closed the door.* LOUISE *comes towards him, smiling, with a small volume in her hand.*)

LOUISE. Mr. Worthington, have you read this new volume of Eastern Poems?

ROBIN (*preoccupied*). Yes.

LOUISE. Do you think we are meant to take them literally or allegorically?

ROBIN. Both.
> (*He passes* LOUISE *and sits on the cushion seat, taking out his cigarette case and helping himself to a cigarette, while* LOUISE *sits on the settee and peruses the volume of Eastern Poems.*)

DICKIE (*coming to* ROBIN). Shall we go and play some more tennis?

ROBIN. Not *yet*.

DICKIE. Why not? What are we waiting for?

ROBIN. Digestion.

DICKIE. You don't need to digest a cup of tea and a handful of buns.

ROBIN. *You* don't. *I* do.

DICKIE. Mag!

MAGGIE. Yes?

DICKIE. Make him come and play tennis. He's slacking.

MAGGIE (*coming to* ROBIN). Don't make him play if he doesn't want to. (*Kindly to* ROBIN.) *I'll* go and play with them while *you* have your snooze.

ROBIN (*jumping up as if he had been shot*). Snooze! I don't want a snooze! (*Gaily.*) Who's coming to play tennis?

BERTHA (*still eating a bun*). I'm ready.

MAGGIE. Come along then.
> (MAGGIE *goes into the garden, running.*)

BERTHA. Wait a tick.
> (*Exit* BERTHA, *running and eating.*)

DICKIE. Come along, Mr. Worthington.
> (*Exit* DICKIE, *running.*)

HENRY. I say, Robin, you'd much better not play again immediately.

# A SINGLE MAN

ROBIN. Why ? *They* do.

HENRY. *They* are a generation younger than *you*.

ROBIN. I wish everybody wouldn't treat me as if I were an old gentleman.

(*He goes out after them.*)

LADY COTTRELL. I declare, Captain Worthington, your brother is the youngest of the party.

HENRY. He'll pay for it to-morrow. He'll be so stiff he won't be able to walk.

LADY COTTRELL. After a few sets of tennis ? He's not as old as all that.

HENRY. It's not the tennis that's going to find him out. It's all that idiotic ragging and jumping about and screaming. It's not natural at his time of life. A man of such sedentary habits, too.

ISABELLA. If he's not very careful he'll break one of his ligaments.

LOUISE. It's so bad for him *intellectually* to mix with such *very* young people. A man of *his* ability ought not to have been so much amused when Miss Sims stuck her thumb in the strawberry jam.

LADY COTTRELL. *I* was exceedingly amused. It was a thoroughly characteristic example of British wit and humour.

(*She goes out.* ISABELLA *glances at* LOUISE, *who is again absorbed in the Eastern Poems, before she says to* HENRY *in an undertone.*)

ISABELLA. I consider the way Louise behaved all through tea was nothing short of scandalous.

HENRY. You'll really have to say something to her. You'd better take this opportunity. (*Exit* HENRY.)

ISABELLA. Louise—I'm ashamed of you !

LOUISE (*in mild surprise*). Why ?

ISABELLA. Everybody must have noticed.

LOUISE. What ?

ISABELLA. The way you run after Robin. (LOUISE *looks affronted.*) Your attempts to wean him away from Maggie—(*with a reproving smile as* LOUISE *is about to retort*) your own words, dear. (LOUISE *hangs her head.*) And it's not only to-day, it's all the time. I don't know what Lady Cottrell must think.

LOUISE (*retorting*). I am only treating Mr. Worthington as I treat every man.

ISABELLA. I hope *not*.

LOUISE. I mean to say—I'm amazed you should see anything to criticise in my behaviour. I am sure *no one*—except *you* who know why you invited me and are therefore, I suppose, on the look-out for *motives* in everything I do—no one else could say otherwise than that I treat Mr. Worthington in a perfectly easy and friendly manner.

ISABELLA. It was the same thing at school.

LOUISE. I don't know what you mean.

ISABELLA. You can't have forgotten the young man with the bicycle who lived opposite!

LOUISE (*angry*). *I* wasn't the only one. You and Jinny and Margaret were just as bad.

ISABELLA. There! *That* is an illustration of what I mean. *You* think *we* were as bad as *you*.

LOUISE. You *were*.

ISABELLA. We were all just as madly in love with him, but we none of us went the lengths *you* did. *We* only smiled at him and waved our pocket-handkerchiefs. *You* used to write him letters and threw nosegays at him out of your bedroom window—till he got in such a fright he told his mother and *she* complained, and *you* were expelled.

LOUISE (*crestfallen*). I don't see why you need rake that up now.

ISABELLA. I only remind you of it because you are still doing exactly the same sort of thing.

LOUISE. When have I ever written a letter to Mr. Worthington? When have I thrown a single nosegay at him?

ISABELLA. You've got beyond *that*, I should *hope*. What I mean to say is—here you are again, making the boldest advances—without apparently realising that you are doing anything out of the ordinary.

LOUISE (*childishly*). I'm very much hurt that you should think such things about me. You've made me feel horrid.

ISABELLA. Let me give you a word of advice, Louise.

LOUISE. Well, what is it?

ISABELLA. It's not the way to succeed in love to be so persevering.

LOUISE (*sitting on the floor at* ISABELLA'S *feet in the*

*attitude of one willing to learn*). What do you think would be a better way ?

ISABELLA. Be more reticent. If you don't encourage a man too much *he* will make advances.

LOUISE (*thoughtfully*). Not always.

ISABELLA. You must show him now and then that you like him.

LOUISE. Of course.

ISABELLA. But don't show him too often. Otherwise he takes fright or gets bored—or says to himself, " I can have *her* any time," and takes no trouble, so nothing comes of it.

LOUISE. That's so true !

ISABELLA (*warming to her subject*). Baffle them a bit. Then they begin to wonder about you till their heads become so full of you they can think of nothing else. That's love. (*As she meets* LOUISE'S *earnest and inquiring gaze she stops short.*) Oh ! (*Uneasily.*) I hope you don't think I am giving you hints as to how to succeed with— any one in particular ?

LOUISE. Oh, no, dear. We were speaking quite impersonally.

ISABELLA. I can't think how I allowed myself to be led away into considering the best ways to attract men except that the subject is so engrossing. But that's not what we are talking about. I'll have nothing to do with helping you to wean Robin away from Maggie. I've told you so repeatedly. I don't think you ought to be here.

LOUISE. Whenever I propose leaving, *Mr. Worthington* invariably asks me to stay on.

ISABELLA. Mere politeness.

LOUISE. I couldn't very well leave by the next train because I found on my arrival that Mr. Worthington was engaged.

ISABELLA. I never suggested you should leave by the next train. The right and proper thing for you to have done was to have stayed here for two or three days, and then had an engagement elsewhere.

LOUISE (*thoughtfully*). I *had* thought of leaving tomorrow.

ISABELLA. That's right.

LOUISE. But I have just heard that the wedding-day

is fixed for August the tenth. It'll look very funny if I leave now.

ISABELLA. It'll look much funnier if you don't.

LOUISE. Every one would say, "Miss Parker stayed until the wedding-day was fixed, then, seeing she had no chance, she left." Oh, no—I can't leave now. It would be putting myself in a very false position.

ISABELLA. You *can't* hang on like this! (*Marching towards* LOUISE *and saying with great determination.*) You really must go—please, dear.

LOUISE (*calmly and seriously*). And do you sincerely believe, Isabella, that Maggie Cottrell will make *him* happy?

ISABELLA. That's nobody's business but *his*. He has chosen her. He is engaged to her, and he is going to be married to her in six weeks.

LOUISE (*moving about, as she says, dramatically*). It must be stopped! Why can't *you* do something? Why doesn't your husband interfere? He ought to *save* his brother. Poor Mr. Worthington is out of his mind. He's infatuated, bewitched. He'll be bored to death in no time by that wretched chit of a child.

ISABELLA (*quite unimpressed by* LOUISE'S *exhibition of feeling*). When *are* you going to leave?

LOUISE (*deliberately*). I haven't made up my mind.

ISABELLA. I shall tell Henry.

(*Enter* ROBIN *quickly.*)

ROBIN (*indignantly*). What do you think? They've got tired of playing tennis, and now they want to play hide-and-seek all over the garden! I won't do it.

(ISABELLA *laughs.*)

LOUISE (*smiling at* ROBIN). Poor Mr. Worthington! *We'll* protect you.

ROBIN (*still speaking indignantly*). I can't keep this up. I've been on the go ever since three o'clock. (*He sits.*) The more they run about the livelier they get, but *I* don't. (*Enter* MAGGIE. ROBIN *does not see her, as his back is towards her.* MAGGIE *puts her finger to her lips as a sign to* ISABELLA *and* LOUISE *not to let* ROBIN *know she is there. She advances towards* ROBIN *smiling, and on tiptoe, then suddenly puts her hands over his eyes and laughs.* ROBIN, *taken by surprise, is exceedingly annoyed, struggles, and says, crossly.*) Don't do that.

Who is it ? (*He frees himself, rises, and seeing* MAGGIE *softens.*) Oh! Maggie, is it you ? (*He takes her hand and says kindly.*) I'm sorry I spoke crossly—but you know, my dear—I think you are getting a little old to do that sort of thing.

MAGGIE (*sweetly*). You said the other day that the way I play and run about is one of my chief charms in your eyes.

ROBIN. I like you to be playful prettily.
(*He talks apart with* MAGGIE.)

ISABELLA (*to* LOUISE *as she goes towards the door*). Come along, Louise. I don't think we are wanted here.
(*She waits for* LOUISE.)

LOUISE (*rising reluctantly, glances at* ROBIN *and* MAGGIE, *and then joins* ISABELLA). He is beginning to get bored with her. I shall certainly not leave yet.
(ISABELLA *and* LOUISE *go out.*)

MAGGIE. Shall we go out ?

ROBIN. Presently.

MAGGIE. It's a sin to stick in the house on a day like this. (ROBIN *invites her in smiling dumb-show to come and sit beside him on the sofa. She comes towards him as she says.*) Very well. We'll sit here just five minutes.
(*She springs on to the sofa beside him and nestles close up to him. He puts his arm round her.*)

ROBIN. This is the nicest part of the whole day.

MAGGIE. I love playing hide-and-seek.

ROBIN. I love having you all to myself.
(MAGGIE *smiles up in his face, then gives his nose a little playful pinch. He kisses her hand.*)

MAGGIE (*counting the buttons down his coat with her forefinger*). One, two, three, four. I feel terribly kiddish to-day. Some days—when it's fine and bright like this—I just want to run about very fast all the time like a field-mouse.

ROBIN. Don't you ever want to sit still and bask like a lizard ?

MAGGIE. Oh, no, never—at least—not for long at a time. I always want to be up and doing. I feel as if I could dance and sing the minute I get up in the morning.

ROBIN. I can't bear being active before breakfast !

MAGGIE. Can't you ? *I* can. (*He puts his arm further round her to draw her closer to him.*) Wait a minute. That's not comfortable. (*She sits up and shakes herself, then leans her back against his shoulder, in a most unromantic position.*) There! That's better! (*She lets her head fall back on his shoulder, which places him in a most uncomfortable position.*) I could go to sleep like this.

ROBIN. *I* couldn't.

> (*Enter* GLADYS *to clear away the tea-things, followed by* MRS. HIGSON. MRS. HIGSON *is the housekeeper; a middle-aged, respectable-looking woman.* MAGGIE *sits up and then goes to the window.*)

MAGGIE. She's come to clear away. We'd better go out.

ROBIN (*also rising*). She'll have finished in a minute. (*To* MRS. HIGSON.) We've made rather a mess there, haven't we, Mrs. Higson?

(*Takes a cigarette.*)

MRS. HIGSON. What does that matter, sir, so long as you enjoyed yourselves?

ROBIN. After all—one is only middle-aged once.

MAGGIE. I *should* enjoy a good game of hide-and-seek.

> (ROBIN *takes out his match-box and strikes a match.* MAGGIE *runs quickly towards him and blows out his match.*)

ROBIN (*taken by surprise, is annoyed*). Oh, don't—please. What a silly thing to do.

MAGGIE (*laughs*). All right. I won't do it again. (*Having gathered up everything* MRS. HIGSON *goes out.* ROBIN *strikes a second match, and while he is doing so* MAGGIE *snatches the cigarette out of his mouth and runs away with it, saying gaily.*) I didn't say I wouldn't do that. I love playing tricks on people. (GLADYS *follows* MRS. HIGSON *off with the tea-cloth and cake-stand.* ROBIN *sits on the settee looking very solemn.*) You aren't cross, are you?

ROBIN. No, dear, but you know—sometimes—you *are* just a little bit rough.

> (MAGGIE *crosses to him and kisses him on the cheek very nicely and gently, then steps back. He smiles at her quite won over.*)

MAGGIE. Shall we go out now?

ROBIN. Soon. (*Leans towards her.*) Sit down and have a little talk first.

# A SINGLE MAN

(MAGGIE, *showing no inclination to be cuddlesome, sits on the cushion seat.*)

MAGGIE. What do you want to talk about?

ROBIN (*smiling*). August the tenth.

MAGGIE. We talked about that this morning.

ROBIN (*wistfully*). Do you remember that evening when we sat in this room for a long time, holding each other's hands and hardly saying a word?

MAGGIE (*cheerfully*). We *were* two sleepy things. We'd been out in the air all day.

ROBIN. It was such a happy, restful evening.

MAGGIE. Wasn't it—but when I'm feeling really strong there's nothing I like so well as to dance till midnight and end up with a good pillow fight.

ROBIN (*slowly and thoughtfully*). There is a great difference—in our ages.

(*Enter* MISS HESELTINE. *She carries a number of loose typewritten pages in her hand.*)

MAGGIE. Hullo, Miss Heseltine.

ROBIN (*to* MISS HESELTINE). Do you want *me* for anything?

MISS HESELTINE. I can come later on, if it's inconvenient now.

ROBIN. If you wouldn't mind.

MAGGIE (*springing up*). No. This is business. (*To* MISS HESELTINE.) You told me I must never interfere with his business. I'll go out and play with Dickie and Bertha. *I* don't mind.

(*She pats* ROBIN'S *arm and goes off to the garden skippingly—and calling " Dickie."*)

MISS HESELTINE (*referring to the pages in her hand*). There seems to be something wrong with this.

ROBIN (*takes pages*). Is that the American article?

MISS HESELTINE. Yes. I wouldn't have disturbed you with it *now*, only it must go to-night.

ROBIN. What's wrong with it?

MISS HESELTINE. You've written parts of it in the first person singular and other parts in the first person plural.

ROBIN. Not really?

MISS HESELTINE. Yes.

ROBIN (*glancing down the sheets*). So I have. How did I come to make such a mistake as that?

MISS HESELTINE (*primly*). You must have had your head full of something else.

ROBIN (*turning over the sheets*). Like when I wrote that article the other day and called beer rice.

MISS HESELTINE. Yes. And in the last chapter of the new novel you called several of the characters by the wrong names.

ROBIN (*looking at her before saying, gravely*). Has *all* my work been careless lately?

MISS HESELTINE. Yes, very.

ROBIN. Sit down, won't you, while I look over this. (MISS HESELTINE *sits.*) It means going over the whole thing carefully from beginning to end, and I *am* so tired! (*Turning over a page or two.*) I can't do any good with it till I've had at least an hour's rest.

MISS HESELTINE. That throws it so late. It has to be typed after *you've* been through it.

ROBIN (*sighing*). Oh, dear, then I suppose I must, but you know—it's not so much that I'm tired physically. It's my brain—it's completely disorganised. I can't concentrate.

MISS HESELTINE. I think *I* could make the necessary changes if you'd trust it to me. (*She comes towards him.*) I could take it home to do and bring it back to you this evening.

ROBIN. Why take it home? Why can't you do it here?

MISS HESELTINE. There's too much noise in the garden.

ROBIN (*with a weary little smile*). It isn't like our usual quiet afternoons, is it?

MISS HESELTINE. No, it isn't—not at all.

ROBIN. It won't be like this much longer. When I'm married and we've settled down—you and I will be able to work together peacefully again—as we used to do. Shan't we?

MISS HESELTINE (*taking the pages from him*). I'm afraid not.

ROBIN. Why not?

MISS HESELTINE. Because when you are married—I shan't be here.

ROBIN (*surprised*). What do you mean? You won't be here?

## A SINGLE MAN

MISS HESELTINE. I'm leaving Farnham.
ROBIN. Leaving?
MISS HESELTINE. Yes.
ROBIN. Where are you going?
MISS HESELTINE. I don't know quite. I think I shall go and live in London.
ROBIN. That's not far away. You can still come and work for *me*—can't you?
MISS HESELTINE. I don't think so.

(*Moves as if to go.*)

ROBIN. Wait a minute. I want to know about this.
MISS HESELTINE. That's all. I find I must leave.
ROBIN (*going towards her*). People don't usually leave without giving a reason. (MISS HESELTINE *hesitates.*) I think you owe me some explanation.
MISS HESELTINE (*looking at the pages in her hand*). I must go and do this now.
ROBIN (*taking her by the arm*). Sit down and tell me why you want to leave me.

(MISS HESELTINE *reluctantly sits again. He watches her all the time, standing.*)

MISS HESELTINE. There's no particular reason—that I can give you.
ROBIN. What do you intend to do after you leave here?
MISS HESELTINE. That hasn't been definitely decided yet.
ROBIN. Then why need you go? (MISS HESELTINE *looks on the ground.*) I don't want to be too inquisitive, but it's so extraordinary that you can't give me any reason.
MISS HESELTINE. I need a change.
ROBIN. If it's a holiday you want——
MISS HESELTINE (*interrupting him*). Oh, no, thank you. I don't want a holiday. I had three weeks in April.
ROBIN. And you'll be having another three or four weeks quite soon—when I go away on my honeymoon.
MISS HESELTINE. I shall have left before that.
ROBIN. I had no idea you were dissatisfied. (MISS HESELTINE *makes a restless, nervous movement.*) If it's a question of earning more money—I shall be very happy to meet you in any way I can.

MISS HESELTINE. It's not that. Please don't think it's that. I'm more than satisfied with what you give me.

ROBIN. Are you going to be married?

MISS HESELTINE (*almost angrily*). Of course not!

(*She turns away from him in her seat.*)

ROBIN. Then what is it? (*With a ring of genuine distress in his voice as he sits on the ottoman at her feet.*) Why—why go away and leave me?

MISS HESELTINE (*distressed by his distress, is greatly agitated*). I must. I'm very sorry—but I must!

ROBIN. But I can't think what I shall do without you. I shan't be able to get on at all. I can hardly imagine yet what it's going to be like here without *you*. I've never thought of you leaving me. You've been coming to me every day for such a long time—five years—it's a long time. (MISS HESELTINE, *unable to control her agitation, rises. He rises almost at the same time as he says.*) Don't decide *yet*—not just yet.

MISS HESELTINE. I can't stay. It's no use pretending I can. I can't. I can't do it!

ROBIN (*puzzled*). Are you afraid your position here is going to be made difficult after my marriage? (*A pause for her to reply.*) Is that it? (*Another pause as before.*) I don't see why it need be difficult. Maggie is very good about not disturbing me in my work hours. She won't interfere with *you*. (*Making light of it.*) If that's all it is—— (MISS HESELTINE *bursts into tears.* ROBIN *is very much distressed to see her in tears and goes to her.*) Miss Heseltine! What's the matter? I can't bear to see you like this. What is it? Is it something *I've* done? Have I hurt you without knowing it? (*Putting his hands on her shoulders and turning her towards him.*) Miss Heseltine! Look at me!—tell me! why must you leave me?

> (*He gently pulls her hands away from her face; she looks up at him appealingly, unable to hide her love for him. He understands and stands looking at her transfixed.*)

MAGGIE (*from the garden*). Robin! What are you doing?

DICKIE (*also from the garden*). Where is he?

MAGGIE. In here. (*When their voices are heard,*

ROBIN *steps back from* MISS HESELTINE. *She makes an undecided step or two as if she didn't know where to go, then begins nervously gathering up the pages. Enter* MAGGIE *followed by* DICKIE *and* BERTHA SIMS, *all darting about and skipping.* MAGGIE, *speaking as she enters and coming towards* ROBIN.) We want to wind up with something really silly before we go home.

ROBIN (*protesting*). Oh, no—my dears—no!

DICKIE AND BERTHA. Yes, yes.

BERTHA (*beginning to dance and sing by herself*). Here we go round the mulberry bush.

DICKIE (*singing*). The mulberry bush.

MAGGIE (*joining in as well*). The mulberry bush!

(*They all laugh.*)
(*While this is going on* MISS HESELTINE, *with the pages in her hand, slowly goes out.*)
(LOUISE *comes in from the garden. Taking in the situation, she says, " Mr. Worthington, too ! " and seizing him by both hands dances him round. He is then swept into the ring between* DICKIE *and* MAGGIE. LOUISE *tries to enter the ring, first on* ROBIN'S *left, in which attempt she fails, and then on his right, this time achieving success. They all laugh and dance in a ring.*)


CURTAIN.

# THE THIRD ACT

SCENE.—*The same as the first act. The scene is arranged as before except that the cradle is no longer there. It is beginning to grow dusk.* ROBIN, *dressed as at the end of the second act, is standing, with his hands in his pockets, staring at* MISS HESELTINE'S *desk.*

ROBIN (*slowly and thoughtfully, as if scarcely able to credit what he says*). Miss Heseltine!

(LOUISE *enters. She wears an elaborate dinner-gown.*)

LOUISE (*in the doorway*). May I come in?

ROBIN (*suddenly brought to himself*). Is it as late as *that*?

LOUISE. I dressed early. I mistook the time. The drawing-room was deserted, so I thought I'd come in here. I hope I don't intrude.

ROBIN (*merely politely*). Not at all.

LOUISE (*smiling as if she had received a most pressing invitation to stay*). Thank you! (*She closes the door and comes towards* ROBIN.) Has she gone?

ROBIN. Yes.

LOUISE (*with a little sigh of satisfaction*). Ah!

ROBIN. She took her work home to do.

LOUISE. Maggie?

ROBIN. Miss Heseltine. Oh, yes; those children have all gone. Thank goodness! (*Hurriedly correcting himself.*) The dears.

LOUISE. Weren't you rather glad—between ourselves—to see them go?

ROBIN. I don't feel safe even yet. I can't help thinking that Bertha Sims is still lurking among the bushes—ready to spring out at me. What's that noise? (*He goes to the window and looks out, then closes the curtains.*) Only the rooks going home.

(*He goes towards the electric switch.*)

LOUISE (*sentimentally*). The twilight hour. (*She leans back luxuriously and says languidly.*) How peaceful it is here! How perfectly harmonious! (ROBIN *turns on the electric light. This surprises and disconcerts* LOUISE.) Oh! (*She sits up.* ROBIN *takes out his cigarette case and helps himself to a cigarette. He is absorbed in his own thoughts, and does not notice* LOUISE.) Have you got a cigarette to give *me*?

ROBIN (*offering her his cigarette case*). I beg your pardon. My mind was full of something else.

LOUISE (*smiles at him as she slowly draws a cigarette from the case*). Thank you *very* much.

ROBIN (*after a moment's pause*). Don't mention it. You want a light.

> (*He moves away for the match-box, which is on the writing-table, brings it to* LOUISE *and offers it to her.* LOUISE *smilingly makes a sign with her hands for him to strike a match. He does so.* LOUISE *does not offer to take the match, but lights her cigarette from it as he holds it.*)

LOUISE. Ta!

ROBIN. I beg your pardon?

LOUISE. Ta! (ROBIN *lights his own cigarette, then throws the match in an ash-tray, and sits on a settee at some distance from* LOUISE.) I hope you don't object to women smoking?

ROBIN. I don't mind one way or the other.

LOUISE. I was afraid you might think it unwomanly.

ROBIN. I shouldn't like my wife to smoke.

LOUISE (*rising*). I practically *never* smoke. (*She puts her cigarette on an ash-tray.*)

(*Enter* GLADYS.)

GLADYS (*addressing* LOUISE). If you please, miss, Mrs. Worthington sent me to say will you kindly come and talk to her while she dresses?

LOUISE (*sweetly to* GLADYS). Tell Mrs. Worthington I will come—presently.

GLADYS. Thank you, miss.

(*Exit* GLADYS.)

ROBIN. If you want to go and talk to Isabella, don't mind *me*.

LOUISE (*reproachfully*). Do you *want* me to go?

ROBIN. Oh, no—I didn't mean *that*—of course.

LOUISE (*archly*). Shall I stay?

ROBIN (*after a pause, reluctantly*). Do.

LOUISE. I know you wouldn't say that unless you meant it. (*She sits by him.*) You and I never seem to be left alone together—do we?

ROBIN (*carelessly*). Don't we?

LOUISE. Never. And I always feel we should have so much to say to each other if we could once break through our British reserve. (*He looks at her in surprise. She smiles at him.*) You have drawn me to you by your writings. I am one of your most devoted readers. I buy all your books. Oftentimes—after reading one or other of your various masterpieces—I have turned from the contemplation of Robin Worthington, the author, to the contemplation of Robin Worthington the man.

ROBIN (*embarrassed*). Oh, yes!

(*Enter* GLADYS.)

GLADYS (*addressing* LOUISE). Mrs. Worthington says will you please come at once. It's most partickler.

ROBIN (*attempting to rise*). Don't let me detain you.

LOUISE (*preventing* ROBIN *rising by laying her hand on his arm, as she turns to* GLADYS *and says impatiently*). Say I am coming—presently.

GLADYS. Yes, miss.

(*Exit* GLADYS.)

LOUISE (*intensely*). I want to see you take your place among the immortals. You *could* if you *would*. But you never *will*—until you have the right woman beside you—a woman of heart, brain, experience—a woman who has lived and suffered—one who would help you in your work, who would be capable of being at the same time your companion and your inspiration. (*She drops her intense tone and says, colloquially.*) Maggie Cottrell can't appreciate *you*.

ROBIN (*rising abruptly, and annoyed*). We won't discuss her, please.

LOUISE (*reproachfully*). You are angry with me.

ROBIN (*turning to her*). No, I'm not angry, but——

LOUISE (*interrupting him by rising and saying frankly*). Forgive me! (*She comes to him and extends both her hands.* ROBIN *reluctantly takes her hands.*)

(*Enter* GLADYS.)

GLADYS. Mrs. Worthington says——

## A SINGLE MAN

LOUISE (*losing her temper*). Tell her I'm *busy*. (*Exit* GLADYS. LOUISE *plants herself in front of* ROBIN *and looks earnestly in his face.*) You *do* forgive me?

ROBIN (*bored*). Oh—yes, of course.

LOUISE. Yes, but *really*.

ROBIN. I must go and dress.

(*He tries to get past her.*)

LOUISE (*planting herself in front of him*). I ought not to have spoken as I did of Maggie Cottrell—but I can't bear to see you throwing yourself away.

ROBIN. I shall be late.

(*He makes another attempt to get past her.*)

LOUISE (*preventing him getting away by laying her hand on his arm*). If only you were going to marry some woman worthy to be your wife!

ROBIN (*trying to free himself*). Yes, but I'm *not*—I mean I *am*.

(*Enter* ISABELLA, *carrying her gloves, and then* HENRY. ISABELLA *wears a smart dinner-gown, and* HENRY *his evening clothes.*)

ISABELLA (*sharply as she enters*). Louise! I sent for you three times.

LOUISE (*sweetly as she goes towards* ISABELLA). I know you did, dear. Was it anything that mattered?

(*They talk together,* ISABELLA *obviously chiding* LOUISE. ROBIN *joins* HENRY *after beckoning him.*)

ROBIN (*drawing* HENRY *aside*). I'm so glad you came in. I was having *such* a time.

HENRY. What's happened?

ROBIN. I don't think I'm naturally the kind of fellow who thinks every woman is in love with him—but really—this afternoon! It must be my lucky day.

(ISABELLA *comes towards* ROBIN *when she speaks, while* LOUISE *sits by the fire.*)

ISABELLA. Aren't you going to dress?

ROBIN. Yes, I'll go now.

ISABELLA. The cab will be here in about ten minutes.

ROBIN. What cab?

ISABELLA. To take us to the Hendersons'.

ROBIN (*addressing* HENRY *and* ISABELLA *in turns during the next speech*). Oh, dear me! yes. We promised to go and dine at the Hendersons'—didn't we? I'd forgotten all about it. I don't want to go a bit. I say, couldn't you three go without me?

HENRY. I don't know, I'm sure.

ISABELLA. What will Mrs. Henderson say?

ROBIN. Tell her I had to stay and work. You don't mind, do you? I really need an evening to myself. I shall dine quietly in my study, and go to bed early. (*He takes his latch-key out of his pocket and gives it to* HENRY.) There's my latch-key. You don't mind, do you? Thanks so much; it's awfully kind of you.

(*He goes out.*)

ISABELLA. How tiresome of him to back out! (*To* HENRY.) Have you got everything?

HENRY. I think so.

ISABELLA. Cigarettes?

HENRY (*feeling his breast-pocket*). Yes.

ISABELLA. Watch?

HENRY (*feeling his watch-pocket*). Yes.

ISABELLA. Pocket-handkerchief?

HENRY. Yes—(*looks in sleeve and pocket*) no.

(*Exit* HENRY.)

LOUISE (*pressing her hands to her temples, and calling out, as if in sudden pain*). Oh—oh!

ISABELLA (*anxiously*). What's the matter?

LOUISE. I've got such a splitting headache. It's as if some one were driving a nail right through my temple.

ISABELLA (*coming towards* LOUISE, *much concerned*). I'm so sorry.

LOUISE. I can't possibly go to the Hendersons'.

ISABELLA (*immediately suspicious, she backs away*). Louise!

LOUISE. You couldn't ask me to go to a dinner-party with my head in *this* state.

ISABELLA (*drily*). You'll feel better soon.

LOUISE. Whenever I have a headache it always lasts all the evening.

ISABELLA. We'll take some menthol with us.

LOUISE. Think of driving in a closed cab!

ISABELLA. We'll have it open.

LOUISE. That would blow our hair about.

ISABELLA. We'll take veils.

LOUISE. It's no use, dear. I'm suffering too much; I shouldn't enjoy myself.

## A SINGLE MAN

ISABELLA (*mercilessly*). I don't *ask* that you should enjoy yourself. I ask that you should come with us.

LOUISE. I really must stay at home.

ISABELLA. Very well, then—we'll *all* stay at home.
(*She sits down facing* LOUISE. LOUISE *looks poutingly at* ISABELLA *a moment before she speaks.*)

LOUISE. There's no dinner for you.

ISABELLA. There's none for *you*, either.

LOUISE. What is enough for one is generally enough for two—but it's not enough for four.

ISABELLA (*muttering*). I thought so.

LOUISE. I have no intention of dining with Mr. Worthington. (*Rising in her queenliest manner.*) I shall ask Mrs. Higson to serve me a snack in my room.

ISABELLA (*calmly, but firmly*). I shall not go and leave you here, Louise.

LOUISE (*reproachfully*). You don't trust me.
(*Sits beside* ISABELLA.)

ISABELLA (*in an ironically affectionate tone*). Darling —you wrong me. I only meant—how could I sit through an elaborate dinner if I knew that my friend was suffering alone in her chamber?

LOUISE. That's very sweet of you. But think of poor Mr. and Mrs. Henderson. They will be *so* disappointed if you don't go.

ISABELLA (*amiably*). Henry must make my excuses.

LOUISE. But if three out of four of their guests don't turn up!

ISABELLA (*assuming gaiety and friendliness*). They won't think much of themselves, will they? (LOUISE *turns away, looking cross.*) You and I will have a nice little mess of something all by ourselves upstairs. It'll be just like the dear old school-days, when we used to have forbidden feasts in our bedrooms. (*She drops the gay and friendly tone, and says, drily.*) Is your head any better?

LOUISE (*seeing that her present line is hopeless, takes a new one, and says solemnly*). Isabella—Belle, dear, I didn't tell you. I have made up my mind to leave tomorrow.

ISABELLA (*unable to conceal her delight*). Not really!

LOUISE (*pained*). I know you wish it.

ISABELLA (*politely*). Not on my own account.

LOUISE. As I am leaving to-morrow, I should like to stay at home this evening.

ISABELLA (*suspiciously*). To say good-bye to Robin?

LOUISE (*coldly*). To pack.

ISABELLA (*eagerly*). I'll help you with your packing.

LOUISE. Thank you, dear; but I never can pack if there's any one in the room.

ISABELLA. I'll sit on the landing and be ready when you want me.

LOUISE (*losing her temper and rising abruptly*). Don't be such a fool.

ISABELLA. You needn't think I don't see through you.

LOUISE. What d'you mean?

ISABELLA. I don't believe you have the slightest intention of leaving to-morrow.

LOUISE. Do you think I'm a liar?

ISABELLA (*cheerfully*). Yes.

LOUISE. How dare you say such a thing?

ISABELLA. As if I don't know what you are up to.

LOUISE (*defiantly*). What am I *up* to—as you term it?

ISABELLA. Do you want me to tell you?

LOUISE (*haughtily*). Certainly.

ISABELLA. As soon as Henry and I have left the house you'll rush upstairs and put on a tea-gown—the white one most likely, with the angel-sleeves—and then—when you have calculated that Robin will just about have begun his dinner—you'll come floating in. You won't have had any dinner. He'll feel obliged to ask you to share his. You'll refuse at first—if you think you stand any chance of being pressed—then you'll sit down. You will begin the conversation by telling him that Maggie doesn't appreciate him. That I believe is the usual opening with those who attempt to make discord between lovers——

LOUISE (*exploding with wrath*). Isabella, you're a beast.

ISABELLA (*with great determination*). You shan't stay here alone with Robin because I won't allow it.

LOUISE (*changing her tactics, turns to* ISABELLA *and says calmly and seriously*). He *asked* me to remain.

ISABELLA (*staring at* LOUISE *in amazement*). *He* asked you. . . .

LOUISE (*going a little towards* ISABELLA). Not in so

many words—but saying he wants to be left alone is an invitation to me to stay.

ISABELLA (*bursting out laughing*). Louise!

LOUISE. I *know* it. While you were upstairs dressing we had the most wonderful talk.

ISABELLA (*immediately sobered*). What about?

LOUISE. It was not so much what we said as what we left unsaid. When you sent for me I asked him if he wished me to leave him, and he said " No." He begged me to remain. He was longing to confide in me. I *felt* it. He knows he has made a mistake. He was just on the point of admitting to me that Maggie Cottrell is *not* the girl for him to marry—when you came into the room.

ISABELLA (*hardly knowing whether to believe* LOUISE *or not*). I think it must be *your* imagination.

LOUISE. *You* are responsible for what has happened. *You* invited me here. *You* encouraged me to fall in love with him.

ISABELLA. There's no harm done, because you are *not* in love with him.

LOUISE. I soon could be. ISABELLA (*turns away.*) Please let me stay behind.

ISABELLA (*with determination*). No.

LOUISE (*falling on her knees in despair and grasping* ISABELLA *by the hand*). Isabella! Isabella! It's a crisis.

ISABELLA (*very uneasy*). Louise! Louise! Suppose somebody comes in! (*She wrenches her hand away.* LOUISE *sinks upon the ground.*)

>(*Enter* MRS. HIGSON, *who has a white linen tablecloth folded over her arm, and a small tray-cloth.*)

MRS. HIGSON. The cab's here, ma'am.

ISABELLA. Thank you, Mrs. Higson. (MRS. HIGSON *lays the cloth down and begins to gather the articles together on the writing-table.* ISABELLA *is very firm as she addresses* LOUISE.) Are you ready?

>(LOUISE *rises slowly and tragically from the ground.* ISABELLA *pulls her up to her feet.* LOUISE *slaps her as she releases herself.* ISABELLA *goes to the door, pauses, turns to* LOUISE, *and beckons her as she says "Louise!" She waits till she sees* LOUISE *begin to follow her, then goes out.*

(LOUISE *pauses at the door, then hastily closes it and turns to* MRS. HIGSON.)

LOUISE. By the way, Mrs. Higson, I may arrive home a little in advance of the others.

MRS. HIGSON (*stiffly*). Indeed!

LOUISE. In case you should want to go to bed early—(*smiles at* MRS. HIGSON *in her most ingratiating manner as she comes towards her*) is there an extra latch-key?

MRS. HIGSON (*mistrustfully*). Oh, no, miss—we've got no extra latch-keys.

LOUISE. Oh! (*Pauses.*) You needn't tell anybody I asked you for one.

(MRS. HIGSON *makes no response, but busies herself with the things on* ROBIN'S *desk. While she is doing this,* LOUISE *fumbles in her bag and takes out a ten-shilling piece.* LOUISE *offers* MRS. HIGSON *the ten-shilling piece with her sweetest smile.*)

MRS. HIGSON (*not offering to take it*). Thank you, miss—it will do when you leave.

LOUISE. Oh! (*She puts the ten-shilling piece in her bag, then goes to the door, where she pauses.*) You needn't tell anybody I offered it to you.

(*Exit* LOUISE. MRS. HIGSON *ironically kisses her hand after* LOUISE, *then unfolds the small table-cloth, and lays it on* MISS HESELTINE'S *desk.*)

(*Enter* GLADYS *with a tray containing the glass and silver, etc., necessary for* ROBIN'S *dinner.*)

GLADYS. They're off. I think they must be late.

MRS. HIGSON. What makes you say that? Mr. Burgess is never late with his cab.

GLADYS. I only thought they might be because Mrs. Worthington was that impatient—wouldn't get into the keb without Miss Parker got in first. Looked as if there'd 'ave bin words if Captain Worthington 'adn't pushed 'em both in from be'ind.

MRS. HIGSON. 'Elp me lay this cloth. (*They lay the cloth together as she continues.*) I'm sure I don't wonder he wants to dine quietly in his study after all the racket there's been this afternoon.

GLADYS (*grinning*). They were playin' 'ide-an'-go-seek.

MRS. HIGSON (*contemptuously, as she smooths the cloth*).

# A SINGLE MAN

'Ide-an'-go-seek! What it's going to be like here after 'e's married, I can't think. Pandemonium, *I* should say, with dirt on all the carpets.

GLADYS. I shan't mind the extra work if it makes things 'um a bit more.

MRS. HIGSON. Careful with that silver.

GLADYS. Cook and I was only saying this afternoon it was quite refreshing to look out upon somethin' besides lawns and flowers and green trees.

MRS. HIGSON. You won't welcome changes so much when you reach my age. And it's not as if you'd known Mr. Worthington the years *I* 'ave. And per'aps you 'aven't got the maternal instinct.

GLADYS (*primly*). No, I 'aven't—an' I 'ope I won't 'ave before I get my marriage lines.

MRS. HIGSON. I think that's everything now.

(*Enter* ROBIN. *He wears a dinner-jacket and a black tie.*)

ROBIN (*speaking as he enters*). I'll have my dinner as soon as it's ready.

(*He takes a book from the bookshelves.*)

MRS. HIGSON. Gladys! Tell cook. (*Exit* GLADYS.)

(*The front door bell rings.* ROBIN *pauses and listens.*)

ROBIN. Who's that?

MRS. HIGSON. Post most likely. What will you take to drink, sir?

ROBIN. I think I could do with some champagne.

MRS. HIGSON. Yes, sir.

ROBIN. A small bottle.

MRS. HIGSON. Yes, sir.

(*Exit* MRS. HIGSON. ROBIN *settles himself to read.* GLADYS *comes in carrying a roll of typewritten manuscript.*)

GLADYS. If you please, sir—with Miss 'Eseltine's compliments.

(*She holds out the roll to* ROBIN.)

ROBIN (*taking it*). Is Miss Heseltine here?

GLADYS. Just gorn, sir.

ROBIN. Run after her.

GLADYS. Yes, sir. (*She hurries to the door.*)

ROBIN. No, don't.

GLADYS. No, sir.

(*Exit* GLADYS. ROBIN *spends a moment or two in indecision, looks at the roll of manuscript, leaves it on the settee, rises, crosses to* MISS HESELTINE'S *desk and lays his book upon it; then he goes to the window, and draws back the curtain. He opens the window and looks out.*)
ROBIN (*calling—not loudly*). Miss Heseltine!
(*After a moment or two* MISS HESELTINE *appears at the window. She wears a long, loose, ready-made coat, a cheap, ordinary-looking hat, and makes, altogether, a somewhat dowdy appearance.*)
MISS HESELTINE (*coming just inside the room*). Did you wish to speak to me?
(*They are both embarrassed and constrained when they meet.* MISS HESELTINE'S *manner is extremely prim, to cover her nervousness.*)
ROBIN (*referring to the roll of manuscript in his hand, which he takes from the settee*). What's this thing?
MISS HESELTINE. The American article. I thought you might like to look it over before it goes.
ROBIN. Why didn't you bring it in?
MISS HESELTINE. I didn't wish to disturb you.
ROBIN. I see—thank you—well—— (*looking at* MISS HESELTINE). *You* know if it's all right.
MISS HESELTINE. I can guarantee there are no mistakes in it *now*.
ROBIN (*giving her the roll of manuscript*). Let it go then.
MISS HESELTINE. I'll take it home and put it up for post.
(*She is going.*)
ROBIN. You might as well do that here—at your desk.
MISS HESELTINE (*hesitating a moment, she glances at him, and then says*). Very well—as I'm here. (*Coming to her desk.*) It won't take me but a few minutes.
(*She sits at her desk, opens a drawer and takes out a large envelope in which she places the American article. She does this with a good deal of fumbling and fluttering of papers, owing to her nervousness.*)
ROBIN. You must have worked very hard to get that ready.

MISS HESELTINE (*without looking up*). It all had to be rewritten.

ROBIN. I hope you haven't gone without your dinner. (MISS HESELTINE *begins to address the envelope, apparently not having heard his last remark.*) You *have* dined—haven't you?

MISS HESELTINE (*still addressing the envelope and not looking up*). Not yet.

ROBIN. Are you going to have some dinner *now*?

MISS HESELTINE. I shan't have time. I'm due at an evening party.

ROBIN. A dinner party?

MISS HESELTINE. Oh, no—only games.

ROBIN. You won't get any dinner.

MISS HESELTINE. There'll be light refreshments handed round most likely.

(*She stamps the envelope.*)

ROBIN (*a little embarrassed and shy at giving the invitation*). Look here! I'm having a bit of beefsteak by myself, and Mrs. Higson is so convinced I don't eat enough, she always gives me twice as much as I can manage. Won't you stay and share it with me?

MISS HESELTINE (*quickly and nervously as she rises*). Oh, no, thank you—I can't do that.

ROBIN. You'd much better. You can go to the evening party afterwards.

MISS HESELTINE. Quite impossible. Thank you all the same.

(*She goes towards the window.*)

ROBIN (*going after her*). I shall be wretchedly lonely all by myself. (MISS HESELTINE *pauses and looks at him.*) You'd be doing me a kindness if you'd stay.

MISS HESELTINE. I don't think I'd better.

ROBIN. You won't enjoy your party if you don't eat something first.

MISS HESELTINE. I'm not expecting to enjoy it much, anyhow.

ROBIN. *I* shan't enjoy *my* steak if *you* go hungry to your party.

MISS HESELTINE. Won't you?

ROBIN (*trying to make her sorry for him*). No. (*A pause.*) Nor my tomatoes.

MISS HESELTINE. Really?

ROBIN. Really.

MISS HESELTINE. Then I'll stay—just a very few moments.

ROBIN (*smiling*). That's right. (*He draws the curtain over the window. Enter* MRS. HIGSON *with a dish containing a steak and tomatoes.* ROBIN *speaks as* MRS. HIGSON *enters.*) Set a place for Miss Heseltine. She's going to have some dinner with me.

MRS. HIGSON. Yes, sir. (MRS. HIGSON *neither shows nor feels any surprise when she hears that* MISS HESELTINE *is going to dine with* ROBIN.) We'd better cook you something extra, sir.

ROBIN. I expect there's enough here. (*He raises the dish cover to see.*) Oh, yes, quite.

MISS HESELTINE. I don't think I *can* stay—really!

ROBIN. Oh, yes, you can! (*To* MRS. HIGSON.) A place for Miss Heseltine.

MRS. HIGSON. Yes, sir.

(*Exit* MRS. HIGSON.)

ROBIN (*smiling at the dish and taking a long sniff*). Smells good—doesn't it?

MISS HESELTINE (*glancing longingly at the dish*). Delicious! But what about this? (*She holds up the envelope in her hand.*) I think I'd better take it to the post. I could slip it in the letter-box on my way to the party.

ROBIN (*taking the envelope out of her hand*). I'll send somebody with that. (*He throws the envelope down.*) Won't you take your things off? (*He brings a chair to the table. When he has done this, he stands with his hands on the back of the chair, watching* MISS HESELTINE *take her things off.* MISS HESELTINE *takes off her hat. Her hair is prettily arranged, quite different from the usual plain style in which she wears it. She next takes off her coat and places it on the chair with her hat. When she has taken off her coat she appears in a pretty, but simple and modest evening dress, in which she looks altogether charming.* ROBIN *cannot conceal his pleasure in her unexpected appearance.*) I've never seen you in an evening dress before. (*Enter* MRS. HIGSON *with the extra glasses, plates, knives, forks, etc., etc., necessary for* MISS HESELTINE, *a small bottle of champagne and a cork-screw.* ROBIN *opens the bottle of*

## A SINGLE MAN

*champagne, indicating the envelope containing the American article as he says to* MRS. HIGSON.) Will you have that thing sent to the post at once?

MRS. HIGSON. Yes, sir.

(*Picks up the envelope.*)

MISS HESELTINE (*murmuring, half-fascinated and half-alarmed*). Champagne!

ROBIN. Now then, Miss Heseltine, are you ready? (ROBIN *sits behind the table.* MISS HESELTINE *sits at the end of it.* ROBIN *speaks next as* MRS. HIGSON *takes off the dish-cover.*) I told you she always gives me much more than I can eat.

(*Smiles at* MRS. HIGSON, *who smilingly goes off with the dish-cover and the envelope.*)

MISS HESELTINE. I only want a very little corner.

ROBIN (*cutting a piece off the steak*). Like that?

MISS HESELTINE. It's too much!

ROBIN. Nonsense! Tomato?

MISS HESELTINE. Yes, please. (*He serves her.*) Thank you!

(*Then he helps himself.*)

ROBIN. I hope you won't find it too underdone.

MISS HESELTINE. Oh, no, thank you; I prefer it underdone.

ROBIN. How fortunate we both like our meat cooked the same way. (ROBIN *offers to pour some champagne into* MISS HESELTINE'S *glass.*) May I give you some champagne?

MISS HESELTINE (*in a flurry, not able to make up her mind whether to accept champagne or not*). Oh—I don't know—no, I don't think so, thank you.

ROBIN. Just a drop. (*He pours it out.*)

MISS HESELTINE. Is it nice?

ROBIN (*filling his own glass*). You know what it's like.

MISS HESELTINE. No, I don't. I never tasted it.

ROBIN (*surprised*). Never tasted champagne?

MISS HESELTINE. No.

ROBIN. How's that?

MISS HESELTINE. Quite a lot of people have never tasted champagne.

ROBIN. Think of that, now. (*He takes a good long drink.* MISS HESELTINE *watches him with curiosity, then raises her own glass to her lips, frowning as she takes a little sip.* ROBIN *watches her with an amused smile till she takes the glass away from her lips.*) Do you like it?

MISS HESELTINE (*her frown relaxing slowly into a beaming smile*). Yes.

(*From here on she becomes much more at home and quite natural and easy in her manner.*)

ROBIN (*eating*). I begin to feel better now. I was nearly dead after those children had gone home.

MISS HESELTINE (*also eating*). I'm not surprised.

ROBIN (*smiling*). I adore their youth and their vigour; the movements of their strong straight limbs; their shouts and their bright, pretty faces. Enchanting! (*With a sigh.*) But it's no use trying to be one of them after forty.

MISS HESELTINE. It's a change to be dining like this.

ROBIN. Such a picnic.

MISS HESELTINE. I mean, it's a change from high tea.

ROBIN (*smiling at her*). How different you look this evening!

MISS HESELTINE. It's because I'm dressed up. *You've* always seen me in workaday.

ROBIN. Your hair looks so pretty. I never noticed before that your hair was so pretty.

MISS HESELTINE (*pleased*). My hair is my best feature.

ROBIN. Do you often go to parties?

MISS HESELTINE. Oh, no—very seldom. I have such a limited circle of acquaintances in Farnham. I don't get much chance of meeting people, for one thing; and, living alone, the way I do, I need to be cautious. It's very easy to find oneself swallowed up in the wrong set before one knows it.

ROBIN (*with deep meaning, thinking of the Cottrells*). Very! I suppose you'll go to plenty of parties when you live in London.

MISS HESELTINE. I don't expect to. I've lived there before, you know. I find London much more dead and alive than Farnham.

ROBIN (*amazed*). London dead and alive!

MISS HESELTINE. Yes.

ROBIN. *I* left because it's so noisy.

MISS HESELTINE. *You* had your friends and your telephone. I only had a bed-sitting-room. I scarcely ever went out with any one except my landlady, and not very often with *her*. We occasionally did a pit if we felt flush.

ROBIN (*sympathetically*). Is that the kind of life you have to look forward to now ?

MISS HESELTINE (*simply*). Yes.

ROBIN. You've lived by yourself a long time ?

MISS HESELTINE. Ever since father married again.

ROBIN (*gloomily*). When *I'm* married, I suppose there'll be jolly tennis parties and gaiety and *fun* every day of the week. (*He looks at her.*) I wonder what is to become of me and my work when *you* go ?

MISS HESELTINE (*troubled*). I don't believe I *could* stay on.

(*She sits back.*)

ROBIN (*nervously*). No.

MISS HESELTINE. It wouldn't do.

ROBIN. No. (*He lays his knife and fork together, and assumes a businesslike manner.*) Have you finished ?

MISS HESELTINE. Yes, thank you.

(*She lays her knife and fork together.*)

ROBIN. I don't think we need ring the bell. *I'll* change the plates.

(*He rises to do so.*)

MISS HESELTINE (*rising and speaking as if she were asking him a favour.*) Let *me*.

ROBIN. Oh, no ; I'll do it.

MISS HESELTINE. I should like to. Please sit down and let me—let me wait upon you.

ROBIN (*humouring her*). Very well.

(*He sits.*)

MISS HESELTINE (*taking his plate as she says, smiling*). " It was Sunday evening, and both the servants had gone to church ; so, as their custom was on these occasions, they waited on themselves."

ROBIN. What's that ?

MISS HESELTINE. A quotation out of one of your books.

ROBIN. Which one ?

MISS HESELTINE. It never had a name. You began it about four years ago, and tore it up after the second chapter.

ROBIN. What a memory you have !

MISS HESELTINE. Yes, for some things.

(*While this conversation is going on* MISS HESELTINE *changes the dishes and plates.*)

ROBIN. It doesn't seem right for me to be sitting here while you do the waiting.

MISS HESELTINE. It pleases me.

ROBIN. I never thought of waiting at table being a pleasure.

MISS HESELTINE (*standing near him with a dish in her hands*). It *is*, if you know how to dream.

ROBIN (*not comprehending—echoes*). To dream!

MISS HESELTINE. More than half a woman's life is made of dreams. She couldn't bear it otherwise.

(*She places the dish on the table.*)

ROBIN. What's the good of a dream?

MISS HESELTINE (*with suppressed exaltation*). Sometimes it grows so vivid it almost seems to have come true. (*She gives a low-toned little laugh as she looks towards her desk.* ROBIN *looks at her and follows the direction of her eyes.*) That's my desk that I work at—our sideboard is. (*She goes to her desk.* ROBIN *watches her, smiling. She carries the dish of fruit and two plates to the table, and places them in front of him.*) I shall never be able to believe this really happened afterwards. (*She returns to her place as she says.*) I expect I shall be trying to remember what story it was, where we dined together. Whenever you dictate a novel to me I always imagine that I'm the heroine.

ROBIN (*offering to refill her glass*). Let me give you some more champagne?

MISS HESELTINE (*putting her hand over her glass*). No, thank you. (*Gravely.*) They tell me it makes one chatter.

ROBIN. Please chatter. I want to know more about you—(*handing her fruit*) what you think, what you feel, what you are like, what you do with yourself when you are away from me. Though I've known you so well for —how long is it?

MISS HESELTINE (*promptly*). Five years last first of June.

ROBIN. And how many hours in all that time have we spent alone in this room together?

MISS HESELTINE (*joyfully*). So many we couldn't possibly count them up.

ROBIN. And yet, after all that, I am only just beginning to get to know you. Why did you never tell me about yourself?

MISS HESELTINE. You never asked.

ROBIN. I wonder why.

MISS HESELTINE. You were always working.

ROBIN (*after a moment's reflection*). What a lot of time one wastes attending to one's work. (*They go on eating before* ROBIN *says.*) I suppose I'm always thinking about myself and my own things.

MISS HESELTINE (*kindly*). That's only because you are a man. (*He laughs. She becomes a little confused.*) Though I'm sure I don't know why I should be talking as if I knew all about it. I've never known any man well with the exception of you and father.

ROBIN. Will you tell me about your father?

(*He takes a cigarette-case from his pocket.*)

MISS HESELTINE. I'd rather not. I was very unhappy at home—and to-night I want to forget all painful things. I am weaving a wonderful memory for the lonely evenings to come. (ROBIN *sighs.*) You want a light for your cigarette. Wait there, I'll get you one.

(MISS HESELTINE *goes to the mantelpiece for a match, which she strikes, then holds while he lights his cigarette.* ROBIN *offers her his cigarette-case.*)

ROBIN. Will *you* have a cigarette?

MISS HESELTINE (*primly*). Oh, no, thank you—I don't think I'll go as far as that.

(*She returns to her place at the table.*)

ROBIN (*after a pause*). How restful you are!

MISS HESELTINE. Will you always think of me so? I should like you to think of me, after I'm gone, a little differently from anybody else.

ROBIN. I can promise you that. (*He smokes in silence a moment before he says gloomily.*) It gets worse and worse the more I think of it.

MISS HESELTINE. What does?

ROBIN. Your going away. I don't see how we shall ever get through when it comes to the last day—our last morning's work. It's so sad doing *anything* the last time if it's something one has done regularly every day for a long time.

MISS HESELTINE. I remember when I left home—the last Sunday evening we sang a hymn. We always sang a hymn on Sunday evening—the same hymn. I *was* so sick of it. I used to have to play the tune. I thought I should be so glad never to have to do it any more; but when it came to doing it the last time, I couldn't see the notes, I couldn't see the words, I couldn't see the others—I was crying so.

ROBIN. I shan't know what has become of you. You might be unhappy or badly off, for all that *I* shall know.

MISS HESELTINE. I might write perhaps—now and again.

ROBIN (*sadly*). Letters! Once a week, once a month, two or three times a year. I shall want to see you every day.

MISS HESELTINE. I shall want to see you, too.

(*They look at each other steadily for some time before he speaks.*)

ROBIN. You look as you looked this afternoon. It's a wonderful look. I have never seen it in a woman's eyes before. (*He pulls himself together, disgusted with himself.*) I'm ashamed—I'm ashamed to have said that.

(*He rises from the table.*)

MISS HESELTINE (*also risen—very gently and kindly*). Don't be ashamed. I'm glad you *know* I love you. (ROBIN *turns and looks at her.*) You've taken it so kindly, I feel as if a great load had been lifted off my heart. I've been set free—after years of oppression. The pain it has been to keep my secret all to myself. Like a child, I had no right to, I hugged it and hid it—fearful lest some one should discover it, and I should be disgraced. And now *you*—of all people—have found me out, and I'm not humiliated—I'm happy. Though I know that to-morrow is coming, to-night I can only feel—how good it is for me that you should know.

ROBIN (*slowly, quietly, and impressively*). It seems to me now as if I had always known. So silently and steadily your influence has grown, it possessed me unawares. (*Speaking with sudden, passionate energy.*) I've made a dreadful blunder. I'm terrified of my future. I can't face it! (MISS HESELTINE *sits on the settee. He moves about as he speaks rapidly and excitedly.*) I was content the way we went on till Henry and Isabella came. It was seeing *them*—their happiness, their affection, their kisses, and caresses. I determined to marry and be happy, as they are. I looked about me for a wife, thought of all the girls I knew—all except *one*. *You* were so near at hand, and I was looking out into the world. I was caught and carried away by the snares of the charm of youth. I only see *you* in my *work-time*—always quiet, always patient, always ready, and never exacting. I took all that as a matter of course—selfishly accepted it. How dull of me never to have thought—what wonderful qualities those in a woman! (*Speaking like a lover, as he sits on the settee beside her.*) I have never seen you as you are to-night. (MISS HESELTINE *rises slowly and steps back from him, fascinated, but afraid. He goes on passionately.*) I ought to be holding my tongue, stifling my heart as *you* did yours; but to-night I can't any more than you can. I *can't* marry Maggie; it's not possible. She's dear, she's sweet, she's lovely; but she's a child. She knows nothing, feels nothing, understands nothing. She has no soul, and very little heart. If I marry Maggie, I shall be finished, destroyed, done for. And *now*—now that I *know* that I love *you* and that *you* love *me*! (*Helplessly.*) What are we to do?

(*They stand looking helplessly at each other; then by a mutual instinct go towards each other, and fall into each other's arms. They remain some moments locked in a close embrace. The curtains over the windows are parted.* LOUISE *is there. She has time to stand and take in the situation before they discover her presence.* LOUISE *advances into the room, then moves slowly and haughtily to the door, observing the dinner-table as she passes it.* ROBIN *and* MISS HESELTINE *watch her dumbfounded.* LOUISE *goes out.* MISS HESELTINE *turns and looks at* ROBIN, *then covers her face with her hands.*)

CURTAIN.

# THE FOURTH ACT

SCENE.—ROBIN'S *study again. It is ten o'clock in the morning on the day after the events of the last two acts.* ROBIN *is seated at his writing-table, his head on his hands. Enter* LADY COTTRELL. ROBIN *rises when she enters.*

LADY COTTRELL. My husband has had a note from you asking him to come and see you—so I came.

ROBIN (*worried*). Oh, but I want most particularly to see *Sir Richard.* That's why I asked him to call on *me* instead of going to call on *him* because—well, you know what it's like at *your* house. There's no privacy. Dickie or Maggie or one of the others is apt to burst into the room at any moment. I must see Sir Richard undisturbed. It's most important. I think I'll run over and see him now—if you'll excuse me. (*He picks up a newspaper and thrusts it into* LADY COTTRELL'S *hands.*) There's the paper. I'll send Isabella to you to keep you company.

(*Exit* ROBIN, *quickly.*)

LADY COTTRELL (*looking after* ROBIN *in surprise*). Odd!

(ISABELLA *enters, followed by* HENRY.)

ISABELLA (*speaking as she enters*). Good-morning, Lady Cottrell.

LADY COTTRELL (*nods unceremoniously to them both without rising or offering to shake hands*). Good-morning, good-morning. What's the matter?

ISABELLA. Nothing.

HENRY. Why?

LADY COTTRELL (*to* HENRY). I thought from your brother's strange manner that something must have happened since I saw you yesterday.

A SINGLE MAN

HENRY (*looking at* ISABELLA). Not that I know of.
ISABELLA. Nothing unusual.
HENRY. We dined at the Hendersons' last evening.
LADY COTTRELL. Nothing else ?
ISABELLA (*looking at* HENRY). No.
HENRY. Miss Parker had a headache and left the party early. When we got home she had gone to bed ; so *we* went to bed, too—and—that's about all. We got up and had breakfast as usual this morning.
LADY COTTRELL. Nothing of any *importance* ?
ISABELLA (*seriously*). Baby was rather fretful in the night.
LADY COTTRELL (*contemptuously*). You won't call that important when you've got fourteen.

(*Enter* LOUISE. *She enters quickly, and with such an air of having something important to tell that she attracts all their attention. They watch her as she closes the door and comes down among them.*)

LOUISE. I waited till Mr. Worthington went out. There is something I think you all ought to know. Sit down.

(*She pushes* ISABELLA *into a chair and waves the others to their seats.*)

LADY COTTRELL. I knew there was something.

(*They watch* LOUISE *expectantly.*)

LOUISE. Last night, when I left the Hendersons' (*to* LADY COTTRELL) I came away before the others. I had a headache. (*To* ISABELLA.) You remember. (*Addressing them all.*) I slipped away without a word, not wishing to make a fuss. I got my cloak and when I came out at their front door I was fortunate enough to find a cab. (*To* ISABELLA.) The one that brought that man who came after dinner. (*Addressing them all.*) I told the cabman to drive me to this gate, where I got out. (*To* LADY COTTRELL.) It was such a fine moonlight night I thought I should like to walk up the drive. When I got near the house I heard sounds of revelry—(*she looks round from one to the other expecting to make a great effect ; they watch her with unmoved faces during the whole of her recital*) issuing from this window— sounds of revelry. (*She looks round at them all again.*) I naturally thought it rather strange, so I stopped outside the window and listened. I thought it might be the servants taking advantage of our absence. Not at all. I distinctly heard two voices—Mr. Worthington's and *a woman's*. (*She looks from one to the other as before expecting to make an effect—they all move forward slightly.*) I was just going to pass on when a little gust of wind blew the curtains apart. There was nothing for me to do then but to walk into the room. I hardly like to tell you what I saw—but I *must*. It's a duty. The table was all in disorder as if two people had been feasting together. I remember noticing a champagne bottle— *empty*. The next thing I saw was—Miss Heseltine— the typewriter—in an evening dress. She was in Mr. Worthington's arms. They were kissing each other.

>    (*She looks round at them all triumphantly expecting to make a sensation. She apparently makes no effect of any kind. They sit still gravely for some moments before* LADY COTTRELL *speaks.*)

LADY COTTRELL (*with perfect composure*). I don't believe a word of it.

ISABELLA. Nor do I.

HENRY. Nor I.

LOUISE (*annoyed at the reception of her story*). But I *saw* it.

LADY COTTRELL. Dreamt it! Robin and his typist— I no more believe it than if you'd told me you'd caught Captain Worthington there kissing *me*.

ISABELLA (*in dismay at the thought of such a thing*). Oh!

LOUISE. If you don't believe *me*, ask the servants. *They* can tell you whether Miss Heseltine dined here or not.

LADY COTTRELL. Why shouldn't Miss Heseltine dine here? (*To* HENRY.) Do *you* see any reason why she shouldn't?

HENRY. No reason on earth.

LADY COTTRELL (*to* LOUISE). We none of us see any reason against it.

ISABELLA. They probably had some business to discuss.

LOUISE. They were drinking champagne.

HENRY. Why shouldn't they drink champagne?

ISABELLA. We drank it ourselves at the Hendersons'.

## A SINGLE MAN

LADY COTTRELL (*to* HENRY *and* ISABELLA). She seems to think it's immoral to drink champagne.

LOUISE. The woman was *décolleté*.

LADY COTTRELL (*to* LOUISE). Is it the fashion where *you* come from to dine high neck?

LOUISE. Oh!

ISABELLA (*to* LADY COTTRELL). I think Louise has gone mad.

HENRY (*to* LADY COTTRELL, *on the other side*). Trying to find a queer meaning to a most ordinary proceeding. It's monstrous!

ISABELLA. Disgusting!

LADY COTTRELL. Foul!

HENRY. If he mayn't dine quietly with his secretary.

ISABELLA. It may be indiscreet.

LADY COTTRELL. Don't be so provincial, Mrs. Worthington. It isn't at all indiscreet. It might be for *some* people if they were that kind of person, but a serious man of *his* age dining alone with his typist to talk about his business, dressed in suitable clothes and drinking what I often drink myself,—I can't see anything in it at all.

LOUISE. They were clasped together in a wild embrace.

LADY COTTRELL. *That* I refuse to believe.

HENRY. So do I, absolutely.

ISABELLA. And so do I.

LOUISE. Can't you see what it all means? We were all to have dined at the Hendersons' last evening—we three—and Mr. Worthington. At the last moment Mr. Worthington backs out—says he wishes to dine *alone*. *We* are packed off. In our absence comes this woman. Not a word to any of us to say she is expected. I arrive home early and find them in this most compromising position. And it's not only what took place last evening. Think of the hours and hours a day they spend shut up in this room together.

HENRY. Working.

LOUISE (*sharply to him*). How do *we* know what goes on? (HENRY *and* ISABELLA *exclaim together*.)

HENRY. What d'you mean?

ISABELLA. Louise!

LOUISE (*ignoring their exclamations, turns to* LADY COTTRELL). You surely won't let your daughter be engaged to a man while he is carrying on an intrigue with another woman.

ISABELLA (*indignantly*). Louise!

HENRY (*at the same time that* ISABELLA *exclaims*). Really, Miss Parker, I——

(*All except* LADY COTTRELL *talk at once.*)

LADY COTTRELL (*with authority*). Leave her to *me*. (*She addresses* LOUISE *calmly but witheringly.*) We decline to believe one word of *your* unsupported testimony against our *friends*. You have told us what is untrue. We *know* Mr. Worthington. He is a man of exceedingly high character. As for Miss Heseltine, I cannot say that I *know her*—but I have observed her. She satisfies me. I am convinced that she is a most respectable young woman.

LOUISE. How can you tell by *observing* a woman whether she is respectable or not?

LADY COTTRELL. I can *sniff* the difference.

LOUISE (*to* ISABELLA). Surely *you* see——

ISABELLA. Hush, Louise. I'm ashamed of you—trying to make a scandal out of nothing.

LOUISE (*excitedly*). But it's *true*, I tell you—it's *true*. They'll deny it, of course, and there's no one to support my word, but it's true, it's true, it's true!

HENRY (*indignantly*). You've said enough and a great deal more than enough. I take it upon myself in my brother's absence to tell you to leave the house.

LOUISE. Oh!

HENRY. How you can do such a thing as this—after accepting Robin's hospitality—I can't trust myself to say what I think of your conduct. You will please leave the house at once.

LOUISE. Do you think I would consent to remain one moment longer in such a house as *this*?

ISABELLA. Louise!

LOUISE (*addressing* ISABELLA). If *you* can't see what's perfectly plain to any intelligent person—that's *your* look-out.

LADY COTTRELL. Hush!

LOUISE. It shall never be said of *me* that I condoned immorality. I leave for Leamington immediately—immediately.

# A SINGLE MAN

(*Exit* LOUISE. *They watch her go out, and then look at each other in amazement.*)

LADY COTTRELL. What is she thinking of to come to us with such a story ? What is her motive ?

ISABELLA. *I* know well enough what her motive is.

LADY COTTRELL. Tell us.

ISABELLA. Something must have happened last night. He probably repulsed her, and this is her revenge.

HENRY. I see.

LADY COTTRELL. *I* don't.

HENRY (*to* ISABELLA). I suppose we had better tell Lady Cottrell everything.

ISABELLA (*in a whisper to* HENRY). I don't want her to know why I invited Louise here.

HENRY (*to* ISABELLA). No. (*He goes towards* LADY COTTRELL.) I am sorry to have to tell you, Lady Cottrell, that Miss Parker has been doing her best all the time she has been here to get Robin away from Maggie.

LADY COTTRELL (*impressed and concerned*). Indeed !

ISABELLA. I've had the most *dreadful* time with her. I haven't known *what* to do. Last evening she actually told me she had had the most wonderful talk with him, and that he had as good as admitted to her that he didn't want to marry Maggie. Of course, I knew it wasn't true ; but fancy her *saying* such a thing. And, later on, when Robin backed out of going to the Hendersons', she wanted me to let her stay behind with him. But I wouldn't *hear* of it. I *made* her come to the Hendersons' with *us*.

LADY COTTRELL. She seems to have found no difficulty in outwitting you when she got there.

ISABELLA. I couldn't keep my eye on her *all* the time. She got out when I wasn't looking. Then I suppose she hurried home, thinking she would find Robin by himself, and would practise her wiles upon him. But, of course, she found him with Miss Heseltine. Then I should think that he either repulsed her ; or, disappointed at not finding him alone, she became so enraged she worked herself into the state of mind in which a woman can make herself believe anything.

LADY COTTRELL. I suppose she'll go and spread this nasty story.

ISABELLA. I shouldn't wonder.

(*Enter* ROBIN. *He halts and looks at them. He is serious and worried.* LADY COTTRELL, HENRY, *and* ISABELLA *watch him in silence for a moment.*)

LADY COTTRELL (*to* HENRY *and* ISABELLA). I think we'd better tell him, don't *you* ? (*They all look at* ROBIN. ROBIN *looks from one to the other for an explanation.* LADY COTTRELL *still addresses* HENRY *and* ISABELLA.) What do you think ? Shall we tell him or not ? (HENRY *goes slowly to* ROBIN, *lays his hand kindly on his shoulder for a moment, then walks away.* ROBIN *watches* HENRY, *wondering, then turns to* LADY COTTRELL *and* ISABELLA *for an explanation.*) Perhaps we had better not tell him after all.

ISABELLA. I think we shall *have* to tell him.

HENRY. I think so, too. It appears, Robin, that last evening——

ISABELLA. I can't think how she *could.*

LADY COTTRELL. Miss Parker says that Miss Heseltine is your mistress.

(ROBIN *is so taken aback and distressed he can't speak for a moment, but looks round helplessly at the others.*)

HENRY (*sympathetically*). *We* don't believe it.

ISABELLA. We told her so.

ROBIN. Of course it's not true. (*He sits at his desk. They watch him anxiously. After a moment he looks up.*) You'd better tell me what else she said.

HENRY. She said that you dined here last evening alone with Miss Heseltine.

ROBIN. That's true.

HENRY. And that you were drinking champagne.

ROBIN. That's true.

HENRY. She also said that you—that she saw you——

(*He hesitates, not quite knowing how to express himself.*)

LADY COTTRELL. Embracing.

ROBIN (*after a pause*). I want to marry Miss Heseltine. (*They all look at* ROBIN, *then at each other, mute with surprise.* ROBIN *addresses* LADY COTTRELL.) That's what I went to tell Sir Richard. I didn't see him. He'd gone out—so I may as well tell *you.* I—I find I've made a mistake, and I don't care for Maggie as much as I thought I did; so the only honourable thing for me to do now is to break off my engagement.

HENRY (*dismayed, then slowly perceiving what he imagines to be the truth*). Bravo! (*They all look at* HENRY *in surprise.*) I call that magnificent. (*To* ROBIN.) To sacrifice yourself in order to save Miss Heseltine's reputation. It's noble.

ROBIN (*bewildered*). But——

ISABELLA (*smiling at* ROBIN). It's just like you, Robin.

ROBIN. But——

LADY COTTRELL (*beaming upon him*). Most chivalrous!

ROBIN (*to* LADY COTTRELL). Bu'——

LADY COTTRELL (*holding up her hand to silence* ROBIN *as she says*). But don't forget that one may carry chivalry too far and become quixotic.

ROBIN. You don't understand. I love Miss Heseltine.
(*They all laugh heartily.*)

LADY COTTRELL. My dear, good man—what *is* the use of trying to bluff *us*?

ROBIN (*coming towards* LADY COTTRELL *as he speaks*). I'm very much in earnest, Lady Cottrell. I realise what a very serious matter it is to break off an engagement, and I don't for one moment want to underestimate my responsibilities—but surely it is better to recognise my mistake *now* instead of later on.

LADY COTTRELL (*preparing to be indignant*). To hear you talk one would suppose—oh—(*remembering he is bluffing, as she thinks*) but of course you don't mean it.
(*She smiles and pats him on the arm.*)

ROBIN. Can't you all see that this is quite a likely thing to happen? It's most unfortunate. I am much to blame—but it's not the first time that a man has got engaged and then found out that he loved some one else.

ISABELLA (*sweetly*). Robin, dear—if it were really true that you love Miss Heseltine—you'd have thought of it before now.

ROBIN. That's the funny thing about it. I have known her for five years, and I never discovered I was in love with her till last evening.

LADY COTTRELL. Most unconvincing!
(LADY COTTRELL *and* ISABELLA *laugh.*)

ROBIN (*distractedly*). Can't I make them understand?

(*To* HENRY.) *You*, Henry. *You* know when I *mean* a thing——

HENRY (*calmly and kindly and rather pompously*). I believe you *would* make this sacrifice, but I shall not let you.

ROBIN (*taken aback by* HENRY'S *superior attitude*). Oh —indeed! (*Derisively.*) *You* won't let me. We'll see about that.

HENRY. It's totally unnecessary. Take the advice of a man of the world; I'm younger than you, I know — but you see — after all — you are only a writer — (ROBIN *turns to him quickly as if to retort.*) I don't mean to be offensive——

ROBIN. I'm sure you don't, Henry; but if I *did* happen to want the advice of a man of the world— I should never think of going to a thick-headed soldier.

ISABELLA (*indignantly when* HENRY *is called a thick-headed soldier*). Oh!

HENRY (*coming to* ISABELLA *and speaking indulgently of* ROBIN). Never mind, dear. The poor old fellow is so upset.

LADY COTTRELL (*reassuring* HENRY *and* ISABELLA). He'll come to his senses directly.

HENRY. I hope so. The trouble with *him* is—he doesn't know life. He lives in a world of his own—a world of romantic books where they indulge in these heroic sacrifices.

ISABELLA (*to* ROBIN). You see, Robin; even if Louise *did* go and spread this story, nobody would be likely to believe her, so it wouldn't do Miss Heseltine much harm.

HENRY. We shall *all* do what we can to protect Miss Heseltine.

LADY COTTRELL. *I* will *befriend* the girl. I will go to her now.

ROBIN (*coming quickly towards* LADY COTTRELL). No.

LADY COTTRELL. Where does she live? (*Rises.*)

ROBIN. I shan't tell you.

LADY COTTRELL. Maggie knows.

ROBIN. Lady Cottrell! I *can't* let you go to Miss Heseltine. You'll talk her round. She'd pack up her little box and go away without a word.

# A SINGLE MAN

LADY COTTRELL. But I'm going to ask her to *stay*. To let every one *see* that there isn't a word of truth in Miss Parker's story—I shall ask Miss Heseltine as a personal favour to *me*—to remain here after your marriage.

ROBIN. Impossible.

LADY COTTRELL. Not at all. Maggie is a sensible girl. She knows that every literary man is closeted for hours daily with a typist. She won't be jealous of Miss Heseltine. I'll soon put everything all right. You shall have them both. (*Exit* LADY COTTRELL.)

ROBIN (*desperately*). I don't *want* Maggie.

HENRY. Why?

ROBIN. She's too young.

ISABELLA. Three weeks ago you were all for youth.

ROBIN. I know I was, but I've had enough of it. Maggie is just as sweet and pretty as she was three weeks ago, but now that I've got to know her better—I can't see anything in her at all.

(HENRY *and* ISABELLA *both look extremely shocked.*)

ISABELLA. If he really feels that way about her.

HENRY (*smiles reassuringly at* ISABELLA). He doesn't. I know exactly how he feels. (*He approaches* ROBIN *and says kindly.*) You have got what we call in my regiment "Bridegroom's Funk." We all get it as the wedding-day approaches. I'd have given anything to get out of marrying Isabella when it came to the last week.

ISABELLA (*indignantly*). Oh—oh!

(*She bursts into tears and hurries towards the window.*)

HENRY (*very much distressed, follows* ISABELLA). Isabella! Listen! I only meant——

ISABELLA (*wailing as she goes out*). You don't love me. (*Exit* ISABELLA.)

HENRY. Isabella! (*Exit* HENRY.)

ROBIN. Idiots!

(*Enter* MISS HESELTINE. *She is without her hat.*)

MISS HESELTINE (*pausing on the threshold*). I didn't know whether to come as usual this morning or not.

ROBIN. I'm so glad you came. Now at last we can talk sense. Shut the door, please. (MISS HESELTINE *shuts the door and meets him.*) She told.

MISS HESELTINE. I knew she would.

ROBIN. They won't believe her.

MISS HESELTINE. Who won't?

ROBIN. Lady Cottrell and Henry and Isabella. They won't believe *me* either when I say that I want to break my engagement and marry you.

MISS HESELTINE. Has Maggie been told?

ROBIN. Not yet. She won't believe it when she *is*, and even if she *does*, they'll all be at her, telling her I don't mean what I say and urge her not to let me off. I don't know what to do. They won't any of them believe anything. It would be awfully funny if it wasn't *us*. (*He paces up and down.*)

MISS HESELTINE. I never thought of them taking it this way. It simplifies it for us very much.

ROBIN (*not comprehending*). Simplifies it?

MISS HESELTINE. If they none of them believe there's been anything between us.

ROBIN. It leaves me more than ever engaged to Maggie.

MISS HESELTINE. I don't want to make trouble.

ROBIN (*anxiously*). Oh, I say, you don't feel differently about me this morning, do you?

(*He holds her hand.*)

MISS HESELTINE (*it is evident that she loves him more than ever*). After what you said to me last night? No. (*With determination.*) But I don't think it right or reasonable that I should come between you and not only Maggie, but your family and friends.

ROBIN (*grimly*). I've got you *all* against me now.

MISS HESELTINE. What could I bring you for all that you would lose? I've got no arts to hold you with, nor beauty. I could only love you and work for you. That isn't always enough.

ROBIN. There's every reason why you and I should marry. Let alone the *great* reason. Leaving love out of the question, it's the only sensible thing to do. We suit each other. We have mutual interests and ideas. The same things make us laugh. Besides which, we've got accustomed. I feel no strangeness in your company, none of that wearisome effort to be a kind of person that I'm nothing like. With *you* I could live my life, I could do my work, I could be myself. Whereas

## A SINGLE MAN

with Maggie—poor Maggie! It isn't her fault she's so tiresome. It's the fault of her youth.

MISS HESELTINE (*troubled*). I can't but remember that it was *I* who sounded her for you—here in this room—three weeks ago to-day.

ROBIN. I don't think she cares for me much. I don't think it's in her to care for any one much.

MISS HESELTINE. That's what we *want* to think.

ROBIN (*with determination*). If I were to marry Maggie now, I should do her a very great wrong. (MISS HESELTINE *shakes her head.*) Oh, yes I should. If I take her away from the home where she's happy, playing with her brothers and her friends, bring her here and don't love her—can't love her—it would be cruel. I *must* tell her everything. I'll go and see her now at once.

MISS HESELTINE (*anxiously*). You will tell her, I suppose, and then let her choose.

ROBIN (*pausing*). Choose?

MISS HESELTINE. Choose whether she will give you up or not.

ROBIN. Suppose she chooses not to?

MISS HESELTINE (*simply*). You would have done the right thing.

ROBIN (*doubtfully*). Yes. (*After a moment's reflection.*) But I should still be saddled with Maggie. I *can't* pass the rest of my days with a young woman who has no idea of life beyond extracting the utmost merriment out of each moment. I shall tell her just as kindly and as gently as I can, but——

(*Enter* MAGGIE.)

MAGGIE. Good-morning.

ROBIN. Good-morning, Maggie.

MAGGIE. I thought perhaps you'd be by yourself.

MISS HESELTINE. Am I in the way?

ROBIN (*to* MAGGIE). Do you want to see me alone?

MAGGIE. What I *really* wanted was to see her first and you after.

ROBIN. Shall I leave you here with Miss Heseltine?

MAGGIE. Let me think. (*She considers a moment while they watch her.*) No; on second thoughts, I'll take you both together. I think I should feel more courageous. And I shall only have to go over the ground twice if I don't. (*To* MISS HESELTINE.) *You* are in the secret because, if you remember, you sounded me about him.

MISS HESELTINE. I haven't forgotten.

MAGGIE (*addressing them both*). Would you mind seating yourselves ? (MAGGIE *watches them seat themselves first, then she speaks very amiably, addressing* ROBIN:) I don't think you are suited to *me*. I like you very much. You are every bit as nice as you were three weeks ago, but now that I've got to know you better, I find that you depress me. (ROBIN *and* MISS HESELTINE *look at each other trying very hard not to smile.*) When you play with us, for instance, I always feel you are trying to be another kind of person from the one you really are, and that you aren't thoroughly enjoying yourself, and then *I* can't enjoy myself either. It isn't your fault. It's the fault of your age. I don't mean to say you are *old*, but you are not quite *this* generation, are you ?

MISS HESELTINE (*protesting*). Oh !

(ROBIN *and* MAGGIE *look towards* MISS HESELTINE.)

ROBIN (*smiling at* MISS HESELTINE *as he says*). There are always *two* points of view.

MAGGIE (*to* MISS HESELTINE). It's no use *half* saying it or he won't catch my meaning.

ROBIN. I catch your meaning all right.

MISS HESELTINE (*to herself in an undertone*). He *is this* generation.

MAGGIE (*to* ROBIN). It was yesterday it was borne in upon me so powerfully the immense difference in our ages. You mustn't think I haven't thought about this very seriously. I sat up quite late last night, talking it all over with Bertha. We came to the conclusion that it isn't fair to ask a girl of my age to marry a man who has had his day.

MISS HESELTINE (*springing up and saying indignantly to* MAGGIE). Oh, no !

MAGGIE (*to* MISS HESELTINE). See here ! *You* were asked to stay in the room to give me your moral support.

MISS HESELTINE. I know I was—but when I hear you talk like that about him—even a secretary has her feelings.

MAGGIE (*kindly to* MISS HESELTINE). I mean to say— *he* has lived and I haven't. The world isn't all new and exciting to him the way it is to me. I want parties and people all the time. He's had all that and wants to settle down. There's the difference between us.

ROBIN. You've hit the nail on the head, Maggie.

MAGGIE (*going to* ROBIN). There's something else I must tell you—something you may not like.

ROBIN (*smiling hopefully*). You've fallen in love with a boy of your own age.

MAGGIE. Oh, no.

MISS HESELTINE. A man of your own age.

MAGGIE. Nothing of that sort. It's this. There used to be some notion that it wasn't honourable for a girl to break off her engagement unless the man were willing to set her free.

ROBIN (*pretending to* MAGGIE *to be seriously impressed*). Indeed.

MAGGIE. People don't hold that notion now.

MISS HESELTINE. You don't say so!

MAGGIE (*to* ROBIN). I thought you might be old-fashioned and want to hold me to my promise.

ROBIN (*airily*). Oh, dear me, no—you'll find me quite up-to-date on that point.

MAGGIE (*looking at* ROBIN *with admiration*). I must say you are taking it splendidly.

ROBIN (*trying to speak gravely*). I am doing my best to disguise my feelings.

(*Enter* LOUISE. *She wears the travelling clothes in which she arrived in the first act, and seems rather hysterical.*)

LOUISE (*crying*). I'm not one to make trouble, but I think you ought to know that I am being turned out of the house for telling the truth. (*Addressing* ROBIN.) I owe it to myself to justify myself before the girl you are engaged to. (*Looking at* MAGGIE.) Last night—

ROBIN (*interrupting her*). No, Miss Parker, no. I can't allow that. Besides, Miss Cottrell and I are no longer engaged.

LOUISE (*greatly surprised*). What?

ROBIN. She has broken it off.

LOUISE. Good gracious!

MAGGIE (*going to* ROBIN, *says kindly*). I do hope you'll be able to find some one to console yourself with— (*with a meaning look and smile towards* LOUISE) some older person; some one who wants to get married as much as you do. (*Whispering.*) We've all noticed how fond she is of you. (*She goes to* MISS HESELTINE *and takes her by the arm.*) Come, let us leave them together.

MISS HESELTINE. No.

> (LOUISE *glides slowly towards* ROBIN *with her most seductive smile. He steps back a step or two, very much embarrassed, as she approaches. Enter* ISABELLA *and* HENRY.)

ISABELLA (*speaking as she enters*). Louise!

LOUISE (*annoyed at being interrupted, says irritably*). What is it?

ISABELLA. Your cab is here.

LOUISE. You may send it away again.

> (*Smiling and unfastening her coat as if she were going to stay.*)

MAGGIE (*to* ROBIN). I'm sure you'll be happy together. I must be off home to tell mother what I've done.

(*Exit* MAGGIE.)

ROBIN (*bracing himself*). Miss Parker.

LOUISE (*smiling up at him*). Louise.

ROBIN. The next time you tell the truth please tell the whole of it, and add that Miss Heseltine and I are going to be married. (*To* MISS HESELTINE.) I suppose we are going to get married, aren't we?

(*Taking her hands.*)

MISS HESELTINE. Yes, please.

LOUISE (*rising majestically and giving her hand to* ROBIN). Good-bye, Mr. Worthington.

ROBIN. Good-bye, Miss Parker. It has been such a pleasure having you here.

LOUISE. Stop the cab!

> (HENRY *and* ISABELLA *bolt out of the door.* LOUISE *stalks out majestically.* MISS HESELTINE *sits down at her desk and begins writing on the typewriter.* ROBIN *comes behind her, gently draws her hands from the machine, and embraces her.*)

CURTAIN.

# DOORMATS

## A COMEDY IN THREE ACTS

PROGRAMME OF THE FIRST PRODUCTION
AT
WYNDHAM'S THEATRE, LONDON

## DOORMATS

A COMEDY IN THREE ACTS

BY

HUBERT HENRY DAVIES

PRODUCED ON OCTOBER 3, 1912

| | |
|---|---|
| *Noel Gale (a Painter)* . . . | MR. GERALD DU MAURIER |
| *Sir Rufus Gale (a Retired Indian Judge, Noel's Uncle)*. . . | MR. ALFRED BISHOP |
| *Captain Maurice Harding (of the ——)* | MR. DAWSON MILWARD |
| *Leila (Noel's Wife)* . . | MISS MARIE LŎHR |
| *Josephine (Rufus's Wife)* . . | MISS NINA BOUCICAULT |
| *Harrison (a Maid-Servant)* . . | MISS GILES |

*The action takes place in Noel Gale's house in Chelsea, and covers a period of ten weeks.*

Act I.—The Studio.

*Six weeks pass.*

Act II.—The Drawing-room.

*A month passes.*

Act III.—The Dining-room.

# DOORMATS

## THE FIRST ACT

SCENE.—*The Studio. This is a well-furnished, comfortable studio on an upper floor of* NOEL GALE'S *house in Chelsea. There is the studio window occupying nearly the whole of the right-hand wall space. In the opposite wall is a door, communicating with the rest of the house. In the centre of the studio is a Model's dais, and to the right of it an easel bearing a large canvas. A chair, an ottoman, and a window-seat running the whole width of the window are the principal pieces of furniture; but upon the walls there are pictures and designs all of a decorative style, while several portfolios of sketches lie about in some disorder.*
NOEL *is standing in front of the canvas. He finishes filling his pipe, lights it, then crosses the studio to the window and draws the curtains.* NOEL *is a young man, a little over thirty years of age, pleasant in face, manner, and disposition, clever and sensitive; and is ordinarily well-dressed in a fairly conventional way.* NOEL *is disturbed by a knock on the door.*

NOEL (*as he is drawing the curtains*). Come in.
(*The door is pushed open timidly and* JOSEPHINE *appears.* JOSEPHINE *is* LADY GALE, *a sweet, kind and unselfish little woman of about fifty. She has a quaint and rather provincial air. Her clothes, which are unobtrusive, are rather old-fashioned. There is nothing smart about her, but she is very neat. She carries a small wicker work-basket, containing her knitting, which consists for the moment of some very small baby's socks.*)

JOSEPHINE (*standing in the doorway and opening the door*). Good-morning, Noel.

NOEL (*delighted to see her*). Good-morning, Aunt Josephine. Have you come to pay me a visit?

JOSEPHINE. If it's quite convenient.

NOEL (*going a little towards her*). Yes—of course. I'm delighted to see you. Where's Uncle Rufus?

JOSEPHINE. He's here.

> (*Enter* RUFUS. SIR RUFUS GALE *is a newly retired Indian Judge. He is a man of about sixty-five, beaming, hale, and rubicund. He appears to be still in the prime of life in spite of his white hair. He is positive and dictatorial in manner, good-humoured except under opposition, which he does not very often encounter. He treats his wife like a child, usually with condescending amiability but sometimes tetchily.*)

RUFUS. Good-morning, Noel. (*Closes door.*) You didn't turn up to breakfast.

NOEL. I always have mine by myself, early. How did you sleep under our roof?

RUFUS. Wonderfully well, thank you.

NOEL. Aunt Josephine too?

JOSEPHINE. I never sleep so well in a strange bed.

RUFUS (*to* JOSEPHINE). You slept splendidly. Never disturbed me once.

NOEL. What has become of Leila?

RUFUS. She left us to go and do her housekeeping. Told us to find our way in here as soon as we had finished our unpacking.

NOEL. Have you finished it already—all those boxes?

JOSEPHINE. Not all.

RUFUS. The maid came and interrupted us in the middle—wanting to do the room.

NOEL. Stay with me till your room is ready. We can have a good gossip. You got here so late last evening we had no time for talking.

JOSEPHINE. You mustn't let us interfere with your work.

RUFUS (*to* NOEL). You go on with whatever you were doing—we'll poke about and look at your things.

NOEL. All right.

JOSEPHINE. If we may.

NOEL (*going back to his easel*). Yes, certainly. Do anything you like. (*Continues working on his picture while* RUFUS *and* JOSEPHINE *poke about.*) I hope you have come to stay with us for a good long time.

JOSEPHINE. Thank you, dear. We hope so too.

NOEL. For as long as you want to be in London, you must use our house as your hotel.

RUFUS. Thank you, my boy, thank you. That's just what your aunt and I had arranged to do.

JOSEPHINE. If we were asked.

RUFUS (*to* JOSEPHINE). We *are* asked. He's just asked us.

NOEL (*amused*). Leila and I will love to have you.

JOSEPHINE (*explaining to* NOEL). We *must* think of saving expenses, you see, now that your uncle has retired and only has his pension. Before you so kindly asked us to stay with you I was afraid I might have to forego the luxury of a visit to London and let Uncle Rufus come without me, which would have been a sad disappointment, I have been looking forward for so long to a little fling in town, before we settle down anywhere—(*goes round the ottoman, picks up a portfolio and carries it to the dais*) theatres and concerts and pictures. That is what I miss so much in India—the arts.

NOEL. Allow me.

JOSEPHINE (*smilingly refusing his assistance*). Don't you bother about *me*. (*Lays the portfolio down on the dais as she says*) I am used to doing things for myself. (*Sits on the dais and puts on her spectacles.*)

> (*As* NOEL *goes back to his easel* RUFUS *comes down between them towards the portfolio.*)

RUFUS. What have you got there, my dear, what have you got there? Let me see. (*Sits on the dais at the other side of the portfolio, which he monopolises.*)

> (JOSEPHINE *yields it meekly.* JOSEPHINE *does not in the least object to yielding the portfolio. She does not visibly object to anything he does. She accepts it all. She has grown so accustomed.*)

NOEL. Have you decided where you'll settle down?

JOSEPHINE. We think of Cheltenham or Tunbridge Wells.

NOEL. Why not London?

JOSEPHINE. Your uncle thought that in London we

should be rather lost—whereas in Cheltenham or Tunbridge Wells—we should be somebody.

RUFUS (*amiably reproving* JOSEPHINE). You needn't go into all my reasons. But we think of Cheltenham—or Tunbridge Wells—or Bath—any of those quiet respectable towns where we should meet refined, nice people—like ourselves.

NOEL. A retired Indian judge and his lady would be quite an important addition to the society of Tunbridge Wells.

RUFUS (*conceitedly—making light of it*). I suppose so.

JOSEPHINE (*looking at a sketch*). You know, Noel, it seems to me—these sketches of yours are very good.

NOEL (*genuinely pleased*). I'm very glad to hear you say so.

RUFUS (*snatching the sketch from* JOSEPHINE). Let me look. (*Holding it off and looking at it.*) Excellent—excellent!

JOSEPHINE (*looking at the sketch over* RUFUS's *shoulder*). You have quite a style of your own.

RUFUS. Just what I was about to say.

JOSEPHINE. Full of distinction and charm.

RUFUS. Full. (*Tosses the sketch on to the portfolio, after which* JOSEPHINE *picks it up and examines it again, as he says to* NOEL.) Why aren't you more famous?

NOEL (*carelessly*). I don't know. There isn't much demand for decorative work. Most people don't understand it or care about it.

RUFUS. Ignoramuses!

JOSEPHINE. But the few who do understand—admire what you do—don't they, Noel?

NOEL. They praise it, but they don't buy it. I sell things, of course—here and there—nothing very much.

RUFUS. You ought to get hold of a big job, such as—er—decorating a church or a town hall.

NOEL. That's what I should like to do, but in England they don't consider you qualified to undertake a commission of that importance—until you are about ninety—unless you are a foreigner. I've been approached lately to go to America to decorate a public library.

RUFUS. Oh! well now—that's something. Are you going?

## DOORMATS

NOEL. It's only an inquiry yet. It may not come to anything.

JOSEPHINE. I think it's very silly of everybody not to overwhelm you with commissions when you do such beautiful work.

NOEL (*coming down behind the dais with some more sketches as he speaks*). Those are old things you are looking at. These are more recent. (*Laying them down on the top of the others between* RUFUS *and* JOSEPHINE.) Tell me what you think of these.

RUFUS (*picking up a sketch at random, holding it off and exclaiming before he can possibly have had time to form an opinion*). First rate—first rate—full of style and distinction and charm.

NOEL (*crosses round dais and sits on the ottoman. Watching* JOSEPHINE'S *face as she examines a sketch without expressing any enthusiasm or admiration*). Not so good—are they?

JOSEPHINE (*weakly, not wishing to hurt his feelings*). Oh, I don't know.

NOEL. You don't like them—do you?

JOSEPHINE (*without conviction*). Oh yes, I do. I like them very much.

NOEL. You are not enthusiastic about them as you were about the others.

JOSEPHINE. I don't think I like them *quite* so well as the others, but—

NOEL. Come and have a look at this. This is the last thing I've done—this portrait. Come and tell me what you think of it.

JOSEPHINE (*following him reluctantly*). What's the good of *my* opinion? *I'm* not an art critic.

NOEL. You are as good a critic as ever I had. You may not know so much about it technically, but you have all the feeling of an artist.

JOSEPHINE (*rises and crosses to the easel, very much pleased*). Oh, Noel dear — how kind of you to say that.

NOEL (*puts a stool in front of the picture*). I shall never forget that you were the first person to recognise that I had any talent. It was *you* who persuaded father to let me become a painter.

JOSEPHINE (*sitting on the stool. Watching* RUFUS *who has*

*been left sitting on the dais and does not at all relish having no notice taken of him*). *And* your Uncle Rufus.

RUFUS (*turns his back to them*). *I* had nothing to do with it—nothing whatever.

JOSEPHINE. Oh, yes, Rufus dear—you had—everything to do with it. *I* may have been the *first* to recognise the boy's talent, but that was only because I saw his little drawings before you did. *You* recognised it as soon as you saw them. (RUFUS *begins to be mollified. She continues.*) I forget now which of us it was who urged his father, but I should think, as he was *your* brother, it would be *you.*

RUFUS (*turning to her, says condescendingly*). I daresay you are right. I've forgotten. It's so long ago.

JOSEPHINE. *Do* come and give us your opinion of the portrait.

RUFUS (*with a haughty glance at* NOEL). My opinion has not been asked. (*Turns away from them.*)

JOSEPHINE (*distressed*). Oh, but Noel wants it—don't you, Noel? (*She glances at* RUFUS, *then drops her voice and says aside to* NOEL.) He likes to think he knows. It's his little vanity.

NOEL (*humouring them both*). Please, Uncle Rufus, I can't go on with my work till I know what *you* think.

RUFUS (*pretending to be more bored than pleased as he swaggers towards the easel*). Oh well, if you really *want* to know—— (*He cocks his eye-glasses on his nose and stands before the picture, too close to it.*)

JOSEPHINE (*as she looks admiringly at* RUFUS). So many people ask him for his judgement on their pictures.

RUFUS (*after putting his head first on one side and then on the other, trying to look like a connoisseur as they watch him, at last says.*) Who is it?

NOEL. Captain Harding, his name is——

RUFUS. Captain Harding— (*Repeating the business of putting his head first on one side and then on the other.*) Oh—well—(*not wishing to commit himself and make another mistake he appeals to* JOSEPHINE) what do you think?

JOSEPHINE. It's so different from his other work.

RUFUS. Not so good?

JOSEPHINE. I don't mean that. I mean—that it's not in his usual decorative style.

RUFUS (*in a tone of condescending chaff*). *Any one* could see that. Rather superfluous to point it out to *me*.

NOEL. I am trying to become a fashionable portrait painter.

JOSEPHINE. Oh—are you ? Why ?

NOEL (*simply*). Leila wants me to.

JOSEPHINE. But what a pity—when you do the other work so well.

NOEL. The other work doesn't pay.

JOSEPHINE. Of course—if you *succeed* at this.

NOEL (*turning to her quickly as he says*). You don't think I have succeeded ?

JOSEPHINE. I don't know. We haven't seen Captain Harding.

RUFUS. I can't tell you till I've seen him.

NOEL. You don't need to have seen Philip the Fourth of Spain to know that Velasquez made a good portrait of him.

RUFUS. Eh ! No.

JOSEPHINE (*looking at the picture*). It's not finished.

NOEL. Very nearly. I shan't do much more to it now. (*Pauses, trying to read the expression on* JOSEPHINE'S *face before he says.*) Rotten—isn't it ?

JOSEPHINE. No, dear—no.

RUFUS (*standing with his arm round* JOSEPHINE'S *shoulders*). Not at all rotten.

JOSEPHINE. It's very clever.

RUFUS. Stylish—that's the word—stylish.

JOSEPHINE (*agreeing with* RUFUS). Yes. (*As she comes towards* NOEL.) But it looks to me a little——

NOEL. Mechanical.

JOSEPHINE. I think perhaps that's it. As if your heart wasn't in your work.

NOEL (*smiles as he says quietly*). I said you were a good critic——

RUFUS. That's exactly the criticism *I* make. His heart's not in his work. That's what I say. Why isn't your heart in your work ?

NOEL. How should I know ?

RUFUS. D'you need a tonic ?

NOEL (*laughing*). No.

RUFUS. It's a very good thing if you've been overworking.

NOEL. I haven't. I don't work hard enough. I spend enough hours in my studio—but I seem lately to have lost my power of concentration. I've known for some time that my work is deteriorating. I didn't know, till just now, that any one else had noticed it. I might as well chuck this game up and go into the City.

RUFUS. What for?

NOEL. To make money.

RUFUS. Why this rage to be rich? You want to get on, of course, and as you get on you'll make money, but you don't depend on this for your living. You've got your private income.

NOEL. Eight hundred a year doesn't go far in London. It was all right when we lived at St. Ives.

RUFUS. Why did you ever leave St. Ives?

NOEL (*simply*). Leila likes London. (RUFUS *looks at* JOSEPHINE—*she looks at him;* NOEL, *remarking their exchange of glances, says to excuse* LEILA.) It was dull for her at St. Ives.

RUFUS. Can't you work as well in London? Plenty of artists do.

NOEL. I could work better—if it wasn't for all these lunches and dinners and parties we go to.

RUFUS. Why d'you go to them?

NOEL (*simply*). Leila likes society. (*Another exchange of glances between* RUFUS *and* JOSEPHINE *which* NOEL *sees —he again excuses* LEILA.) And it's right that she should have it. Leila is a great social success. She's enormously popular.

JOSEPHINE. I don't wonder. She is so charming and pretty——

NOEL (*smiles at* JOSEPHINE, *delighted to hear* LEILA *praised*). Isn't she?

RUFUS (*who can't bear to be left out of the conversation even for a moment*). I haven't said she's not—have I?

JOSEPHINE (*soothingly to* RUFUS). No, dear—no.

RUFUS. I don't deny that she is charming and pretty. It is quite natural that she should be popular. But what I do say is—if all this gadding about is too expensive for him, and has an injurious effect upon his work she ought to be content to stay at home.

NOEL. She might get bored.

RUFUS. Let her.

NOEL. I shouldn't like her to be bored when she's with me.

RUFUS. Well then—if she *must* have society—can't she go about by herself, without dragging *you* along ?

NOEL. I shouldn't like that. I don't want Leila to go about without *me*. That is the way so many couples in London become estranged.

JOSEPHINE. He's quite right there, Rufus.

RUFUS (*ignoring* JOSEPHINE'S *remark—says to* NOEL). You are being sacrificed to Leila.

NOEL. There's a difference between a sacrifice and an offering.

RUFUS. The more we do for people the less they think of us.

   (JOSEPHINE *looks at* RUFUS, *but he is not thinking of her.*)

NOEL. One doesn't only do things for people in the hope of getting a reward—if I do anything for Leila it's because——

RUFUS (*interrupts him*). Because she exacts.

NOEL (*protests*). No.

JOSEPHINE. Because he loves her.

NOEL (*smiles*). Yes.

   (*Enter* LEILA—*she is a delightful young married woman, gay and good-humoured, charming and smart—a woman of spirit and abundant vitality —accustomed to having her own way without fighting for it. She carries a visiting card in her hand—*JOSEPHINE *makes a movement to rise as she enters.*)

LEILA. Noel ! Don't get up, Aunt Josephine. Noel dear, this man has called to see you. (*She offers him the card with her right hand.*)

NOEL (*instead of at once looking at the card, takes her left hand and kisses it*). Dear Leila !

LEILA (*smiling*). That is my hand. This is his card.

NOEL (*smiling at her*). Let's see who he is. (*Before he looks at the card he says.*) You've got your hair done in a new way.

LEILA. D'you like it ?

NOEL. Yes. I like that saucy little twist just there.

LEILA (*laughs and thrusts the card at him*). There !

NOEL (*taking the card from her*). What's his name ?

LEILA. Mr. Welkin. I think he's an American by his accent.

NOEL (*reading the card*). Elisha P. Welkin. Yes, he must be. What does he want?

LEILA. I don't know. I didn't see him. I only heard him. Harrison put him in the drawing-room and brought his card to me.

NOEL (*after puzzling over the card, says to* LEILA). Oh, I know. It's about that library. (*To* RUFUS *and* JOSEPHINE.) That library in America that I told you they might be wanting me to go and decorate.

RUFUS. Oh yes, yes, yes—to be sure. (*To* JOSEPHINE.) You know.

JOSEPHINE. Yes, dear.

NOEL (*adopting an American accent for fun as he says to* LEILA). I guess I'll go and interview Elisha P. Welkin right now.

(*He goes out.* LEILA *sits on the dais and fingers the sketches as she speaks.*)

LEILA. Have you been looking at Noel's things?

JOSEPHINE. Yes, dear.

RUFUS (*coughs and clears his throat, then turns to* LEILA). I am sorry to have to say, Leila, that in *my* opinion his work is not as good as it used to be. Even your aunt notices it.

LEILA (*in mild surprise as she looks at* JOSEPHINE). Oh.

JOSEPHINE. He says himself that it is deteriorating.

LEILA. He hasn't said so to *me*.

RUFUS. Can't you see for yourself?

LEILA. I don't notice any change.

RUFUS. Perhaps you don't take very much interest in his work.

LEILA (*smiles at him, rather surprised at any one taking this tone to her, before she answers*). I take an interest in it from the point of view that it's *his*. I want him to succeed. I daresay I don't appreciate it as much as some people do, because I don't understand it properly. It would be affectation for me to pretend to be an authority—like Aunt Josephine.

JOSEPHINE (*meekly*). *I* don't pretend to be an authority on *anything*.

RUFUS (*importantly, as he turns to* LEILA). We can't all be connoisseurs. (LEILA *looks at him and smiles.*)

Don't you think it's unwise to make him go about so much in society—wasting his time and frittering away his talents?

LEILA (*putting the sketches together*). *I* don't make him go about. On the contrary, I'm always urging him to stick to his work and let me go out without him.

JOSEPHINE. He wouldn't like that.

LEILA. Why not? I'm quite as well able to take care of myself.

RUFUS (*more to himself than her*). So I see.

LEILA. And I'm sure he ought to be able to trust me.

RUFUS (*tries playfulness as he sits on the dais facing her*). If *I* were your husband, my little Leila, and I wanted you to stop at home with *me*—I'd make you.

LEILA (*gaily*). Oh, would you! I should like to see any one try to make *me* do anything I don't want to. (*Looking from one to the other and seeing that they disapprove of this remark, she explains herself.*) It's a good thing for Noel for me to go about and meet people. It makes him known. I get clients for him. It's all through *me* that Captain Harding is having his portrait painted— (*checks herself, then continues*) Oh—but don't tell Noel that. I shouldn't like him to think that it was more for *my* charms than *his* talents that Captain Harding gave him the commission. It would hurt his feelings, and I hate hurting people's feelings. It makes me feel such a brute——

RUFUS (*pompously*). You need not fear, my dear Leila, that I shall say anything calculated to turn your husband against you.

LEILA (*with exaggerated sweetness*). Oh, thank you, my dear Uncle Rufus. It wouldn't matter if you did, because you couldn't if you tried. What are you making, Aunt Josephine?

JOSEPHINE. Socks for my grand-daughter. (*Holding up a very tiny sock.*) Isn't she growing tall?

LEILA (*taking and smiling at the little sock*). How sweet!

RUFUS (*continues in his important manner*). I don't want you to run away with the idea that Noel has been *talking*—about you.

LEILA (*turns to* RUFUS). I'm sure he has. (*Smiles.*) He never does anything else.

RUFUS. Complaining, I mean.

LEILA (*gaily*). Noel—complain of *me*! He thinks I'm perfection. (*Turns her back on* RUFUS *again as she says to* JOSEPHINE.) How long does it take you, on an average, to make a little sock like that?

RUFUS (*trying to recall her attention*). Leila!

LEILA (*ignoring him, says to* JOSEPHINE). About a fortnight?

RUFUS. Leila!

JOSEPHINE. Leila!

LEILA. 'M?

JOSEPHINE. Your uncle is speaking.

LEILA. Oh—still? (*Turning to* RUFUS.) Yes?

RUFUS. I want you to give me your attention.

LEILA (*turning and facing him*). Of course I will. What is it?

RUFUS. We are often selfish, without meaning to be.

LEILA (*pretending to be impressed*). How true that is. It reminds me of something I wanted to speak to you about. I wonder if I dare. (*She glances from* RUFUS *to* JOSEPHINE *while* RUFUS *speaks, and at last goes over to him and takes his arm.*)

RUFUS. Of course, dear Leila. Out with it. Don't be afraid.

LEILA. Well. This morning, when Aunt Josephine and I were breakfasting together, before you came down, we were talking about her wardrobe, which sadly needs replenishing—I was advising her where to go and what to get—and what do you think she said? That she could only afford *one* new dress because *you* wanted so many clothes. (RUFUS *begins to grow restive, gets his arm free, and* JOSEPHINE *lays down her knitting and looks alarmed.*) I know you don't mean to be selfish, but I thought if I put it before you—poor Aunt Josephine!

(*To hide a mischievous smile, she turns away from him, hiding her amusement from them both.*
JOSEPHINE, *very much upset, rises and goes towards* RUFUS *as she speaks.*)

JOSEPHINE. Don't mind anything she says, Rufus dear. One new dress is quite enough; if I could have one nice evening gown—prune silk, I thought.

RUFUS (*haughtily*). If you require more, you have only to say so.

# DOORMATS

JOSEPHINE. But I don't, dear, I don't—(*looking down at her rather old-fashioned gown as she continues*) I'm sure I shall do very well as I am when we get to Cheltenham or Tunbridge Wells. *You must* have good clothes, to go to your clubs in.

RUFUS (*turning to her*). You make me look so selfish. (*He walks about in some perturbation, while* JOSEPHINE *shakes her head and feels thoroughly in the wrong.*)

LEILA. I'm so sorry I said anything. It's always a mistake to give unsolicited advice. It's never appreciated.

> (*Enter* MAURICE—*this is* CAPTAIN HARDING. *He wears his full-dress uniform, in which he is being painted, and makes a most brilliant appearance—he is a fine young fellow of twenty-eight—with a handsome appearance and charming manners—*LEILA *goes towards him to greet him when he enters.*)

Oh, here's Captain Harding. Good-morning.

MAURICE. How d'you do ? (*They shake hands.*)

LEILA. May I introduce you to my uncle and aunt ? Captain Harding—Lady Gale.

MAURICE. How d'you do ?

LEILA. And my uncle—Sir Rufus Gale.

MAURICE. Oh !—the Judge—how d'you do ? (*They shake hands.*) I heard you were expected.

RUFUS. You saw it in the papers ?

MAURICE. No ; your nephew told me.

RUFUS. Oh, yes ! It was in the papers.

> (*He joins* JOSEPHINE *in the window—he shows her a letter.*)

MAURICE (*lays his cap and gloves on the chair beside the ottoman. To* LEILA). Where's the master ?

LEILA (*coming towards him*). He's engaged with a man on business. I don't expect he'll be long.

MAURICE. Oh ! (LEILA *picks up a portfolio with sketches.*) May I help you ? (*Under cover of putting the sketches away in the portfolio they talk in low tones, so as not to be heard by* RUFUS *and* JOSEPHINE). Will you lunch with me to-morrow ?

LEILA. Is it a party ?

MAURICE. No.

LEILA. Then I can't.

MAURICE. Why not?
LEILA. I have a jealous husband.
MAURICE. Did he object the other time?
LEILA. When?
MAURICE. There's only once that you ever lunched with me alone. Did he make a row?
LEILA. Of course not. He didn't say anything. I didn't tell him.
MAURICE. Can't you do the same to-morrow? (LEILA *shakes her head.*) Why?
LEILA. I don't like being underhand.
MAURICE. There'd be no harm in your meeting me somewhere.
LEILA. Of course, there'd be no harm in it.
MAURICE (*with a sigh*). Unfortunately.
LEILA (*smiles*). You are a devil.
MAURICE (*smiles*). So are you. That's why we get on so well. (LEILA *is tying the tape of a portfolio. He tries to take her hand.*) If your jealous husband went away?
LEILA (*avoiding his hands*). He never does.
MAURICE. But if he did?
LEILA (*lifts up the portfolio and holds it out to* MAURICE *as she says in an ordinary tone*). Will you please put that portfolio back in the corner for me? (*As* MAURICE *takes the portfolio.*) Thank you. (*Crosses to* RUFUS *and* JOSEPHINE.)
    (MAURICE *replaces the portfolio in the corner, where it originally came from. Enter* NOEL.)
NOEL. Good-morning, Harding.
MAURICE. Good-morning.
NOEL. I'm awfully sorry to have kept you waiting. Shall we begin now, so as not to waste any more of your time? (*Turning, he sees* RUFUS *and* JOSEPHINE *standing together near the picture.*) Oh! (*To* MAURICE.) Do you mind my uncle and aunt being here?
MAURICE (*amiably*). Not a bit.
JOSEPHINE (*politely*). Wouldn't you rather we went away?
RUFUS. No, my dear, no; certainly not. Let us stay where we are. This may amuse me.
            (JOSEPHINE *still looks undecided.*)
LEILA. It's all right, Aunt Josephine. I often sit in

the studio while Captain Harding is being painted—don't I, Noel?

NOEL (*innocently*). Always. (*To* MAURICE.) Come along. Let's begin.

MAURICE (*gets on to the dais and sits on a stool facing* NOEL. *Speaking from the time he picks up his cap from chair*). I'm afraid I shall only be able to stay for a short while. I have an engagement directly. But you said if I could come for five or ten minutes, it would be better than nothing.

NOEL. I know. I needn't detain you long this morning.

JOSEPHINE (*speaking to* LEILA). I suppose we mustn't speak.

LEILA (*gaily*). Oh! yes you may. I chatter away whenever I feel like it. Don't I, Noel?

NOEL. Yes, dear.

MAURICE. *I'm* the only one who mayn't speak. It's such a bore—sitting here like a waxwork—not allowed to open my mouth.

NOEL. Would you mind not moving your lips? There, that's it; now you're splendid.

LEILA. Let me hold some of this wool for you.

JOSEPHINE. Oh! thank you, dear—that would be a great help.

LEILA (*holds the wool while* JOSEPHINE *begins to wind it*). Noel!

NOEL. Yes.

LEILA. What did Mr. Welkin have to say?

NOEL (*working on his canvas*). A great deal. He says—if I'll go out to America—have a look at that library—see what I can make of it, and submit my designs, and so forth—he'll pay all my expenses. I shall have to compete with two or three others—but he thinks I stand a first-rate chance.

LEILA. How splendid!

NOEL. If I got the job—it would be a great thing for me, excellent terms—much better than I expected. The worst of it is—they are in such a hurry. They want me to go out at once.

MAURICE. To America?

NOEL. Yes. (*Becomes intent upon his canvas, so that he does not see* MAURICE *deliberately turn his head and look at* LEILA—*their eyes meet for a moment—then* LEILA *looks* away. *Nobody notices this.* JOSEPHINE *is intent upon her knitting, and* RUFUS *is watching* NOEL. NOEL *looks up from his canvas at* MAURICE *and says, quite unsuspectingly.*) Would you mind looking this way? (MAURICE *resumes his correct position. After a moment's pause,* NOEL *says to* LEILA, *working as he speaks.*) Well, Leila, what do you say?

LEILA. It sounds most promising.

NOEL. So *I* think. (*After a moment's silence.*) How soon could you be ready?

LEILA (*surprised at this question, then says, after an appreciable pause*). I?

NOEL. Yes.

LEILA. Am *I* to go too?

NOEL (*surprised by this question, pauses in his work and says*). I suppose so. I don't know. I never thought of anything else. (*Continues working.*)

LEILA. Wouldn't it make it rather expensive for you if I went too?

NOEL. Welkin pays. He understood that you would be going too. At least, I took it for granted you would when I made the arrangements. He has invited us to stay at his house—with him and Mrs. Welkin—for as long as I have to be there.

LEILA. Oh, yes.

NOEL. Very kind of him, isn't it?

LEILA. Very—very kind. When does he want you to sail?

NOEL. What he said was (*assuming an American accent*) " Come right back with me to-morrer. Bring Mrs. Gale along—glad to have you—bully, fierce—fine." (*The others smile at this. Continues in his natural voice.*) I told him we couldn't leave as soon as that, but that we'd follow him in a week or two—as soon as you could get ready.

LEILA. Oh, yes.

(*There is a pause, during which* MAURICE *turns deliberately and looks at* LEILA.)

NOEL (*looking up from his canvas at* MAURICE, *says, unsuspectingly*). Eyes right, please.

(MAURICE *resumes his correct position.*)

LEILA (*after a moment's silence*). What about Uncle Rufus and Aunt Josephine?

## DOORMATS

JOSEPHINE (*to* LEILA). Oh, but you mustn't think of us.

NOEL. I thought if Uncle Rufus and Aunt Josephine wanted to stay on in London after we left, they could take care of the house for us. (*Not thinking what he is saying.*) We should have to put *somebody* in.

LEILA. Noel!

(RUFUS *grunts.*)

NOEL (*afraid he has given him offence, turns to him quickly and says*). I mean—you know what I mean.

RUFUS. Of course, my dear Noel, of course. Such an arrangement as you suggest would suit us admirably.

NOEL. There, Leila! You see. There's no need for you to stay behind on *their* account.

JOSEPHINE (*to* LEILA). None whatever.

LEILA. I'm afraid you'd find me rather in the way.

NOEL. You! Leila! What an idea!

LEILA. Suppose I can't get on with Mrs. Welkin. How dreadful that would be—having to be civil to her every day for. . . . How long do you expect to be gone, Noel?

NOEL. About a month—six weeks with the journeys.

LEILA. I'm sure I should be sick all the way over.

JOSEPHINE (*to* LEILA). I know of such an excellent remedy; I tried it on our last voyage from Bombay! Marvellous! And always before—I've been such a martyr. Sir Rufus can tell you.

RUFUS. Don't recall it, my dear. It was horrible—disgusting!

JOSEPHINE (*in an aside to* LEILA). No injurious after-effects.

RUFUS. Josephine! Please!

(JOSEPHINE *says the rest in a whisper to* LEILA.)

NOEL. You were all right last summer, Leila—in the Mediterranean—and we had a most awful squall.

RUFUS. *I* should have thought she'd be glad to go. Such a chance to see the world. It improves one so—a residence abroad—makes one so interesting and entertaining.

NOEL. Never mind, Uncle Rufus. She'll go with me if she wants to—and if she doesn't—I don't want her to do anything that she doesn't want to.

RUFUS (*looking severely at* LEILA). I should also

have thought that she might consider it her *duty* to go.

JOSEPHINE (*echoing* RUFUS'S *sentiments with great conviction*). Yes.

NOEL. I hope you will never do anything for *me*, Leila, from a sense of duty.

JOSEPHINE (*lays her hand timidly on* LEILA'S *arm and says, appealingly*). He *wants* you to go with him.

LEILA (*smiles at* JOSEPHINE *to make it all right, then rises and comes towards the easel as she says, amiably, to* NOEL). May I come and see how you are getting on, Noel, dear?

NOEL (*pleased by any attention from* LEILA). Do, dear. Come and tell me what you think of it. (*Steps back from the picture to look at it.*)

LEILA (*takes* NOEL'S *arm and stands beside him, looking at the picture*). Oh! isn't that good? Splendid! You *have* improved it. (*Glances at* MAURICE *as she says.*) You've made him much too handsome. (*Looking at the picture again.*) It's wonderful! It really *is*—wonderful—— I'm so proud of you. (*Kisses him.*)

NOEL. Oh, Leila! Leila!

LEILA (*withdrawing her arm from* NOEL'S). Now I must go and answer letters. (*Goes to the door, where she pauses and says vaguely to anybody.*) I shall be in the drawing-room if anybody wants me.

(*She goes out. There is a silence of several seconds after* LEILA *goes out before* MAURICE *speaks, during which* NOEL *continues working.*)

MAURICE. Does anybody know what time it is? (*He pauses, but no one notices his question.*) Never mind. It's sure to be time I flew. Awfully sorry I can't stay longer.

NOEL. So am I; but it can't be helped if you've got an engagement. Very good of you to have come in for these few minutes.

MAURICE (*rises and steps off dais*). Not at all. (*Looking at the portrait, says, pleasantly.*) Getting on—isn't it? (*Shakes hands with* NOEL.) Good-bye.

NOEL. Good-bye, old man.

MAURICE (*shaking hands with* RUFUS). Good-bye, Sir Rufus.

RUFUS. Good-bye.

MAURICE (*shaking hands with* JOSEPHINE, *who rises as he approaches*). Good-bye, Lady Gale.

JOSEPHINE. Good-bye, Captain Harding.

MAURICE (*speaking to* NOEL *as he goes towards the door*). Let me know when you go to America—won't you?

NOEL. Of course. As my wife is not coming—I shall probably sail to-morrow—with Welkin.

MAURICE. I see. (*Smiles round at every one*). Good-day.

(*He goes out.*)

NOEL (*speaking as* MAURICE *goes out*). Good-bye. (*Throws palette down on shelf under paint table, his expression is thoughtful and despondent.*)

JOSEPHINE (*watches him, then sits on the dais. Sympathetically*). She may decide to go with you, Noel, after she has had time to think it over.

NOEL. No, she won't.

JOSEPHINE. You haven't discussed it properly yet.

NOEL. She has made up her mind not to go—so she won't go. I know Leila. I'm not going to press the point to be refused again. It's quite reasonable of her not to come. It would be inconvenient. It's a long way. I see all that. I shouldn't mind her refusal so much if she'd only said she would *like* to go with me. It's no use *pretending* to *you*. Staying here in the house, you'll very soon see for yourselves how things are. You've seen already. I daresay my disappointment is partly due to pride. It's not very pleasant to have you all sitting round and noticing—how it's nothing to her—if *I* go away—to the other side of the world.

JOSEPHINE (*sympathetically*). She's fond of you, Noel —I'm sure she's fond of you.

NOEL. She's what's called " Fond of me in *her* way " —that means—she doesn't dislike me——

JOSEPHINE (*a little shocked by the suggestion*). Noel!

NOEL. She thinks I don't matter. It's just what Uncle Rufus said, " The more we do for people, the less they think of us."

RUFUS (*rising and coming towards them as he says, pompously*). Very true—that remark of mine! To be always suppressing one's own will and desires in favour of somebody else is no doubt extremely noble—but it doesn't pay.

JOSEPHINE (*quietly*). It's the only way to get on with *some* people.

NOEL. Bad-tempered people. But she's not *that*. If I have given in to Leila, it has been without a struggle—from affection—I wanted to please her. It began when I fell in love with her. We both began like that. When Leila and I were first married, there was quite a race between us to see which could do most for the other for about two months.

JOSEPHINE. It always *begins* like that.

RUFUS. How foolish to let it continue on one side only.

NOEL. Very foolish.

RUFUS. Why do you do it?

NOEL. Aunt Josephine understands.

RUFUS. It's ridiculous for *you* to be at the mercy of Leila. You are much cleverer than she is.

NOEL. Oh, yes — much — (*pointing to his brain*) — here.

RUFUS. Ridiculous! And look what it's bringing you to. Your life is confused, upset, unsatisfactory. You are gradually becoming less interesting as an artist and as a man. Worst of all, less and less able to interest the very person for whom all these sacrifices are being made.

JOSEPHINE (*rises, seeing how troubled* NOEL *is by the truth of these remarks, protests gently*). Rufus!

RUFUS (*to* JOSEPHINE). He's got to have it. (*To* NOEL.) What you need is—mental detachment.

(JOSEPHINE *sits on the ottoman.*)

RUFUS. You should cultivate a spirit of independence.

NOEL. I know all that, just as well as you can tell me. But how is one to change habits while circumstances remain the same? You can't turn round suddenly after breakfast one morning and become a new man—*apropos* of nothing at all.

RUFUS (*thoughtfully*). No. It needs a crisis—some definite point to come to issues upon. Well, here is your opportunity.

NOEL. Where?

RUFUS. This voyage.

## DOORMATS

NOEL. You mean—make this a test case! Insist upon her coming along with me?

RUFUS. No; go without her—the sooner the better—to-morrow—with Mr. Welkin. (NOEL *assents, and is impressed and interested by all that* RUFUS *says in the following speech.*) While you are away, you'll be hard at work. You'll be successful. You'll be made a fuss of. That will give you confidence. Your old powers will reassert themselves. When you have gained the mastery over yourself, you'll be able to gain the mastery over her.

NOEL. I shouldn't wonder if you are right. (*To* JOSEPHINE.) You'll stay here and look after Leila while I'm away, won't you?

  (JOSEPHINE *is about to assent, when* RUFUS *interrupts.*)

RUFUS. Now, now, now—none of that. Never mind her. Think of yourself.

NOEL (*smiles at* RUFUS *as he says*). I don't want her to feel lonely while I'm away.

RUFUS. Yes, you do. That's exactly what you *do* want. Let her be lonely, miss you, long for you. Then she'll remember your goodness to her. She'll appreciate you when you are not here. And when you come home (*with an expansive smile*) she'll give you *such* a welcome. (NOEL *smiles, too, as* RUFUS *gives him an encouraging slap on the back, then goes up to door, speaking to* JOSEPHINE *as he passes her.*) Come along, Josephine. The room must be ready now. Come and help me with the unpacking. (*Opens the door wide and stands waiting for* JOSEPHINE.)

  (JOSEPHINE *obediently gathers up her work and goes to the door, speaking as she does so.*)

JOSEPHINE. You shall sit on the bed, dear, and direct me where to put the things. (*When she is in the doorway she pauses and says.*) Oh! (*She says it in such a way as to attract* NOEL'S *attention.* JOSEPHINE *turns to* NOEL *and says, without any suspicion, just as if it were a piece of news.*) There's Captain Harding just coming out of the drawing-room now.

NOEL. Oh! I suppose he's been talking to Leila.

JOSEPHINE. Very likely.

RUFUS (*who is still waiting for* JOSEPHINE *to go out*).

Out of the way, my dear; out of the way. Either go out or come in—one of the two; but don't block up the doorway.

> (JOSEPHINE *and* RUFUS *go out of the room, leaving* NOEL *before the easel.*)

CURTAIN.

# THE SECOND ACT

SCENE.—*The drawing-room. This is a charming room on the first floor. The windows afford a view of the upper parts of the trees in* NOEL'S *small front garden. The room is decorated and furnished in the most excellent taste, but not too expensively. The walls are panelled and painted white, and all the furniture consists of old and carefully chosen pieces. There are windows in the back wall of the room, and between the windows is a cabinet. Across the corner of the room there is a writing-desk with a chair in front of it. Near the fireplace is a sofa, and one or two smaller chairs stand about a table upon which are a few books. It is early in the afternoon, six weeks later than Act I.*

(RUFUS *is seated at the writing-desk, writing, while* JOSEPHINE *is seated on the sofa sewing. Enter* HARRISON, *a neat young parlourmaid.*)

HARRISON. Beg pardon, my lady, I came in to look for Mrs. Gale.

JOSEPHINE. I think you will find Mrs. Gale upstairs in her bedroom, Harrison.

HARRISON. Thank you, my lady. (*Turns to go.*)

RUFUS (*turning round in his chair to* HARRISON). Who wants her?

HARRISON. Captain Harding, Sir Rufus.

RUFUS. Why don't you show Captain Harding in?

HARRISON. He asked me to tell Mrs. Gale that he would wait for her downstairs, in the hall.

RUFUS. Has he come to take her out?

HARRISON. I couldn't say, Sir Rufus—he didn't tell me.

(RUFUS *grunts.*)

JOSEPHINE. Thank you, Harrison.

(HARRISON *goes out.*)

RUFUS. He comes every day now.

JOSEPHINE. Nearly every day.

RUFUS. This isn't at all what I meant. Instead of pining for Noel she's consoling herself.

JOSEPHINE (*earnestly*). I wish Noel would come home.

RUFUS. What did he say about that in his last letter?

JOSEPHINE. He was still uncertain. He hoped he might be able to return this week or next. He couldn't be sure.

RUFUS. It must be nearly six weeks since he went away.

JOSEPHINE. Six weeks to-morrow. (*Sighs, and resumes her sewing.*)

RUFUS (*rises and brings his letters to the table*). She's out to lunch more often than she's in; tea too.

JOSEPHINE (*trying to excuse* LEILA). She has a great many friends.

RUFUS. I *believe* she has been to see Captain Harding at his rooms—from something they said the last time he dined here.

JOSEPHINE. I gathered from what they said that when she visited him there were others present.

RUFUS. It needs more than their saying so to convince me.

JOSEPHINE. Let us think the best we can of her.

RUFUS. Let us not be made fools of. (*Goes to* JOSEPHINE, *and pats her shoulder.*) I have felt reticent about discussing this matter with you before. (*He sits upon a stool near the sofa.*)

JOSEPHINE (*laying her work down*). I have seen how it is weighing upon you, Rufus dear. I know how you must feel your own responsibility. I too feel mine most keenly. We were left in charge of Leila by Noel. It is most difficult to know what we ought to do. I have ventured on one or two occasions to drop hints—but she ignores them, and as soon as I get at all pressing, brushes me aside, in her imperious way. Could *you* speak to her?

RUFUS. You remember how, on the morning after our arrival, I began reproving her for her selfishness, and how artfully she turned the tables upon me—

started talking a lot of rubbish about you not having enough clothes. Almost succeeded for one moment in making me believe that I am selfish. (*Laughs at the absurdity of the idea as he repeats.*) I! (JOSEPHINE *laughs too, a little tinkling, echoing, obedient laugh.*) I don't want that to occur again.

JOSEPHINE (*thoughtfully*). No.

RUFUS. I'm not afraid of her.

JOSEPHINE (*playing up to him, scouts the idea*). You! Afraid?

RUFUS. I think she would find her match in me.

JOSEPHINE. I should just think she would indeed!

RUFUS. You remember how I went for that Mrs. Coles in the alimony case?

JOSEPHINE. You did make her look small.

RUFUS. And that fellow Higgins?

JOSEPHINE. You polished him off pretty neatly, too. (RUFUS *is about to speak.*) (*Trying to bring him back to the subject.*) But about Leila?

RUFUS. Yes, I have wondered several times whether I ought not to speak to her, but on consideration I came to the conclusion that it was more dignified merely to let her read my disapproval in my tone and manner. My position here is most delicate—not only am I Leila's uncle by marriage—but her guest.

JOSEPHINE. The way she keeps on urging us to stay makes me think there can't be anything *seriously* doubtful.

RUFUS (*ridiculing* JOSEPHINE *in his superior manner*). My dear Josephine, how simple you are! Don't you see that she couldn't be having Captain Harding daily to the house if you and I were not installed here as watch-dogs? We are being made a convenience of. I wouldn't stand it—if it were not that it suits me so well to remain here.

JOSEPHINE (*sighing*). I must try again!

RUFUS. I'm afraid she's too sharp for you. I will speak to her. You can be by and support me if you like.

> (*Enter* LEILA. *She appears radiant as ever, smartly dressed for out-of-doors. She carries her gloves in her hand, and lays them for a moment on the table.*)

LEILA. Oh, here you are, Uncle Darby and Aunt Joan! I thought you were going out.

RUFUS (*expressing his disapproval by addressing* LEILA *in his most solemn manner*). There is a gentleman waiting for you in the hall.

LEILA. Captain Harding—I know. It won't do him any harm to wait. I wouldn't have arranged to go out with him this afternoon only I understood you were both going to the Wallace Collection. (*Pauses a moment, and then, as they do not reply, says.*) Aren't you?

RUFUS (*solemnly and mysteriously*). We don't know.

JOSEPHINE (*taking her cue from* RUFUS). We can't say—now.

> (LEILA *turns and looks at them, then* RUFUS *shakes his head at* LEILA *in solemn disapproval.* LEILA *looks from* RUFUS *to* JOSEPHINE. JOSEPHINE *takes her cue from* RUFUS, *also shakes her head at* LEILA. LEILA *takes no notice of this, but bends down to scribble a note of something.*)

RUFUS (*aside to* JOSEPHINE). She ought to ask us what's the matter with us.

JOSEPHINE (*aside to* RUFUS). They never will—people like her—if they know we want them to. It's part of their plaguiness.

> (LEILA *turns to them, folding up the note she has scribbled as she speaks, then picks up her gloves from the table.*)

LEILA. I was merely going for a walk. We thought we'd go to Battersea Park—to see the birds. Won't you put on your things and come with us?

RUFUS (*explosively*). No, we won't. And let me tell you, Leila, we most heartily disapprove of your conduct—your aunt and I. Every day—somewhere or other with this young man.

JOSEPHINE. Dreadful!

RUFUS. Abominable!

JOSEPHINE. Shocking!

RUFUS. What will people say?

LEILA. I'm afraid I never trouble much about what people say.

RUFUS. It's a pity you don't!

JOSEPHINE. A great pity.

LEILA. I suppose you haven't been in London long enough to notice that there are some women—it doesn't matter what they do—it's all right; and others, it doesn't matter what they do—it's all wrong. I'm one of the former.

RUFUS. There are things that are done and things that are not done—even in London.

LEILA. Everything is done, Uncle Rufus. It never matters what one does but only how one does it.

RUFUS. Of course if you are simply going to argue with me and justify yourself——

(LEILA *smiles at him,* RUFUS *grunts, goes up to the window, and stands looking out.* JOSEPHINE *removes her glasses, rises and goes to* LEILA.)

JOSEPHINE (*speaking very gently and sincerely, and naturally*). It is Noel we are thinking of, Leila—our dear Noel—not what people say, nor what may be done or not done in this new London of yours, where everything is so strange to me. A generation has passed away since I lived here before, so that my ideas of propriety have become old-fashioned. But think a little of Noel, working for you in America and thinking of you very, very often, I feel sure.

LEILA. Dear Aunt Josephine, Noel and I understand one another perfectly.

RUFUS (*coming down behind sofa*). I shall speak to Captain Harding.

(*Enter* MAURICE. *He is now, of course, wearing civilian clothes. He speaks as soon as he enters, and strolls towards* LEILA.)

MAURICE (*good humouredly, only pretending to be annoyed*). How much longer must I wait? I've been cooling myself for the last ten minutes on one of your hard hall chairs. (*Shakes hands with* LEILA.) How d'you do? (*Going to* SIR RUFUS *to shake hands.*)

(RUFUS *gives him a most formal bow, then crosses and stands by fireplace.* MAURICE *is naturally surprised.*)

Oh! (*Strolls towards* JOSEPHINE, *offering to shake hands.*) How——

(JOSEPHINE *cuts him short by giving him a frigid little nod.*)

Oh! (*turns to* LEILA *wondering what this means*).

LEILA (*explaining to* MAURICE). It's because I go about with you so much. They think it's wrong. What do you think? (*Addressing* RUFUS *and* JOSEPHINE.) It would be interesting to get all our points of view. (*To* MAURICE.) Of course, as Aunt Josephine says, her ideas of propriety are a little old-fashioned, while Uncle Rufus's notions of wifely duty are positively prehistoric!

RUFUS (*hurries to the door and throws it wide open—in a commanding tone*). Josephine!

(JOSEPHINE *obediently rises, gathers up her work, and scurries out.*)

LEILA (*as if nothing was happening continues to* MAURICE). —As you see.

(RUFUS *casts an indignant look at* LEILA, *then goes out after* JOSEPHINE, *closing the door after them.*)

(LEILA *and* MAURICE *both smile.*)

Silly old man!

MAURICE (*coming to* LEILA *who is sitting on the sofa*). But isn't this really rather serious?

LEILA. Why?

MAURICE. Their reception of me.

LEILA. D'you think it matters?

MAURICE. Not to *me*— (*Taking her hand and raising it slowly as he says.*) But I wouldn't for the world do anything to compromise *you*! (*Kisses her hand.*)

LEILA (*confidently*). I'll see that you don't do that.

MAURICE. I'd better not come here so often if this is the way they take it. Only that, of course, means snatched meetings out of doors, and all kinds of subterfuges which we both hate—and might end in our running away together.

LEILA (*gravely*). It isn't in my scheme of things to run away from home with any man.

MAURICE. It isn't in my scheme of things to run away with any man's wife (*looking at her*), but we may not be able to help ourselves.

LEILA (*looks at him*). Then I suppose we shall do it.

MAURICE (*sits on sofa beside her*). It's stupid to muck up one's career, but when I'm with you like this, I think it would be worth all the sacrifices I should have to make to have you near me always.

LEILA. If I lived with you I should be yours— shouldn't I?

MAURICE (*smiling at her*). Yes.
LEILA. I should belong to you.
MAURICE (*takes her hand*). Altogether—all the time.
LEILA. I should belong to you much more than I ever did to Noel, because I should be kicked out by everybody and therefore be much more dependent upon you. I don't believe I *could* belong to any one completely. Nor could you! We are both alike in that.
MAURICE. We are both alike in so many ways. It's wonderful how natural we are together. (*Moves nearer to her, transferring her hand from his right to his left, and slipping his right arm round her waist.*)
LEILA. Not here!
MAURICE (*removing his arm and sitting back in a corner of the sofa*). I'm much fonder of you than I ever thought I was going to be. When I first began coming here to have my portrait painted, I used to look at you when you came to sit in the studio, and think you were awfully attractive. But I wasn't anything like as much in love with you as I am now. D'you know, I sometimes find myself stopping in the middle of things to wonder what you are doing.
LEILA (*smiling*). Do you?
MAURICE. Do you do that about me?
LEILA. Sometimes. (*She smiles at him and he kisses her hand.*)
MAURICE. What have you done to-day?
LEILA. This morning I got up, had breakfast, did my housekeeping, then I did some telephoning——
MAURICE. Who to?
LEILA. Friends—and people. I cultivate a lot of bores because I think they might be useful to Noel. I'm rather good about that.
MAURICE. What did you do when you'd finished telephoning?
LEILA. Talked to Uncle Rufus and Aunt Josephine for about half an hour. Then I did some mending. I have plenty of that to do—being a poor man's wife—I'm rather clever at it.
MAURICE. It all sounds rather dull.
LEILA (*lays her hand on his arm for a moment and is very charming and sincere*). When I know you are coming to see me it brightens up everything else.

MAURICE (*very much pleased*). How nice of you to say that. (*Thoughtfully.*) It's not so bad for us now, of course. (*Rises and sits on the arm of the sofa.*) It's rather as if we were secretly engaged—tantalising, but pleasant. But when he comes home.

LEILA. You must trust me to manage the situation then.

MAURICE. Shall you tell him?

LEILA. I shouldn't mind. I'd rather—in a way. It's more honest. But of course one can't. Apart from everything else—it would hurt him so—that's really what I couldn't bear! He has always been so good to me, and I'm so fond of him. (*Half smiles as she adds.*) He's a very great friend of mine.

MAURICE. It's extraordinary how I don't hate him!

LEILA. Why should you hate him? I don't see how anybody could hate Noel! You'd love him if you knew him well. He's got so much character and he's such good company. I'm devoted to Noel—devoted! It's so silly of people to suppose that a woman only falls in love with another man because her husband is either a brute or a fool!

MAURICE (*looking at the door*). Who's that?

LEILA. The Uncle and Aunt coming out of their bedroom. I hope they won't come spying in here.

MAURICE (*rises*). I don't want to meet them.

LEILA (*rises*). What do you care?

MAURICE. If the old boy is rude to me again, I shall be ruder still to him.

LEILA. Oh, well—we don't want a fight. We shall meet them if we go that way. (*Nods towards the door.*) Shall we go and sit in the studio? (*Crossing to the other door.*) They won't think of looking for us there.

(*She goes out by this door.*)

MAURICE (*following her as he speaks*). Right-oh! Happy thought—they'll think we've gone to Battersea Park. (*He follows, closing the door behind him.*)

(*The door upon the opposite side of the room is pushed open cautiously.* RUFUS *pokes his head in. He now wears his frock-coat and has his gloves on. He carries his silk hat in his hand. He advances cautiously into the room, and when he sees there is no one there, he beckons to* JOSE-

PHINE, *who is dressed also in her best outdoor clothes. She makes a much less splendid appearance than* RUFUS.)

RUFUS (*lays his hat carefully upon the table, and, turning to* JOSEPHINE, *says solemnly*). Gone!—while I was putting on my boots.

JOSEPHINE (*timidly*). Ought we to pursue them, do you think?

RUFUS. To be ridiculed and set at defiance—publicly in Battersea Park! No. I wash my hands of Leila. There is only one thing to do—write to Noel. (*As she does not respond, he turns to her after a moment and says.*) Don't you agree?

JOSEPHINE. You know best.

RUFUS. Have an opinion!

JOSEPHINE. I think that to write to Noel would be rather going to extremities. It might make mischief, and would be sure to upset him.

RUFUS (*petulantly*). All the onus on *me*, as usual!

JOSEPHINE. I will support you, dear, of course, whatever you do.

RUFUS. I don't want your support if you give it unwillingly.

JOSEPHINE (*distressed, goes towards him*). I give it most willingly, Rufus dear. (*Lays her hand on his shoulder.*)

RUFUS (*brushing her hands away from him, not to be won over all in a moment*). Now you are trying to humour me as if I were a child. You don't really agree with me.

JOSEPHINE (*knowing what she is expected to do does it as if she really meant what she said*). Yes, dear, I do. On reflection I think that much the wisest thing to do is to write to Noel.

RUFUS (*turning to her*). Then why bandy words? (*Indicating the writing-desk.*) There is the desk and the paper. (JOSEPHINE *hurries to the desk and sits.*) Write to my dictation. (*Standing behind her, facing the window.*) Or would it be better to cable? No, too expensive. Write! " My dear Noel "——

JOSEPHINE (*writing*). Noel——

(*Enter* NOEL. *He stands in the doorway smiling at them and looking very cheerful. His visit to America has done him a great deal of good. He is bronzed by his sea voyage, and has much more assurance of manner. The despondency which oppressed him in the First Act has vanished, and he is now buoyant and in high spirits.*)

NOEL (*in an unconcerned manner, as if he had seen them ten minutes before*). Hullo!

RUFUS (*turns, and is greatly surprised to see* NOEL). Noel!

JOSEPHINE (*turns quickly and rises, and is also greatly surprised*). Noel!

NOEL (*shakes hands with* RUFUS). Why so surprised to see me?

RUFUS (*coming towards him*). We didn't expect you yet.

NOEL. I wrote.

JOSEPHINE. We never received any letter.

NOEL. Oh, I wonder how that is. (*Embraces her.*) Perhaps it's coming by a slow boat. I must have overtaken it on the way. That's it, that accounts for it. That's why Leila wasn't at the station to meet me. Where is she? Where's Leila?

RUFUS (*solemnly*). Gone out!

JOSEPHINE (*hastily to* NOEL). She didn't know you were coming, you see.

NOEL. Of course not. How long will she be?

JOSEPHINE. She didn't say.

NOEL. How is she—well?

JOSEPHINE. Very well.

RUFUS (*solemnly*). She is in excellent health.

NOEL (*cheerfully*). Splendid! It is nice to be home again. I've had a most glorious time. I was no end of a success. They chose my designs out of all the rest. You should have heard some of the things they said. (*Assuming an American accent.*) " Say, Mr. Gale, what are they thinking of in Europe to let you come over here?" " I reckon these drawings of yours are among the most remarkable works of art in the United States." (JOSEPHINE *laughs a little at this.*) They dined me and lunched me and made speeches to me and at me. (*Speaks more seriously, but all the time exhilarated.*) You were quite right, Uncle Rufus. It was what I needed. I can't tell you how it has bucked me to be made such a fuss of. I'm too old a bird, I hope, to have my head turned, but it has given me assurance, confidence in my

own powers ; and I remember so well what you said—
" Mental detachment "—without which one is of no
value. I'm only home for a few weeks, while they get
the library in shape. Then I shall go back, of course,
to do the work—the actual painting. I shall take Leila
with me then. (*With great determination, but humorously and assuming an American accent.*) " Yes, sir! " (*In his natural voice.*) If she says she doesn't want to come
I shall tell her gently, but firmly, that—(*American accent*) " I'm the ' borss.' " (*Growing anxious and impatient.*) I wish she'd come in. What a long time
she is. Where has she gone to—did she say ? (*Goes to the window and looks out.*)

    (RUFUS *and* JOSEPHINE *exchange an uneasy glance before* JOSEPHINE *speaks.*)

JOSEPHINE. She said she was going to Battersea Park.

RUFUS (*by fireplace, with great solemnity*). To see the birds.

    (NOEL *turns to them quickly, struck by their reticent and solemn manner.*)

NOEL. What's the matter ?

JOSEPHINE (*hastily*). Nothing, dear—nothing !

NOEL (*hardly waiting while* JOSEPHINE *speaks*). Why are you both so—(*looking at her*) mysterious ? (*looking at him*) and solemn ? (*Pauses for them to reply before he says.*) Is anything up ?

JOSEPHINE (*weakly*). No.

NOEL (*to* RUFUS). She's not ill ?

RUFUS. I have told you that her health is good——

JOSEPHINE (*anxiously, as she sees* NOEL'S *uneasiness*). She'll be in soon, Noel. You'll see her directly.

NOEL (*going again to the window, and looking out*). I hope so.

    (*Enter* LEILA. *She is amazed to see* NOEL, *whose back is now towards her, and stops still a moment before she speaks.*)

LEILA. Noel ! ! (*Goes towards him.*)

NOEL (*at the sound of her voice he turns to her—joyfully*). Leila ! (*He folds her in his arms and kisses her, overcome with emotion at the joy of seeing her again.*) Oh, Leila ! I was so afraid you were ill or that something had happened. (*Looking in her face.*) You are all right, aren't you ?

LEILA (*smiling at him*). Yes, dear—of course I'm all right.

NOEL. Oh, I'm so thankful—and so glad to see you,—dear Leila. (*Hugs her again.*) (*Enter* MAURICE. *He enters very soon after* LEILA, *but not until she is folded in* NOEL'S *arms, so that* NOEL *does not see him until he and* LEILA *have released themselves. When he sees* MAURICE *he becomes very reserved.*) Oh! (*Crosses to* MAURICE.) (MAURICE *comes forward a little to meet him, and shakes hands politely but without cordiality.*) How d'you do?

MAURICE. This is a surprise!

NOEL. Yes.

MAURICE. We didn't expect you yet.

NOEL. Didn't you? (*Turns to* LEILA *as she speaks.*)

LEILA. Have you had a good voyage, Noel?

NOEL. Excellent, thank you.

LEILA. I thought you would have cabled, or something?

NOEL. I wrote, dear—(*hesitates and looks at* MAURICE) I wrote you a long letter. I was explaining to Uncle Rufus and Aunt Josephine, as you came in.

(*Everybody is embarrassed.*)

JOSEPHINE (*rises, and goes to* LEILA *as she says*). It was a slow boat—not his, the one that brought his letter, or, rather, that didn't bring it—that hasn't brought it yet, I mean.

(*The situation is too much for* JOSEPHINE. *Finding everybody's attention upon her, she is overcome with confusion and emotion, and hurries out. They all see this. Every one is a little more embarrassed till* LEILA *comes to the rescue.*)

LEILA. Why don't we all sit down? (*Sets the example.*)

NOEL (*to* MAURICE, *laconically*). Won't you sit down?

MAURICE. Thanks. (*Looking at* LEILA.) I must be off. I have an appointment. (*Not knowing whether to shake hands with* NOEL *or not, making a hesitating movement towards him.*) Good-bye!

NOEL (*nods to* MAURICE). Good-bye.

LEILA (*annoyed by the behaviour of* NOEL, *towards* MAURICE, *defies him by extending her hand cordially to* MAURICE). Good-bye, Captain Harding. (*As they shake hands.*) Come and see us again soon.

MAURICE. Thanks, I will. (*Crosses down below the sofa to* RUFUS, *who turns his back on him, then looks round the room awkwardly.*) Thanks.

(*He goes out.*)

LEILA. We've been seeing a good deal of Captain Harding while you've been away. He often comes to the house—almost every day!—as Uncle Rufus has no doubt already told you. (*Rises and goes towards* NOEL.) It seems so natural to see you again—almost as if you had never been away. And how well you are looking! (NOEL *smiles at her, but it is a reserved, sad smile.*) (*Appeals to Rufus.*) Isn't he looking well? (RUFUS *is solemn and unresponsive.*) I'll go and take my things off now. Then I'll come back to hear all about what you've been doing in America. (*Humming to herself.*)

(NOEL *makes a movement as if to call her back, but* LEILA *does not see it, and goes out.*)

NOEL. What does it mean?

RUFUS. What?

NOEL. Your reticence—your embarrassment—as soon as I asked for Leila. Aunt Josephine rushing out of the room in tears. His coming to the house every day. If there's anything wrong, why didn't you write and tell me?

RUFUS. I was just going to when you came in.

NOEL. What?

RUFUS (*adds hastily*). I don't know that there's anything wrong. She's with him continually—but I must say, in fairness to her, I've seen nothing suspicious; it's all very frank and open. I've done everything a man could. But you know what your wife is—does exactly as she likes, whatever anybody says. *You've* never been able to control her.

NOEL. I've never had an occasion like this. If she's had her own way before, it has been about things in general, not about a man. Comes every day, does he? I'll soon put a stop to that.

RUFUS. Don't jump to conclusions. This may be one of these new-fashioned *friendships* between men and women.

NOEL (*with great emphasis*). *Friends* don't need to meet *daily*. They can get along quite comfortably without a sight of each other for weeks at a time—

It's *lovers* who *must meet*. I won't have him coming to my house.

RUFUS. You must settle that with Leila.

NOEL. You think she'll get her own way over this as she used to do over other things. I've not been away for nothing. If Leila won't submit to me, there'll be a row. (*He is crossing to the door, and is stopped by* RUFUS.)

RUFUS. Don't lose your temper; it's fatal. She never loses hers. You want to meet this situation wisely—so don't be too tragical. Anger won't answer, nor will kindness, nor appeals to her better nature. You'll still be at her mercy, *manage* her—outwit her. And there's only one way to do it successfully.

NOEL. What's that?

RUFUS. Retaliation.

NOEL (*blankly*). Flirt with the first woman I meet?

RUFUS. If she's pretty enough.

NOEL (*scornfully*). It's contemptible. I'm surprised at you suggesting such a thing.

RUFUS. Remember, she has this great advantage over you, she is doing something she knows she shouldn't, while you are only trying to stop her. You are like an anti-society chasing after something that runs faster than it does. No anti-society was ever known to suppress anything yet. The most it ever did was to divert it—that's what you've got to do.

NOEL. Yes; but to deliberately set to work to make her jealous. It may be the clever thing to do—but it's not sincere, it's not real—I don't like it.

RUFUS. I know what I'm talking about. I haven't sat on the bench for fifteen years without gaining unusual insight into the workings of the human heart. (*Impressively.*) If she wants to be off—nothing you can do will stop her. But if you should show signs of wanting to be off, she'll come running back like a hare.

NOEL. I don't know who to flirt with. I daresay I could find some one—but to begin—all of a sudden—now.

RUFUS (*slyly*). Has there been nobody in America?

NOEL (*indignantly*). No. Certainly not.

(RUFUS *shrugs his shoulders.*)

RUFUS. Oh! Well, you must pretend there has been.

Is there no woman at all that you've been seeing a good deal of—all the time you've been away?

NOEL. Only Mrs. Welkin.

RUFUS (*seizing brightly on the notion*). Why not Mrs. Welkin?

NOEL (*laughs, rather joylessly, before he says*). You haven't seen her. She's all bones and gristle—with a receding chin.

RUFUS. Invent! You are an artist. Create charms for Mrs. Welkin. Give her a neglectful husband—be in a hurry to get back to her. Don't care whether Leila goes with you or not—you'd rather she didn't. It's the only way, my boy, the only way. If you do what I suggest, you can twist Leila round your little finger.

(*Enter* LEILA. *She smiles at them as she enters.*)

RUFUS (*attracted by her entrance*). Ah! here's Leila! (*Opens book.*) (LEILA *lays her hand on* NOEL'S *shoulder. He is just about to take her hand when a glance from* RUFUS *stops him.*) I'll go and take your aunt out now and leave you young people together. (LEILA *strolls up to the window and looks out. When he has got half-way to the door, he stops and says.*) Oh, my hat—I was forgetting it. (*He goes back to the table for his hat and stick which* NOEL *hands him, glances at* LEILA, *then says aside to* NOEL.) Remember Mrs. Welkin. (*Speaking as he goes to the door.*) It's too late for the Wallace Collection. We'll take a little walk on the Embankment. Bye-bye.

(*He goes out.*)

LEILA (*crosses down behind* NOEL *and puts her hands on his shoulders*). Well, Noel?

NOEL (*is about to take her hands, but alters his mind—indifferently, but not rudely*). Well, Leila!

LEILA (*she is at first more puzzled than annoyed, though also a little annoyed. She sits upon the sofa and settles herself before she speaks*). What kind of an experience did you have in America?

NOEL. Very agreeable, thank you. Very busy! No time to feel lonely or homesick.

LEILA. You found time to write me some nice long letters.

NOEL. I tried not to forget my duties in the midst of my pleasures. (*Begins to roll a cigarette.*) (LEILA *looks more puzzled still.*) Charming people, the Welkins.

LEILA. How many of them are there? I forget if you told me.

NOEL. Only Welkin and (*tries to appear guiltily confused*) Mrs. Welkin.

LEILA. What is she like?

NOEL (*smiles, turns towards her, and says, with calculated enthusiasm*). Delightful! so intelligent! Not half appreciated by her husband. *He* is just the ordinary business man. She—the sensitive, cultured, misunderstood wife.

LEILA. Pretty?

NOEL. Like Beauty and the Beast—she and Elisha.

LEILA (*puzzled*). Elisha?

NOEL. Welkin.

LEILA. Oh, yes—Elisha P.—what's her name?

NOEL. Ella—(*corrects himself hastily*) Elaine.

LEILA. I suppose you call her Ella. (NOEL *smiles an elaborate, guilty smile, then turns his face slowly away from* LEILA. LEILA *doesn't like this, and says with some asperity*.) I'm glad you've been enjoying yourself. It makes me feel less guilty.

NOEL (*looks up suddenly with a very serious expression of face only seen by the audience, controls himself and then says carelessly*). You have been enjoying yourself?

LEILA (*still annoyed*). What d'you expect? If you go away and leave me for weeks at a time?

NOEL (*seriously*). I asked you to come with me.

LEILA. What a good thing I didn't. You wouldn't have had half such a good time with—Ella.

NOEL (*remembering his rôle, tries to laugh it off by saying*). Oh, no—of course—I shouldn't—no!

LEILA (*watches him before she speaks*). You are going back again soon, aren't you—to America, (*pointedly*) to your *work*.

NOEL (*carelessly*). Quite soon.

LEILA. I suppose you won't want *me* to go with you *this* time?

NOEL (*is on the point of saying what he feels, then checks himself, and says indifferently*). My dear, please yourself.

LEILA. I shouldn't think of going—to be in the way. I've no wish to play gooseberry.

NOEL (*cautiously, trying to appear indifferent, but*

*wanting very much to know*). What shall you do if I leave you behind?

LEILA (*recklessly*). Enjoy myself!

NOEL (*suspiciously*). With— (*Puts cigarette away on ash-tray—checks himself.*) How? What do you mean by enjoying yourself?

LEILA. Flirting. Having a man I like to take me about and make love to me.

NOEL (*angrily*). Leila!

LEILA (*flaring up*). Well! *You* have Mrs. Welkin. Why shouldn't I have my friend?

NOEL. That's different.

LEILA. Oh, no, it isn't—not at all! I'm modern.

NOEL (*rises, goes to her behind the sofa, and says soberly*). Look here, Leila. I'll give up Elaine—if you'll give *him* up.

LEILA (*jeering*). Ho! You can't think very much of her to throw her over like that.

NOEL. There's such a thing as duty.

LEILA (*sarcastically quoting him*). I hope you will never do anything for *me*, Noel, from a sense of duty. (*In her natural voice.*) You once said that to me. If your inclination doesn't hold you—you needn't think you *have* to love me. I see what it is. You've found some one you like better than me (*nearly in tears*). Well, it can't be helped.

NOEL (*sits beside her, and says with a sudden burst of affection*). Leila! Leila! I do love you, I never loved any one but you. I never shall! She's nothing to me. I don't care a fig for the woman—I love *you*. (*He dries her eyes with handkerchief.*)

LEILA (*momentarily touched by his outburst, and very much relieved to know that he is still in her power, smiles upon him and says kindly*). I know that, Noel. You were trying to make me jealous. I knew you couldn't mean it. But I thought I'd like to make you say so. (*Stands up and moves away.*)

NOEL (*bangs his knee, is vastly annoyed with himself when he realises that he has given himself away*). Oh! Why aren't you jealous? You ought to be! (LEILA *smiles at him.*) If I thought *less* about you you'd bother a bit about *me*. (*Turns sharply to her as she does not answer.*) Eh? Isn't that it?

LEILA (*plaintively*). I think you might be nicer when you've just come home.

NOEL (*rises also, looks at her lovingly and then with a tenderness that betrays itself in his voice says*). I should like to be nicer, Leila—but it's a tremendous disappointment to me—this home-coming. (*He is hurt by this move away of hers.*) I've been thinking things over while I've been away. I've been thinking a good deal about our marriage. I'm not going to say it's been a failure—we've been very happy together—but we've been happy at my expense. It's a good deal my own fault, I know. I've spoiled you. I've always given you your own way. It has been my pleasure to do so. But the result of it is you have come to think that *I* don't have to be considered. You take my gift as your right. You forget to thank me. It's not right, Leila. In marriage there should be give and take—which doesn't mean that one should do all the giving and the other all the taking. That's what our marriage has come to. There's going to be a change, Leila—a drastic change. (LEILA *begins to show veiled defiance.*) I didn't realise the extent to which you had ceased to consider me—till the day you refused to come with me to America. (LEILA *is about to protest, but he interrupts her.*) Oh, you didn't refuse in so many words, I know—but you showed me very plainly that you didn't want to come. (LEILA *looks on the ground.*) I didn't like to tell you—nor let you see—how much I cared, but you must have seen, you must have known, you couldn't help it! I tried to make myself believe that a short separation wouldn't be altogether a bad thing for either of us. I half hoped that when I was gone—you'd be sorry—perhaps—miss me a little, (*resentfully*) but you seem to have had a very merry time. (LEILA *still looks on the ground.*) You're not fond of this man, Leila?

LEILA. Who?

NOEL (*irritated, says sharply*). You know who I mean—Harding.

LEILA. Fond of him?

NOEL. Yes, fond of him. Leila, I want you to tell me— Has there been anything? Is it anything that makes any difference to you and me?— Is there anything that you're *ashamed* to tell me?

LEILA. What's the good of all these questions, Noel? Suppose I had done anything—that I ought to be ashamed of—d'you think I'd be such a fool as to let any one know? You'd have to accept what I told you—whatever it was. I can tell you anything I please—the truth, or a lie, or nothing.

NOEL. No, Leila, no. No, you can't! I won't be put off like that! You must tell me. I mean to find out. I'm going to get to the bottom of this. (*Before he has finished speaking,* LEILA *has risen and is strolling towards the door.*) Where are you going?

LEILA (*speaking as she goes*). I'm going out till you are in a better temper.

NOEL (*shouts at her*). Stay where you are. (*This surprises her so much she does as she is told.*) I know what you always do—your kind. Avoid a row—refuse to have it out. I'm being tiresome—so you think you'll go where it's more amusing—and leave me to worry by myself.

> (LEILA *crosses slowly towards the table.* NOEL *watches her without moving from his place. At the table she pauses, picks up a book, looks at the title, turns over a page or two to see what it is, saunters to the sofa with it, arranges the cushion, sits down, puts her feet up, settles herself, opens the book, and begins to read, ignoring* NOEL *altogether.* NOEL *watches all this before he speaks.*)

I want to know *exactly* how we stand.

> (*She turns a page of her book and still ignores him. He walks deliberately, but with great determination to the sofa.*)

You must tell me what I think I ought to know.

> (*He pauses, watching her, but she still ignores him. He sits down on the side of the sofa, near the foot of it, beside her legs, then says with quiet determination.*)

I'm going to have *my* way this time.

> (*She still ignores him. He takes the book from her firmly, but not snatching it, and pitches it away. She offers no resistance, he then takes her two hands in his, gripping them firmly and forcing her to face him.*)

If you won't tell me—I shall go straight to him!

LEILA (*affecting a calm and leisurely indifference, says quietly*). What good would that do you, Noel? He would deny that there had been anything—(*pausing deliberately to choose her expression*) wrong. You wouldn't know whether to believe him or not, but you'd have to take his word.

NOEL. Why can't *you* deny it?

LEILA (*as before, but with decreasing self-control*). Why should you believe me? If I were guilty I should lie—shouldn't I? And if I were not, you'd believe what you chose.

NOEL (*getting more and more insistent*). Leila!

LEILA (*losing her temper*). Believe what you choose.

NOEL. Leila, Leila—remember!

LEILA (*pushing him away with her left hand and tearing her right from his grasp. He does not want a physical struggle and lets her free herself. While she is freeing herself she says furiously.*) Stop it, Noel! I've had enough. (*Rising, and moving away from him.*) Think what you like— (*Turning to him, says menacingly.*) Go to Captain Harding if you like—only I warn you—if you do, it *will* make a difference. If you've no more respect for me than to go to him behind my back and ask him if he's my lover, I'll have nothing more to do with you. Why d'you stick me on a pedestal, where I don't belong, and never wanted to be— (*Turns and comes towards him without stopping in her speech.*) And then go and break your heart when you find I'm not a saint? I never set up to be a saint. I'm no different from other women. We all flirt and philander. All of us who get the chance. Why not? Why not? D'you suppose it's amusing to sit at home all day and mind the house? (*Half turns to him, stretching out her left hand towards him as if to stop him saying something.*) Oh, don't begin the usual thing—if only I had a child—(*passionately, her tears rising*) I wish I had! I wish I had! It would be something to satisfy my heart. (*Turning to face him, forcing back her tears by raising her voice still more.*) But not everything! Even the women with children!—they want more than that. They want companionship—they want life, excitement! (NOEL *comes towards her as she continues recklessly.*) And adventures—yes, adventures. Forbid him the house. It's your house. But don't forget—I can see him outside if I want to. I can meet him *without* your knowledge. You can track me with detectives if you like. They won't find anything out. I may not choose to give up my friend. I may not choose— (*Her head up, proud and defiant and rebellious, she moves away from him.*)

NOEL (*after a long pause, during which he is considering his position*). If you don't want to stick to me, I can't *make* you. I'm not going to watch you every minute. It wouldn't be worth it. I haven't the time.

LEILA (*turns to him, and goes towards him while she is speaking*). Noel! Noel! Can't you understand? Nobody could take your place—no one. You must know that. (*As he pays no attention to her, she is very near to tears, but still defiant and always justifying herself.*) I'm not good enough for you. (*She sits on the sofa.*) I'm frivolous and spoilt. But it's not altogether *my* fault. You've always given in to me and let me do exactly as I liked. *You've* made me what I am. (*Breaking down and crying.*) Don't turn against me. (*Appealingly.*) Noel! (*Buries her face in her hands and sobs.*)

NOEL (*unable to resist her, goes towards her, pauses, and looks down at her*). It's been my fault, too—mine more than yours. (*Drops on one knee beside her and says imploringly.*) But, oh, Leila—tell me—let me think! Let me feel—let me *know*—that it's all right.

LEILA (*drying her eyes as she looks at him and says*). Yes, Noel—of course—of course it's all right.

NOEL. D'you swear it—that there's been *nothing*——

LEILA (*becoming restive and offended*). I've told you. If you're not going to take my word—— (*Makes a movement away from him.*)

NOEL (*taking her hands and drawing her round to face him again*). No, Leila—Leila—don't turn away. I take your word. You say it's all right. I believe you. But I love you so desperately. I'm so jealous. If I thought that any one was pushing me out and taking my place — I'd — I'd— (*Dropping his voice almost to a whisper.*) No, no! Listen to me. I shouldn't be afraid—only lately—I've seen—for some time past I've noticed—it's not the same—not quite the same. There are little signs—little things that make me think—and then—you say something, or you do something—something so sweet and tender—and then I think you *are* the same—and that it's only my fears and my jealousy and my love for you. You say it's all right. You say so. I hope it's all right.

LEILA. Poor old Noel! Dear old boy, I wish I was more what you want.

(*He is kneeling on the ground beside her.*)

NOEL. I wouldn't have you any different—but I *wish* we were back at St. Ives. Have you forgotten how it was then? You are everything in the world to me still—just as you were then—just as I was to you *then*. Your mind was given up to me—your hands were always finding my hands. When we looked into each other's eyes and kissed each other—I was enough—I was everything. What a long time ago that seems. Nothing can hurt me now, you said, neither poverty, nor age, nor pain—so long as I have you. (*She drops her eyes.*) I have never forgotten that. (*He rises and stands, looking away.*)

LEILA. I'm fond of you still, Noel.

NOEL (*speaking kindly to her, but very sadly, and as if he were thoroughly disillusioned*). I know, dear. I know all about it. You needn't explain. You like me as one likes a faithful friend. I've been kind, and so you thank me. But the old impulse has gone. It's no use pretending. We can't hide these things from each other. I don't inspire you any more. It must be a great disappointment to you, too.

(*Enter* RUFUS *followed by* JOSEPHINE.)

RUFUS. Well, Leila! We've had our walk. Up and down the Embankment twice, from the church to Chelsea Bridge.

(*While he is saying this* LEILA *goes to the door, taking no notice either of* RUFUS *or* JOSEPHINE, *who remains, looking anxiously at the others.* RUFUS *watches* LEILA *go out of the room before he says expectantly.*)

Well, Noel! You've succeeded?

(*The question comes as a shock to* NOEL. *He has gone through so much since his scene with* RUFUS, *he has to let his mind travel back to that.*)

NOEL (*echoes*). Succeeded?

RUFUS. You've conquered her?

NOEL. No, Uncle Rufus, no, I've not conquered. I've done—what I've always done—given in, given in, given in—all along the line.

> (*As* NOEL *goes out of the room* JOSEPHINE *comes to* RUFUS *and takes his arm. Both stand looking towards the door through which* NOEL *has passed.*)

CURTAIN.

# THE THIRD ACT

SCENE.—*The dining-room. A square, comfortable room and, like the other rooms in* NOEL'S *house, decorated and furnished in excellent taste, but without extravagance or any great outlay of money. There is a door in the right-hand wall and a fireplace opposite, with a fender in front of it. In the centre of the room there is a round dining-table, now set for breakfast for four persons. The coffee-pot, etc., stands before the place laid on one side of the table. On the table are jam dishes, butter dishes, an egg-stand with boiled eggs, cruets, etc., and all the necessary knives, forks, spoons, china, etc. Against the wall is a sideboard with a white cloth spread over it. On the sideboard are plates, knives, forks, and spoons, and two dishes with covers standing on heaters. There are two armchairs and six other dining chairs, which are all alike. Three of these stand against the walls ; the others are at the table.*
JOSEPHINE *is seated, but has not yet begun her breakfast. She has a cup of coffee beside her, but nothing on her plate. She is reading a letter.*
*It is about a month later than Act II.*

RUFUS (*who is by the sideboard, helps himself to sausage and bacon, then crosses and sits at the table. In loud and petulant tones he demands*). Why don't they give us more variety in our food ? Nothing but sausage—every morning, sausage. (*Pushing his plate away.*) I'm sick of sausage.

JOSEPHINE (*as soon as* RUFUS *speaks, lays down her letter and becomes anxious about his comfort, but says brightly*). We had haddocks yesterday, darling.

RUFUS. I detest haddocks. That's well known.

## DOORMATS

JOSEPHINE (*cheerfully*). Have an egg?

RUFUS (*grumpily*). No.

JOSEPHINE. You used to be so fond of sausages.

RUFUS. I like sausages when they are properly cooked, but not when they are burnt or burst! (*Holds up a sausage on his fork.*) Look at that!

JOSEPHINE (*adjusting her eye-glasses on her nose, peers at the sausage*). It is not well cooked, certainly.

RUFUS (*indignantly*). It's a disgrace! (*He puts the sausage on his plate again, pushes it about with his fork.*

JOSEPHINE *takes up her letter and continues reading it while* RUFUS *sulks. After a short silence* RUFUS *exclaims in a loud voice of lamentation, sounding almost as if he were ready to burst into tears*). Why can't she give us kedgeree?

JOSEPHINE (*laying her letter down again, and always speaking cheerfully*). Would you like me to ask her to?

RUFUS. How can you ask her? We are visitors. We must eat what's provided.

JOSEPHINE. But I'm sure Leila wouldn't mind me asking her. She'd be only too pleased to give you some of your favourite dishes if she knew what they were.

RUFUS. I don't suppose her cook understands kedgeree. There's only one way to make it! Besides—it's too late for this morning. (*Pulls his plate towards him again, as he mutters.*) Sausage! (*Continues eating his sausage and bacon.*)

JOSEPHINE (*rises and puts her arm round his shoulder*). Shall I see if there's anything on the sideboard that you could fancy?

RUFUS (*with his mouth full*). If you like! (*Pats her cheek.*)

     (JOSEPHINE *crosses to the sideboard, raises the covers and looks inside the two dishes.*)

JOSEPHINE. Here's a delicious-looking little mess of something; fish, I think.

RUFUS (*indignantly*). The haddocks from yesterday.

JOSEPHINE (*sweetly*). Do try some of it.

RUFUS (*mutters*). No, thank you.

JOSEPHINE (*putting some of the mess from the dish nearest to the audience on to a plate*). I think *I* must have a little. It looks so very nice.

RUFUS (*eating*). This *bacon's* as brittle as glass.

JOSEPHINE (*returning to her place with the plate she has filled and putting it down on the table as she says anxiously*). Isn't there *anything* that tempts you ? (*She stands surveying the table as* RUFUS, *having finished his sausage and bacon, lays his knife and fork together*). Marmalade ?

RUFUS. Ugh !

JOSEPHINE. Toast ?

RUFUS (*after a pause says sullenly*). An egg.

JOSEPHINE (*about to pass* RUFUS *the egg-stand, says cheerfully*). That's right.

RUFUS (*reaching across the table for the egg-stand*). Don't bother. I can reach. Better get on with your own breakfast. You haven't had anything yet.

JOSEPHINE (*sitting in her place again and taking her knife and fork up as she speaks*). Never mind *me*. I can begin now though ; now that you've got what you like.

RUFUS (*drinking coffee—draining his cup*). I'm ready for some more coffee.

JOSEPHINE (*lays down her knife and fork and rises quickly as she speaks*). I'm so sorry. (*Takes his coffee cup*). I didn't notice. How thoughtless of me !

 (*As she pours out coffee for* RUFUS *he puts on his glasses, peers at her plate, takes it up and smells it.*)

RUFUS. This doesn't smell so bad. (*He puts his plate on one side, replaces the egg in the egg-stand, places her plate in front of him and begins to eat her breakfast.*) I hope you've left enough in the dish for yourself ?

JOSEPHINE (*cheerfully as she crosses behind* RUFUS *and sets his cup of coffee on the table beside him*). I think so, dear. I'll just see. (*Crossing to the sideboard.*) I think there was a little. (*Lifts the cover from the dish nearest the audience and lays it down as she says.*) Oh, yes. Just a mouthful. Quite enough for *me*. (*As she puts the few remaining scraps from the dish on to a plate.*) Noel must have fancied this too. (*Returns to her place, lays her plate in front of her, sits down and at last begins her breakfast.*) I shall be so glad when we are in a house of our own. Then I shall be able to give you everything you like for breakfast.

RUFUS. I don't see how we are ever to find a house.

JOSEPHINE. I thought you had decided on that one in Tunbridge Wells !

RUFUS. So I have. Signed the lease yesterday. Didn't I tell you?

JOSEPHINE. No, dear.

RUFUS. Oh!

JOSEPHINE (*kindly*). You must have forgotten.

RUFUS. I thought you knew.

JOSEPHINE. But if you have signed the lease the house is ours.

RUFUS. We shan't be able to stay in it.

JOSEPHINE. Why not, dear? Have you found out something about the drains?

RUFUS. The drains are all right. But the rates! Preposterous! Wicked! I never saw such a Government.

JOSEPHINE. I thought it was the County Council who fix the rates!

RUFUS. I don't care who it is, I won't pay.

JOSEPHINE. Well—at all events—it's a good thing we've *found* a house, for we shan't be able to stay *here* much longer—if Noel goes back soon to America.

RUFUS. Has he said when he's going?

JOSEPHINE. Not to *me*. But when he came home he said he should go back almost immediately. It's nearly a month since he came home.

RUFUS. Is he going to take Leila with him?

JOSEPHINE. I don't know, dear. He hasn't said. Nor has she. They are both so reticent now—about everything.

>(*Enter* LEILA. *She is graver and paler than before; she seems to have lost her gay and smiling manner.*)

LEILA. Good-morning.

JOSEPHINE. Good-morning, dear.

>(LEILA *crosses to the sideboard, raises the dish-covers, and looks inside the dishes.*)

RUFUS (*who has now finished his breakfast, says facetiously*). Overslept yourself this morning, Leila?

LEILA (*having decided not to have anything from the sideboard, goes to the table as she speaks*). I didn't sleep at all—the early part of the night, so I stayed in bed a little longer.

JOSEPHINE. What a very pretty dress you are wearing.

LEILA (*taking a very apathetic interest in her clothes*).

This? Yes—it is rather nice—isn't it? (*Pours herself out a cup of tea.*)

JOSEPHINE. I admire it extremely.

RUFUS. If you two are going to talk clothes, it's time I hooked it. (*Gathers up his paper and rises.*) I'll go and smoke a pipe with Noel. I suppose I shall find him in his studio.

LEILA (*helping herself to toast*). I expect so. He's always there at this time of the morning.

RUFUS. I'll go and rout the beggar out.

(*He goes.*)
(LEILA *eats her breakfast of tea and toast—* JOSEPHINE *watches her.*)

JOSEPHINE. Are you only eating toast, Leila?

LEILA. Yes. I'm not hungry.

JOSEPHINE. You look pale, dear!

LEILA (*not wishing to pursue this subject*). I'm all right, thank you.

JOSEPHINE. D'you think you go out enough?

LEILA (*looks up at* JOSEPHINE *as she says*). I thought I used to go out too much.

JOSEPHINE (*slightly embarrassed*). I meant—to take the air. (*Enter* HARRISON. HARRISON *pauses near the door when she sees* JOSEPHINE. JOSEPHINE, *attracted by* HARRISON'S *entrance, glances at her, then says.*) Oh—here's Harrison—come to clear away. (*Rises, picking up her letter.*) I'll go upstairs now and finish reading my letter. It's from Alice.

LEILA. Your daughter? Is she well?

JOSEPHINE. Very well, thank you. (*Going to the door.*) Very good news of them all, I'm glad to say!

(*She goes out.*)
(HARRISON *holds the door open for* JOSEPHINE, *then closes it after her, then comes towards* LEILA, *rather mysteriously, as if she had something important to say.*)

HARRISON (*behind table*). If you please, ma'am. It's Captain Harding. He's at the door. (LEILA *shows surprise and concern, but conceals her emotion from* HARRISON, *who continues without a pause.*) He wants to know if you can speak to him for five minutes.

LEILA. Why didn't you put him in the drawing-room?

HARRISON. He said he would stay where he was if I'd

bring you the message. I asked him if he didn't wish to go to the studio to Mr. Gale, and he said "No," he wanted to see *you.*

LEILA. You'd better show him in here.

HARRISON. Yes, ma'am.

(HARRISON *goes out, leaving the door open, and a moment later* MAURICE *enters. He looks pale and nervous and carries his hat and stick.* LEILA *and* MAURICE *are both agitated when they find themselves alone, face to face.*)

LEILA. You shouldn't have done this.

MAURICE. I couldn't help it. I *had* to see you. I waited in the whole of yesterday afternoon. You neither came nor sent word. I've been up nearly all night.

LEILA. What doing?

MAURICE. Watching your windows. (*She heaves a sigh and turns away from him, turning a little in her chair—much troubled.*) There was a light, till four o'clock this morning.

LEILA. I was reading—I couldn't sleep.

MAURICE. I can't go on like this. I never see you now. If you were here by yourself, or with the two old ones, it wouldn't matter so much. As it is—it's hell.

LEILA (*rising and moving a few steps from him*). I must be at home and behave myself properly—mustn't I?

MAURICE. If you cared for *me*—you couldn't! If you knew what I suffered—all day and all night. I shall clear out, change my regiment, and get sent abroad. It would be better never to see you if I can't have you to myself. I hate what I'm doing; making love to another man's wife. Does he know you've seen me since he came home?

LEILA. Yes.

MAURICE. Did you tell him?

LEILA. No. But I'm sure he knows.

MAURICE. What did he say?

LEILA (*turning to him*). Nothing. He *never* says anything. He hasn't said one word of anything *real* since the day he came home. It's simply awful the constraint between us. (MAURICE *looks at her, deliberately lays down his hat and stick on the chair, goes towards her, seizes her in his arms and kisses her passionately. She yields. When he releases her he kisses her hands.*) I'll meet you somewhere to-day.

MAURICE (*holding her hands*). Leila, listen, I'll bring the motor. Not here. I'll meet you with it opposite Chelsea Barracks at one o'clock !

LEILA. Why the motor ? Where are we going ?

MAURICE. We could go anywhere in the motor. We could go to Scotland or Dover and take the afternoon boat to France !

LEILA (*stares at him in amazement before she says*). Oh, but think—think ! That would be the end of everything !

MAURICE. I'm ready if you are.

(*Enter* NOEL. *He advances into the room, unsuspectingly, before he sees them, stops short suddenly, makes a dart towards* MAURICE, LEILA *gets between them.*)

LEILA. I asked him to come—I asked him to come and see *me*. (NOEL *stares at* LEILA, *while he thinks what to do, restraining himself from following his natural impulse to go for* MAURICE. LEILA *turns to* MAURICE.) I'm afraid you had better go.

(*She looks anxiously from* MAURICE *to* NOEL, *who speaks while* MAURICE *picks up his hat and stick.*)

NOEL (*to* MAURICE). Don't go. Wait for me—wait for me, please, in the drawing-room. (*As he turns away.*) I expect you know your way there !

(MAURICE *goes out, drawing the door to after him but not latching it.* NOEL *moves across the room.*)

LEILA (*as* MAURICE *has gone*). If you say one word to him about coming here or about anything at all to do with *me*—I'll take his part against you. You've a right to have *whom* you like in your own house or to turn any one out. You can order *me* out—but I won't have my friends insulted as long as I'm mistress here.

NOEL. Sit down, Leila, and listen to *me*. (LEILA *comes and sits in a chair, while* NOEL *goes to the door and latches it, then turns to her.*) This can't continue.

LEILA. It's the first time he's been here since you came home.

NOEL. I know that. I'm not talking about *him*—

but about *us*. No two people with any respect for themselves or each other, who once lived together from choice, could consent to live like this.

LEILA (*frightened by his intensity*). Noel! Listen! I've been careless. I've been indiscreet. I daresay you could scrape up evidence that would *ruin* me. I've been to his rooms, but he's not my *lover*. I swear— I *never*——

NOEL (*repudiating the suggestion*). I don't suspect you of *that*. Oh, no. Not *you*. But you're fond of him. You love him. Your thoughts fly to him though your body's here. (*She drops her eyes.*) You are a prisoner in my house. I'm your gaoler. When I was away and you were free to see him every day you were gay and light-hearted and happy. Now that I am at home again and you see him—seldom—you are listless and melancholy. I haven't asked you not to see him. I left you to judge for yourself. I don't *believe* you asked him here to-day. He *forced* his way into the house. I don't believe you asked him, because—since I was at home again—you *have* considered my position, and for that I thank you—for not humiliating me before people; but I can't accept *sacrifices*. If you think that *he* could make you happy. If you are both set on this—if it's serious— if it's for life—go to him. I'll serve you in the only way that's left me. I'll get out of your way. I shall be going back to America soon in any case. I can arrange to go—next Saturday. My work will keep me there some time—some months—perhaps a year. After that —I could take up with some woman or other for a bit— and stay over there. You can do the regulation thing —write me a letter—urging me to come back; I shall, of course, refuse—then—you can divorce me.

LEILA. I can't accept that, Noel. It isn't right that *you* should be put in the wrong for *me*—for what *I've* done.

NOEL. You *must* accept it. (*With great determination.*) I must ask you, please, to do this in the way I wish. (*With strong suppressed emotion.*) I won't have you dragged through the mud. Now—you had better go and talk it over with him. Arrange between you what you want to do—then—let me know. (*Enter* HARRISON *with a large tray. She hesitates when she sees* NOEL *and*

LEILA. NOEL *turns to* HARRISON *and says quite naturally.*) You can come in, Harrison. We've finished.
> (HARRISON *lays her tray on a chair and begins to put the things from the table on it.* LEILA *rises, pauses one moment, then goes slowly out of the room.*)
> (*Enter* JOSEPHINE *with her work-basket, as the maid is going.*)

JOSEPHINE (*stops near the door to say*). Oh! You haven't cleared the table yet. I'll take my sewing into the drawing-room.

NOEL (*turns to her quickly*). No, Aunt Josephine—please. Stay here—won't you? The drawing-room is occupied.

JOSEPHINE. Oh—very well, dear, I'll stay with *you* if I shan't be in your way.
> (*She sits in the armchair beside the fireplace. There is a short silence while* JOSEPHINE *takes her work out of her work-basket and begins to sew.* NOEL *stands on the hearth with his back to the fireplace, smoking.* HARRISON *returns, and continues clearing the sideboard.*)
>
> (*Enter* RUFUS.)

RUFUS (*excitedly as he comes towards* NOEL—*not noticing* HARRISON's *presence*). Do you know who's in the drawing-room?

NOEL. Yes, Uncle Rufus, I do. I sent them there.

RUFUS (*explosively*). What! (*Is checked by noticing* HARRISON's *presence.*) Oh! (*He watches* HARRISON, *staring at her every moment till she goes out with her tray. As soon as she has gone out* RUFUS *closes the door, then comes back and begins again.*) But what are you thinking of?

NOEL. I'll tell you directly. (*As* HARRISON *returns.*) Wait a minute.
> (HARRISON *finishes clearing.* RUFUS *watches her, then assists her by handing her plates, etc. He then grunts and sits down, with his left elbow resting upon the table. When* HARRISON *takes the cloth she tugs it a little to try and get it from under* RUFUS's *arm.* RUFUS *testily pushes up his side of the table-cloth when he feels* HARRISON *tugging, and the maid retires finally. As*

## DOORMATS

*soon as she has gone,* RUFUS *rises, closes the door; then he comes back to his chair.* RUFUS *and* JOSEPHINE *both turn to* NOEL, *looking at him for an explanation.*)

NOEL. Leila and I are going to separate.

(RUFUS *and* JOSEPHINE *stare in amazement, then look at each other, then at* NOEL.)

JOSEPHINE. You are going to divorce her?

NOEL. No. I am going to let her divorce *me*!

RUFUS (*in a perfect scream of fury*). What! You are going to let *her*—? Good heavens! Good heavens! Oh, no, Noel, no—you can't mean that. You don't mean that. (*To* JOSEPHINE.) He doesn't mean that!

NOEL. What else would you have me do? *I* can't make her happy.

RUFUS. What else would I have you do? Divorce *her*, of course. Expose her. *Threaten* her, anyway. Frighten her out of her wits. That would bring her to a standstill. Divorce you! As if *you* were the guilty party! Oh! it's grotesque! Of course she never considers you if this is the way you go on. If she knows that every time it comes to a pinch—you'll give way. For heaven's sake, Noel—reconsider!

(JOSEPHINE *rises*.)

NOEL (*goaded by* RUFUS's *violence*). It's no use talking, Uncle Rufus, I've made up my mind. I must do things my own way.

RUFUS. *Do* things your own way—but I hope you'll excuse me if I refuse to stay here and listen to such—*childishness.* I'll go to some place where it doesn't matter *who* hears my language.

(*He bangs out of the room.*)

(NOEL *leans on the mantelpiece, turned away from* JOSEPHINE. JOSEPHINE *glances at* NOEL. JOSEPHINE *moves across the room. She has nearly reached the door when* NOEL *speaks.*)

NOEL (*sits down*). Don't go, Aunt Josephine, please. (*She stops and turns to him.*) I'd rather not be alone while I'm waiting. (JOSEPHINE *looks at him as if she would like to go and comfort him, but she is too timid to do that, so she sits down again, lays down her workbasket on the table, and goes on with her sewing.*) Always working at something—aren't you?

JOSEPHINE (*as brightly as she can*). There is plenty to do. After the children, you know, there are the grandchildren.

NOEL. Do you think Uncle Rufus is right ?

JOSEPHINE (*stops sewing and considers her answer before she gives it, quietly but impressively*). What you are doing is the logical outcome of everything else.

NOEL. I've *always* given in ?

JOSEPHINE. You couldn't help it.

NOEL. She's the stronger ?

JOSEPHINE. It's not that. It has nothing to do with strength or weakness. Some people have a genius for giving. Others a talent for taking. You can't help being whichever kind you are, any more than you can change your sex. You and I are amongst those who *must give*. (*Quaintly, as she resumes her sewing.*) Doormats, I always call them to myself.

NOEL. I'm not a doormat, not usually—not in my business—nor in my dealings with *most* people—only with her.

JOSEPHINE. Every doormat is not everybody's doormat. But everybody is either a doormat—or else—the thing that tramples on the doormat.

NOEL (*suggests vaguely*). A boot !

JOSEPHINE (*with a faint smile*). Yes, I always wanted a name for them. Leila is a boot. So is your Uncle Rufus. They can't help it. Just as every one is either a man or a woman—not in the same degree of course—but there are *men* and *women*—(*illustrating with her hands*) at either end, as it were, of a long piece of string ; very mannish men at one end and very womanish women at the other. Then—as you go along—men with gentler, what we call feminine qualities—and women with masculine qualities—some with more and some with less—right along—till you come to a lot of funny little people in the middle that it's hard to tell what they are. Just so, it seems to me, is every one a more or less pronounced doormat or boot.

NOEL. She wasn't always a boot. When we were first married and while we were engaged—Leila was quite as much of a doormat as *I* was.

JOSEPHINE. Oh, my dear ! that's where they are so clever. (*Turning more directly to* NOEL.) Leila wanted your love. So she set to work the surest way to gain it. She pretended to be a doormat. That's what they do, if it serves their own purposes. Oh, *yes*; they come after *us* just as often as we go after them.

NOEL. When she got me where she wanted me—she gave up! She didn't need to trouble any more.

JOSEPHINE (*removes her spectacles, speaking slowly and impressively, as if she were formulating a new idea*). It is not so much that *they* dominate *us*. They don't, as it were, knock us down and trample on us. It is *we* who wilfully lay ourselves down to be trampled upon. We *love* being trampled upon. It thrills us to give and it bores us to take. It's of no use *knowing*—with one's brain—how to take if one hasn't got their *instinct*—for as soon as a great emotion surges within us, it sweeps all our knowledge away and reveals what we are —doormats!

NOEL (*rises and goes over to the fireplace*). It's not very comforting to know that if I had been as wise as Solomon—I couldn't have helped it.

JOSEPHINE. I'm sorry for *you*.

NOEL. Don't *you* ever find it hard?

JOSEPHINE (*smiles happily, but a serious, contented smile*). Oh, no! So long as I have somebody to serve— I am content. They were always very good to me about that—your uncle and the children—they always allowed me to do things for them. It must have been very tiresome for them at times to have me fussing after them so much. One can be just as exacting in giving as in taking. It wouldn't have amused me at all to be married to another doormat. I want some one who will take from me and indulge my passion for giving. (*Very gravely, as if she were looking far away.*) I'm sure I don't know what I should have done if Rufus had ever wanted to leave me. I gave him everything I had— long ago. (*Very humbly and gently and quietly.*) Thank God! he never strayed from me.

> (LEILA *comes slowly into the room, leaving the door open behind her.* JOSEPHINE *looks from one to the other, then gathers up her work, rises, and crosses to* NOEL, *squeezes his arm, goes towards the door, and pats* LEILA'S *arm as she passes her; then she goes out.*)

LEILA. He's coming directly. He will tell you himself—what we have decided. (*Sits down at the table, turned rather towards the audience so as not to face* NOEL.)
     (*Enter* MAURICE. *He looks from one to the other, closes the door, then goes quietly towards* NOEL *as far as the upper corner of the table.*)
MAURICE. Mrs. Gale has told me what you have offered to do, and I must say—before I go any further—it is most generous——

NOEL (*interrupting him impatiently*). Cut all that, please! (*Controls himself, then says quietly.*) All right, go on, I'm listening. Please sit down.
     (MAURICE *sits.* NOEL *remains standing on the hearth.*)
MAURICE. I can't accept your offer. I cannot allow *any* man to blacken himself for *me*.

NOEL. It's not for *you* I'm doing it!

MAURICE (*conciliatingly*). I'm aware of that! But I can't in any way take advantage of it. We should prefer to go away — and for *you* to divorce Mrs. Gale!

NOEL. That's not my offer.

LEILA. We can't accept your offer, Noel.

MAURICE. We have decided to take this step with a full knowledge of the consequences. I quite realise all that it means—leaving the army—and giving up—practically everything. (LEILA *turns her head slowly to look at* MAURICE. *He looks at her as he says.*) I am more than willing. (*She looks away. He says to* NOEL.) I shall endeavour in every way to do *my* part.

NOEL. And my wife? what about *her*? Her future? What is *that* to be?

MAURICE (*rather surprised*). I shall marry Mrs. Gale—of course—as soon as ever she is free. You don't doubt that, surely?

NOEL. We are none of us doubting each other's words or right intentions. But I'm looking beyond. (*Turning to* MAURICE.) I want to know what provision you propose for *her*?

MAURICE. As to that—I don't mind telling you exactly what my income is. I can't say to a penny without referring to some books, but I'll get my lawyer to draw up a thing and send it you. (*He says the following quite modestly, merely stating a fact, not very tactfully, but with no intention to give offence.*) I can assure you *now*, though, that Mrs. Gale will be considerably better off than she *has* been. And it's all *mine*. I mean to say— it's not an allowance. It's all right.

NOEL (*who has been taking this in carefully and considers thoughtfully as he replies*). Yes, yes, I see. Thanks. I knew that you could offer her much more than I have as yet been able to. But her *life* ? Her future position ?

MAURICE (*puzzled*). Settlements ? I shall be delighted to make a settlement.

NOEL. I'm sure you'll do all that's correct and even generous, but——

LEILA (*to* MAURICE). He means that the position of a divorced woman is—well—you know what it is. That's what he's thinking about.

MAURICE. I know. So am I. But I told you all along that I couldn't accept his offer.

LEILA. Neither can I. He mustn't be allowed to sacrifice himself for *us*.

NOEL. Please leave *me* to decide what *I* should do. I want to know what *he* proposes for *you*.

MAURICE. We should go abroad, I suppose, at first. We haven't decided where yet. Eventually, we may, I hope, be able to live it down. Some people do. Especially—(*glancing at* LEILA)—people like *us*—who, if I may say so, are both rather popular.

NOEL (*facing them*). Some people never live it down. (*To* MAURICE.) You are rich, I know, but you aren't rich enough to buy your way back. (*To* LEILA.) Some divorced women are for ever shunned and despised and condemned. (*To both.*) It's to make provision against that that I say unless you accept my conditions she stays here. Until I am satisfied that she goes to a better home than she leaves, I won't set her free. If you take things in your own hands, I won't divorce her. What shall you do then ?

MAURICE (*after a little reflection*). Of course—if you say you *won't* divorce her—we *must* accept your conditions.

LEILA (*positively*). No ; I refuse.

MAURICE (*to* LEILA). But we can't, for *your* sake——

LEILA (*interrupting him*). *I* am the best judge of that. It is for *me* he proposes to sacrifice himself.

MAURICE. I know—but don't you see—if *you* won't divorce *him* and *he* won't divorce *you*—and we go away together—it means—we can never be married.

LEILA. I quite realise what *my* position would be.

MAURICE. It is hardly necessary to assure you, I hope, that—under all circumstances—I should stand by you—but still, I don't think it is out of place to remind you that there is also *my* position to be considered. You see—in any case—I'm giving up a great deal.

LEILA. I'm giving up more than *you* are.

MAURICE. I'm not so sure.

LEILA. What! Look what I'm losing. Everything a woman holds dear.

MAURICE. I know—I know—but still—you'll have *me*.

LEILA. Yes—and you'll have *me*.

MAURICE. Couldn't you persuade her to accept your terms?

NOEL. *I? I* persuade her? Why should she heed me now? She never did in the past. If she were willing to be led by me—should we be where we are? *I can't persuade her*—but *you—you*—you are made of such different stuff. (MAURICE *turns again to* LEILA, *who is still uncompromising.*) Ask her.

LEILA. It's no use.

NOEL. Tell her. Impose your will on hers. That's what women adore. They don't like men to give in to them.

MAURICE. We had better discuss this quietly later on.

NOEL. Oh, no. I must know now.

MAURICE (*rising*). You know *my* decision.

LEILA. And you know *mine*.

MAURICE. We can't *both* have our own way.

LEILA. No—we *can't*.

MAURICE. How are we ever to get on——?

LEILA (*interrupting him and finishing his sentence*). Exactly. If as soon as I make up my mind and am *thoroughly determined*, you take the other side and oppose me. What sort of a life should we have together?

MAURICE. That's what I'm beginning to ask myself.

LEILA. We should fight every day of the week—if you are never going to give in to me.

MAURICE. I am not accustomed to giving in—to any one.

LEILA. Nor am I.

MAURICE. He offers to sacrifice himself. He's willing.

LEILA. And you? Aren't you willing to sacrifice *yourself*? Isn't it worth everything in the world to get me?

MAURICE. Well——

(MAURICE *hesitates.* LEILA *draws back from him with a prolonged*)

LEILA. Oh!

MAURICE (*seeing his mistake, goes towards her and says quickly*). Of course it is—listen—look here.

LEILA (*avoiding him*). No, no, don't come near me. I've done with you.

MAURICE. You might at least let me explain.

LEILA. You have explained. You'll take me all right if I'll come on your terms, as long as you don't suffer. At last I see you as you really are—thoroughly selfish.

MAURICE. Selfish! I selfish! If either of us are selfish, it's not me. However, if that's your opinion, there's nothing left for me but to go. (*Opens door.*) If you change your mind I am still at your service, always ready to do the right thing.

(*He goes out.*)

LEILA. What a mercy I found him out in time. Think, think, what a life he'd have led me. Nothing but rows, incessant rows—the—the—I don't know any name bad enough to call him.

NOEL. He's a boot.

LEILA. Oh, don't talk nonsense. How could I ever be so mad as to think, even for one moment, of giving up—all that I have—for him. Oh, Noel, Noel! (*Lays her head on her arms on table.*)

NOEL. How can you turn to me for comfort now, after all that you've done to me? Because some one else doesn't want you, you think you can come back—and that I shall be waiting just where you want me. How can you expect such a thing? Before you tired of me and preferred him, no sacrifice was hard—because I loved you, and you were mine. You've never realised what it means to be able to get on with a man like that, or with a woman like yourself—constant patience, self-effacement, sacrifice—oh, not unwilling sacrifice, when it is for love—but still somebody's got to be always playing up to you, if you are still to remain the splendid, dashing, wilful creatures the world admires. You can't do it without us.

LEILA. It's too late, now. What a thing it's been for me always having you. When I was sitting at the table there, and you defended me and looked after all my interests so—I realised how you had always thought of me before yourself—and the difference between you and him, and I couldn't let you degrade yourself—Noel, whatever became of him; I didn't do that.

NOEL. I haven't forgotten.

LEILA. I need you, Noel. I do, indeed. I'm no good without you. (*Buries her head on her arms on table.*)

NOEL. You're finding it out at last, Leila.

LEILA. What?

NOEL. That the boots need their doormats just as much as the doormats need their boots.

(NOEL *goes up to the door, hesitates once or twice, then suddenly comes down behind* LEILA, *takes her face in his two hands, bends down and kisses her. Then he goes quickly to the door.*)

CURTAIN.

# OUTCAST

A PLAY IN FOUR ACTS

PROGRAMME OF THE FIRST PRODUCTION

AT

WYNDHAM'S THEATRE, LONDON

OUTCAST

A PLAY IN FOUR ACTS

BY

HUBERT HENRY DAVIES

PRODUCED ON SEPTEMBER 1, 1914

| | |
|---|---|
| *Geoffrey* | MR. GERALD DU MAURIER |
| *Hugh* | MR. ARTHUR WONTNER |
| *Tony* | MR. GEOFFREY KERR |
| *Taylor* | MR. JULES SHAW |
| *Miriam* | MISS ETHEL LEVEY |
| *Valentine* | MISS GRACE LANE |
| *Nelly* | MISS UNA VENNING |
| *Maid* | MISS MAUD BUCHANAN |

Act I.—Geoffrey's flat in Piccadilly.

Act II.—The same, three months later.

Act III.—Miriam's Maisonette, fifteen months later.

Act IV.—Same as Acts I. & II., three weeks later.

# OUTCAST

## THE FIRST ACT

SCENE.—*The sitting-room of a small bachelor's flat, several floors up, overlooking Piccadilly. There is visible a small entrance hall with an outer door opening on to the landing and an inner door opening into the sitting-room. There are some overcoats and hats hanging on pegs in the entrance hall and an umbrella-stand with walking-sticks and umbrellas. Nearer at hand is a door opening into the bedroom. At the back there is a window which overlooks Piccadilly. There are some thin curtains drawn over the lower half of this window. There is on one side of the room a fireplace with a low fender which one can sit upon with comfort, and upon the other is a sideboard, with whisky and brandy decanters, several syphons of soda water, and some tumblers, also a plate of sandwiches, and a dish of fruit. A table, with writing materials and a disorder of papers upon it, is in the centre of the room. An ordinary chair stands behind this table, and armchairs are near it. On the far side of the room from the fireplace is a sofa; there is also other furniture, including a window-seat. This is the sitting-room of the small flat which* GEOFFREY SHERWOOD *rents furnished. The furniture is good enough, but ordinary. The room has an air of comfort owing to the presence of* GEOFFREY'S *own belongings. It is late at night, almost midnight. The electric light is turned off, and the curtains are drawn over the lower half of the window. The room is empty, and is very faintly lighted by the fire in the grate and the lights in the street below.*

*The electric bell at the entrance rings.*
*Enter* TAYLOR.

TAYLOR *is the valet to* GEOFFREY *and also to the other men who occupy the other flats in the building. He is a middle-aged man, and a good creature with a well-trained servant's manner. He enters from the bedroom stealthily, treading carefully so as not to make a noise. He closes the door after him noiselessly, then crosses to the entrance, turns on the electric light, and opens the front door.*

*Enter* HUGH BROWN.

HUGH *is a young barrister about thirty—about* GEOFFREY'S *age. He wears his day clothes—his high hat and his black coat.*

HUGH. Good-evening, Taylor.

TAYLOR. Good-evening, sir.

HUGH (*coming down towards the table*). Is Mr. Sherwood in?

TAYLOR (*closes the outer door and comes towards* HUGH *before he answers*). Mr. Sherwood is asleep, sir.

HUGH (*a little surprised*). Gone to bed—has he?

TAYLOR. No, sir, not yet—not properly. He's lying on his bed half-dressed. He's been there for the last four hours.

HUGH. All evening?

TAYLOR. Yes, sir. It was soon after seven that he dropped off.

HUGH (*laying down his hat and umbrella*). I'm glad to hear that he *could* drop off. I was afraid that to-night he'd be feeling like anything else but that. I suppose you know what's been happening to-day?

TAYLOR. Yes, sir — not from anything that Mr. Sherwood told me, but I saw in the evening papers that Miss Valentine Guest had been getting married.

HUGH. Yes. I thought Mr. Sherwood might be feeling depressed. That's why I came round so late.

TAYLOR. I see, sir.

HUGH. I rang him up several times during the evening, but they told me they could get no answer.

TAYLOR. That was because the last time I came up to have a look at Mr. Sherwood—hearing the telephone bell ringing—and being afraid it might wake him up,

I took the receiver off the hook and laid it on the table.

HUGH. He must have been sleeping soundly if he didn't hear the telephone.

TAYLOR (*looks steadily and gravely at* HUGH *as he replies*). Oh, sir! It isn't real sleep. It's drugs. (*Takes a small box of cachets from his pocket and shows it to* HUGH *as he comes towards him.*) I found this box in his room—cachets, I think they call them.

HUGH (*takes the box from* TAYLOR *and looks at it before he says*). I've urged him over and over again not to take these things.

(*Lays the box of cachets on the table.*)

TAYLOR (*picking the box up as he speaks*). I know you have, sir—so have I. But if he won't listen to *you*, it's not much use *me* talking. I do what I can. Whenever I find the nasty things I take them downstairs and pitch 'em behind the kitchen fire. If he asks me for them I say I don't know anything about them—haven't seen them. (*Puts the box in his pocket again as he continues.*) That may be very wrong, sir, but I don't know what else to do. I haven't the time to look after Mr. Sherwood as I'd like to. It's not as if I was only his servant. There's the other gentlemen in the other flats to attend to. It would take a man all his time to keep Mr. Sherwood away from the drugs and the drink. It's a sad pity, sir, to see a nice gentleman like him going this way.

HUGH. He's only begun it since—well, the last few weeks?

TAYLOR. I never knew him to so much as look at a drug before, nor to take a drop too much of anything on any occasion. It's only since—lately.

HUGH. Since his engagement was broken off?

TAYLOR (*discreetly making a pretence of arranging some of the things on the table as he replies*). I can't say, sir. I don't know exactly when that was, Mr. Sherwood didn't tell me.

HUGH. Oh, I thought you'd be sure to know.

TAYLOR. I guessed what had happened. I couldn't help noticing when the letters and telephone messages stopped coming and going. And also—Miss Valentine used to come here to tea sometimes, with her mother or some other lady. She hasn't been since Christmas, and one day, it was somewhere about the end of January, all her photos, which he used to have stuck about his rooms, disappeared. That was the way I guessed—from things like that and from the change in Mr. Sherwood. He never chaffs me now when I call him in the morning.

HUGH. But it wasn't all at once—I mean—it wasn't *immediately* after his engagement was broken off that he began taking drugs?

TAYLOR. No, sir. He kept up bravely for a time—and then—I suppose he found that he couldn't sleep. And it's only in the last three weeks that he's always at the whisky, I suppose that's to stop him thinking.

HUGH. He attends to his business. He goes to the City every day—doesn't he?

TAYLOR. Mostly every day. This afternoon he was working at home—studying his financial reports and writing letters at this table here—from two o'clock on.

HUGH (*more to himself than to* TAYLOR). While Valentine was getting married!

TAYLOR. He finished at about six. Then he had a bit of something to eat. He'd had no lunch. When I came up to clear away he was lying down on his bed asleep, where he is still.

HUGH. Aren't *you* wanting to go to bed? Isn't it getting rather late?

TAYLOR. It's past my usual time, sir—and if you were thinking of staying——

HUGH. Yes—all right—I'll stay. I'll be here when he wakes up.

TAYLOR. Thank you, sir. I should feel easier in my mind if I knew that one of his friends was with him.

(*The entrance bell rings, and immediately afterwards there is a violent knocking on the door and a young man's voice shouting.*)

TONY (*without*). Geoffrey! Geoffrey!

HUGH (*hurriedly to* TAYLOR). That's Mr. Hewlett. Go and open the door at once and tell him not to make such a noise.

(TAYLOR *opens the door.*)

(*Enter* TONY HEWLETT. TONY *is a cheerful, nice-looking boy of twenty-three. He is smartly dressed in his evening clothes. He wears an overcoat and an opera hat set rakishly on his head.*)

(TAYLOR *makes signs to* TONY *to come in quietly, but* TONY *does not notice these, and comes gaily towards* HUGH, *exclaiming.*)

TONY. Hullo, Hugh! Where's Geoffrey?

HUGH. Don't make such a row, you fool. Geoffrey's asleep.

TONY. Oh, is he? I'm awfully sorry.

HUGH. You should come in more quietly.

TONY. How was I to know he was asleep? This is no time to be in bed—midnight.

HUGH. He's not in bed. He's lying down. He's been taking a sleeping draught.

TONY. Poor old thing. (*Taking off his overcoat and hat, and laying them down near* HUGH's *hat and umbrella as he speaks.*) He must have been having a devil of a day.

TAYLOR. If you two gentlemen are staying I'll bid you both good-night.

HUGH. Good-night, Taylor.

TONY. Good-night, Taylor. Pleasant dreams.

TAYLOR. Thank you, sir.

(TAYLOR *goes out, shutting the inner and outer doors after him.*)

TONY. I'm awfully sorry for poor old Geoffrey. I wonder where he keeps his cigarettes?

(*Hunts about for cigarettes.*)

HUGH (*taking his cigarette case from his pocket*). I've got some here.

TONY. All right, thanks. I've found them.

(*Helps himself to a cigarette from a box which he finds on the sideboard, lights it, and then sits down.*)

(HUGH *watches him, but does not speak until* TONY *is seated.*)

HUGH. Are you going to stay?

TONY. Yes, of course. I'm going to stay till Geoffrey wakes up. Aren't you?

HUGH. Yes, but I wonder if *you'd* better.

TONY. Why shouldn't I if *you* do?

HUGH. Well, because you're a very nice child, Tony,

and we're all very fond of you, but you do sometimes get on our nerves, and if I were in Geoffrey's situation I doubt if I could stand *you*.

TONY. Geoffrey wants livening up. I'm better at that than *you* are. You are all very well in your way, Hugh. You are one of the knobs on the backbone of England, and I'm more the life and soul of the party. Will you have a drink?

(*Goes to the sideboard and proceeds to pour out two whiskies and sodas.*)

HUGH. Yes, please. A little one.

TONY. It was seeing the light twinkling in this window that brought me up here: that and my thirst, and feeling so sorry for poor old Geoffrey. I couldn't help thinking about him all the time at the wedding.

HUGH. Were you at the wedding?

TONY (*bringing the two tumblers of whisky and soda to the table*). Yes. I thought I should have seen you there.

HUGH. You thought I'd have gone to Valentine's wedding! Good heavens! I should think not, indeed.

TONY. Weren't you asked?

HUGH. They asked every one they knew, I think, but *I* wasn't going to be seen there—after the way she's treated Geoffrey.

TONY. It wasn't very nice I must admit, but, after all, if Valentine chooses to break off her engagement it's none of my business. And then, you see, her family and mine are very old friends. I've known Valentine much longer than I've known Geoffrey, and I'm very fond of her. I think she's a dear.

HUGH. Do you? I think she's hateful.

TONY. You only say that out of loyalty to Geoffrey. Everybody else thinks she's charming.

HUGH. Charming! Oh, yes. She is pretty and attractive, she knows how to please—(*getting more and more incensed as he continues his speech*) but a girl who could be engaged for over a year to a good fellow like Geoffrey and then throw him over for no other reason than because he's poor and she gets a chance to marry a rich baronet!

TONY. He's not such a bad sort of fellow—Sir John Morland.

HUGH. He's a bore.

TONY. He's a good sportsman, and he's done his share of public service—been a magistrate and the High Sheriff of his county and something or other in the Territorials.

HUGH. Don't make excuses for her, Tony.

TONY. I'm *not* making excuses. I don't want to take sides one way or the other, but you must see that she's only done what people do. I don't say she's right to throw over Geoffrey in order to make a good marriage, but, after all—there's a good deal of difference between being Lady Morland or the wife of an obscure business man.

HUGH. Geoffrey's clever and young. He'd have got on if she'd given him time. I'm told by people who ought to know that he shows quite unusual ability in finance, and is likely to do extremely well—*was* likely to do well.

TONY. I shouldn't wonder if old mother Guest has a good deal to do with breaking off Valentine's engagement.

HUGH. Girls marry whom they like nowadays and not whom their mothers tell them. I can't make any allowances for her when I think of Geoffrey. When I think of what he was and what he is—going to the devil as fast as he can with drink and drugs. That's Valentine's work. We have to thank *her* for that.

TONY. Does he talk to you much about it?

HUGH. No. Never a word. When she broke it off he wrote and told me, and asked me never to mention it to him. When we meet it's understood between us, taken for granted, that's all. I can see he doesn't want me to condole with him.

TONY. Fancy loving a girl as much as that!

HUGH. And fancy that girl not caring!

TONY. I'm rather sorry I went to her wedding now. I think I ought to have taken a stand like you.

HUGH. I shouldn't let Geoffrey know you were there if I were you.

TONY (*consciously putting on airs*). My dear fellow, how can I hide the fact? It is published in half the evening papers. "Among those present were Lady Crowborough, General Ames, Sir Charles Trotter, *and* Mr. Anthony Hewlett."

HUGH. Look out, Tony. I think I hear him moving about in the next room.
> (*They both pause and listen, looking towards the door.*)
> (*Enter* GEOFFREY SHERWOOD. GEOFFREY *is a young man of about thirty, and the traces of his recent way of living are clearly visible in his face and demeanour. He is pale and hollow-eyed. His movements are slow and uncertain, and he hardly seems to attend to what is said. He wears a smoking-suit and bedroom slippers and a silk handkerchief round his neck, and he hasn't brushed his hair. He tries to appear at ease before the others, but he cannot smile. He looks at them before he speaks, and they both appear rather anxious and nervous though determined to appear normal.*)

GEOFFREY. Hullo. (*He closes the door, and then goes towards* HUGH *as he says.*) It's very good of you to come and look me up. Have you got what you want to drink?

HUGH. Yes, thanks.

TONY. We helped ourselves.

GEOFFREY. Don't you want some cigarettes?

TONY. Thanks.

HUGH. Thanks.
> (GEOFFREY *carries the cigarette-box to the table and sets it down between them, standing between them behind the table.*)

GEOFFREY. What have you been doing all day, Hugh?

HUGH. I was in court most of the time.

GEOFFREY. Were you briefed?

HUGH. Yes. We had rather an amusing case.
> (HUGH *tells the following story with exaggerated animation, not because he thinks it is a particularly good story, but in his attempt to appear cheerful.*)
> (TONY *plays up to him with smiles and nods and occasional laughs and interjections.*)
> (GEOFFREY *standing between them appears to be attending, but he hardly hears. He looks from one to the other when they speak, but the ex-*

*pression of his face makes no response to what is said. Part way through the narrative he goes slowly to the sideboard, pours out a whisky and soda, then turns to them, leaning against the sideboard with his glass in his hand as the narrative finishes.)*

HUGH. It was an action brought by a firm of upholsterers against a man called Thompson for some work they had done in his house, which he said they hadn't done properly, and so he refused to pay. It wasn't a large amount, sixty pounds — nothing to Thompson. He's rich and a good business man, but, like most of us, he prides himself most on being what he isn't. He wanted to shine as a wit. When the case was being prepared he made a joke. This morning in court I was leading him and he wouldn't be led. I couldn't think what he was up to. He was leading up to his silly joke. I'd forgotten all about it till—*apropos* of nothing—out it came. The judge was furious, pounced upon him and rebuked him severely for levity. Poor Thompson spat and spluttered and went purple in the face, and gave his evidence so badly the jury thought he was lying and he lost his case which he ought to have won.

TONY. I wish I'd been there to see him make an ass of himself.

GEOFFREY (*to* TONY). *You* were at the wedding.

TONY (*taken by surprise is a little disconcerted and echoes weakly*). The wedding!

GEOFFREY. Valentine's wedding. I read in the paper that among those present was Mr. Anthony Hewlett.

TONY. Oh, yes. I looked in for a minute.

GEOFFREY. Did you go to the church?

TONY. Yes. I looked in there too.

GEOFFREY. Did Valentine look nice?

TONY. Very—very nice indeed.

GEOFFREY. Radiant, happy—smiling?

TONY. I didn't notice that she smiled much.

GEOFFREY. She had a fine day.

TONY. A lovely day.

GEOFFREY. The sun shone on her. Why are you looking so glum, Hugh?

HUGH (*smiles*). Was I looking glum? I didn't know it.

GEOFFREY (*addressing both of them*). You thought you'd find me sunk in the depths of despair on Valentine's wedding night. Oh, no—that's all over. I *was* in despair three months ago—naturally. It's not nice to be chucked. It's damned disagreeable. But I hope I've got more pride than to break my heart over losing a girl who cares no more about me than *she* does. I should be a mean-spirited devil if I were still crying my eyes out because my girl went off with another fellow. Besides—you don't love a girl the way I loved Valentine —if you can't respect her. I don't respect her. How can I ? Neither she nor any of the women of her class who do what she's done—sell themselves for a title and three houses. I see no difference between them and those poor wretches down below there walking the pavements of Piccadilly. (*The passion goes out of him. He becomes listless again as he says.*) Have another drink, Hugh.

HUGH. No thanks, old boy.

GEOFFREY. Tony ?

(HUGH, *unseen by* GEOFFREY, *shakes his head at* TONY.)

TONY. No thanks.

GEOFFREY. Then I must drink by myself. (*Goes to the sideboard and fills up his glass again as he says.*) That's how I feel about Valentine. (*Sits on the end of the sofa with his glass in his hand as he continues.*) So don't waste your sympathy on *me*, you fellows. I know why you came here to-night, to sit with me, to cheer me up, to pity me. It was very nice of you. I appreciate it, but it's not necessary. I'm all right. (*Drinks.*)

TONY (*pleasantly*). Would you rather we got out—Hugh and I ?

GEOFFREY. No, no. Stay here—stay just as long as you like. I'm not going to bed for hours yet. I've had my sleep. (*Drinks again.*)

HUGH. Would you like a game of anything ?

GEOFFREY (*echoes*). A game ?

TONY. Auction ?

GEOFFREY. We're only three.

HUGH. We could ring up Basil and see if he's there.

TONY. Yes. Bright idea, Hugh. Basil's a late one. He's sure not to be in bed yet.

GEOFFREY. He won't be at home.

HUGH (*making a move to rise as he says*). I'll find out—shall I ?

GEOFFREY. No—never mind. I don't think I want to play cards. My head's queer. I was working rather hard this afternoon. (*Drains his glass again, then says after a pause.*) I'm sorry I'm not better company. It must be damned dull for you here.

TONY. No—it isn't.

HUGH. We're quite happy.

GEOFFREY. I wish you'd drink up. Tony !

TONY. No, thank you.

GEOFFREY. Hugh !

HUGH. I don't want any more, thanks. (GEOFFREY *rises, turns to the sideboard and begins to refill his glass.* HUGH *watches him rather anxiously.*) I say, old fellow, don't have any more.

GEOFFREY. Why not ?

HUGH. Don't you think you've had about enough ?

GEOFFREY. I want it. I'm thirsty.

HUGH (*rises and goes towards* GEOFFREY *as he speaks*). It's so bad for you—taking one drink after another. You've got a headache already. You'll only make yourself ill. It's senseless.

(GEOFFREY, *setting his glass down, turns angrily on* HUGH. *He moves about during his speech to give vent to his feelings. When once he gets started he is so nervous and wrought up he seems as if he couldn't stop, keeps coming to a full stop as if he had finished and then returning again to the attack.* HUGH, *near the sideboard, bears it all patiently.*)

(TONY *leans his head on his hands and looks down at the table-cloth, embarrassed.*)

GEOFFREY. Shut up, Hugh ! You're always at it, telling me what I ought to do. . . . Last week I was to go out of London—see fresh scenes and new faces. A lot of good *that* would do me. . . . How can I get away ? I'm not a millionaire, I've got to stay here and work. I can't afford to go away. You know that perfectly well . . . and there's no need for me to get out of London. . . . Now I'm not to have a drink ! Good heavens ! Haven't I lived by myself and looked after myself for ten years? I can take care of myself all right without any interference from you or from any one, I don't want telling. (*At his loudest and angriest.*) Leave me alone, Hugh—d'you hear? *Leave me alone!* (*The rest is an angry mumble as he goes to the window, opens it, and sits on the window seat looking out.*) I'm sick of being told what I ought to do and advised and interfered with.

> (*There is a long pause after this outbreak before* TONY *speaks. During the pause* HUGH *sits on the end of the sofa nearest* TONY.)

TONY. Suppose we all go out? What d'you say, Geoffrey?

GEOFFREY (*whose anger is now spent, says drearily*). Whatever you like. I'll go out with you or stay here—it's all the same to me.

HUGH. What's the good of going out now? Every place is shut.

TONY. We could prowl about the streets.

GEOFFREY (*grimly*). Yes—and insult people. Why not? I should rather like to insult some one.

TONY. Come on then. Get some clothes on.

> (GEOFFREY *is leaning out of the window, so he does not respond to this.*)

> (HUGH *rises to detain* TONY, *speaking aside to him.*)

HUGH. Don't let us take him out.

TONY. Why?

HUGH. He'll only get us all locked up.

> (HUGH *and* TONY *separate when* GEOFFREY *speaks.*)

GEOFFREY. It's raining.

TONY. Is it?

GEOFFREY. Let's stay where we are.

TONY. All right.

> (*Kneels on the window seat looking out.*)

GEOFFREY. Give me a drink, Hugh. (*Sits watching* HUGH, *taking a savage pleasure in making* HUGH *bring him a drink.* HUGH *obediently but reluctantly fills up* GEOFFREY'S *glass and gives it to him.*) Give yourself one.

> (HUGH *pours out a drink for himself, then sits down again by the table. After a moment's silence, during which* GEOFFREY *and* HUGH *sip their*

*drinks,* TONY *turns suddenly to them and exclaims.*)

TONY. I think I could pot that policeman.

(*Hurries to the sideboard, seizes a syphon, returns to the window with it, takes aim, and squirts at somebody down in the street.*)

(HUGH *is amused by this little diversion and watches what* TONY *does, but* GEOFFREY *sits gloomily holding his glass.*)

(*When* TONY *has squirted the syphon through the window he peers cautiously out, then draws back, suddenly horrified as he exclaims to the others.*)

Oh, I say! I hit a woman. I squirted it right on her hat. (*Peers out of the window again and calls down.*) Sorry!

HUGH. What does she say?

TONY. Nothing. She's just standing there looking up.

GEOFFREY. What's she like?

TONY. Not bad.

GEOFFREY. Tell her to come up here.

TONY (*turns to* GEOFFREY). D'you mean it?

GEOFFREY. Yes. She might be amusing. It's some one to talk to anyway.

TONY (*calls through the window*). Come up!

GEOFFREY. You'll have to go down and let her in, the front door's closed.

TONY (*calls through the window*). Wait a minute.

(TONY *hurries to the sideboard, deposits the syphon, then goes out, leaving both doors open.*)

GEOFFREY. I'm sorry I lost my temper with you, Hugh.

HUGH. That doesn't matter. I've forgotten all about it.

GEOFFREY. I know you think I drink to drown my sorrows. That was what made me angry—because I don't—it's not for that. That may have been the reason once—but not now. I don't care now; I don't feel anything. I'm like a man who has had his arm or his leg amputated. He recovers; he doesn't feel pain; but he's not the same man that he was before: he's marked; he's maimed for life. Something vital has gone out of me—and left me so bored. If I could only think of anything to do that would be the least bit interesting. (*He drinks slowly.* HUGH *watches him, then drinks to keep him company. Then* GEOFFREY *says in a matter-of-fact tone.*) I wonder what Tony's up to.

HUGH. I'll just see if I can see him. (*Goes to the window and looks out.*)

TONY (*heard outside*). Come along, here we are. This is it. Come in. (*Enter* TONY, *grinning. He says to* GEOFFREY). I think she's a bit suspicious.

GEOFFREY (*calls out*). Come in. It's all right.

(*Enter* MIRIAM. *She is a young woman, tawdrily dressed in cheap and ostentatious finery, but with an eye for effect. She carries a small metal bag. In spite of the vulgarity of her dress she looks interesting. Her face is sensitive and intelligent though too flagrantly " made up." She enters very slowly and is reserved and suspicious and rather hostile at first. She does not advance very far, but remains standing near the door as she looks at the room and at her three unknown companions.*)

GEOFFREY. Good-evening.

(MIRIAM *looks at* GEOFFREY, *and gives a half nod in answer to his salutation, but without smiling.*)

HUGH. Good-evening.

(MIRIAM *looks at* HUGH *and repeats the same business.*)

MIRIAM (*suspiciously*). What is it? What d'you want?

GEOFFREY. We thought you'd come and talk to us.

MIRIAM. That all?

GEOFFREY. That's all. Sit down—won't you?

MIRIAM (*ungraciously*). I don't mind.

GEOFFREY. Have a drink. (*She looks at* GEOFFREY, *who says to* TONY). Get her a whisky and soda, Tony.

(TONY *goes to the sideboard prepared to pour out a whisky and soda.*)

MIRIAM. No.

TONY (*pleasantly*). Don't you want a whisky and soda?

MIRIAM. No.

GEOFFREY. There's brandy.

MIRIAM. I don't want brandy.

GEOFFREY. Won't you have anything to drink at all?

MIRIAM. If you had some coffee, I'd take a cup.

GEOFFREY. I haven't got any up here, and it's too late to ask for it. Everybody's gone to bed.

MIRIAM. Never mind. It doesn't matter much. (*She slowly takes off her hat, examines it carefully, then looks at* TONY.)

TONY. I hope I didn't do much damage.

MIRIAM (*with the faintest smile curling her lips*). It don't exactly improve it to have it trimmed with soda water.

TONY. Let me dry it for you by the fire. (*Holds out his hand for the hat.*)

MIRIAM (*giving him the hat with some reluctance*). Careful.

TONY (*taking the hat*). All right. (*He holds the hat to the fire to dry.* MIRIAM *leans forward in her chair watching him anxiously.*)

MIRIAM. Shake it. (TONY *shakes the hat in front of the fire.*) Not that way. Give it to me. (*Takes the hat from* TONY *and shakes it gently in front of the fire, sitting on the fender as she does so. She looks up at* TONY *and smiles faintly again as she says.*) Sorry to be so fussy, but it's an only child.

> (*As* TONY *moves away* GEOFFREY *idly takes up* MIRIAM'S *metal bag which she has left on the table and examines it.* MIRIAM *cranes her neck to see what he is doing to her bag.*)

GEOFFREY (*becoming conscious that she is watching him, realises what he is doing*). Oh! I wasn't thinking what I was doing. (*Lays the bag down on the table again.*)

MIRIAM. Look inside.

GEOFFREY. I don't want to.

MIRIAM. Go on. Look inside.

GEOFFREY (*opens the bag and takes the things out as he says*). A pocket handkerchief and twopence. (*Puts the things back in the bag again while* MIRIAM *speaks.*)

MIRIAM (*with affected jauntiness*). I always carry my fortune about with me. I don't trust the banks.

GEOFFREY (*lays the bag on the table again as he repeats*). Twopence.

MIRIAM. It's a rotten climate here in London—especially after Monte Carlo.

TONY (*looks at* GEOFFREY *as he says incredulously*). Monte Carlo!

MIRIAM. I've been spending the spring in Monte. (*Grins as she says to* GEOFFREY.) He doesn't believe that.

TONY. Yes, I do, it's a nice place to *be* in—Monte.

MIRIAM. It's a nice place to be *left* in.

TONY. Left?

MIRIAM (*impatiently*). Yes—left—plaqué—dumped, if you like.

TONY (*making himself comfortable on the sofa*). How did you come to be dumped there?

MIRIAM. Woke up one fine morning and found he'd gone.

TONY. What a brute!

MIRIAM. It wasn't *his* fault. He'd got to go back to his wife. He treated *me* all right. I lived like an actress for two months. The night before he went away he gave me twenty pounds. Alone in Monte with twenty pounds. It costs you that much to get out.

GEOFFREY. What have you been doing since?

MIRIAM. The less I tell you about that the better.

GEOFFREY. Where are you living?

MIRIAM (*telling a lie so impertinently and apparently that she isn't telling a lie at all*). At the Ritz!

GEOFFREY (*seriously pursuing his questions*). Haven't you got a room somewhere?

MIRIAM. If you'd asked me that this time yesterday, I should have said " Yes," and it wouldn't have been a lie.

GEOFFREY. Have you no place to go to?

MIRIAM. I had—till this morning. She turned me out at two o'clock to-day.

GEOFFREY. What for? What had you done?

MIRIAM (*impatiently*). What had I done? What hadn't I done? Hadn't paid my rent, of course. Why d'you ask me so many questions? I didn't come here to complain. I was asked up to chat—wasn't I? To be merry, and make you laugh. I was doing my best.

GEOFFREY. Have you had any supper to-night? (MIRIAM *turns sullen and won't answer. He waits before he says.*) When did you last have a meal?

MIRIAM (*sullenly*). I had my tea.

GEOFFREY (*rises*). Get up, Tony, and clear this table. (TONY *rises and goes to the table.*) Help him, Hugh. (HUGH *and* TONY *clear the table, putting the things on the window-seat while* GEOFFREY *crosses to the sideboard, saying.*) Let's see what we've got here to eat. (*Taking up the dish of fruit and the plate of sandwiches as he speaks.*) There are the sandwiches and some fruit. (*Bringing the sandwiches and the fruit to the table.*) I've got a cake in the cupboard. Could you tackle that?

MIRIAM. I guess I could tackle most anything.

GEOFFREY (*speaking as he goes to the sideboard, and takes out a cake on a dish and a plate and knife and brings them to the table*). All right. I'm sorry I haven't got more to offer you, but it's all I can manage at this time of night. There you are.

>   (*While he is doing this* MIRIAM *rises, goes to the table, looks at the food; then, a little overcome with emotion, says gratefully.*)

MIRIAM. Thank you. I thank all of you. (*Sits down and begins to eat.*)

GEOFFREY. You've got nothing to drink. I've only got soda water if you won't have spirits.

MIRIAM. I wouldn't mind a drop of whisky now. (GEOFFREY *pours out a whisky and soda as she continues.*) I didn't like to touch it before I'd had something to eat. It affects you so queer on an empty stomach. I wasn't for finding myself in a strange place without knowing what I was doing. (*As* GEOFFREY *places the tumbler beside her on the table, she smiles as she says.*) It don't seem so strange now — with all you boys being so kind.

>   (GEOFFREY *takes a cigarette from the box which is still on the table, lights it, then sits down on the end of the sofa. He lounges there smoking while the following dialogue goes on, his face well seen by the audience.*)

HUGH (*to* MIRIAM). Are you a stranger in London?

MIRIAM. I ought not to be. I've been here often enough—but not for some time. I was in Paris most of last year—at the Rat Mort. D'you know it? It's in Montmartre.

TONY. I know it. I've often been there.

MIRIAM. Did you ever see me?

TONY (*sitting in an armchair and making himself comfortable*). I don't think so. I can't remember.

MIRIAM. I was dancing there till I took sick. Then of course I lost my job—through having to go to hospital.

(*She continues eating. She is very philosophical as she tells her story, and does not feel sorry for herself.*)

HUGH. You've had a hard time.

MIRIAM. Not so bad as some girls. There's many has a worse time than *me*.

HUGH. Who?

MIRIAM. All those poor devils who can't see that life has its comic side.

HUGH. Do you find life comic?

MIRIAM. Many a time.

HUGH. Not lately.

MIRIAM. What about you three nuts waiting on *me*? Ain't it a scream?

(TONY *laughs*. MIRIAM *looks at* TONY *and laughs too*.)

HUGH. I think it's rather wonderful that *you* should be able to see anything comic in that.

MIRIAM. You wouldn't have me go through the world sighing. I can't afford it. It's *my* business to be gay.

HUGH. " And if I laugh at any mortal thing,
'Tis that I may not weep."

MIRIAM (*cheerfully*). Lord Byron.

HUGH (*rather surprised that she should recognise the quotation*). Yes.

TONY. *I* didn't know that.

HUGH. No one supposed you did, Tony dear.

MIRIAM (*thoughtfully*). There've been times, though, when I haven't been able to raise a laugh about anything.

HUGH. I believe you.

MIRIAM. I remember once when my sense of humour was of no use at all.

TONY. When was that?

MIRIAM. When I was fool enough to fall in love. That's an old story. It happened in America. I was raised in America; I didn't tell you that. Oh, I was properly in love. I got over it—pretty quick, too.

HUGH. It didn't go very deep, I expect—your love? You soon forgot all about him? You were lucky.

(MIRIAM *looks steadily at* HUGH, *and finishes masticating what she has in her mouth before she speaks. She says her speech with a dry intensity which is more impressive than if she had spoken emotionally.*)

MIRIAM. My man quit me to marry a rich old woman. I and my baby were left to starve. When you're starving for food you haven't much time to think about being in love. Love doesn't kill — but hunger does —and hunger killed my baby. (*She continues eating. There is a long silence.* GEOFFREY *and* TONY *and* HUGH *all sit quite still, smoking, not looking at each other while* MIRIAM *eats. After a few moments she looks slowly at each of them before she says.*) There now! I've gone and depressed you all—damn it. I didn't mean to do that. It's your own faults for being so sympathetic. I was feeling so low I just out with the truth. I'd have done better to have told you stories. I guess you are all three wishing me far enough. All right. I'll be getting on my way.

GEOFFREY. You needn't go yet. I'd like you to stay and talk to me some more—if you will.

MIRIAM. Just as you like. (*Sits down again and goes on eating.*)

HUGH. I must be getting to bed. It's very late.

GEOFFREY (*speaking as* HUGH *goes to get his hat and umbrella*). All right, old boy. Thank you so much for coming round.

TONY (*getting out of his chair*). Wait a minute, Hugh, and I'll come with you.

HUGH. All right.

(TONY *puts on his hat and coat, and speaks aside to* HUGH *near the door.*)

TONY. Can you lend me a sovereign? I haven't got anything on me.

HUGH (*taking the money from his pocket*). I think I can. Give her two. (*Gives two sovereigns to* TONY, *who quietly lays the money beside* MIRIAM *on the table as he speaks.*)

TONY. That'll help to repair the damage I did to your hat. (*Goes to the door without waiting for* MIRIAM'S *thanks as he says.*) Good-night, Geoffrey.
GEOFFREY. Good-night, Tony.
HUGH. Good-night.
(*Both* HUGH *and* TONY *go out. There is silence for a few moments afterwards.* GEOFFREY *continues smoking and* MIRIAM *eating. She glances at him once or twice before she speaks.*)
MIRIAM. *You* look a bit down on your luck. What's the matter? Money?
GEOFFREY. No.
MIRIAM. Your girl? (*He turns his face away from her. She looks at him very sympathetically before she continues.*) Been chucked—have you? That's tough—specially if it's the first time. You get used to it after awhile. You get used to anything after awhile.
GEOFFREY. Think so?
MIRIAM. The only way to be happy—it seems to me—is just not to expect anything from anybody. Then, when somebody does you a kindness—like *you've* done *me*—it comes as a lovely surprise. But you don't get down to *that* kind of happiness till you've had all the pride kicked out of you and lost most all your fine feelings. I was as nice a girl as you could wish to meet once—modest and quiet and obliging. They could have made what they liked of *me*. That was my trouble. They made *this* of me.
GEOFFREY. Have you ever tried to give it up—this kind of life?
MIRIAM (*rises suddenly, her tone instantly changing to one of suspicion and resentment*). Now, look here! If you're going to try and save me, I shall clear out—now—this minute. Even if I wanted to be reformed, it wouldn't be no use. It's been tried. And what was the end of it? As soon as I turned respectable and took to honest work—I was found out—then I was a fraud—not fit to associate with the others. I was turned away—put back to where I come from—only I was worse off than before because of the time I'd lost. It's no use, I tell you, I must go on.
GEOFFREY. I don't see that *you* need reforming much more than the rest of the world. What about girls who

marry men they loathe in order to live in luxury—and then don't keep to their bargains—half of them—take lovers on the sly ? I don't think you're worse than *they* are.

MIRIAM (*reassured*). That's all right, then. Now we understand each other. May I help myself to one of your cigarettes ?

GEOFFREY. Yes, of course.

>   (MIRIAM *takes a cigarette from the box and lights it, then sits in an armchair, curling herself up comfortably as she speaks.*)

MIRIAM. You must tell me when you want me to get out. Otherwise I'm liable to outstay my welcome. It's so dry and warm in here.

GEOFFREY. You needn't be in a hurry. I'm not tired. I was fast asleep all evening.

MIRIAM. That's a funny time to go to sleep.

GEOFFREY. I took something.

MIRIAM. Drugs ?

GEOFFREY. Yes.

MIRIAM. That's bad. I could see there was something of that sort the matter with *you*. Have you been at it long ?

GEOFFREY. The last few weeks.

MIRIAM (*very kindly and very earnestly*). Since your trouble began—eh ? You've been hard hit about something or other—so you thought you'd take to drugs, I suppose, and whisky to make you forget. Don't you do it, it's a shame to see a young fellow like you beginning such habits as those—a gentleman, too—with everything just as it should be—your nice flat and your nice friends and all. Break away from it now, old man, before it gets a hold on you : you won't be able to stop it by and by. You'll go down and down, till you get like the drunken brutes who come after *me*. *You* mustn't be one of the no-goods. It's the respectable folks who make the world go round. We're only a drag. (*She pauses, but as* GEOFFREY *makes no response, she says apologetically.*) I beg your pardon for talking like that to *you*; you must think I've got a nerve. I don't suppose *you* want advice from any one—specially not from *me*. (*She puts on her hat.*)

GEOFFREY. Wait a minute. (*Going towards his bed-*

*room door as he says.*) I've left all my money on my dressing-table.
(*He is at the door before she calls him back.*)
MIRIAM. Pss! Here! (*He turns to her. She comes towards him.*) Don't you give me anything. (*Shows him the money in her bag.*) Your friend gave me these. That's plenty for the present. I can go back and pay my rent now, and sleep in my own bed to-night. If you wouldn't mind not giving me anything yourself—it would make me feel as if I'd been your pal—if you wouldn't mind. (*She lays her bag on the sideboard, then arranges her hat in front of the looking-glass, " fixing " herself with great care. When she has finished, she picks up her bag, and in a cheery and matter-of-fact tone says to* GEOFFREY.) So long and many thanks, and good luck. (*Goes towards the door.*)
(*She has opened the inner door and is just going out when* GEOFFREY *calls her back.*)
GEOFFREY. Come back. (*She stops and turns to him.*) I can't let you go like this—down the street and out of sight — after you've done me such a good turn. (*She comes a little towards him, surprised by this last remark.*) Sit down again while I tell you what I mean. I'm down on my luck—as you saw—hard hit. I can't tell you what about but it's something I shall never get over. I'm knocked out—completely—everything's finished. Those two friends of mine that you saw here, knew I'd be having a bad time to-night—so they came round, like good fellows, to cheer me up—to take me out of myself. But everything they said and did only irritated me—because — *they've* got no troubles — *they've* got nothing on their minds. I wanted to be with some one as miserable as I am myself. Then *you* came—and by different things that you said you brought it home to me—that there are millions of people in the world who are having a worse time than I am. *That* took me out of myself. I wondered how *I* dare complain. Now I want you to listen carefully while I tell you something about myself—about my circumstances. I'm in the city and I don't make much. You see how I live—it's simple—and I've only got what I earn. The reason I had for saving my money is gone, so I may as well spend it if it's going to do any one any good. I want you to let

me do this. Take a room for you somewhere—or two rooms if I can afford it—and pay your rent and your food. You shall be well fed every day. (MIRIAM *breaks down at this. She buries her face on her arm on the table and cries.* GEOFFREY *pauses at this, much distressed and goes on when he is sure he can speak without betraying how much he is moved.*) You're too good a girl to turn out again on the streets. I can't do it. So that's how we'll manage for the present. We'll try it at any rate and see how it works—if *you* agree. (MIRIAM *looks up at him and smiles consent through her tears but is too overcome to speak*). Very well then. You've got the money to pay for your room. (*She nods her head.*) You'd better go there now. (*He rises. Taking her cue from him she rises too.*) And to-morrow—come back here and ask for *me*. Geoffrey Sherwood. (*She nods again.*) I'll tell the porter to expect you and bring you up. Then we'll go out together and find you a place to live. To-morrow at three o'clock.

> (*He holds out his hand as he might to a man friend. She shakes hands with him, but is still too overcome to speak a word. Then she turns away and goes out slowly, still crying.*)

CURTAIN.

# THE SECOND ACT

SCENE.—*The same as Act I.*
*It is late in the afternoon about three months later than the events in Act I. As it is summer-time it is still quite light. The stage is empty; the inner door being open shows the hall.*
*Enter* GEOFFREY *looking very smart in his city clothes: a short black coat with the side-pockets stuffed with evening papers and letters, a silk hat, and his umbrella. He looks very bright and well with no traces of his dissipated habits of three months ago. He walks with a springy step and whistles or otherwise shows his lightheartedness. He closes the outer door, then comes to the table, lays down his umbrella and his hat on the table, pulls out the letters and papers from his side-pockets and throws them on the table. He then crosses to the sideboard, opens the cupboard door with a key and takes out the decanter of whisky, gets a tumbler, takes the stopper out of the decanter and is about to pour some whisky into the glass, then pauses.*

GEOFFREY. No, Geoffrey! (*Puts the stopper back in the decanter and the decanter back in the cupboard, closes the cupboard, then pours a little soda water into the tumbler and drinks it off. He then crosses to the table, where he sits down and writes.*) (*There is a knock on the door.*) (GEOFFREY *calls.*) Come in.
      (*Enter* TAYLOR, *leaving the outer door open so that*
                HUGH BROWN *is seen standing in the hall.*)
  TAYLOR. If you please, sir, are you at home to Mr. Brown?
  GEOFFREY (*cheerily*). Oh, yes, indeed. (*Calls.*) Come in, Hugh. (*Holds out his hand to* HUGH, *who comes forward: shakes hands with him without rising, talking*

*fast all the while.*) How are you ? Awfully glad to see you back. Sit down—do. I'll be with you in a minute. (*As* HUGH *crosses towards the fireplace* GEOFFREY *calls out to* TAYLOR *to stop him before he goes out of the door.*) Don't go, Taylor, I want you. (TAYLOR *remains.*) (GEOFFREY *continues speaking while he puts the note he has written in an envelope and addresses it.*) I'd like this to go at once. It's only round the corner. Have you got any one to send ?

TAYLOR. I'll take it myself, sir.

GEOFFREY. Thank you, Taylor. I wish you would. (*Handing the letter to* TAYLOR.) Ask if there's any answer ?

TAYLOR. Yes, sir.

GEOFFREY (*turns to* HUGH *as* TAYLOR *goes towards the door with the letter*). Well, Hugh. (*Suddenly remembering something.*) Oh! half a minute. (*Calls.*) Taylor !

TAYLOR (*coming towards* GEOFFREY *again*). Yes, sir.

GEOFFREY. Those shares of yours are going up.

TAYLOR (*evidently very much pleased to hear this*). No !

GEOFFREY. They've gone up five points since yesterday.

TAYLOR. Oh !

GEOFFREY. I think they'll keep on rising.

TAYLOR. You don't say.

GEOFFREY. So you'd better hang on for a bit.

TAYLOR. Whatever you tell me, sir, I'll do. " Hang on " or—what's that other term they use—" get out."

GEOFFREY (*bantering* TAYLOR *as he says to* HUGH). Taylor's having a flutter on the Stock Exchange. He's a terrible fellow to gamble. There's no holding him in.

TAYLOR (*laughs a little as he says to* HUGH). He *will* have his little joke. (*Then gravely to* GEOFFREY.) I'll go with your letter now, sir.

GEOFFREY. All right, Taylor.

(TAYLOR *goes out, closing the inner door after him.*)

HUGH. What's he fluttering in ?

GEOFFREY. It's a land and irrigation scheme in Texas. (*Taking a report from among his papers on the table.*) There ! That's the report. (*Hands it to* HUGH.) Take it home and read it. It's a very good thing.

HUGH. Speculative ?

GEOFFREY. Yes—rather.

HUGH. No thanks. (*Smiles as he throws the report back on the table without reading it.*)

GEOFFREY (*smiling*). Dear old Hugh, I should hate to see you do anything that wasn't thoroughly safe and conservative. It would be out of your character. (*Taking up the report.*) I won't advise you to put anything in this, anyway, because it's an untried scheme, so it carries a certain amount of risk, but I think it's going to turn out all right. I've taken up a good few of the ordinary shares on my own account—apart from the firm—and I'm hoping to make a bit.

HUGH. You can take care of yourself all right, but how about Taylor?

GEOFFREY. He's only bought fifty pounds' worth. I'm hoping he'll make a bit too.

HUGH. He may lose his fifty pounds.

GEOFFREY. He'll never know it if he does, the silly old ass.

HUGH. That's very generous of *you*—but is it the way you conduct your business?

GEOFFREY (*good-humouredly*). No, you fool, of course it isn't. (*Gravely.*) But when I was so bad three months ago and had gone most of the way to the devil, Taylor did a lot for me that wasn't included in the service for which I pay him. That wasn't business on *his* part. It sometimes pays to be unbusinesslike. (*He lays down the report he has held in his hand and takes up another which he offers to* HUGH.) Look here. Here's something else. This is hardly at all speculative——

HUGH (*interrupting* GEOFFREY *by pushing the report away with his hand*). I don't want to hear about your old companies, I want to hear about *you*. I haven't seen you for six weeks.

GEOFFREY (*laying the report on the table and then sitting down near* HUGH). No,—no more we have.

HUGH. And you never wrote me a single line all the time I was away.

GEOFFREY. Didn't I?

HUGH. No.

GEOFFREY. Oh. Well, you see, I've been so busy—up to the neck in all these schemes. (*Indicating the reports on the table.*) It's a good thing for me. It's exciting and amusing and takes my mind off—other things.

HUGH (*after a momentary pause*). How's Miriam?

GEOFFREY (*smiles as he says*). She's all right.

HUGH. It's still a success—is it?

GEOFFREY. Can't you see for yourself that it is?

HUGH. How d'you mean?

GEOFFREY. Look at me. (*Leans towards* HUGH *as he pulls down his lower eyelid to show him his eye.*) Clear. (*Holds out his hand to show* HUGH *that it does not shake.*) Steady. (*Waves his hand towards the papers on the table.*) Busy. (*Seriously and generously.*) And it's all thanks to Miriam. But for *her* I should have gone completely under. She's cured me of taking drugs,—not by hiding my cachets like Taylor—nor by preaching at me——

HUGH. Like me.

GEOFFREY (*kindly*). You were splendid, Hugh,—so was Tony—so was every one, but I suppose I needed some one different — some one altogether unlike any friend I'd ever had—to take me out of myself just then. It was fortunate for me that I came across Miriam when I did. Think of it — the very girl I needed — coming up here like that, by accident—that night——

HUGH. I'm very glad she's turned out so well.

GEOFFREY (*cheerfully*). You must come and see her in her little flat. She's made it so attractive. She has a kitchen. She cooks quite well. Come and try one of her dinners some time.

HUGH. All right.

GEOFFREY. I dine with her several times a week—either there or in a restaurant.

HUGH. Do you?

GEOFFREY. Yes. And then we often go to a music-hall or a cinema. *You* thought I'd get tired of her in no time, but I don't. She's wonderful — such good company—a sense of humour and sometimes a tact and a delicacy of feeling and taste that would surprise you. There are fine qualities in Miriam, only no one had ever taken the trouble to discover and develop them before.

HUGH. You are not falling in love with her—are you?

GEOFFREY. No, of course not. That's out of the

question. She attracts me and she needs me. We are both lonely. I see no reason to remain virtuous—now —for nobody's sake, and it's very much better that I should be having an affaire with Miriam than with some woman of our own class who'd expect more from me. It wouldn't be right for me to devote myself to any one like that now, nor to marry what is called " a really nice girl," for if it should ever come to a choice between any one else and Valentine, it would be Valentine every time. But we needn't go into that. She's not for *me*. (*There is a knock on the door.* GEOFFREY *calls.*) Come in. (*Enter* TAYLOR. *He carries a visiting-card.* GEOFFREY *speaks as soon as* TAYLOR *enters.*) Did you take it?

TAYLOR. Yes, sir.

GEOFFREY. Any answer?

TAYLOR. No, sir. The gentleman was out.

GEOFFREY. Oh. All right, thanks. (*Turning to* HUGH.) Now tell me about yourself.

TAYLOR (*still standing near* GEOFFREY *interrupts him with*). If you please, sir——

GEOFFREY (*turning to* TAYLOR *again*). What is it, Taylor? (TAYLOR *hands the visiting-card to* GEOFFREY. GEOFFREY *takes it, looks at it, and is much surprised and troubled. He turns the card over and examines it, and after a long pause says quietly to* HUGH.) It's Valentine. (*After another pause, during which* GEOFFREY *and* HUGH *look at each other,* GEOFFREY *says.*) Where is she, Taylor?

TAYLOR. Her ladyship is downstairs in the hall, sir, waiting for me to bring her your answer.

GEOFFREY (*undecided*). Well—wait a minute.

TAYLOR. Yes, sir. (*Turns towards the door.*)

GEOFFREY. No—don't go.

TAYLOR. I will wait outside till you call me, sir.

(*He takes* GEOFFREY'S *hat and umbrella; then goes into the hall, closing the inner door after him.*)

GEOFFREY. She's scribbled on the back of her card to know if I'm here and if she can come up and see me if I'm not busy.

HUGH. Do you want to see her?

GEOFFREY. I don't like to send her away. I think I'd better see her.

HUGH (*rising*). Give me time to get out of the way first.

GEOFFREY (*rising*). Don't go, Hugh. Stay a few minutes at any rate. It'll take some of the edge off if you are in the room when we meet.

HUGH. All right. Just as you like.

(GEOFFREY *goes to the door and opens it.*)

GEOFFREY (*speaking to* TAYLOR, *who is outside*). Ask her ladyship to come upstairs.

(*He comes towards* HUGH *again, leaving the door ajar. He listens for* VALENTINE'S *approach only half paying attention to what* HUGH *says.*)

HUGH. While I think of it, Geoffrey—will you dine with me this evening?

GEOFFREY. This evening—very well,—yes—thanks.

HUGH. Tony's coming. He has to catch a train to Stafford at ten o'clock so we are not going to dress.

GEOFFREY. Not dress.

HUGH. No. We shall dine at the Savoy Grill Room at eight.

GEOFFREY. That's the lift coming up. Did you hear it?

HUGH (*listens, then nods*). Yes. (*Then he adds.*) We'll call for you here about half-past seven—Tony and I.

GEOFFREY. All right.

(*Enter* TAYLOR.)

TAYLOR (*announces*). Lady Morland.

(*Enter* VALENTINE. *She is tall and beautiful and distinguished and is expensively and fashionably dressed. Her manner and poise are so perfect that she does not betray any of the embarrassment she feels in meeting* GEOFFREY *again, but is charmingly gracious and natural as she greets him.*)

VALENTINE. How d'you do, Geoffrey.

GEOFFREY. How d'you do, Valentine.

(*They shake hands, then* VALENTINE *sees* HUGH, *crosses to him and shakes hands with him.*)

VALENTINE. Oh, how d'you do, Mr. Brown; I haven't seen *you* for quite a long time.

HUGH. No. It must be nearly six months.

VALENTINE. More than that, I think.

GEOFFREY. Won't you sit down?

VALENTINE. Thank you. (*She sits before she continues. The others also sit.*) I've been to a concert this afternoon and then I went to a tea-party at the Ritz,—and as I had a little time to spare before going home to dress for dinner, I thought I'd drop in and see you.

GEOFFREY. Very kind of you.

VALENTINE. I hope I'm not interrupting something. You weren't talking business or anything?

GEOFFREY. Hugh won't do business with *me*. I've been trying to make him invest his money in some of our companies but he's too wary.

(VALENTINE *looks from* GEOFFREY *to* HUGH.)

HUGH. I just looked in to let Geoffrey know I was back in London.

VALENTINE. Have you been away?

HUGH. On circuit.

VALENTINE. Oh, yes. Did you have any interesting trials at any of the assizes?

HUGH. Nothing extraordinary — except the Trent murder.

VALENTINE. What was that?

HUGH (*without any intention of being personal or realising that he has been so until* VALENTINE, *and then* GEOFFREY, *speak*). A tragedy of a young man and his sweetheart. They'd been keeping company for a couple of years and then she got a chance to marry some one with more money, so she jilted her lover and he stabbed her.

VALENTINE (*remarks quickly*). Yes, yes, I remember reading about it.

GEOFFREY. What a fool he must have been to take it so much to heart as that.

HUGH. They were rough sort of people without much self-control.

GEOFFREY. Not like *us*.

HUGH. No. (*There is a moment's embarrassment, then* HUGH *rises.*) I must be getting along now, Geoffrey.

GEOFFREY. All right, old man.

HUGH (*shaking hands with* VALENTINE). Good-bye.

VALENTINE. Good-bye.

HUGH (*speaking to* GEOFFREY *as he goes towards the*

*door*). Tony and I will be round here about half-past seven.

GEOFFREY. All right. I'll be ready for you. You can let yourself out, can't you ?

HUGH. Yes, thanks. (*He goes out.*)

VALENTINE. D'you know, Geoffrey, I hadn't the slightest intention of calling on you when I left home. It was as I was leaving the Ritz—standing on the steps there—waiting for my car, I had an impulse. I suddenly thought I should like to see you again, so I told the chauffeur to go home and said I was going to walk—and I walked straight here.

GEOFFREY. Is that the first time you've thought of me since our last meeting ?

VALENTINE. Of course not. I've often thought of you. One of my reasons for coming here was—I knew we were bound to meet somewhere or other, sooner or later—and it's best to get it over like this first.

GEOFFREY. I don't see why we are bound to meet.

VALENTINE. We have so many mutual friends.

GEOFFREY. I never see them now.

VALENTINE. Have you dropped them all ?

GEOFFREY. Completely.

VALENTINE. I'm sorry.

GEOFFREY. Why ?

VALENTINE. They were so fond of you.

GEOFFREY. People who go out a great deal and entertain a great deal don't miss any one. One young man more or less at their parties makes no difference to them.

VALENTINE It's a pity to lose one's friends.

GEOFFREY. My *friends* have stuck to me. Those others are only my acquaintance. I only went to their houses to meet you and because you wished it. I never cared about society for its own sake.

VALENTINE. I see—and then—I suppose you are very busy.

GEOFFREY. Very.

VALENTINE (*after a moment's pause*). I had another reason for coming.

GEOFFREY. Oh !

VALENTINE. Nothing very special—only—I wanted to see how you were.

GEOFFREY. I'm very well.
VALENTINE. You look very well.
GEOFFREY. You seem disappointed.
VALENTINE. A little surprised.
GEOFFREY. Oh!
VALENTINE. Only because Tony Hewlett told me three months ago that you were—not very well.
GEOFFREY (*coolly*). He told you I'd taken to drink?
VALENTINE. Yes.
GEOFFREY. That was a phase. I soon got through it. I'm a reformed character now.
VALENTINE (*in a low voice*). I'm glad to hear it.
(*There is a pause during which* GEOFFREY *looks at her searchingly before he speaks.*)
GEOFFREY. Why *did* you climb up here to find me, Valentine?
VALENTINE (*surprised by this question*). For the reasons I've told you.
GEOFFREY. Are you sure?
VALENTINE. Of course. Why? What do you mean?
GEOFFREY. Wasn't it rather to see for yourself if I'm still suffering from broken heart, and if you think I'm recovering too easily to try and bring about a relapse?
VALENTINE (*hurt and indignant*). No.
GEOFFREY. Think.
VALENTINE. I didn't stop to examine my motives. I came, as I told you—on impulse.
GEOFFREY. You'd like to count for something in my life still—though I'm to count for nothing in yours. You don't want me, but at the same time you don't want to let me escape you. You'll keep me in your power if you can, isn't that it?
VALENTINE. I suppose you'll believe nothing but what's bad of me now.
GEOFFREY. I wish you hadn't come. It would have been much kinder of you if you'd left me alone. I've been doing my best to forget you—avoiding every place where there was a chance of meeting you—trying to fill my life full of all kinds of interests and amusements so that I shouldn't have time to think about you and regret you. And I was succeeding. I was well on the way to forgetting all about you. There's no sense in our

remembering each other. It's no satisfaction to either of us to meet like this.

VALENTINE. I know how you must feel about everything and towards me. It's only natural you should be hurt and angry, but don't be unjust. It isn't only vanity that makes me want not altogether to lose sight of you. I miss you, Geoffrey. Nobody but you has ever understood me. It seems such a pity—after all that there used to be between us—if there's nothing of it left—if we can't ever meet as friends.

GEOFFREY. I'm in no mood to sit down and talk sentimentally about the past. Much better cut me out of your thoughts and stand by what you've done.

VALENTINE. You are very practical, Geoffrey.

GEOFFREY. So were you when you threw me over to marry Sir John Morland.

VALENTINE. I was ignorant then—ignorant of what marriage means. (*He turns to her surprised.*) That surprises you. Modern girls are supposed to know. We *do* know—in the sense that we are told—but with so little experience of life and so little imagination as many of us possess—we often understand very imperfectly.

GEOFFREY (*with a good deal of hesitation and incredulity*). You haven't come here to tell me, I suppose, that you find, when it's too late, that you've made a mistake?

VALENTINE (*evading his question*). My husband treats me very well — much better than I deserve. He's extremely generous and attentive—too attentive. (GEOFFREY *turns away distressed and indignant, controlling his feelings with difficulty.* VALENTINE *becomes ashamed of what she has said and begins to apologise, but grows more and more agitated as her feelings carry her away.*) I'd no business to say that. I'm sorry—but if you knew how intolerable it becomes at times not to be able to speak out my thoughts to any one; I've no one to talk to—no one. Mother won't listen. She encouraged my marriage and she won't hear anything that sounds like criticism of what *she* did. I can't blame her. She didn't force me. Nobody forced me. I chose for myself, and I daresay my marriage is as happy as most—but with no one to confide in—turned in upon myself—I feel so lost and lonely. (*Breaks down.*)

VOL. II          R

GEOFFREY. I can do nothing to help you. You've gone right out of my world. You are the wife of Sir John Morland, and after having been your lover I'm not going to sink down to being your confidant. (*Greatly distressed to see her distress.*) I wish you hadn't come.

VALENTINE (*pulls herself together, dries her eyes, and rises as she says*). You've told me that—already, Geoffrey, I'll take you at your word. It's time I was getting home anyway. (*Regaining her composure as she continues.*) It was a mistake my coming here to-day. I shan't act on impulse again. As we aren't likely to meet anywhere, it seems—I should like to tell you, and I want you to try to believe this, for I *really* mean it—I'm glad that losing me hasn't ruined your life, and that you seem to be getting over your disappointment.

GEOFFREY. Would you be glad if you heard I'd consoled myself?

VALENTINE (*a little surprised by this question*). I hope and fully expect that you'll do that some day—but you aren't engaged to any one else yet?

GEOFFREY. No. I'm not engaged.

(*Enter* MIRIAM. *She walks straight into the room a few paces, then stops short suddenly when she sees Valentine. There is a great change for the better in* MIRIAM'S *appearance, nothing tawdry about her now. She looks like a quiet, well-behaved woman. She is very well dressed, quietly and simply, but with everything in excellent taste. There is a long pause when she appears. All three of them are acutely embarrassed.* VALENTINE *freezes, but is complete mistress of herself in spite of her anger and resentment.*)

MIRIAM. How d'you do, Geoffrey. I thought I'd pay you a surprise visit.

VALENTINE. I really must be going now. (*Goes towards the door.*)

GEOFFREY. Let me show you to the lift.

VALENTINE. Oh no, please don't. I'd much rather you didn't.

(*She goes out, leaving both the doors open.* MIRIAM *watches her till she has gone, and then watches*

# OUTCAST

GEOFFREY *as he closes the doors and comes back to her side.*)

MIRIAM. Aren't you glad to see me, Geoffrey?

GEOFFREY. Yes, dear, of course I'm glad to see you.

MIRIAM. You didn't look much like it.

GEOFFREY. I was taken by surprise. It's the first time you've come in like that—unannounced.

(*He embraces her and kisses her, then stands with his arm round her. She fingers his clothes as she speaks.*)

MIRIAM. There was no one at the lift when I arrived, so I walked up the stairs; I was just going to ring your bell when I noticed that the door wasn't latched—so I didn't see why I shouldn't come right in. You aren't cross, are you?

GEOFFREY. No, dear. Of course I'm not cross. (*Kisses her.*) But I think it's better if you don't come up when I'm not expecting you, because, you see—any one might be here.

MIRIAM (*a little chilled by this remark, moves away as she says*). All right, I apologise. I wouldn't have done it if I'd thought you'd mind.

GEOFFREY (*kindly*). That's all right, my dear, don't worry. You look very nice this afternoon. What have you been doing with yourself all day?

(MIRIAM *takes off her hat, sticks the pins through it, and lays it on the table as she talks racily and good-humouredly with a half-amused perception of what she is saying.*)

MIRIAM. I had a charwoman in this morning. I was ordering her around for a while. By the time she was through it was one o'clock—so I asked her to stay to lunch.

GEOFFREY. The charwoman? Oh, well—after all—why not?

MIRIAM. She looked kind of half-starved. I thought it would be fun to feed her up, and there wasn't such a heavy rush of guests to my lunch table that I couldn't squeeze one more in.

GEOFFREY (*amused*). What did you talk about, you and the charwoman?

MIRIAM. Told each other a pack of lies. *She* said she didn't drink and *I* said I was a widow. (GEOFFREY smiles at her. *She continues with mock gravity.*) My husband was a ship's officer on board an Atlantic liner. He was washed overboard in a squall — year before last — so I'm now living on the pension granted to me by the company — I don't think. (GEOFFREY *laughs.* MIRIAM *continues as she crosses to the sideboard, fixing her hair in front of the glass there while she talks.*) I had to be respectable or she wouldn't have sat at my table on account of her social position. I rather fancied myself, as that officer's widow, being kind to the poor old thing.

GEOFFREY. You have the best heart in the world.

MIRIAM. What about you?

GEOFFREY (*disclaiming her praise*). Oh! (*She turns to him smiling. He holds out his hand to her as he says.*) Come here. (*She sits on the arm of his chair, settling herself with her arm round his neck.*) Get comfortable. That all right?

MIRIAM. Lovely.

GEOFFREY. Go on. Tell me some more. What did you do after lunch?

MIRIAM. I went to hear the band play in Hyde Park. That was a penny for my chair, and another penny for my programme, that's twopence. I don't want you to think I'm scattering pennies as if they were peanuts——

GEOFFREY. Rubbish! You are very good indeed the way you keep down your expenses.

MIRIAM. I thought I ought to know what they were playing — that's why I bought a programme, so as to improve my musical education and be able to spot the classics when I hear them, like you and Hugh.

GEOFFREY (*smiles at her*). I see.

MIRIAM. You're making fun of me.

GEOFFREY (*kindly*). No, I'm not. Don't be silly.

MIRIAM. I was enjoying myself fine, listening to that band — when a young fellow came along and sat himself down in the next chair to mine.

GEOFFREY. Well——

MIRIAM. He got mighty fresh.

GEOFFREY. Oh!

MIRIAM. He asked me to tea.

GEOFFREY. What did you do?

MIRIAM. You don't think I went with him—do you, Geoffrey?

GEOFFREY (*reassuring her*). No, of course not.

MIRIAM. Not that there'd have been any harm in it if I had gone to tea with him, but I didn't think you'd like it.

GEOFFREY. You thought right.

MIRIAM. So I withered him.

GEOFFREY. With a look?

MIRIAM. Yes—and a few well-chosen words.

GEOFFREY. Then did you get up and go?

MIRIAM. No, but *he* did.

GEOFFREY (*laughs, then says*). Have you had any tea? Do you want some now? You can have it up here if you like.

MIRIAM. Oh, I *should* have enjoyed that, but I've had tea already, thanks, Geoffrey. I went to an A.B.C. near Victoria. I took a bus ride as far as there. (*Breaking off suddenly as she thinks of something.*) Oh and say—I was nearly forgetting. (*Getting off the arm of the chair.*) Let me get at my bag. (*Crossing behind his chair to get her bag which is on the table as she continues.*) When I came out of the tea-shop I went and bought something. (*As she dives her hand into her bag.*) Wait a minute. Sit still and I'll show you. Here we are. This is it. (*She produces a tiny paper parcel from her bag and gives it to* GEOFFREY.) There! It's for *you*. It's a present.

GEOFFREY (*smiling at her as he takes it*). For me?

MIRIAM. Yes. (*She watches him unwrap the paper and take out a pencil which slides into a metal sheath—worth about three-and-sixpence. She waits till he is examining it before she says.*) It's a pencil, to carry about in your pocket. It might come in useful some time.

GEOFFREY. How very kind of you. Dear Miriam, I'm quite touched.

MIRIAM. D'you like it?

GEOFFREY. Very much.

MIRIAM. Will you use it?

GEOFFREY. Yes, indeed.

MIRIAM. I'm glad. (*Watches* GEOFFREY *for a moment as he plays with the pencil and examines it before she says.*) Well now, Geoffrey, tell me, what have *you* been doing with yourself this afternoon?

GEOFFREY. I got home from the city about half-past five : then Hugh Brown came to see me.

MIRIAM. And then ?

GEOFFREY. Then—oh, then, *you* came.

(*There is a pause before* MIRIAM *speaks.*)

MIRIAM. Who is she ?

GEOFFREY. Who ?

MIRIAM. The one who was here just now.

GEOFFREY. A friend of mine.

MIRIAM. I might have guessed that by myself. (*Pauses again before she says.*) Funny you can't say who she is.

GEOFFREY. You shouldn't have come up here unexpectedly.

MIRIAM. No. I see that. It was a bit of a shock to both of us—and I daresay to her too. (*Moves away as she says.*) Oh, well, I suppose you do what you like up here. (*Faces him as she says very sincerely.*) But I want you to know that I'm true to you. There's nobody but you comes to my place.

GEOFFREY. I hope you don't think she came here for anything but just to call on me—just as Hugh or Tony or any of my friends might call.

MIRIAM. If that's all she came for I wonder you can't tell me who she is. What am I to make of it ? It don't matter to *you*, I suppose, what I make of it. It's none of my business *who* comes here. But I can't help having my own thoughts and feelings about the matter. It makes it pretty difficult for me to be your friend, if you're never going to tell me anything about yourself.

GEOFFREY. I've told you a great deal about myself.

MIRIAM. Things you could tell to the whole street.

GEOFFREY. I told you, a long time ago, that I was once engaged to be married.

MIRIAM. Was that *her* ?

GEOFFREY. Yes.

MIRIAM. She's beautiful.

GEOFFREY. Yes—but I'd rather not talk about her. I don't like discussing that part of my life with any one. Now that you know who she is you ought to be satisfied that her coming here means nothing, because—as I've told you already—everything was ended between her and me —long ago.

MIRIAM. She's married now, isn't she ?
GEOFFREY. Yes.
MIRIAM (*with a sudden outburst of jealous anger*). What does she want to come back for ? Isn't one man enough for her ?
GEOFFREY (*angry in his turn, says as he rises*). No more of that. I won't have it. You must understand that I can't allow you to say anything disrespectful about *that* lady.
MIRIAM (*resentfully*). She's a *lady*—she is—and I'm not a lady, so it don't matter if she walks out as soon as I come in—passes me by as if I was dirt. You don't defend *me*—only *her*. I've seen it before, this—freemasonry that there is among ladies and gentlemen to stand by each other and protect themselves. (*Dejectedly as she sits down.*) I'm not in on that.
GEOFFREY (*comes towards her, feeling very sorry for her, lays his hand on her shoulder and says very kindly*). Never mind. Come along. Cheer up. I'm sorry, but you know how it is. She was my first love. You can't get away from the memory of things you've grown up with. I knew her so well for so many years. The first time I saw her she was a girl of sixteen with her hair down her back. She came to stay with us for her summer holidays. After that I used to go a lot to their house in London. We were always seeing each other and writing—then we were engaged—and then—you know what happened. She has no use for me now—and it gives me no pleasure to see her now. It's all over and done with. I've left it behind me, but meeting her again this afternoon stirred everything up, and I still can't bear to hear any one say anything against her—so you won't—ever—will you ? (*He holds out his hand to her to make friends again. She takes his hand.*) I know you won't. (*He is going to move away after that, is about to withdraw his hand, when she draws it impulsively towards her and lays her cheek against it. He is touched and says kindly.*) I'm sorry I was cross and spoke sharply.
MIRIAM. It isn't that. (*Drops his hand and looks very forlorn.*)
GEOFFREY (*kneels beside her as he says*). What is it then ? What's the matter ? Mm ?
(*She looks mournfully in his eyes.*)

MIRIAM. I wish I was more to you, Geoffrey.

GEOFFREY. But you *are*—a great deal to me. You know that. I've never pretended that my affection for you is more than it is—but I've shown you over and over again, in all sorts of ways, how fond I am of you. You're the greatest comfort to me. You are really.

MIRIAM. Some one to take out evenings when you've nothing better to do.

GEOFFREY (*hurt and chilled by this remark*). How can you say that?

MIRIAM. Isn't it true?

GEOFFREY. I'm in the city all day.

MIRIAM. I know it.

GEOFFREY. And you have plenty to do in the daytime, too, looking after your flat.

MIRIAM. It's an old woman's job, that is, keeping two rooms clean and cooking meals for myself.

GEOFFREY. It's the daily life of many a wife whose husband goes out to his work.

MIRIAM. Yes—but there's a difference. When he comes home from his work they go out together.

GEOFFREY. So do we.

MIRIAM. I know, but I mean—*she* goes where *he* goes.

GEOFFREY. Well?

MIRIAM. No. I don't go where *you* go. When *we* go out together, it's to some little out-of-the-way joint where your friends won't see us. I'm not expecting you can take me with you *everywhere*—but I wish you didn't feel you must hide me. (GEOFFREY *is embarrassed by hearing the truth put into words. She continues appealingly.*) I've been at such pains to make myself fit to be seen with you. Isn't my language much better? Don't you notice it? And my clothes! Did you ever see anything more quiet and ladylike than this? So chic too. Then I study the papers to know what's going on in the world—and I read books, not only novels—history and books of travel and lives. All so as I won't disgrace you by appearing too ignorant—(*tentatively*) in case you should ever want to show me off. (*She watches him hopefully, but as he does not notice her, but seems absorbed in his own thoughts, her hope turns to disappointment. She is very resigned as she says.*) Of course if you think it's best to keep me dark, it's all right. Whatever you say goes. (*She still watches him as he moves slowly away, evidently in deep thought.*)

GEOFFREY. I never thought of you being dissatisfied with things as they are. It comes as a kind of surprise.

MIRIAM. I'm well off. I know that. I should be an ungrateful girl if I was to think anything else after all that you've done for me. It's only that—if I had the chance and if you wished it—I think I might be rather more of a companion to you than I am. See what I mean?

GEOFFREY (*slowly*). Yes. I see what you mean.

MIRIAM (*cheerfully as she rises and gathers her things, except her bag, from the table*). Shall we go to dinner now, Geoffrey? It must be getting about time.

GEOFFREY (*embarrassed*). I'm afraid I'm not free this evening.

MIRIAM (*disappointed*). Can't you dine with me?

GEOFFREY. I'm awfully sorry.

MIRIAM (*cheerfully*). If you can't you can't. That's all there is to it; I'd better fly along though before the shops shut and buy myself something to eat.

GEOFFREY. I wish I hadn't made that engagement with Hugh and Tony.

MIRIAM. Are you dining with them?

GEOFFREY. Yes.

MIRIAM. Just you three?

GEOFFREY. Yes, I've promised to go with them to the Savoy Grill Room.

MIRIAM (*wistfully*). It's a nice place that—so they tell me. I've never seen it. (*In a matter-of-fact way.*) I must hurry and fix myself up a bit before I go out. (MIRIAM *goes into the bedroom and as* GEOFFREY *stands looking after her the entrance bell rings.* GEOFFREY *opens the door. Enter* HUGH, *followed by* TONY HEWLETT.)

HUGH. Are you ready for us?

TONY. Good-evening, Geoffrey, don't let me be kept waiting.

HUGH. I telephoned down to tell them to keep us a table.

GEOFFREY (*after closing the door, comes down between* HUGH *and* TONY). Look here, I want to ask you some-

thing. (HUGH *and* TONY *both turn to him.*) Shall you mind if we take Miriam with us ?
(HUGH *and* TONY *both look surprised.*)
HUGH. Miriam ?
TONY. To the Savoy ?
GEOFFREY. Yes. She's just been here. She's in there now. (*Indicating his bedroom.*) She seems to have counted on me dining with her this evening. I don't want to break my engagement with *you,* and I don't want to send her home alone.
TONY. Couldn't we take her somewhere else ?
GEOFFREY. I don't want to do that either. I told her we were going to the Savoy and if we change she'll think it's because we're ashamed of her. (*To* HUGH.) Should you mind very much ?
HUGH. Not personally, but I think it's a mistake.
GEOFFREY. She looks all right.
TONY. She's damned smart now, Hugh. You haven't seen her lately.
HUGH (*to* GEOFFREY). I wasn't thinking of how it would *look.* I don't care twopence about that. Besides —nobody knows about her past except us three, and we shall never give her away.
TONY (*to* HUGH). Then what's the matter with you ?
HUGH (*ignoring* TONY'S *remark, says to* GEOFFREY). I think you'll be making a mistake if you let her think she can interfere with your engagements. She'll encroach and become inconvenient.
GEOFFREY. That's what *I've* been thinking about— protecting *myself,* but what about *her* ? D'you think she doesn't notice it ? And hasn't she a right to feel sore, if after I've encouraged her to improve herself, and when she's doing everything she can to make herself presentable and companionable, I only take her out to places where I shan't be seen with her ? You see, I've made a friend of her—and I can't treat a friend that way—I—I can't.
(*Enter* MIRIAM *from the bedroom. She closes the door after her while* HUGH *speaks.*)
HUGH. Hullo, Miriam ! Will you dine with us three at the Savoy ?
(*She looks from one to the other to see if they really mean it.*)

GEOFFREY (*smiling at her*). Do!
TONY. We wish you would.
MIRIAM (*crossing to the table to get her bag*). Thanks very much, boys, but I have an engagement.
GEOFFREY (*good-humouredly*). What are you talking about? You know you haven't got an engagement.
MIRIAM. It's very kind of you all, but I think I won't come.
GEOFFREY. We shan't enjoy ourselves a bit if you go off by yourself.
TONY. You *are* such good company, Miriam. You always make me laugh.
MIRIAM (*with a little smile at* TONY). Bless you.
HUGH. Why won't you come?
MIRIAM. There's something I want to say to Geoffrey, something I was thinking of in there. I didn't know you two were with him, but it don't matter, I may as well say it in front of you; you're his friends.
HUGH. We're your friends, too, Miriam.
TONY. Yes.
MIRIAM (*with a grateful little nod to each of them*). I know—I know— (*Then she addresses herself to* GEOFFREY.) I should hate more than anything in this world that you should ever find me an encumbrance.
GEOFFREY (*draws her towards him and says in a tone of affectionate reproach*). Miriam!
MIRIAM. Listen, Geoffrey. I think I see things pretty well as they are. If you think it would be best for yourself to be quit of me, for good, I'll clear out. And I'll go with no other feelings towards you but those of love and gratitude.
GEOFFREY (*murmurs*). Miriam!
MIRIAM. I thought, for one moment, I'd take myself off without a word of explanation to any one.
TONY. Without saying good-bye to us?
MIRIAM (*to* TONY). Yes. (*To all of them.*) It's so simple for me, my children, to slip away and leave no trace. No relatives to think of; no letters to be sent on. (*To* GEOFFREY.) Then I thought—perhaps it wouldn't be quite fair to *you*—to leave you that way—without giving you the choice, if I really have, as you say I have, been of some use in helping you pull yourself together. But I guess you can get along without me now, so let

it be whatever is best for *you*, and you needn't worry about *me*, *I* shall be all right.

GEOFFREY. Please stay with me. I want you. You've been so kind to me, and loyal, I didn't realise till now that, though it's been all right for *me*, it isn't much of a life for *you* at present. If you'll trust me I'll see what I can do to give you a rather better time, I'll take you about more in future. We'll have no end of fun, if you'll only stick to me and put all those silly notions out of your head about me not wanting you. (*He puts his arm round her and hugs her to him a moment and then says, intending to speak cheerfully but with a strong undercurrent of emotion.*) And now I think it would be a good plan if we all went out to dine.

MIRIAM (*addressing all of them*). You really want me to dine with you?

HUGH. Of course we do.

TONY. We insist.

MIRIAM. Watch me walk into the Savoy!

(*She walks to the door with an exaggerated, easy, and indolent grace.* GEOFFREY, HUGH, *and* TONY *watch her, laughing.*)


CURTAIN.

# THE THIRD ACT

SCENE.—*A sitting-room in* MIRIAM'S *Maisonette. This room is decorated and furnished in a flamboyant style. Everything is ornate and expensive and is in exquisite taste within its own style. On either side of the room there is a door, and in the wall opposite the audience a fireplace. There is a divan heaped with cushions, and a chaise longue in the middle of the room with a small table and a chair near it. Other chairs, cabinets, bookshelves, and small tables to complete the scene. Cupids and festoons of fruit and flowers appear largely in the decorations; there are several small statuettes of nude or semi-nude figures; some beautifully bound books and some French novels in paper covers: the pictures on the walls are all amorous subjects.*
MIRIAM *is reclining on the chaise longue and* GEOFFREY *is sitting on the side of it, leaning against her and holding her hands, which he kisses.* MIRIAM *is wearing a very elaborate tea-gown. She is as smart as a woman can be in every detail of her dress and coiffure, and has gained immensely in style and distinction of manner and bearing.* GEOFFREY *wears an ordinary business suit as it is afternoon.*

MIRIAM. Must you go back to the city this afternoon?

GEOFFREY. No, my darling, I'm going to stay here with you. There's nothing much I can do in the city to-day.

MIRIAM. I should think you've made enough money by now to last you for a little while.

GEOFFREY. I haven't done so badly lately.

MIRIAM. Clever little head! (*She caresses his head while she says.*) When I think that it was *your* brains provided *me* with my beautiful home. (*Leans back and surveys the room.*)

GEOFFREY (*surveying the room with satisfaction*). Everything paid for! (*He takes his cigarette case from his pocket and takes out a cigarette while* MIRIAM *speaks.*)

MIRIAM. I love to remind myself that all the things I have about me—*you* gave me—and every stitch of clothing that I wear.

GEOFFREY. What should I do with the money I make if I hadn't got you to dress up and surround with nice things?

MIRIAM. I used to feel afraid—when first you began making money—afraid that you wouldn't think so much of me now, but might be wanting to look around you for some smarter girl.

GEOFFREY. I did look around.

MIRIAM. You didn't?

GEOFFREY. Yes, I did — but I couldn't find her. There wasn't a smarter girl to be found in the whole of London or Paris.

MIRIAM (*squeezing his hand in both of hers*). You dear!
    (GEOFFREY, *delighted to have scored off her, makes a face at her and laughs.*)

MIRIAM. Will you be going to Paris again soon?

GEOFFREY. I might have to go next week. Do you want to come with me?

MIRIAM. Sure. I had a grand time when you took me there before.

GEOFFREY. All those hats and new dresses—eh?

MIRIAM. Yes.

GEOFFREY. Maxim's and the Café de Paris?

MIRIAM. Yes—and the evening we went to dine with those business friends of yours—Monsieur and Madame Duval, and you passed me off as your wife.

GEOFFREY. I'm rather ashamed when I think of *that*.

MIRIAM (*anxiously*). Why? Did *I* make you ashamed?

GEOFFREY (*scouting the suggestion*). You! You were wonderful. I never saw anything like it, " ravissante " he said you were, and she said, " elle est délicieuse, si élegante, si spirituelle." Oh, *you* were a great success—but all the same, I oughtn't to have done it—only when Duval had called to see me at the hotel he had fallen so violently in love with you and taken it so for granted that we were married——

MIRIAM (*finishing his sentence for him*). You didn't like to give me away—did you?

GEOFFREY. No.

MIRIAM. That was real sweet of you, Geoffrey. And what are those people anyway? Only the bourgeoisie. (GEOFFREY *smiles at her and kisses her hand, then she continues gravely.*) I think that the *chief* reason why I like going to Paris with you so much is that you call me your wife in the hotels. It makes all the servants and every one treat me with such marked respect.

(*Enter* BEAMISH.)

(BEAMISH *is a plain-faced parlourmaid, very correctly dressed, with a little white cap on her head, but with most inferior manners. She saunters in and out and speaks as if she were addressing nobody in particular. She is not so much deliberately rude as indifferent.*)

MIRIAM. You should knock on the door.

BEAMISH. So I did.

MIRIAM. I didn't hear you.

BEAMISH. That's not my fault. Would you like to see Miss Essex? She's just called.

MIRIAM (*to* GEOFFREY). Nelly.

GEOFFREY. Do you want to see her?

MIRIAM. No, but I think I'd better because she's in trouble.

GEOFFREY. Very well.

(*Rises, takes a book from the table, and then sits upon the divan.*)

BEAMISH. Shall I bring her in?

MIRIAM. Yes. Bring her in.

BEAMISH. All right.

(BEAMISH, *in going out of the room, leaves the door open.*)

GEOFFREY. What's Nelly's trouble?

MIRIAM. Same old thing.

GEOFFREY. Jack Soames?

MIRIAM. Yes. He's been drunk again for over a week and knocking her about something cruel.

GEOFFREY. Why doesn't she leave him?

MIRIAM. She's fond of him. (*Rises and comes towards* GEOFFREY *as she says.*) I'm sorry she's called *now*—but it does her good to pour out her woes to me—

though I guess it makes her envious, too, to see me so happy.

(*Enter* BEAMISH.)

BEAMISH. Miss Essex.

(*Enter* NELLY ESSEX. *She is a pretty girl of twenty-five, very fashionably dressed, who looks and behaves almost like a lady. As soon as* NELLY *has entered,* BEAMISH *goes out.*)

NELLY. I've only popped in for a moment,

MIRIAM (*as she meets her*). We're glad to see you.

NELLY. Hullo, Geoffrey.

GEOFFREY (*kisses his hand to* NELLY). Hullo.

NELLY. I've come to tell you some news.

MIRIAM. What? Is Jack sober?

(NELLY *playfully threatens to strike* MIRIAM. GEOFFREY *laughs.*)

NELLY (*crossing towards* GEOFFREY). Don't laugh. It's serious. (*She looks from* GEOFFREY *to* MIRIAM *before she speaks, but it is evident from her happy expression that her news is not tragic.*) I'm going to be married.

MIRIAM (*incredulously*). You're not?

NELLY. Yes I am.

GEOFFREY. Who to?

NELLY. Jack, of course.

MIRIAM. He's going to make you his wife? (*She is almost overcome with emotion.*) Oh, Nelly, I *am* glad. That's fine. The man you're so fond of—and you're going to bear his name.

GEOFFREY. I suppose I ought to congratulate you.

NELLY. Thanks, Geoffrey. Thanks ever so much.

MIRIAM. Sit down, Nelly, and tell us more about it.

NELLY. It was yesterday that he made me the proposal — yesterday afternoon. He's been ill, you know, for the past week—oh, very bad indeed he's been this time—right up to the night before last. Then he became himself again, and went to bed and slept. All the morning he was very quiet and—you know—full of remorse, and I suppose felt that he hadn't been treating me quite as he should—anyway, towards evening, he said he'd marry me. It all came from himself; I never suggested anything—and to make a long story short, (*smiles and looks very happy as she says*) we're to have our wedding in a fortnight's time.

MIRIAM (*wistfully*). I guess I shan't see much more of you after that.

NELLY (*a little embarrassed*). I don't know, I'm sure. I hope so—but of course that'll have to depend on what Jack says about it.

MIRIAM. Naturally. I quite see that. It isn't to be expected he'd let you come to see me as his wife.

NELLY. We won't be in London much, you see. Jack's got property in Lancashire—somewhere near Liverpool, I believe. We're going to live there mostly.

MIRIAM (*smiling pleasantly*). You'll have your country house then and entertain the gentry?

NELLY (*smiling*). P'raps.

MIRIAM. Sell at bazaars and sit on committees with the other ladies.

NELLY. Who knows?

MIRIAM (*wistfully*). Things will be changed with *you*, I can see that.

NELLY (*impulsively*). But I shan't forget you, dearie. I shall never forget your kindness to me. I don't know what I should have done sometimes—when things were at their blackest and I didn't know what way to turn—if I hadn't known I could run in here and be sure of kind words and a welcome.

MIRIAM. No need to thank me. I'm sure if I've ever been any comfort—I'm very pleased.

NELLY. I must be going now. Jack's waiting for me to go shopping. He's going to buy me an engagement ring. Good-bye, Geoffrey.

GEOFFREY. Good-bye, my dear. Best of luck.

NELLY. Thanks. Good-bye, Miriam.

MIRIAM. Not yet. I'll go with you as far as the front door.

(*They go out.* GEOFFREY *then returns to his book.* MIRIAM *re-enters almost immediately and closes the door after her, while she speaks cheerfully.*)

MIRIAM. Isn't that grand? Poor old Nelly—as I used to call her—making that splendid marriage.

(*She comes towards* GEOFFREY, *but stops when he speaks. He sits up on the edge of the divan.*)

GEOFFREY. Tied up for life with a drunkard! I should think she'd do much better for herself if she remained free. Jack Soames for all his faults is generous, and he knows that if he tries her patience too far she can leave him. She has *that* hold over him. Nelly's an attractive girl. She'd have no difficulty in finding some one else.

MIRIAM. I've no doubt it's sense you're talking—but married!

GEOFFREY. What kind of a marriage is that? I can imagine nothing more awful than Nelly's future. Shut up in a gloomy house in the country, with a husband who's almost certain to go from bad to worse. He'll have nothing else to do but drink, because nobody will know them.

MIRIAM (*simply*). He might reform himself for *her* sake—for the sake of his bride.

GEOFFREY (*smiles and goes towards her as he says*). He might. (*Kisses her.*) But I wouldn't be too optimistic. (*Replaces his book on the table, and then lies down on the chaise longue.*) I've seen such marriages as theirs before.

MIRIAM. As for people not wanting to know Nelly,— I daresay it'll be hard for her at first—perhaps always. But on the other hand, her neighbours may not know properly who she is. She speaks well and she dresses well, and if they don't know for certain, and she makes herself agreeable, and they like her— (*Pauses before she says, speaking with a slightly forced lightness of tone, not looking at him.*) It's almost—you might say—in a way—as if *I* were to be married to—any one—and we went and lived far away from London—somewhere in the country. (*He glances at her, but when at this point she turns to look at him he takes his book from the table again and pretends to be partially engaged with it so as not to be under the necessity of looking at her.*) Who'd know for certain? *You* and the boys wouldn't give me away,—and if any one else were to do such a thing, it might not be believed. (*She takes her eyes off him and looks in front of her as she continues, and he, knowing that she is not watching him, glances at her from time to time as he idly turns the pages of his book, but should not give the impression that he is reading.*) It would be much easier for *me* though than for Nelly, because—as I come from America—they wouldn't expect to know all about me. I should be—vaguely—an American woman who has lived in Paris,—a widow or a divorcée — they wouldn't be sure which— (*Turning to him again and speaking rather eagerly.*) And it wouldn't really matter, because in America we can get divorces for all sorts of reasons—incompatibility or any old thing. It doesn't necessarily mean that a woman has been guilty.

GEOFFREY (*unable to ignore her meaning any longer, smiles at her and says very kindly*). You're a good girl, Miriam.

MIRIAM (*looking in front of her again and speaking very gravely and definitely*). I don't say a man ought to marry his mistress, however well she's behaved herself,—nor whatever she's done for him. I don't see any reason why he should, I don't think it's her due. It's entirely a matter of his own wishes. (*Pauses and looks at him again while she says.*) But there's something to be said for people knowing one another thoroughly before marriage. Jack and Nelly already know the best and the worst—(*very lightly as if it were an afterthought*) like you and me.

GEOFFREY (*lays his book on the table and gives her his whole attention as he says*). I don't exactly expect Nelly will be able to stick it long. She'll miss the noise of London too much—the restaurants and music-halls and parties—all the gaieties and frivolities and excitements which are like food and drink to her. How can she settle down to a quiet, dull, domestic life after the kind of life she's been leading here?

MIRIAM. There are *some* girls like that. Most of those who have ever gone in for the gay life are like that. It's in their blood. They *can't* settle down. (*Slowly.*) But there's others too. I don't know about Nelly, I'm sure—but I know there are *some* who'd give much to get away, who are sick and tired of it all, who've come to see that it's only passing the time and trying to forget and being of no real use to themselves or any one—girls who want peace and rest and to be good. I know there are *some* like that.

GEOFFREY (*sits on the side of the chaise longue, towards her, and says very gravely and kindly*). It's the reaction, my dear. It's the discontent we all feel at times, whatever life we have chosen. But I fear that it doesn't last. You'd want to be back again as soon as your rest was over. It's only reaction.

(*He rises intending to move away, but she rises almost at the same time to detain him. He stops and waits for her to speak, seeing by the expression on her face that there is something important she wishes to say.*)

MIRIAM (*very earnestly and appealingly and at the beginning timidly*). Mighn't it be the woman in me—the woman I smothered for so long—struggling—trying to live still — asking to come out and show herself? Couldn't it be that? Love works such wonders. I long so to be something better, Geoffrey — since I've known *you*—to be of some good in the world—to take my place among the helpful ones. (*She is nearly crying as she says.*) But they won't have me. I can't even help to raise the poor and the fallen because of what I am. There's no true woman's life to be found outside of marriage.

(*She breaks down and cries, using her handkerchief.*
GEOFFREY, *distressed, goes towards her and puts his arms about her, trying to comfort her.*)

GEOFFREY. Don't cry, dear, don't cry. Oh, it's dreadful, I know, it's horrible. Poor Miriam! I'm so sorry for you. I'll take you out to some nice place this evening, and I'll buy you those black pearls.

(*She makes a movement away from him. Then* TONY HEWLETT *and* BEAMISH *are heard speaking outside the room.* GEOFFREY *listens as soon as he hears their voices, but their words need not be distinctly heard.*)

TONY. Is she at home?

BEAMISH. I believe you'll find her in there.

TONY. Will it be all right for me to go in, do you think?

GEOFFREY (*listens, then says warningly to* MIRIAM). Some one's called. It's Tony.

(MIRIAM *goes out of the room, drying her eyes. Enter* TONY HEWLETT.)

TONY. How are you, Geoffrey? Where's Miriam?

GEOFFREY. Only gone to her room. She'll be back soon. How are you?

TONY. I came to ask her if you'd both come and sup with me to-night. I'm having some people to meet Ida Mason—the girl who does that Egyptian dance in *Over the Way.* She's so pretty and awfully nice. I'm sure Miriam would like her. D'you think you can come?

GEOFFREY. *I* shall be very glad to come, thanks, Tony —and I expect Miriam will too. It'll do her good. She wants cheering up. Sit down and keep me company till she comes and then ask her.

TONY. All right. If I'm not in the way. (*Makes himself comfortable on the chaise longue while* GEOFFREY *brings a box of cigarettes*).

GEOFFREY. There! Help yourself.

TONY. Thanks.

GEOFFREY. Where have you come from?

TONY. Now?

GEOFFREY. Yes.

TONY. I've been lunching with Valentine.

GEOFFREY. Oh. How's Valentine? Going strong?

TONY. Not very.

GEOFFREY. What's the matter with her?

TONY. She's all right as far as her health is concerned, but of course she's miserably unhappy.

GEOFFREY. What about?

TONY. I suppose you know that she's left her husband?

(*This comes as a tremendous surprise to* GEOFFREY. *There is a pause before he can speak.*)

GEOFFREY. No. I didn't know that.

TONY. About a month ago. Perhaps I oughtn't to have told you, but I thought you'd be sure to have heard.

GEOFFREY. I never see Valentine now. I've only seen her once since her marriage. She came to call on me at my rooms one day—ages ago. Why has she left her husband?

TONY. I don't know whose fault it is, I'm very sorry for both of them. *She's* bored to death with *him* and he's crazy about *her*—and there it is—I suppose she couldn't stand him any longer. They aren't separated permanently, not legally I mean. *He* believes she'll come back to him and *she* swears she won't, and it's all like that. He's up in Scotland somewhere fishing and *she's* at Claridge's with her mother.

GEOFFREY. What line does her mother take?

TONY. She sides with the husband. She's at Valentine day and night to try and make her go back to him.

GEOFFREY. Poor little Valentine!

TONY. I really was awfully sorry for her. She feels so much, too, that it's all her fault that *you* are living like this with Miriam and flaunting her about everywhere so openly.

GEOFFREY. She talked about *me* then?

TONY. Oh, yes—most of the time. She told me how she went to call on you that day and met Miriam as she was leaving. I didn't let her know, of course, how you happened to come across each other in the first place, but I told her what a good sort Miriam is and how fond we have all become of her.

GEOFFREY. What did she say to that?

TONY. Nothing. She just cried and cried as if her heart would break. It was awful.

(GEOFFREY *rises and moves away to hide his own emotion before he turns to* TONY *again and speaks.*)

GEOFFREY. D'you think she'd like me to go and see her?

TONY. I'm sure she would. It would mean everything to her, I know—because you see—she talks to *me* about you. There's only *me* she *can* talk to about you. She's got you so dreadfully on her mind, I believe she's in love with you still.

GEOFFREY. Tony! Think of what you're saying. Don't use expressions carelessly.

TONY (*rather surprised by* GEOFFREY'S *tone*). No—of course not. I didn't think there was any harm in saying I believe she's in love with you still—now that it's all over on *your* side.

GEOFFREY. What makes you think that it's all over on *my* side?

TONY. You seem so happy with Miriam.

GEOFFREY. You really think it would be all right for me to go and see Valentine?

TONY. She told me she never would *ask* you to come —because that day when she went to call on you, you said that you didn't want to see her any more.

GEOFFREY. Tell her that I'll come to see her soon.

(*Enter* MIRIAM. *She shows no traces of her recent tears, but is gentle and subdued.* TONY *rises as she enters and smiles at her.*)

MIRIAM. How d'you do, Tony?

TONY. I'm all right, thanks. (*They meet and kiss; then* TONY *says.*) I came to see if you and Geoffrey would come to supper to-night at Oddy's ?

GEOFFREY. He's got Ida Mason coming—the girl you admired so much when we went to see *Over the Way*.

MIRIAM. Oh, yes.

TONY. Basil will be there too, and three or four other people that you know already.

MIRIAM. Shall we go, Geoffrey ?

GEOFFREY. Yes, dear, I think so. It sounds rather fun.

MIRIAM. All right. Thanks very much, Tony. I'll wear my new frock in your honour.

TONY. Splendid ! So glad you can come. I must be off now, I'm supposed to be working ! Oddy's to-night then. Good-bye.

MIRIAM. Good-bye, dear.

TONY. So long, Geoffrey, old thing. (*When he opens the door he turns to* GEOFFREY *and says as an afterthought.*) And I'll tell Valentine you'll be round to see her.

> (*Exit* TONY. *He has made his last remark quite innocently and has no reason to believe that he has said anything indiscreet, but he has left a bomb behind him which* GEOFFREY *realises as much as* MIRIAM. *They begin the scene very slowly, both attempting to speak casually, but all the same there is great constraint.* MIRIAM *does not speak until* GEOFFREY, *after watching the door close after* TONY, *turns and sees her standing with her eyes fixed upon him.*)

MIRIAM. Valentine ?

GEOFFREY. Lady Morland.

MIRIAM. I know. (*After a pause.*) Are you going to see her ?

GEOFFREY. Yes—some time.

MIRIAM. Do you meet then, occasionally ?

GEOFFREY. Never. I haven't seen her since that day she came up to my rooms and you came in while she was there.

MIRIAM. Why begin it again ?

GEOFFREY. She's unhappy and she wants to see me.

MIRIAM (*echoes*). Unhappy.

GEOFFREY. Yes.

MIRIAM. Has her marriage turned out badly?

GEOFFREY. Very.

MIRIAM (*after a pause, says quietly*). I'd rather you didn't go to see her, Geoffrey.

GEOFFREY. Oh—but I must.

MIRIAM (*with more emphasis*). I'd much rather you didn't.

GEOFFREY (*kindly*). Please be reasonable. I appreciate your feelings and can understand why you dislike the idea of our meeting again—even now—though it's so long since we were engaged, but remember, dear, she's in very great trouble.

MIRIAM (*does not move away from him, but neither does she respond to his advance. She is very determined as she says*). I should have thought that if she's unhappy because her marriage has turned out so badly, you'd be the very last man that she ought to see.

GEOFFREY. You don't know the sort of terms that she and I used to be on. I wasn't only her lover, I was her best friend. You can't quite realise, I expect, what we were to each other.

(*As he gets no response from* MIRIAM *he moves away again. She waits until he has moved away before she speaks.*)

MIRIAM. I can realise that it's dangerous for you to go near her while she's in this state.

GEOFFREY (*turning towards her*). Why dangerous?

MIRIAM. Because you love her. Because you've never ceased to love her. D'you think I haven't got eyes?

GEOFFREY. But I never see her now. I scarcely ever mention her name.

MIRIAM. Never—to *me*—but you hug the thought of her to your *own* breast. Many a time have I seen you sitting there, when you thought I wasn't observing you —with your mind far far away. I knew full well what your trouble was. I never spoke to you about it, because I respected your silence as something sacred. I saw that there are chambers in your heart where I must never penetrate—so I sat still and said nothing—but I've shed some bitter tears behind your back.

GEOFFREY. I've often felt very grateful to you, Miriam, for your tact in not referring to Valentine.

MIRIAM. It was to me as if she had died. One isn't jealous of the dead. (*Pauses, controlling herself with difficulty, and looking menacing and desperate as she continues.*) But if she's coming back again to claim you—I don't know that I can sit still and keep quiet and be tactful.

(*Moves away, trying to control herself.*)

GEOFFREY (*going towards her*). Now, Miriam—don't distress yourself like this. She doesn't claim me. I don't know what you mean by that.

MIRIAM (*close to him, facing him*). You're determined to go to her?

GEOFFREY. Yes—quite—(*she turns away*) to go and see her—to let her know that I'm still her friend. (*She darts a mistrustful look at him. He takes hold of her arm as he continues.*) Oh, Miriam—please be good and patient as you've always been—please—for *my* sake.

MIRIAM (*pulling her arm away*). I've been patient a long while for your sake. I've said not one word against her—ever—because you once asked me not to, I've never so much as spoken her name—have I—never once—tell me—have I—ever?

GEOFFREY. No. Never. Not once.

MIRIAM. No—and I never would have done so long as I thought it was her *memory* you were cherishing, but if it's *herself*——

GEOFFREY (*protesting and trying to control her*). Miriam! Stop! Please! I can't let you go on like this.

MIRIAM (*raising her voice and getting away from him*). Why can't she stick to her own man? What does she want with *you*? And you must run to her—the minute she calls—because she's in trouble—never mind how she's treated you in the past. If she made a bad bargain—let her keep it. And if that's more than her flesh and blood will stand—she isn't the first woman who's had to go through with it and she won't be the last. She made her own bed. Let her lie in it. (*Pauses to choke back the sobs which threaten to overcome her utterance.*) Much she cared about you! She despised you because you were poor. Pranced off to church with a millionaire and left you then with a broken heart to drink yourself to death. Fine leavings you were when I found you. (*Pauses again, struggling to keep back the sobs which increasingly threaten to overcome her.*) I took care of you in those dark days. I looked after you like a child, and now when you're a man again and strong, she wants you back—to ruin you a second time. (*Shouts in a hopeless attempt to keep back her sobs.*) She shan't do it—she shan't! Not if I have the power to stop her.

(*Walks up and down sobbing. There is a lengthy pause before* GEOFFREY *speaks. He waits until* MIRIAM *has partially recovered herself.*)

GEOFFREY (*very seriously, but not angrily*). You make our whole position towards each other extremely difficult.

MIRIAM. Whose?

GEOFFREY. Yours and mine.

(*This surprises her. She comes a little towards him when she speaks.*)

MIRIAM. *I* make it difficult?

(*During the following speech* GEOFFREY *speaks carefully and sometimes haltingly. He finds it difficult to express his meaning without being offensive, and also, to put his meaning clearly into words.* MIRIAM *is bewildered at first. She listens and tries to take in his meaning, but it only comes to her gradually.*)

GEOFFREY. I'm not blaming you, my poor Miriam. I don't see how it would be possible for you, under the circumstances—to feel or behave differently, but you see, on *my* side—looking at it from *my* point of view—I can't agree to accept the position you are trying to place me in. What I want to explain — to point out to you — has nothing to do with whether I should go to see Valentine or not. About that—I must of course do—whatever I think proper. I don't propose to pay her a clandestine visit. I propose to pay her a call, but I needn't, I think, enter into my reasons for wishing to go and see Valentine. If Tony hadn't happened to say something about it as he went out, I shouldn't have thought it necessary to tell you I was going—nor afterwards to say that I'd been ; not from a wish to be anything but entirely straightforward—but I shouldn't have thought of mentioning it to you, I should have looked upon it as altogether my own business. (MIRIAM *sits on the foot of the chaise longue and listens quietly, giving him all her attention.*) This may seem rather—if not unjust—unkind—to *you*. You were thinking—I am sure—not so much of yourself as of *me*—of protecting *me*. I don't want you to protect me. (*He pauses a moment as she turns up her piteous face to look at him.*) It's no use deceiving you by *pretending* to give in to you—just to please you and for the sake of peace—if I don't feel like it. You deserve more honest treatment than that. You deserve so much more than I can give you. Our positions are too unequal. I know what you would say—what any one, not looking at our situation through my eyes would say. I give you food and clothes, a house to live in and plenty of amusement—but all that is nothing compared to what *you* give *me*. To feel so greatly in your debt — oppresses me. You are not unduly exacting—I'm sure you don't mean to be exacting—but your love instinctively makes claims on me—I feel it as much as you do—and if I'm to remain independent, which I insist upon—it will mean that I must constantly inflict suffering on *you*. I can't do that. It would be more than I could endure. I'm not cruel by nature. I can't deliberately hurt your feelings by taking you to my heart one moment and holding you at arm's length the next—I'm too fond of you—I respect you too much. I can't any more insult you by doing that. (*Pauses before he says slowly.*) So it comes to this. I don't see how I am to continue my life with you any longer.

(*He waits a moment, then, as* MIRIAM *makes no movement, he crosses slowly to the divan, where he sits down.*)

MIRIAM (*after a long pause, says slowly, and as if she had scarcely grasped the full meaning of his words*). D'you mean you want to leave me—altogether—for good and all ?

GEOFFREY. We agreed to stay together for as long as it suits us—and as soon as it suits us to separate—for any reason whatever—we are perfectly at liberty to do so—either of us.

MIRIAM. I've always been faithful to you, Geoffrey—and I haven't been extravagant nor run up bills, I hoped that might count in my favour. I've cost you a lot of money in clothes, I know—but I thought you liked to see me the smartest-dressed woman in the room—when we go to a restaurant or any place. I thought men liked that.

GEOFFREY. I have no fault to find with you. You've been very good. You've been wonderful. It's my own shortcomings which are troubling me.

MIRIAM. I know you never loved me as I love you—not every day and all day. (*Rises and comes slowly towards him as she continues.*) But sometimes in the night I've made you love me—when we're alone in the house and the streets are quiet—I've made you forget—I've made you forget everything but me.

(*She puts her arms about him. He puts his arm round her and lays his head against her.*)

GEOFFREY. I know you have. I'm not ashamed to own it. (*As he raises his head and drops his arm.*) But what is love like that worth afterwards?

MIRIAM (*gently*). If I'm content with such love as you give me—why be so proud?

GEOFFREY. It isn't only my pride which rebels against this state of things. It's more than that. It's my self-respect. I can't bear being beholden. I don't want to be made to feel that I ought to be answerable to you for any of my actions. I want to feel free. I shan't forget you after I leave you. You know you can count on me to be generous, I shall do whatever I can afford.

MIRIAM (*bitterly*). I'm not calculating. I'm not engaged in wondering how much you'll give me. These aren't crocodile tears I'm shedding to see what I can *make* out of you. So you've had your fun and now it's time to pay me off. (*Turns to him quickly, angry and menacing.*) What if I won't be paid off! Suppose I turn nasty! You don't know me yet. You've always brought out the best that is in me, but there's plenty in me that's not of the best—so I warn you—for I stick at nothing, *I'm* not afraid. *I've* got nothing to lose, but I know those who have. I know *one* who's got plenty to lose if I can ever *prove* anything against her. I'll fix *her*. (GEOFFREY *goes towards her to strike her. She dodges him and continues raging.*) Shame on you, Geoffrey—shame on you! What have I done but love you? And for that, you must turn on me, spurn me, kick me out like trash——

GEOFFREY (*breaks in on her speech so loudly and angrily that he frightens and then subdues her*). That's not fair! It's untrue! You're making out that I have no heart—that I'm treating you badly—when I'm *not*. I protest against any one thinking so, I never deceived you, I never pretended more than I feel, I've always been honest about it. You've always known perfectly well that our life together was only for a time—that it wasn't meant to last. You must have foreseen that sooner or later this would happen. (*She is completely subdued now as she listens to him.*) It's very sad and very difficult—for both of us—but if I'm generous and considerate—as I mean to be—as I'm trying to be—it isn't just to me to say you won't accept my help, and won't let me behave well towards you now—as I've always done in the past, Miriam—always. (*Turns to go.*) I'll leave you now. I'll go home. It'll be better if we both think this over—separately.

MIRIAM (*clutching at his coat to stop him going*). Geoffrey!

GEOFFREY. What is it?

MIRIAM. Am I not to see you again?

GEOFFREY. Oh, yes, you'll see me again—but I want to be alone now.

MIRIAM. Geoffrey! I have no claims—no rights—but I'm a woman in love. Have pity! You're the only man who's ever treated me fair and now you're turning out just like all the rest. Don't lay it on your conscience that you raised me up and made me better, and then went and threw me down. Don't send me back to the old life. Don't send me back to the streets.

(GEOFFREY *frees himself and goes out.*)

CURTAIN.

# THE FOURTH ACT

SCENE.—(*The same as Acts I. and II.*)
    *The room looks exactly as it did in Act II. except that it is now in very neat order. There are no papers nor litter of any kind to be seen, and there is a great profusion of flowers in vases: large bunches of the choicest and most expensive-looking blooms adorn the room wherever they can be placed to advantage. It is the early afternoon of a fine sunny day, so that the room is well lighted. The curtains are drawn well back from the windows. The stage is empty when the curtain goes up. A few weeks have passed since Act III.*
    Enter GEOFFREY *from his bedroom. He is very well dressed as if he had been careful to look his best. He looks at the flowers and moves about slightly rearranging a few of them so that they may show to even better advantage. The entrance bell rings.* GEOFFREY *pauses and looks surprised. He looks at his watch, then goes and opens the door.*
HUGH BROWN *is at the door.*

    HUGH. May I come in?
    GEOFFREY (*politely, but not very cordially*). Yes. Do. I can see you for a few minutes.
    HUGH (*advancing into the room*). I've just come from seeing Miriam, so I thought I'd better look in and tell you about it.
    GEOFFREY. Oh, yes. I'm glad you've come. Sit down—won't you?
    HUGH. What gorgeous flowers!
    GEOFFREY (*taking no apparent interest or pleasure in his flowers*). Aren't they nice? I went out and bought them just now. I like having flowers about.

HUGH. I told—Miriam what you are prepared to do for her.

GEOFFREY. What did she say?

HUGH (*tells of his interview with* MIRIAM, *gravely but dispassionately, as if the whole business were a legal case*). Not much of anything. She neither accepted nor rejected the offer you told me to make her. Indeed she hardly spoke a word all the time I was there. She listened to what I had to say, but even when I gave her the cheque you told me to let her have to go on with, she didn't say thank you, nor put out her hand to take it,—so I left it on the table and came away.

GEOFFREY. Did she want to know why I hadn't come myself?

HUGH. She didn't ask. I told her you thought it would be very painful, for both of you, to go into all the details of a settlement together, and so I had come to discuss it with her instead.

GEOFFREY. It was very kind of you to undertake it, Hugh.

HUGH. That's all right. I suppose you'll hear from her. If you don't—let me know if you want me to see her again.

GEOFFREY (*who does not appear to have heard* HUGH'S *last remark, says slowly*). Do you think I'm being an awful brute?

HUGH (*considering the question, says doubtfully*). No— I suppose not. (*Then confidently.*) No—of course not. You are behaving very handsomely towards Miriam. You are doing far more for her than any girl in her situation has a right to expect. There is nothing at all brutal or unusual in the way you are treating her. The only unusual thing about it is your extreme generosity.

GEOFFREY. I want to do what I can for her.

HUGH. Naturally—but I mean to say,—she has no claim on you. It isn't as if you had betrayed an innocent girl in the first place—or had ever led her to believe that you were likely to marry her. You have a liaison with Miriam, during which you treat her very well. You think it's time to end it—but you still continue to treat her very well. There's nothing that any one can blame you for. Of course—in these cases—if the girl is mercenary or even legitimately doing the best she can for herself, it's a simple matter soon settled—but if she loves you, it's bound to be a cruel business.

GEOFFREY. Yes. It's a cruel business. (*With quiet determination.*) But I can't go back on it now.

HUGH. It would be no advantage to either of you if you did. You'd only make it more difficult for yourself later on—the next time you want to get away. She'd be all the more determined to keep you—if she remembered that you had given in to her *this* time. And it would be no real kindness to Miriam—to keep on with her for a little while longer, and then make her go through all this again. It would only be postponing and prolonging trouble and wasting her time.

GEOFFREY. That's true enough.

HUGH. Suppose you were leaving her to get married! No one would expect you to let consideration for Miriam stand in the way of your making a suitable marriage.

GEOFFREY. If I were leaving her to be married, I expect she'd be reasonable. She always said she would be. She has told me more than once that she would never try to stand in my way if I ever wanted to make a good marriage. She said—when the time came—I had only to tell her, she'd go away quietly—whatever it cost her.

HUGH. I've no doubt that she meant that. I've no doubt that she'd do it. But on the other hand—I shouldn't have thought it was for Miriam to say that if you wish to leave her for a reason of which she approves, you may, but that if you wish to leave her for any other reason—you may not.

GEOFFREY. No. Of course it's not.

HUGH. Suppose you intended to have an affair with some other woman! (GEOFFREY *glances surreptitiously at* HUGH, *but it is easy to see that* HUGH *had no ulterior motive in saying this.*) Some one you didn't want to marry—or could not marry for any reason—and that it was a tremendous event in your life — that you really loved her and felt that existence without her was worthless! Is Miriam to stand in the way of *that*?

GEOFFREY. I'm morbid about Miriam. That's what it is. I ought to think more of myself and my own happiness and not quite so much of her. We are much

# OUTCAST

too soft-hearted nowadays, Hugh. That's what's the matter with most of us.

HUGH. It's hard not to be soft-hearted when one has just come away from seeing Miriam. She's suffering tortures.

GEOFFREY. I know she is, but it can't be helped. As you say yourself, *I'm* not to blame. No man is expected to be at the mercy of any woman who happens to fall in love with him. Simply because I took her up for a time, and encouraged her to improve herself, doesn't mean that I'm *always* to be responsible for her, does it?

HUGH. Now you are entering upon a very large question! the amount of responsibility we involve ourselves in by our actions — both conscious and unconscious responsibility—foreseen or unforeseen. If one has given one's word, of course there's no question—one must keep it, however unpleasant the consequences, though even then, I don't know—circumstances might possibly arise, in certain cases, which make it more honourable to break one's word. That's a dangerous doctrine. But there *have* been cases when it would have been wrong to keep one's word. The responsibility for the effect of our examples upon others, or how far we are responsible to people we have taken a special interest in and advised or encouraged to be this or that, is much more difficult to define. Undoubtedly we are responsible, to a certain degree, for *all* our actions—but then we are not all wise! we are not seers: we can't foretell results—and no man can be held *wholly* responsible for other people, however weak and dependent they may be. They too have wills and personalities of their own—and are not to be absolved by what he does, from *all* responsibility on their own account. (*At this point* GEOFFREY *deliberately looks at his watch, then looks at* HUGH. HUGH, *taking the hint, rises as he says.*) It is too complicated a question to generalise about. We all have to decide our own individual cases. And it's time I was off. I ought to be at my chambers now.

GEOFFREY. All right. Good-bye.

HUGH. I'll see you some time.

GEOFFREY. Drop in or ring me up. (*Enter* TAYLOR. *He comes in without knocking and carries over his arm a folded suit of clothes of* GEOFFREY'S. *He has walked into the room before he stops when he sees* HUGH *and* GEOFFREY *and when* GEOFFREY *speaks.*) (*Impatiently.*) Why d'you bring those now?

TAYLOR. I took them downstairs to brush, sir. I was just going to put them away, I didn't know there was any one here. You are not generally at home, sir, at this time in the afternoon.

GEOFFREY. You don't want to stay in the bedroom for anything? It's only to put these clothes away?

TAYLOR. That's all, sir. Would you rather I came and did it another time?

GEOFFREY. No, no. Never mind. Go along. Hurry up.

(GEOFFREY *goes towards the inner door waiting for* HUGH *to go out. As he goes up* TAYLOR *crosses towards* HUGH *on his way to the bedroom.*)

HUGH. Good-afternoon, Taylor.

TAYLOR. Good-afternoon, sir.

(*He is nearly at the bedroom door when* HUGH *speaks again.*)

HUGH. Have you been having any more flutters on the Stock Exchange?

TAYLOR. No, sir. Only that one. I ventured fifty pounds and by the kindness of Mr. Sherwood increased it to a hundred. That's more than a year ago.

HUGH. I should have thought your experience would encourage you to try again.

TAYLOR. I own it made me feel a little giddy,—for the moment, but when I told my wife what we had made she was not at all pleased.

HUGH. Wasn't she?

TAYLOR. Not at all, sir. On the contrary. She was greatly put about. She said fluttering might be a safe enough pastime for *gentlemen*, but not for people like *us* and that I ought to know better. I have never seen my wife in such a taking in all the thirty years that we've been married. We almost had words—till I promised to stick to the savings bank in future, which I mean to do.

GEOFFREY. Don't waste time, Taylor. I want those things put away.

(TAYLOR *goes into the bedroom as soon as* GEOFFREY *speaks. He leaves the door open behind him.*)

HUGH. Be sure you let me know, Geoffrey, if you want me to do anything more for you about Miriam's business.
GEOFFREY. All right. Thanks. Good-bye.
(*He shakes hands with* HUGH *to get rid of him, and as* HUGH *goes out* GEOFFREY *looks at his watch and then towards the bedroom door. He is evidently labouring under great agitation. He takes a cigarette from a box then goes somewhere else to get a match and lights it and keeps glancing towards the bedroom door.*)
(*Re-enter* TAYLOR *from the bedroom. He closes the door behind him.*)
GEOFFREY. Don't come up again unless I ring.
TAYLOR. No, sir.
(TAYLOR *crosses towards the entrance hall. He is nearly there when* GEOFFREY *speaks again.*)
GEOFFREY. I don't want any one to come up unless I ring.
TAYLOR. I will see that nobody comes up, sir.
(TAYLOR *closes both the doors after him as he goes out.* GEOFFREY *moves aimlessly about for a moment or two, smoking, then sits down. No sooner has he sat down than he gets up again, goes and opens the inner door of the entrance and sets it wide open, then he sits down again, somewhere else, and smokes. Almost immediately he is up again. He goes to the window and looks down into the street. Then he comes to the table, opens a drawer in it, and takes out some joss-sticks. He lights these and puts them in a pot on the mantelpiece to burn. He looks at his watch again then wanders about smoking his cigarette and looking at his flowers. He is re-arranging the position of one of the vases when the entrance bell rings. He throws his cigarette into the grate and at once goes and opens the outer door of the entrance.*)
(*Enter* VALENTINE. *She is plainly dressed in quiet colours and wears a veil over her face. She walks straight in without greeting* GEOFFREY, *who shuts the outer door and locks it as soon as* VALENTINE *has passed through it. Then, without noticing her, he goes to the window and*

*pulls the curtains right across it. While he is doing this* VALENTINE *raises her veil. He then comes straight towards her. She goes towards him. They throw their arms round one another and stand locked in a close embrace with their lips joined for several moments. They look in each other's eyes and still cling to each other when they speak.*)

GEOFFREY. My darling.

VALENTINE. I love you, Geoffrey; I love you.

GEOFFREY. I know it at last: now that you've come to give yourself to me.

VALENTINE. I'm yours, absolutely—my darling.

GEOFFREY. My dear one — my girl — my beautiful Valentine. (*Then the entrance bell rings.*) (*They move apart and then stand looking at each other and listening. After a moment or two* GEOFFREY *signs to* VALENTINE *to stay where she is and keep quiet. Then he goes on tiptoe to the outer door and listens.* VALENTINE *watches him. After he has listened for a moment or two he appears reassured. He comes into the room and softly closes the inner door. Then he comes towards* VALENTINE. *They speak in low tones.*) I heard steps going away. I expect it was only some one with a parcel or a telegram or something. No one else is likely to come up.

VALENTINE (*almost in a whisper*). I thought it was my husband.

GEOFFREY. But he isn't in London.

VALENTINE. No.

GEOFFREY. Then how could he follow you here?

VALENTINE. He couldn't, of course. It's silly of me, but I can't help feeling as if every one knows what I'm doing. All the way here I felt as if every man and woman I passed in the street knew where I was going.

GEOFFREY (*smiling at her*). That's only because it's the first time.

VALENTINE. But I've been here before and not felt like that. (*Stops when she sees* GEOFFREY'S *smile and smiles a little herself as she says.*) Oh—I see what you mean. (GEOFFREY *goes towards her to take her in his arms, but she holds up her hand in a very engaging manner to stop him, smiling at him as she says.*) Wait a minute.

(*She then takes off her hat and veil and lays them on the table.*)

GEOFFREY (*speaking while* VALENTINE *is taking off her hat and veil*). Your hair! Your beautiful hair! I always loved your hair.

(VALENTINE *comes to him smiling. He puts his arm around her and leads her gently to the sofa, where they sit down close together with their hands locked in each other's as they talk.*)

GEOFFREY. Do you feel at your ease now, Valentine? Are you happy?

VALENTINE. I'm happy to be with you again, Geoffrey.

GEOFFREY. No qualms?

VALENTINE (*slowly*). Of conscience?

GEOFFREY (*hurriedly*). No, no. I didn't mean that. I meant, are you still in a fright lest any one should come and ring the bell?

VALENTINE. No, dear—not if you say it's all right.

GEOFFREY. There's no one there now. I heard some one walk away. If it was a messenger boy or some one from a shop, they'd ring once and then, if nobody came to the door, go and leave whatever it was downstairs. That's what's happened.

VALENTINE. I see. (*After a momentary pause.*) I thought you meant, have I any qualms about what I'm doing.

GEOFFREY. It isn't wrong for you and me. You were mine first. You were my girl before you were his. And you know I wouldn't have persuaded you to come back to me if you hadn't left him already. You told me you never would live with him again.

VALENTINE. I put up with him for as long as I could. I tried to make the best of things—but I think it's degrading to live with a man as his wife without loving him.

GEOFFREY. Poor Valentine!

VALENTINE. Mother tried to arrange for us still to live under the same roof, but he wouldn't agree to that. He said he expected his wife to be his wife.

GEOFFREY. I don't know that I can blame him.

VALENTINE. I didn't realise until after I was married the mistake I was making, because I didn't realise till then how dearly I love *you*. And when you came to see me the other day—we *both* realised—didn't we—how greatly we need each other? Is it right to refuse happiness and life when they call us and bid us enjoy ourselves?

GEOFFREY. No, dear, no. Only fools do that. We'll live and be happy, you and I. (*He touches her hair as he says.*) Such lovely hair! I always thought so, even when you wore it in a pigtail.

VALENTINE (*smiling at him*). I never wore my hair in a pigtail.

GEOFFREY. Oh, Valentine! How can you say such a thing?

VALENTINE. Never.

GEOFFREY. I can prove it.

VALENTINE. How?

GEOFFREY. I took a snapshot of you once—running.

VALENTINE. When?

GEOFFREY. That time you came to stay with us for your summer holidays. Do you want to see it?

VALENTINE. Have you got it? (GEOFFREY *seeks and produces an unmounted snapshot, smiling all the while.* VALENTINE *rises and goes to him as she says.*) Let me look at it.

(*She slips her arm through his and they stand close together side by side looking at the photograph which he holds, and smiling.*)

GEOFFREY. What's that thing flying out behind if it isn't a pigtail?

VALENTINE (*laughing as she looks at it*). That tam-o'-shanter and those boots!

GEOFFREY (*drawing the snapshot away from her*). I won't have her laughed at.

VALENTINE (*putting out her hand to take it*). Let me have it back.

GEOFFREY (*putting it out of her reach*). What for?

VALENTINE. It's so hideous. (*Tries to grab it.*)

GEOFFREY. No. (*Steps back and holds it in his hands behind his back. They are both laughing a little.*)

VALENTINE. You have plenty more pictures of *me*.

GEOFFREY. I wouldn't part with this one for the world. (*Takes out his pocket-book. Puts the snapshot carefully inside and replaces his pocket-book in the pocket of his coat.*) And I haven't got *any* more pictures of *you*.

VALENTINE. What's become of them all?
*(They become serious and both smile rather sadly and wistfully during* GEOFFREY'S *next speech.)*
GEOFFREY. There was a bonfire. Everything went on to it: photographs, letters, flowers, Christmas cards, New Year cards, birthday cards——
VALENTINE. I can't remember ever sending you a birthday card.
GEOFFREY. On my twentieth birthday.
VALENTINE. Poor Geoffrey! I'll do everything in my power now to make it up to you. Oh, what a fool I was to ever let you go!
*(She throws her arms round him and presses herself against him.)*
GEOFFREY *(putting his arms round her)*. You can't get on without me, any more than I can get on without you. We've both tried. *(Then the entrance bell rings.)* *(They move back but still hold each other as they look at each other and listen. Then* GEOFFREY *leaves her and goes up noiselessly as far as the inner door, where he stands and listens.* VALENTINE *stays where she is and watches him. He turns to her and with gestures motions her to move to the other side of the room so as to be out of sight if he should open the door.* VALENTINE, *understanding his meaning, goes across the room.* GEOFFREY *opens the inner door quietly a few inches and listens without going outside, then quietly closes the door again and goes towards* VALENTINE. *He speaks in a low voice.)* Nobody can hear us in here if we keep our voices low.
VALENTINE. I don't think mother can possibly know I've come here. She has no suspicions of you and me. I don't believe she knew when I went out, I didn't tell her I was going. I didn't want to see her. I didn't want to have to tell her lies.
*(There is a few moments' silence after* VALENTINE *has finished speaking, and then the entrance bell rings again. They both turn quickly towards the door, then look at each other, then listen. There is a considerable pause before* GEOFFREY, *leaning across the table, speaks to* VALENTINE.)
GEOFFREY. If it should ever be discovered that we meet, would you have the courage to come away with me?

VALENTINE. Where?

GEOFFREY (*glances towards the door before he continues rapidly*). Yesterday I had an offer made me to go and take charge of a large business in Buenos Ayres. Of course I refused it——

VALENTINE. Why?

GEOFFREY. You'd said you'd come here to-day.

VALENTINE. Am I preventing you taking something you ought not to miss? Was it a great chance for you?

GEOFFREY. It was very good — but that doesn't matter, I'm doing very well indeed here. I refused their offer, as I said—but they seem so keen for me to accept it, they told me it should be left open for me until to-morrow. (*Pauses before he says.*) Wouldn't it be better to accept and for you and me to go out there and live together always?

> (*The entrance bell rings three distinct times in rapid succession. At the first two peals of the bell they both sit perfectly still, staring at each other. At the third they both rise together instinctively.*)
> (*There is a distinct pause after the third peal before* MIRIAM'S *voice is heard outside raised in protest and pleading. All her words need not be heard.*)

MIRIAM. No, no. Let me be. I'm doing no harm. I was only ringing his bell. I wasn't making a disturbance. I wasn't annoying any one. No, no. Don't push me away. Don't push me away, etc.

> (TAYLOR'S *voice is also heard, but none of his words are recognisable.*)
> (*The following scene passes very rapidly between* GEOFFREY *and* VALENTINE *while the disturbance is going on outside.*)

GEOFFREY (*as soon as* MIRIAM'S *voice is heard exclaims*). Miriam!

VALENTINE. Let her in. She'll rouse the whole building, she'll draw a crowd.

> (GEOFFREY *crosses quickly to his bedroom door and opens it.*)

GEOFFREY. Go in there.

VALENTINE. No. I'm not going to be caught there. (*She turns to the table, picks up her hat and veil and puts them on her head as she says.*) I've been seen here like this before. (*She seats herself as she says.*) Let her in.

(GEOFFREY *runs towards the entrance leaving the bedroom door open. When he is nearly at the entrance* VALENTINE *exclaims suddenly.*) Wait. (*He stops and turns to her. She rises and runs to the bedroom door and shuts it, then runs back to her chair and sits as she says.*) Now.

(GEOFFREY *opens the inner door and then unlocks the outer door and opens it.*)

(*Enter* MIRIAM. *She looks haggard and desperate but is exceedingly smartly dressed. She turns round in the entrance and enters the room backwards, with her hands out in front of her, protesting, so that she does not see* VALENTINE.)

(TAYLOR *only appears in the hall,* GEOFFREY *remains near the inner door.*)

MIRIAM (*vociferating first to* TAYLOR *and then to* GEOFFREY *as she enters*). No, no, no, no! Don't touch me. Leave me alone. I wasn't going to make a disturbance. I was ringing the bell and waiting there till you came, Geoffrey—till you came and opened the door. I haven't come here to make trouble. I was standing there quite quietly when he came and tried to make me go away. He took hold of me, Geoffrey. He tried to *push* me away. He——

(*She has backed as far as the table. When she comes into collision with that she turns and sees* VALENTINE *sitting calm and apparently unmoved in her chair.* MIRIAM *gives a violent start and then drops her arms by her sides. She supports herself from falling by placing her hand on the table, and then stands motionless and speechless, staring in front of her.* GEOFFREY *dismisses* TAYLOR *with a gesture. Exit* TAYLOR, *closing the outer door after him.* GEOFFREY *closes the inner door and then stands staring at* MIRIAM *till she speaks.*)

MIRIAM. I didn't know you had any one with you. (*She looks at* VALENTINE *before she says.*) There's nothing to fear from *me*. (*To* GEOFFREY.) Once upon a time I threatened you. I told you that if I could ever *prove* anything there'd be trouble. I want you to know that I only said that in my excitement. I wouldn't really hurt you, nor any one you love. (GEOFFREY *sits down on the sofa still staring at* MIRIAM. MIRIAM *pauses before she proceeds.*) I've come on a matter of business, as I wanted to see you—not Hugh. (*She then opens her bag and fumbles in it while she says.*) I called here a few minutes ago and rang the bell. But there was no answer, so I went away. I'd got as far as Piccadilly Circus when I stopped and turned back again. I thought I might as well have another try instead of going all the way home. (*She turns to* VALENTINE *and says to her most politely.*) I must apologise for having made such a commotion. (*She then produces from her bag a several-times-folded cheque, carefully unfolds it then holds it towards* GEOFFREY.) What's this?

GEOFFREY (*without offering to take the cheque*). It's the cheque I asked Hugh to give you to be going on with. I thought you might run short.

MIRIAM. Keep it. (*She still holds it towards him, but as he does not offer to take it, she lets it flutter to the ground at his feet.*) I don't want it, and I don't want any of your settlements or allowances or whatever it was Hugh called them—either. So long as you kept me with you and made me feel I was worth the expense—I was glad enough to help you spend your money. But I've no wish to be a burden, now that you've got no further use for me.

GEOFFREY. You know I can well afford it, and that I want to do whatever I can for you.

MIRIAM (*indifferently*). I daresay you do.

GEOFFREY. Then why be so proud?

MIRIAM. I once asked you that question, and *you* made answer—that it wasn't only your pride which prevented you accepting my love. You said it was something more than that. You said it was your self-respect. It isn't only pride which prevents *me* accepting your money. It's something more. (*She pauses before she says.*) Do you remember the very first time that ever I came up here? (GEOFFREY *nods his head.*) You offered me money *then.* But I told you—if you recollect—that I'd rather you didn't give me anything—if you wouldn't mind, as I wanted to feel as if I'd been your pal. It's the same still.

VALENTINE (*kindly*). But if you won't accept his help, what will you do in the future?

MIRIAM (*vaguely*). The future! I'm one of those who

never troubled much about the future. I wasn't brought up that way. I've long since become accustomed to living from day to day. "A hand-to-mouth existence" I think they call it. I've got my furniture—and some good clothes, and some jewels he gave me from time to time. When I've spent those, there's always two courses *open* to me.

VALENTINE (*echoes*). Two?

MIRIAM (*as if looking far away in front of her*). The river is always flowing under the bridges. (*She closes her eyes, then puts her hand to her head and reels slightly as she says faintly.*) Oh, I've come all over queer. (*Drops her hand and says to* GEOFFREY.) I'm afraid I must ask you to let me lie down.

GEOFFREY (*rising*). Come and lie down on my bed.

(*He crosses to his bedroom door, opens it and goes out leaving the door open.*)

MIRIAM (*to* VALENTINE). It's the want of food.

VALENTINE (*echoes*). The want of food?

MIRIAM. I've had no appetite of late. (*Trying to speak lightly she says with a strange little laugh.*) I'm like a dog who's lost his master—can't eat.

(*Assisting herself by the edge of the table she goes slowly towards the bedroom door. When she is about to pass in front of* VALENTINE *she falls on the floor in a dead faint and lies perfectly still at* VALENTINE'S *feet.*)

(VALENTINE *sits in her chair, staring at* MIRIAM. *It never occurs to her to do anything.*)

(GEOFFREY *comes in from the bedroom and, taking the situation in at a glance, stoops down beside* MIRIAM, *picks her up in his arms, and carries her into his bedroom.*)

(VALENTINE *watches everything he does, but she does not otherwise move. When* GEOFFREY *and* MIRIAM *have gone out* VALENTINE *sits rigidly still for a moment staring in front of her. Then her breast heaves, her face relaxes, and she sobs.*)

(GEOFFREY *appears at his bedroom door; but he does not leave the threshold.*)

GEOFFREY. She's only fainted. She's coming round. Will you please get me some brandy? You'll find it in the cupboard in the sideboard.

(GEOFFREY *retires into the bedroom.* VALENTINE *rises, opens the sideboard cupboard door, takes out the brandy decanter and pours some brandy into a tumbler which she finds on the top of the sideboard. She does all this fumbling because of her agitation and also because she does not know the sideboard. She does not appear to be crying except that from time to time a sob escapes her. She crosses quickly to the bedroom with the tumbler in her hand, disappears for a moment, then reappears beginning to cry.*)

(GEOFFREY *re-enters from the bedroom and stands near the threshold, looking gravely at* VALENTINE *as she cries. They go towards each other when she speaks, but do not stand near together.* VALENTINE'S *whole speech is broken with sobs.*)

VALENTINE. I'm not crying for that poor girl. It's my husband. I know how *he* feels now—hurt and abandoned and forlorn, but he can't put his grief into words. He never could express himself properly. I heard from him only this morning, such a dull stupid letter it was. He told me how many trout he'd caught, and what the weather was like. I can see him now, wandering along the bank of the stream, stopping to cast his line, hooking his fish, landing it—with his heart breaking. (*She pauses to press her handkerchief to her eyes before she continues.*) I never gave him a fair chance. He was very kind. He was really kind to me always, but he was tactless and he bored me, so I grew impatient and then angry, until at last I refused to see any good in him at all, because I compared him with *you.* I scorned him, but I took his name, and I spent his money; I'm using them both still. I'm going back to him.

GEOFFREY. I've been trying to persuade myself that I am under no obligation to Miriam—that I have undertaken no responsibility because I have made her no promises. I'm wrong. I am responsible for what I have made of her. I mustn't drag her out of the depths, encourage her to do her best, then leave her to go back to where she came from. I ought never to have helped her to rise at all if I wasn't prepared to see her through. I ought to have left her alone.

VALENTINE. Life is so hard for all of us, so hard and so unfair.

GEOFFREY. We don't quite know why we're on the earth, and we none of us know for how long, but I think we'll be glad when we're old, or when death comes, if we can say we played the game—though it tear the hearts out of our bodies now. (*He has a movement away to regain his self-control before he says.*) I don't know Sir John Morland, I've seen him but I never was introduced to him, but I know he's an honest upright man who has done his duty to his country—and it's more important that his home should hold together and that his marriage should remain intact and that Miriam should be saved—than that you and I should be happy.

VALENTINE. I'm weak—I always have been weak. I look back in vain for a sign of strength in anything I've done. I loved you and promised to marry you and then I broke my word. I promised to love and honour him and again I broke my word. And now I haven't the courage to stick to you at all cost. Is it worth while even trying to make anything of myself?

GEOFFREY (*with quiet confidence*). You'll try.

VALENTINE. I shall try, but—— (*Pauses.*)

GEOFFREY (*as before*). You'll succeed.

VALENTINE. Do you believe in me?

GEOFFREY. Yes—now.

VALENTINE. Will you think of me as doing the best I can in the midst of great difficulties?

GEOFFREY. Yes.

VALENTINE. Good-bye, Geoffrey.

GEOFFREY. Good-bye, Valentine—for ever.

VALENTINE. For ever. (*She puts her arms round his neck and draws his face down to hers. They kiss each other—rather as children kiss each other. Then* VALENTINE *draws back and lowers her veil over her face. While she is doing this* GEOFFREY *goes up and opens the inner door and then the outer door, looks out along the passage, then turns and nods to* VALENTINE. VALENTINE *walks out without pausing or looking at* GEOFFREY *as she passes him.* GEOFFREY *looks after her along the passage, and then slowly closes the outer door. He comes back into the room and closes the inner door. He goes and stands in front of one of the vases of flowers, smells them, then goes to the window and draws the curtains right back.*)

(*Enter* MIRIAM *from the bedroom. She is pale and looks weak and tired.* GEOFFREY *turns when he hears her enter.*)

MIRIAM. I'm well enough to go home now.

GEOFFREY. You'd better stay a little while longer and rest.

MIRIAM. I think I shall be all right if I have a taxi.

GEOFFREY. Sit down for a few minutes. I'm sure you oughtn't to go yet.

MIRIAM. You're all alone?

GEOFFREY. Yes, I'm all alone.

MIRIAM. Very well. For a few minutes. (*She sits in the chair he has offered her.*)

GEOFFREY. Take off your hat and lean your head back. (*While she slowly takes off her hat which she afterwards holds in her lap,* GEOFFREY *sits at some distance from her.*) (*There is a long pause before he speaks.*) I'm going away, Miriam.

MIRIAM. Yes.

GEOFFREY. Out of England. Out of Europe. I'm going to Buenos Ayres.

MIRIAM (*echoes*). Buenos Ayres?

GEOFFREY. To-morrow I must make arrangements with a firm in the city who want me to go out there and take charge of their business for them. I shall live out there. I might come to London occasionally—for a visit—but I shall make my home in Buenos Ayres. (*Pauses before he says.*) You'd better come with me. (*He pauses again, but as* MIRIAM *neither moves nor speaks he continues.*) You can come as my wife if you like. I'm quite willing to marry you.

MIRIAM. There was a time when I'd have jumped at that—but it's past. No, thank you. I won't marry you —but I'll go with you to Buenos Ayres or anywhere else if you really want me.

GEOFFREY. I won't make protestations—and I'm not going to pay you compliments, but I'm speaking the truth when I tell you that I shall be glad to have you if you'll come with me.

MIRIAM. Thank you, Geoffrey.

GEOFFREY. You might as well marry me. I don't

think you need be afraid. I shall never see Valentine again. I shall settle down and do my best to make my wife happy and contented.

MIRIAM. I'm sure of it.

GEOFFREY. Nobody out there need know.

MIRIAM (*as if weighing the question.*) No. That's true. (*Then after a pause.*) But I wasn't looking at it quite in that light. (*She pauses again and turns to him before she says.*) Did you ever read the marriage service?

GEOFFREY. Yes.

MIRIAM. I never did, till the other day. It was after the last time I saw you, one afternoon. I was wandering along and I passed a church. I heard singing, so I stood and listened. Then I thought it could do us no harm if I prayed for us both, so I went inside. That was how I happened to come across the marriage service. It seemed as if it opened my eyes. It made me see—that whether you think marriage is something religious, or only human—it's a solemn business, it's for the protection of good women, it's their reward. I'll cleave to you, Geoffrey, as long as you wish; but I won't marry you.

GEOFFREY. All right.

CURTAIN.

THE END

Lightning Source UK Ltd.
Milton Keynes UK
UKHW040602091219
355029UK00001B/10/P